MW01244410

Silk & Swords

A Thurian Chronicles Novel

Christopher Stires

DDP
DEEP DESIRES PRESS

Winnipeg, Canada

Copyright © 2020 by Christopher Stires
Cover design copyright © 2020 by Story Perfect Dreamscape

All characters are age 18 and over.

This is a work of fiction. Names, characters, business, places, events, and incidents are either products of the author's imagination or used in a fictitious manner. Any resemblances to actual persons, living or dead, or actual events is purely coincidental.

Published November 2020 by Deep Desires Press, an imprint of Story Perfect Inc.

Deep Desires Press
PO Box 51053 Tyndall Park
Winnipeg, Manitoba R2X 3B0
Canada

Visit http://www.deepdesirespress.com for more scorching hot erotica and erotic romance.

Subscribe to our email newsletter to get notified of all our hot new releases, sales, and giveaways! Visit deepdesirespress.com/newsletter **to sign up today!**

Silk & Swords

The Queen

and the Oracle

"I wish to hear new tales of *herstory*," Queen Igraine said.

The oracle nodded as she reviewed the leaves at the bottom of the teacup.

The Queen knew what people noted when this ancient woman appeared. They only saw her bald head with brown spots dappling her skull and face, the ornate brass coils encircling her long neck, and her dress made with patches of different materials and colors. She, however, was always mesmerized by the woman's piercing green eyes that seemed to observe things around them that no one else could see.

Igraine settled comfortably into her chair. These readings happened once a year and had for the last six and twenty. She was a lass when they first met and her arranged betrothal to King Richard had recently been announced. A dear friend, concerned about Igraine's worrisome turns of mood, had taken her to see this mystic woman whose gifts the friend raved about.

Igraine had been an uneasy bride-to-be. The lineage of Richard's family and hers went back 400 years to when her knight ancestor rode beside their first king, D'Arth, to forge the kingdom that would become Thuria. She knew, and admired, Richard the king, but she barely knew Richard the man.

She had had three questions for the oracle. First, would she be a good queen? And second, was there true love and, third, if so, would she find it with this man?

The oracle had replied that visions of Igraine's future as woman and respected queen were a whirlwind. Some images were strong as if they had already occurred, but others were like running water in winter, not yet frozen in time and place.

Then the oracle said, to answer her second question, she would tell a *herstory*.

Igraine had been puzzled. There was no such word. It was history. His…story. The past written by men for men. Few women were ever recorded in the writings. That was the way of the world. But the tale she heard—about a proper family aunt she had believed she knew well—was told from the aunt's view and was about the true love she had found. Igraine had been spellbound by the tale, listening to every detailed description. She never suspected the deep passions within her aunt, and the utter joy the aunt had found in partnership with her husband. Since that first reading, since she had become Richard's wife and the realm's queen, she had the oracle come every year to inspire her with new kingdom tales of *herstory*.

The oracle set the cup on the table upon a laced mat in the midst of a circle of white crystals.

Then she looked across the table at the Queen.

"The names of three women have appeared to me," she announced. "The first ye knew when she was babe in arms. She has now reached womanhood. The second ye have never met but yer Majesty's decree changed this woman's life forever, and ye may alter it again if ye wish to. The last is about a woman, and her husband, my Queen is well acquainted with. However, this tale involves a mystery that ye may not wish to hear."

"All if ye please."

"The rebellion of the Usurper is now six months into our kingdom's past and the traitorous nobles have met their fates."

"Yes. Good fortunes are once more on the rise for Thuria."

"'Tis so, yer Majesty. But some of yer subjects are still haunted by what they saw, did, and had done to them during the war."

"Most of us will never be what we were. Myself included. Continue."

"I shall also attempt again to answer your private question. Is there true love?"

"And include the risqué," Igraine added. "I enjoy those parts of the tales."

"Of course, yer Majesty."

The Queen noted that the oracle no longer seemed focused on her. It appeared by the gleam of her green eyes that the ancient woman's spirit had gone far outside the walls of this chamber.

"I shall begin the first one," the oracle said. "It involves a gentle lass and one of the King's men who proved to be most valuable during the war, but ye find him to be without any honor…"

Bree O'Darrow: The King's Enforcer

1

HE ARRIVED AS THEY TOLD BREE HE WOULD.
She heard three voices outside the gaol and knew immediately who the stranger was, and what his duty was for King Richard. Her end was now at hand and she should have been sobbing and shivering in fear. That was exactly how she would have reacted only two months ago, but today, she no longer wept, no longer trembled.

The angels had abandoned her, her soul had withered.

And she was ready for all to be done.

She was not the reason the stranger had been sent here. But she would soon, most assuredly she reasoned, be added to his tasks.

Lord Fitzgerald and Magistrate Baltimore were talking to the stranger in a rush with their words hurtling into the other's speech. These men—two among the most powerful and influential persons in the valley—were terrified of her.

At first glance, she did not appear to be a vessel of evil. She was a tiny lass; barely seven stone in weight and only a smidgen over five foot in height. Yet she frightened all around her. Sincere prayers for her demise were pleaded daily.

Outside, the two prominent men stopped talking.

"Not here for some local matter," the stranger said.

"This is most grave," Baltimore responded.

"More so than the reason I was sent here?"

"Both are of high import, sire."

"Not a sire. I hold no title."

"We have sent our swiftest messenger to King Richard with a new petition," Lord Fitzgerald added. "King's answer should arrive at any time."

"If instructed to do your petition's bidding, then I will. Not before."

Bree felt disappointed. She had truly believed this day would be her last in life. Had welcomed it. Now it appeared she would have to wait. Mayhap until tomorrow. Then again, tomorrow might be more fitting for that day was her eighteenth birthing day and had been the date chosen for her wedding.

She noted that the stranger talked quietly. While he spoke the royal Thurian as most did in the kingdom, his words had the lilt of a dialect spoken in the northernmost highlands of the Rivenran monarchy. Most distinctive was that he talked matter of fact with no nuance in his speech. That made sense. The King's enforcer would not be an emotional and sensitive person. He was a killer.

"An additional fee to enhance your usual stipend could be agreed upon," the lord proposed.

"Besides gold, we have many fine horses," added the magistrate. "You can have your pick. More than one if desired. And a woman to satisfy your bed while you are here attending to our first petition."

Bree was not surprised at their offers. They, and all the citizens in the valley, wanted her removed from their lives as soon as possible, and with finality.

"Insulting," the stranger said.

"We did not mean to besmirch your character," the lord responded quickly. "But we are in desperate need of your services."

The magistrate cleared his throat. "We know your value to the kingdom. Situations do arise that few men would undertake. You have honor. That we know. 'Tis just that you adhere to a code much different from most and that is good. The world is a dangerous place, and the King is most fortunate to have a loyal man such as you serving him when those circumstances arise."

"Bribes and flattery."

"Not false flattery. Truth."

"Do this yourselves. Surely there must be one man here who is willing to end this threat to your valley."

"Nay. We need the King's enforcer."

"Now I'm intrigued. So, *gentlemen*, show me this evil terror."

Bree, without conscious thought, brushed her hands at the wrinkles in her dress and took note of her dirty, bare feet. She shook her head. There was no need to appear presentable. Those days were over. Still, from habit, she glanced about the one-room gaol to see if all in her cell was neat and tidy. She knew the King's enforcer would be surprised at the furnishings. She had humbly requested a comfortable bed and it had been brought to her posthaste. As had table and chair, wash basin and mirror, a few poetry books that she had not touched and, of course, a leather-bound Holy Book that she often held when praying. In one corner was a tall shielding screen and behind it was the necessity pot. She had been given all these because the citizens wanted her placated and docile. They had been horrified by what had happened and feared what more might come.

As for her personal appearance, she knew what the man would see. She had been told often that she had a lovely, enchanting face haloed by a beautiful, silky reddish-brown mane that reached down to her small bottom. Her eyes were a deep smoky gray, and her best friend, Trish, the same age as she, who was youngest daughter of the House of Blackwell, had teased her by saying she had bedchamber eyes. There was a tiny mole beside the left corner of her full lips. A kissing mouth if there ever was one, Trish had joshed. The same face, eyes and mouth, her friend continued, that Delilah must have had that aided the temptress in seducing Samson and her other many admirers. She had a slender and trim frame—for the most part. Trish's coarsest tease, the one she repeated quite often, which always had embarrassed Bree, was that she carried a quarter of her body's weight in her pillows. Each time Bree responded that she was not that big on top. Yet Bree knew she was more endowed than most of her size. She never wore dress or gown with plunging neckline. Trish joked about that, too, saying if she had Bree's magnificent bosom, with her freckles that ran from oval nipple to oval nipple and down, she would wear gowns with décolletage cut to navel. Mayhap lower. Bree had always wished her body were fuller and more curved like the goddesses and ladies portrayed in ancient paintings and sculptures. Her heart clenched. She wished Trish were here to plague her with her teasing. She would be more accepting and good humored if she were. Bree still had a difficult time thinking of Trish, and the others she loved, in the past tense.

Bree heard the lock being turned.

Then the door opened.

He alone stepped inside. The lord and the magistrate remained outside.

Bree had half-expected the King's enforcer to appear as artists often portrayed Death, in hooded black robe and skull face holding a giant reaping scythe. Instead, this man looked like many other men she might have encountered in the fields or at the market. He was six foot in height, and not muscled like a blacksmith or a tree cutter. Yet there did not seem a pinch of fat on him. While he moved with an almost sloth-like demeanor, she intuited he had a quickness within him that most seasoned warriors would envy. His dark clothing, from an unusual wide-brimmed hat to his tall spurred boots, were cloaked in trail dust. There were two short swords sheathed on his hips. The brim of his hat was pulled low on his weather-tanned brow shielding his seemingly black-hued eyes. He was more handsome of face than most, despite the three-days of whisker growth, with a firm but not square jaw, full lips, high cheeks, and a slender straight nose. He was not glorious as her beloved Ian had been but would attract the apt attention of earthy women. Yes, unless a person knew who he was, he would not cause one to tremble in dread nor make small children run away in fear.

The stranger studied her. Once a blatant appraisal such as this would have embarrassed her to her very core. No longer though.

"They call me Quinn," he said.

She curtsied. "I am Bree, House of O'Darrow."

Over his shoulder, Quinn said, "This slip of a lass is the one who frightens you?"

"She is more than she appears," the lord answered.

"Is she a witch? Demon? Or mere blood-thirsty cutthroat?"

"Nay. She is cursed."

"Explain."

"She can say three words and the one she is speaking to will perish soon thereafter," the lord replied. "Five persons are dead because of her."

"What are these *deadly* words?"

Neither his lordship nor the magistrate answered.

So, Bree said the words to the ceiling.

"I love you."

2

BREE WATCHED THE KING'S ENFORCER WALK back outside to gather again with Lord Fitzgerald and Magistrate Baltimore.

Why, she wondered for the thousandth time, had her life come to this wretched station? She had tried to live a good and proper life. She had. Yes, she had sinned upon occasion. She admitted that in church confessional and accepted the penance priest gave her without protest or grumble. But what had she done that was so egregious that her act merited *this* punishment? What sin had been so dreadful that it led to the deaths of those she cherished most.

Was it because she had fallen in love?

Was it? she asked again for the thousandth time.

Bree sat down on the floor with her back against the side of the bed. No tears came, she had none left to weep. Her mind followed a now well-traveled path.

She was the only child of the Baron and Baroness of the House of O'Darrow. Their valley, christened Bella Verde, was in eastern-central Thuria near the great Io River and the unmapped Frontier border. It had the richest, most fertile soil in the entire western regions. The O'Darrow neighbors were the House of Blackwell with its prized wine vineyards and the House of MacLeod with its esteemed Angus cattle. But 'twas her papa's wheat and barley that brought more buyers to the valley at harvest than any other farmhold estate. The yield every time sold well. The royal purchaser would always outbid the other buyers at auction for the bulk of the crop. He had to, no matter how high the bidding went. 'Twas said Queen Igraine would only eat bread, pies and cakes made from O'Darrow grains and could tell the difference if a substitution was made in baking. One year, the purchaser's predecessor had thought the bidding had grown too extravagant and allowed the Zar king's buyer to take the bulk. The current purchaser had said aloud that he would not make that error. But most of the O'Darrow revenue came from the Baron's casks of aged whisky. Noble households throughout the western regions paid her papa to allow their representatives to study under his tutelage. So far, none of the apprentices was able to match his fine whisky.

Her mama and papa were well-respected in their valley. This she knew from overhearing many conversations. They had not grown arrogant with their success and wealth. Papa had declined offer of dedicated private balcony seating for Sunday gatherings at church. Mama said those seats would show they thought they were above the other hard-working citizens of the valley. They were not, only more fortunate than most. Mama did not comment about the families of Blackwell and MacLeod having private balcony seats beside the Queen's brother and his family, House of Fitzgerald. Papa, she saw, was often sought out for advice about farming and his political views about events such as the recent uprising to overthrow the King. Mama was much admired for the charity gatherings she hosted with the township priest, Father Genovesi, for their congregation's poor. Twice, when Bree was still babe-in-arms, Mama had played piano concertos for the King and Queen at Citadelcourt in the capital city of Blackwater.

Bree recognized she was blessed in the life she had been granted. And was grateful. Gave sincere thanks in prayer every day. She could not have had a better Mama and Papa. They loved her and she loved them without respite. They were always encouraging in her endeavors including the ones they knew would turn to folly. She had never been seriously ill or injured. Still vivid was the memory of the winter Trish nearly drowned when she fell into an icy stream. 'Twas thought Trish would perish from the illness that followed. She survived but, from that time on, Trish had weakness in her lungs and could not participate in the strenuous for long. Some of their friends stopped including Trish in outdoor events because of the frailty. Bree did not. Many said that if you saw one of the two lasses, you soon saw the other.

Bree honestly thought her life could not be improved.

Then all changed. And 'twas for the *better*.

On her seventeenth birthing day, Mama and Papa hosted a celebration gathering at their manor with dinner and later dancing. The valley noble houses, save one, and several outside-the-valley doyens and doyennes attended. All was well until they adjourned to the small ballroom and the music from a stringed quartet began. Bree was disheartened. The young gentlemen were clustered together across the room from the young ladies. No one was dancing. She knew Papa and Trish's father would come and escort them onto the dance floor. She would cherish the moment, but she did not want her only dances to be with Papa and, mayhap, Father Genovesi.

Then, late, as had become their custom, the MacLeod brothers arrived in their usual loud bluster and all the valley noble houses were accounted for. No one had spurned the O'Darrow invitation. Trish was whispering into her ear about how rude the MacLeod brothers were, but she was only half-listening to what her friend was saying.

Bree became enthralled at first sight of the MacLeods' visiting cousin. Ian MacLeod, at five and twenty, was the eldest son and heir of the MacLeod part of family that lived and conducted business in the capital. He was beautiful, with his longish golden hair, deep blue eyes, and exquisite handsome face. She realized her body was a tingle with her heart pounding, her mouth agape. And she could not divert her eyes from him.

She saw the MacLeod brother, Hew, tap his cousin's arm, and

point directly at her. She was petrified, but unable to look away from him. Ian MacLeod gazed at her for a long breath then smiled—a dazzling, warm smile. Without further pause, he walked to her, introduced himself and asked if she would honor him with a dance. They danced for most of the evening. Ian only allowed Papa to cut in on them and that he did with an accepting but reluctant grace. Later she knew they had talked but could not recall a single word said except that he was charming and sweet. She was in a gentle daze when she went to bed that night and her dreams were about Ian MacLeod. She thought she remembered that Trish had said, before Trish left the celebration, she would learn the cousin's history.

A few days later, Trish and she gathered in the indigo garden sitting knee to knee, holding hands.

"I learned a little, but not much, from Hew MacLeod and two MacLeod maidservants," Trish said. "Then I found a treasure trove about your Ian. You should remember that I told you the Lady Glass of Blackwater is visiting our estate. Father and she are planning a business venture together. She overheard me talking about Ian MacLeod and took me aside. She said Ian and she were part of many of the same social circles at the capital and often crossed paths. She asked why I wanted to know about him. I explained about you and him meeting at your celebration. She said she would tell me about him because good and proper young ladies needed to be warned." She sighed. "The Lady Glass is old. She is at least thirty, mayhap even forty. Still, she is one of the most beautiful women I have ever seen, and she is always perfectly dressed and groomed. Every gown she has worn is more wondrous than—"

"Trish!" Bree interrupted.

Trish smiled. "Oh. Yes. Your Ian." She paused, but only for a half-second. "He has quite a reputation in Blackwater as a ladies' man. His lovers have been titled young women as well as commoners. No illegitimate babes yet. 'Tis said, and it cannot be proven nor disproven, that he killed the brother of a lady he ruined in a duel. Also, that he was well-known at the notorious Harp House brothel."

Bree felt her heart clench and her eyes verging on tears.

Trish continued. "His father became angry when he had to pay off a second titled family when Ian seduced their daughter and refused to marry her. His father, the High Lord MacLeod, sent Ian here to ponder and mend his ways. His uncle, the Viscount, informed Ian that if he took a single woman at the MacLeod valley manor to his bed, he would be flogged. This was not idle warning. Can you imagine anyone punishing the man who would one day be the head of the entire clan?" She paused again. "You're not interested a tad in that part either, are you?"

Bree tightened her hold on Trish's fingers.

"Very well. Ian quickly found one of our township tavern women to tend his fleshly desires. 'Tis said the trollop refused his coin and stated the only payment she wanted was for him to lay in her bed often. He did regularly. Until the day after your party celebration. Then he went to *that* woman and gave her gold with his thanks. Told her that he would not be returning. He had met the lass of his dreams."

"W-Who is this lass?" Bree asked, suddenly chilled.

Trish laughed. "Ye, you silly goose."

She was overwhelmed. Could this be true? She and a few of the local lads had practiced courting intimacies after she had turned four and ten and her pillows had begun to blossom. These clandestine rendezvous resulted in a handful of awkward tries at kissing that never went beyond pressing of lips. Mayhap once or twice, a tap of tongue occurred. Along with the kisses came, always outside of clothing, fumbled strokes to her pillows and her quick touch of exploration to small, erect cocks. These pairings never lasted long. Ian MacLeod was a man of the world, not a ham-handed, blundering lad. Did she dare dream that Ian was captivated by her? She wanted it to be so. But Trish had never, ever, lied to her. Then again, what Trish had learned from old Lady Glass could be mere gossip and nasty chinwag from jealous and envious parties. None of it true.

Her questions were soon answered.

Her Papa and Mama received a written note from the Viscount MacLeod asking if he and his nephew could call upon them the following afternoon. 'Twas granted.

The two men came to the front door and not the back as friends and neighbors did. Bree understood this was an official visit. They gathered in the seldom used but immaculate guest parlor that the maids had been cleaning ever since the note arrived. She watched as the Viscount introduced his nephew to Mama and Papa, although Papa had met him at her party celebration. His uncle recited Ian's blood lineage and bona fides. He included his nephew's future prospects. Ian presented his card to Papa, as was becoming the fashion in the capital, and gave a small bouquet of white carnations to Mama. For Bree, he only had his smile. More would have been considered forward and ill-mannered. His smile was enough.

As Bree listened, she chastised herself. She had been outside too long before the visit and the sun had given her face a pink tint. And she had to consciously keep herself from fidgeting. When she heard the reason for the calling, she nearly swooned.

The Viscount announced his nephew, with Mama's and Papa's approval of course, wished to be allowed to court their daughter.

Bree was beside herself, twitching in her skin, as Papa crossed his arms over his chest, appearing very fatherly, and seemed to take forever and a day to respond. He looked to Mama for agreement before answering.

"Yes, a courting will be allowed," Papa, at long last, replied.

She nearly squealed in delight and wanted to run to Papa and hug him. But she remained where she was, appropriate and modest.

"However," Papa said, "there will be standards adhered to. All visits will be planned beforehand. No unannounced callings. There shall always be a supervising escort to ensure proper, respectable decorum. Never will the two be alone together." He looked at the young man. "You, sire, may join us for Sunday gathering at church. My wife will sit between you and our daughter."

Mama added, "The Baron and I courted for two full years before we were wed."

"If this is agreeable," finished Papa, "and if you gentlemen have the time, I would like to show you about our property and fields. This season's yield of wheat and barley is very promising."

When the three men departed, with Papa and the Viscount enthusiastically discussing the coming harvest auctions and livestock judging, Bree was in the utmost delightful of swirls. Life was wonderful.

That evening, before bed, Mama took her aside.

"Daughter, Ian MacLeod is a most handsome and charming man," her mama said. "He is also a bit of a scoundrel. I recognize this firsthand because your papa was the same in his youth. It took my guiding hand to smooth his rough edges and inclinations."

She nodded. Mama had never shared such intimate knowledge with her before.

"I want you to remember this," Mama said. "Your Grandmama gave me this advice and warning. A man will not buy the cow, if he gets the milk for free."

In bed, she pondered that for the briefest moment. But for the most part, before drifting into sleep and glorious dreams, she inventoried and scrutinized every facet of Ian's beautiful face and strong body. He was never found lacking. She even giggled aloud as she pictured them at a royal gala and, dancing a vassedanse in the Citadelcourt grand ballroom. Ian would lift her at the waist above his head in midst of the dance's final twirl and she, wearing an elegant snow-white gown, with her body straight and arms outstretched, would appear as lovely as a dove soaring in the clouds. The entire crowd, led by the Queen, would applaud them.

The following evening, Mama gave her a chastity belt.

"You shall wear this daily," she instructed. "Even on days when Ian MacLeod is not calling on you. I want you to become used to it on your person."

Bree was mortified. "I would never do anything improper…or sinful."

"Believe this, at a time that shall come, Ian MacLeod will make his seduction feel proper and most natural. Sin will not be among your thoughts. I know this to be true. This garment will protect and serve you well. I wish Grandmama had given me one when your papa was courting."

Bree blushed. She loved Mama and Papa with all her heart and soul, but she did not wish to know even a hint about their physical life together.

"When Trish and you were young girls," her mama continued, "the two of you often went swimming with the boys. I watched. Those days were innocent times. Do you still swim with the boys?"

"Nay. Not since the coming of my first moon-flowing. Now Trish and I swim alone and always in secluded spot."

"Does anyone, save Trish, see you unclothed?"

"No, Mama."

"Good. If Papa and I are not with you and Ian when he calls, Matron Harriet shall be your chaperone. You will not try to deceive or fool her to be alone with Ian. She has my permission to use switch to your backside if you misbehave."

"I won't!"

Mama sighed deeply. "Your papa and I have sheltered you too much. The world you see is not the true world."

"I do not understand your meaning, Mama."

"I pray you never do."

Bree was confused by Mama's words.

Mama patted her hand.

Then she said, "Trish and you have, since blooming into womanhood, kept abreast of the latest clothing fashions and styles coming out of our capital and the other kingdoms, are aware of the popular grooming rituals. The noble ladies of Zar were the first, I believe, to adopt one grooming in particular, but it has taken hold in our capital, too. 'Twas a standard in the ancient Memphi dynasty of

Moses' time, an expected one among both royal women and men. Do you, daughter, remove the hair on your legs and under your arms? Do you trim the hair at your intimate?"

"U-Uh…uh," Bree stammered.

"You do. I shall not share this with Papa. He would be mortified. Listen to me. If Ian MacLeod, with his own eyes or touching by hand, becomes aware of your grooming, I will end the courtship."

Bree nodded. She understood this.

And the courtship began.

Ian and she took long walks together in the coming days and weeks. Always with watchful Matron Harriet between them. They engaged in carriage and horse rides, had picnics under shade trees. She watched as Ian and Papa played chess after evening dinner. Ian joined the family every Sunday for church service. Once Mama hosted a gathering to make quilts for the poor. Ian was there. He read poetry, refined and genteel prose without a tad of scandalous verbiage, to the ladies and lasses. Still, he caused a delighted titter among the elder women when he had paused on a very tame word and smiled as he raised one brow. Bree loss track of how many times she stabbed her fingers with needle as she gazed at him.

Trish had heard, and of course shared, that Ian MacLeod's return date to the capital had been extended. By his request.

Bree was delighted.

On the days when Ian was not calling, Trish and other valley lasses would gather around Bree. They would relentlessly pepper her with questions about the relationship. With each response, they would smile and say how blessed she was. Then one day, Trish quieted all. She had learned of a recent event that involved Bree's courting beau.

"Two evenings ago, Ian and Hew MacLeod went to our township tavern to engage in games of chance and, of course, for the spirits. A bounder, well into his whisky, made a discourteous and loud remark about Bree's physique. Ian took the man outside and throttled him speechless."

The lasses sighed and told Bree how gallant her beau was.

But Bree, tight-lipped, looked at Trish.

Trish smiled. "I knew you would ask so I inquired. Yes, *that* tavern wench was there. Ian and she had no exchanges save for the trollop placing mugs of ale on his table."

Bree relaxed, pleased.

'Twas during the very next calling, walking along the wooded stream on the estate, when Ian and she eluded Matron Harriet for a few minutes. Alone for the first time, Ian took her in his strong arms and kissed her. The kiss was gentle and slow, so ever slow. With his lips and tongue, Ian placed his claim on her mouth. Bree basked in their embrace, her heart swelled, and a pleasant warmth blossomed at her intimate under the chastity belt. 'Twas well worth the scolding she received from Matron Harriet later. Each stolen kiss after that day was better than the one before. Their longest kiss came during a picnic when Matron Harriet had fallen asleep after eating her meal.

After that kiss, as Ian caressed her cheek, he suggested a secret rendezvous. "I wish to show you magnificent pleasures and I cannot wait until our wedding night. I swear, my love, being so close to you but with a wall still between us shall cause me to perish in misery and agony. You, and only you, can save me from this fate."

Bree nearly melted into bliss.

Before she agreed to the secret and special rendezvous, Trish and she had a lengthy talk about such a gathering. Trish was firm in her belief that Bree should wait until she was wedded.

"Remember," she said to Bree, "Ian lost interest in the other women he laid with."

Bree smiled. "But I am different. I am his true love. He has told me that."

"I am sure," Trish continued, "the other females had the same thought."

Soon however Trish was as enchanted as her friend as she listened to Bree's dreamy words about Ian's kisses and the wondrous warmth he caused to her person. She wanted more, and she wanted to learn to pleasure him. They were in love and what they were planning could not be a sin. Besides, Bree added with a sigh, they could only go so far. She was wearing chastity belt.

One warm morning, weeks after their courtship had begun, with Trish and Hew MacLeod standing guard, Ian and she met without another single person at the estate knowing it.

They lay at a secluded cove that they would come to call the Oasis, on a blanket over a thick patch of moss. They remained clothed. Ian kissed her mouth and neck and caressed her pillows. Then, with the most charming words, he lifted the hem of her dress. Bree knew their lovemaking would go no farther. Nay. She had trouble removing the chastity belt at bedtime using the lock's key. Which was, at the current, secured in Mama's jewelry box. Ian smiled and rubbed his right thumb over the tips of his index and middle fingers then he showed her a thin sliver of metal. Moments later, as if by divine magic it seemed to her, Ian removed the belt from her body and set it aside. Ian's strokes to her intimate were heavenly. She tensed as he moved over her. Bree had been told that the first joining was painful for the female. Theirs was not. 'Twas like a pinch. Of course, she should have known that coupling with Ian would be different than the usual and expected. She did not know how long being-as-one should last until Ian withdrew his erection from within her and seeded the ground. Bree was mildly disappointed with the coupling. She did not have to tell Ian because he intuited it. She had not pinnacled. He promised that the next time he would bring her to woman's glory. It did not happen, nor did it during the third joining.

It was not until their fourth time together that she soared with unexpected bodily pleasure. They had returned to the Oasis, and in the moonlight, they lay fully unclothed for the first time beside one another. He caressed her body with a sure hand, and she explored his with tentative and shy touches. Ian found his rhythm this night. He stroked her intimate until she was moist before moving over and inside her. His member caused a rising within her body that she had never known. When she pinnacled, she cried out aloud as wondrous glory rippled through her. Ian withdrew, and seeded the ground. He laid beside her and she kissed him as she never had before. All was grand.

Bree told Trish that her life was perfect, and she wanted it to remain as 'twas now, forever.

Then changes came once more.

At the end of the ninth month of their courtship, Papa and Mama received a second written request for Ian and the Viscount MacLeod to be allowed to call upon them the following day.

Bree was sitting in the guest parlor beside her Mama when Papa showed the two men into the room.

Immediately, a silent but gripping dread grabbed her by the throat. She had never seen such a serious and solemn demeanor surrounding her beloved. For the past week, Ian had been talking about letters from his father and his future responsibilities for the House of MacLeod. Tears threatened her eyes. She knew he had been called home. He had been here much longer than originally planned. How could their courtship continue at such a distance? How would she survive not seeing his glorious smile regularly? Not sharing kisses and intimate caresses? She would wither from a parting.

Nay, an angel whispered in her mind's ear, Ian has come today to fulfill your heart's desire.

Bree nearly shouted in joy. She held Mama's hand more firmly. Yes, that was why the gathering was formal.

Ian faced Papa.

"Too long," Ian said. "Too long."

Papa furrowed his brow. "What is too long, sire?"

"The Baroness and you courted for two years."

"Aye."

"Too long, too long."

Papa smiled but only for a moment. He then adopted his stern, fatherly deportment.

"Say what you have come to say, sire. If you do not so in short order, I will escort you out the door."

Bree saw the Viscount hide a chuckle behind his hand.

Ian inhaled deeply, held the breath, then exhaled.

"Two years is too long a time, Baron and Baroness O'Darrow. I know a respectable amount of time is protocol before the date is set but it must be sooner than later. I cannot continue living as I have been."

"You are still unclear in what you intend to convey. Come to the point, sire, and be distinct in your words."

The Viscount laughed.

And Ian nearly shouted. "I have fallen in love with your daughter. I am asking for her hand in marriage."

Bree swooned, and collapsed into Mama's embrace.

During the next few days, there were several gatherings between the houses of O'Darrow and MacLeod. Ian's father, the High Lord of House of MacLeod, came for an extended visit to meet her, and hold talks with Mama and Papa. Bree was in a blissful daze, would give oath that her feet were not touching the ground when she walked. She could recall most of the subjects discussed in the meetings but not their answers. After the first, she had Trish beside her to review later what was talked about. The matters discussed, and occasionally debated, were her dowry, when the wedding would be held, whether the ceremony would occur in their valley or at the capital, if Father Genovesi—who had been Bree's priest her entire life—would perform the Holy Book bonding or if Blackwater's High Vicar would. Even discussed were possible journeys the bride and groom could take to celebrate their first weeks of wedded bliss.

In-between those gatherings, Mama would talk to her about the perfect wedding dress; that, of course, Trish would be her maid of honor but who else would be asked to be bridesmaids; what foods would be served at the wedding dinner. The date most mentioned for the wedding was her birthing day.

On a Saturday four weeks after Ian's proposal, Mama sat Bree down.

"Tomorrow, at the church," Mama said, "after the priest's

sermon, Papa, in front of the township, will officially announce your engagement to Ian."

Bree was happier than she had ever been.

The next day, Sunday, sitting in first pew of the crowded church, Bree knew Father Genovesi's sermon—about the testing of Job, no less—was slower and longer than the usual oration spoke by their priest. And Mama, sitting between Ian and her as usual, kept raising her spread fan to block Bree's view every time she glanced at Ian.

Finally, after announcing the birth of a healthy son to a ground's family at the estate of Blackwell and the upcoming feast day of St. Benedict, Father Genovesi called Papa and Ian forward. As the three men gathered on the steps in front of the pulpit, Bree saw that Ian was wearing a new tailored suit. The clothing was both conservative and handsome. Bree heard a titter among the lasses in the church before Papa spoke.

Papa stood upright straight and held the lapels of his Sunday coat between his fingers. She thought he looked like an artist's depiction of the perfect father, which he was.

"I am most proud to announce," he said, "the betrothal of my daughter, Bree Suzanne, House of O'Darrow, to Mister Ian Michael Stephen, House of MacLeod."

"*NAY!*"

The shrill cry filled the church from floorboard to rafter.

The congregation, most seated and some standing, turned swiftly toward the doorway.

In the entryway was a young lass. Mayhap, Bree reasoned, thirteen or fourteen years of age. The lass was wide-eyed, and her dark hair was twisted in wild tangles. As she spoke with spit flying from her mouth, she rended madly at her clothing and exposed a nail-clawed breast.

"Ian is my true love," the lass shrieked, "and I am his!"

She pointed with both hands, index and little fingers extended, directly at Bree. "This…this creature has bewitched and stolen him from me!"

Later 'twould be determined that the lass was named Loki and she was kitchen serving maid at the House of MacLeod. Other maidservants would reveal they often saw Loki gazing, enchanted, at Ian. She even peeked at him from around corners. No recollection, including Ian's own, could recall any discourse between the two. Ian swore to this on the Holy Book, and Bree believed him without single doubt. Yet Ian must have given Loki an empty wine chalice at some point. The glass, along with two linen napkins that Ian had used, were found under the kitchen maid's bed pillow.

Also found was an upside-down black cross with a satanic goat's head and pentagram carved on it.

Loki marched forward, hexing hands continuing to point at Bree.

Several men rose and started for the lass. Then they froze as she screamed:

"I curse ye Bree O'Darrow! I give my soul to Satan, and with the master's aid, all who Bree O'Darrow loves and all that she treasures will perish! Ye shall live a long life to dwell on yer treachery, Bree O'Darrow! If ye are slain, the person who ends yer life shall inherit the curse!"

Ian, Father Genovesi and Hew MacLeod ran toward the lass.

Loki smiled at Ian. "Ye were my destiny. I love ye."

A dagger suddenly appeared in Loki's fist, and she slit her own throat from ear-to-ear.

Bree stared, in shock, at the corpse and barely felt Mama take her into embrace. Nor did she recall Papa, and moments later Ian, come to her.

The following day, the first tragedy came.

3

I LOVE YOU," QUINN REPEATED TO BREE AS THEY stood in the gaol cell.

Then he chuckled. It had always been amazing to him the things people chose to believe in. During his three and thirty years, he'd never seen a single event he attributed to black, or white, mystical. He admitted he had witnessed happenings—several acts of nature and some amid battle—he couldn't explain. These events, however, he just didn't have the knowledge to reason them. Never had he considered the happenings to have been orchestrated by Heaven or Hell.

Bree brushed at a wrinkle in her dress. "Those outside do not care if you inherit my curse."

"I know."

"If you are ordered to execute me, I shall not fight or run from you."

Quinn nodded. "To fight or run you have to want to live."

"I do request time for Lord's prayer beforehand."

"Makes no never mind to me."

Bree furrowed her brow. "You do not believe in Heaven and Hell, do you?"

"I believe in Hell. We live in that world."

"I feel sad for you."

"Don't bother. I need to talk more with the two outside."

Quinn walked from the cell. He had been sent to the valley to find and kill a man. A straight-forward task. Now he was being strayed, a little anyway, from that assignment by this young lass. Why was that? Why her? Bree O'Darrow had no life left within her, actually believed she was cursed, and yet she felt *sad* for him. When had any person ever told him that? Never. She intrigued him. And he could not remember the last time he had been curious about another person. Even the coin-paid women at the capital who lay with him— the few not afraid to—held no interest for him once the deed was done. He considered altering his usual routine before he reached the lord and the magistrate. Once again, when had he done that before? He swiftly adapted to an unforeseen event or turn in a task but this change in habit was different.

Why did this sorrowful lass intrigue him so?

Quinn had been told he was abandoned as babe, left in a trough teeming with refuse and rats. That history no longer bothered him. He'd placed it on a dark shelf in his mind and rarely dusted it off. When he did, he cursed the unknown Good Samaritan who rescued him. He had grown up in the highlands in the northern kingdom of Rivenran. 'Twas a hard life there that created a strong people. He had been shuffled between the mountain kinfolks. No one wanted a most troublesome, angry lad for long. After he turned seven or so, he walked to Rivenran's capital, Balmoral, and fended for himself on the streets of the city. He'd never been religious despite the sincere kindness of persons like Friar Joseph. The missionary was from First Church, who braved the high mountains for his order to share the word of the Gospel. The friar always had a hot meal and warm bedding for any who wished it. But if one accepted, and sometimes it was the only meal and bed Quinn had had for a week, one had to endure the friar's sermons. He often talked about the teachings of a man called Jesus. But most of the tales did not make any sense to him.

If one turned the other cheek when slapped, one would more than likely get that cheek punched, too. No, he was the one who did the hitting.

And that was his best ability.

He was a good fighter. When he learned to use blades and clubs, the weapons became extensions of his body. By the time he was five and ten, even grown men no longer challenged him in any way despite his disrespectful manners.

That was the age when he began, always alone, to wander the western kingdoms and provinces.

He hired out to different persons and clans. All that mattered when he did so was the amount of coin offered. His reputation as a skilled, ruthless fighter grew among those who traveled in that low rogue world.

He plainly remembered his first meeting with Matthias Duncan.

During the summer of his thirtieth year, he was in Thuria's capital of Blackwater looking for new employment. He was down to his last silvers and counting closely each spending.

One night he had been sitting in a crowded city tavern, in the corner with back to wall, slow nursing a mug of ale, hoping to overhear a conversation that might lead to a job, when a man approached him. The man, while not wearing the usual noble finery, was plainly one of that class.

"My name is Matthias Duncan," the man said. "Member of the royal high council and on a task for the King. May I buy you ale and talk?"

Quinn beckoned the noble to join him. But, as Duncan sat, he walked away from the table. He left his hat to show he'd be back.

A few minutes later, he returned. He saw a fresh stein of ale before his place but continued slow drinking from his original mug.

"You are who you say you are," Quinn said.

"You went to verify who I was."

Quinn did not respond. What he'd done was obvious.

He noted that Duncan had no ale or whisky for himself. He'd

encountered a few before who did not imbibe spirits. Most could not be trusted, deeming they're not drinking to their superiority over others who did. He also surmised from the furrow on the noble's brow that this member of high council detested the task he'd been given. He knew immediately this man and he would not like one another.

Duncan cleared his throat and began. "Our King Richard has me searching for a man of proven and skilled fighting ability."

"He has an army at his disposal."

"Not for this position."

"Ah. There are several assassins for hire in the capital if the King wishes to remove a political rival or a Queen's lover."

"Nay. Not that either. However, and I must be clear on this point, assassination will play a role in the position."

"Explain."

Duncan inhaled deeply. "The position would be called the King's enforcer, but no knighthood or rank will come with it. 'Twould be a permanent position with room at Citadelcourt and meals. An agreed-upon stipend would be paid each month even if no task were given for that time. The enforcer would have to swear fealty to the King, always be available for any task, willing to travel anywhere. All tasks would remain secret. The King shall never, in person or by written message, give the enforcer assignments. The enforcer would be assigned King's tasks only by me acting as go-between."

"But again, the King has an army to choose a man from."

"Here is how 'twas presented to me. There is right and wrong. Sometimes wrong must be done for the safety of the kingdom and her citizens. Occasionally evil needs to be done. No knight of honor would accept these tasks and the assignments would be condemned from highest station to lowest if known. King Richard understands this. He wants me to find a man who does not follow our code of honor. One who has his own. Or none. While the specific tasks undertaken would remain secret, the position and duties of the enforcer would be announced. An outsider would have mystery surrounding him that one of our knights would not, and this would add to the fear of him. The King believes this knowledge would keep some citizens from breaking the law."

"These tasks? Explain."

"The kingdom has enemies. Some within our borders, some outside. These persons are always beyond the law, or the enforcer would not be needed. And, for the welfare of our kingdom, these persons must be dealt with in the harshest means."

"Ah." Quinn finished his ale. "If considered for this position, I would have one demand and two questions to be answered. I would demand meeting—once—with King Richard to determine if he were a man I could give my oath to."

Duncan frowned. "Acceptable."

"I assume a test of my ability would be required?"

"Yes, and if task is concluded satisfactorily, before I would recommend you to the King, you and I would have long discussion."

"To talk philosophy and my view of the world? Boring."

"Your other question?"

"You are to be go-between. How would I know if assigned task was given by the King or by you for your own benefit?"

Duncan bristled.

Quinn knew trust and so-called honor would be paramount between the three men. Later, Quinn was to learn the high-principled counsel did, in fact, detest his role in Quinn's position, yet he never discovered the reason Duncan accepted it. The 'why' didn't really matter.

The testing task was simple in many aspects. There was a wealthy merchant in Blackwater who supplemented his fortune with dastardly endeavors. Dastardly was the word Duncan used. The high counsel said this merchant would soon be arrested and convicted of crimes in a lawful court. The target was the businessman's assassin partner. This killer would, more than likely, walk away from arrest and soon be plying his trade with another partner. Rough justice was called for.

Quinn followed the assassin for a full day. The next morning, he found the man lounging in a tub as he was being washed and groomed by two battered, bruised women. He walked silently up on the assassin and without saying a word slid his dagger into the assassin above his collarbone and cut him up to his chin. The women did not scream nor call for help. One blessed him before they scampered away.

Afterward, Duncan and he had the discussion the counsel had threatened. 'Twas more boring than Quinn had anticipated. But his blunt, short answers must've satisfied the counsel, because soon after came audience with the King. He found Richard to be a good and practical man who understood the way of the world. The King even joked with him a couple times during the meeting. He was offered and accepted the position as enforcer.

For him, the main benefits were steady coin, comfortable room with good bed, and regular meals. In the beginning, he knew, in the back of his mind, he could always walk away from his pledge of fealty if things turned to his disliking. Over the next three years, he discovered he would honor and keep his oath given to King Richard.

Tasks, at first, were few. All were outside the borders of the kingdom. Then came the rebellion of the Usurper. He went among the traitors and plied his skill. Twice he was nearly killed by the King's own men mistaking him for an enemy soldier. He accomplished the slaying of one noble when, in the guise of rebel standing sentry, he put an arrow into the heart of the man as the traitor lord rode past his guard station.

It would always amuse Quinn when Duncan used words like justice and right when giving him his assignments. The conservative, high-minded man was exactly as he first judged him. Duncan surprised him only once. That was when he heard that the counsel had wedded a woman from a barbarian clan. That was most out-of-character for the man he had come to know.

He had no friends amongst the Thurians, and only a handful of steady acquaintances—a tavern ale tender who only talked about the weather and women's teats, a trio of coin-paid females that he never saw except when he followed them to their brothel room, and a knight named Beaudry who was often at the same gambling tables he frequented. He maintained the mystery about himself as the King and Duncan wanted. He corrected himself. He did have one friend. The room he'd been given had been adopted, before he arrived, by a mangy, stray cat. The tom grudgingly allowed him to stay. The stray, who vanished for days at a time then returned bloody but with strut in his walk, he named Mouser. He and Mouser accepted, reluctantly, the other's presence. Mouser never demanded food, only a spot on the bed to recuperate and sleep and made clear that he was never to be touched. The bowl of water Quinn put out was drank but never acknowledged with gratitude.

Today, after three years as enforcer, his latest task had brought him to Bella Verde Valley in eastern-central Thuria. He admitted, on first arrival, the name was fitting. This was a beautiful green valley.

And so was the young woman he had just met, despite the curse.

Quinn stopped beside Lord Fitzgerald and Magistrate Baltimore.

He nearly smiled at them. He could tell they had gathered some iron in their bollocks. Bribery and flattery had not worked. Now would come power position. These two were predictable. 'Twas a surprise they had not used this tactic first. He decided to put them off their game. Just for his own amusement.

"I came to you using the main road," he said. "It appears to me that your valley was spared from the ravages of the Usurper's rebellion that many others in the kingdom were not."

"We lost several valley sons to the war," interjected Fitzgerald.

"Which side were they fighting for?"

He heard the lord gasp at the insinuation.

"Did the estates here do well during the rebellion?" he continued.

"I protest," replied the lord. "We did not use the war to turn profit."

"I'd wager that you, however, took in a goodly fortune. That is why the brigands decided to plague your valley."

"We have two plagues to contend with," corrected Baltimore.

Quinn glanced at the open doorway of the gaol. He could not see the lass inside. "I wonder what the third shall be."

"Enough," the lord said, having regrouped himself, now solemn and with much import. "I am House of Fitzgerald, brother of the Queen and overseer of the largest estate in the valley. I order you to render final decree on Bree O'Darrow."

"Nay," Quinn replied, simply.

Fitzgerald appeared thunderstruck, as if the enforcer had spat on him.

"I c-command you," the lord stammered.

"I follow the orders of one man, and no one else," Quinn said. "And our King has not instructed me one way or t'other in this matter."

"I am titled personage and the Queen's brother."

"So?"

Quinn knew the lord would retreat in his stance. The man did not know how to proceed. His orders were never refused nor disobeyed. He had two options open to him. To either accept the refusal, or to send his men to punish Quinn. But how would the lord explain to the King that he had his enforcer slain? If they could do so.

That left the magistrate to pick up the banner.

"We are confused, sir," said Magistrate Baltimore. "The King has already sent knights to aid in our first petition. I do not disparage your skills in any manner but why would one man come as reinforcement for the troop?"

Quinn allowed them to wait for his response. He studied the gaol with its hard-packed, barren ground circling it then the township. The town had only a few buildings, centered around a two-story tavern-inn, and were all on the same side of the roadway. The other side had no structures, not even a corral for horses. Then he saw three upright carved pillars among the tall grasses and weeds. All were broken and not near their original heights. Pillars such as these, as well as other ruined structures were scattered across the kingdom. Before the first Thurians had walked this land, an ancient people had lived here. What had ended their reign, their very existence, was mystery.

"I'm not here to join with the knights," he replied, at last.

Hell, he thought, Sir Bryce Lakesnow was in command of the troop and the knight captain didn't need, nor would want, the aid of the enforcer. Before the rebellion, the army had been at maximum strength. Back then Lakesnow would have arrived at the head of a fifty-man troop for this campaign. Today, he had ten knights under his command. Still, Lakesnow was more than able to render justice upon the villains calling themselves the Watchdogs. The brigands were plaguing a 200-kilometer stretch of the border between Thuria and the Frontier. The band numbered forty to forty-five men and growing. The Watchdogs had come to this valley and to the townships and farmholds outside and informed the citizens that they would protect the people of the region from barbarian raiders and bandits. For this service, they would charge a tax and be paid in coin and food on regular basis. The ones who refused were murdered and their homeholds burned. The valley citizens and those outside had sent petitions to the King for aid. Lakesnow and troop had been dispatched to resolve the situation.

Quinn's task was related to the Watchdogs. Seton Martell was the leader of the brigands. Duncan said that the dastardly—there was that word of his again—Martell had once been a battle-decorated veteran of the King's knights. During a Frontier mission, he'd been seized, with others, by the fierce Nikota clan. He alone escaped and this was touted as miracle never done before. Then the evil began. He had, in a drunken rage 'twas said, savaged and murdered a fellow knight and the knight's wife before disappearing from the capital and eluding the hunters chasing him. 'Twas known he'd served the Usurper, although Quinn had never seen him in his among-the-rebels tasks, but when the traitor nobles were captured the once-knight was not among the prisoners. 'Twas repeated by several witnesses, that Martell would walk a battlefield after fight and slay any wounded knight he found. With Martell's knowledge of army ways and training, he would dodge the knight troop for quite a while. Quinn's task was clear cut. Find Seton Martell and slay him. The risk of Martell escaping justice was too great given his history. Quinn was to kill Martell even if Lakesnow had taken the once-knight prisoner. He had clarified that last detail with Duncan. 'Twas so, the high counsel had said reluctantly.

"My task is to stay here at first," he told the two men outside the gaol. "The people in this valley are respected and our King wants to ensure you remain unharmed."

"No disrespect intended, sir," the magistrate replied. "How can one man, even with your skills, guarantee our safety?"

"I believe the Watchdogs are due soon to collect their tax."

"In a few days," said Fitzgerald, finding his voice once again.

"I'll meet with them on your behalf. Just tell me where the tax is to be delivered."

"There's always a dozen or more when they come."

"That's my concern."

"They'll kill you."

Quinn shrugged. "Then you'll be on your own again."

The two men moved away and whispered to one another.

He gazed at the gaol again, pondering. His thoughts were once again about the lass. Was he really going to do this? Aye, she was a lovely lass, but he'd seen more beautiful. He'd even lain with one in the capital of Cordoba who he'd paid triple the usual amount to do so. That was not his reason. Although he would admit that the one sad look the lass had thrown him had caught him square at the lacing of his breeches. He wasn't a monk after all. That wasn't it. And he wasn't a do-good rescuer of the downtrodden and fallen. His charity did not go beyond *not* kicking beggars out of his way when they blocked his city path. What was it about this lass that intrigued him so?

The lord and magistrate turned back to him.

"We shall do as you instruct," Baltimore said. "A room has been prepared for you at the tavern. The cook prepares good meals of the common variety."

He'd decided. "I'm going to stay here. Put a bed inside the cell that will accommodate a man of my size."

"Place it besides the lass's?" asked Fitzgerald.

Quinn stepped in front of the lord. Only mere breath separated them. "In her state of mind, that would be rape. Are you calling me rapist?"

The Queen's brother backstepped. "Apologies, apologies."

"Place the bed on the opposite side of the room from hers. I also want a gentle pony with sidesaddle. Don't know your valley. Need to see the lay of the land. I will use her as my guide."

"We have men who would be excellent guides for you," the magistrate responded.

"The lass was born here. She knows the valley, too."

"Our people would be dismayed and angered to see her riding about."

"My task is to protect your people, not to please them. I shall use her as my guide."

"We cannot do that," said Baltimore flatly.

"Why?"

"We discussed putting her on a horse and telling her leave the valley. Even considered leaving gaol door open so she could just walk away. If she were killed, thrown by the horse, the man who gave her horse would inherit the curse."

"Or the one that left the door open."

"Aye."

"Shite," Quinn muttered. "Bring a half-dozen ponies and I will choose the one she rides."

"It shall be done. Will there be anything else, sir?"

"Eventually," he said, walking toward the gaol. "I shall let you know when I need it."

T WAS DARKFALL AND BREE SAT, WITH HANDS
folded in lap, on the edge of her bedstead watching Quinn in
the candlelight. This was a most improper arrangement.

Earlier a bed was brought to the gaol and pushed against the far
wall from hers. The men delivering the stead kept their backs to her
and had not, as far as she witnessed, stolen even a swift glance at her.

She did not understand the enforcer. Why a second bed? If he
intended to have his way with her body, he would just use her bed
afterward. But, thus far, he had not touched her and his looking at
her, except for that first appraisal, had not been for long or
disconcerting. Well, mayhap a little distressing.

They had talked, and she had told him in simple words about
how the curse had happened at the church. She was exhausted when
she finished the recital.

After eating the bowl of stew with bread and drinking the stein
of ale provided for him—she'd hadn't touched her own meal—he had
removed his boots, tunic, and weapons. He'd placed the short swords
on the ground beside his bed then she was surprised to see he carried
a third weapon—a dagger he kept sheathed at his spine—and he put
it under the bed pillow to keep within easy reach. He wore a leather
cord around his neck that held a man's straight shaving razor. Now,

he was stretched out on the mattress, head upon pillow with hands clasped behind and eyes closed. But she knew he was not sleeping.

"You told them to leave the door unlocked," she said.

"Aye."

"You have now taken responsibility for me, and if I am somehow killed, you will inherit the curse."

"So, you and the people of this valley believe. Anytime you wish to leave, lass, do it. I won't stop you."

Bree shook her head. He truly did not believe and that would lead to his damnation.

Quinn opened his eyes and turned onto his side, placing his raised head against the palm of his hand. "You wish your life ended, are ready for it. So, tell me why you haven't killed yourself?"

She frowned and responded immediately. "That is mortal sin. The taking of one's own life sends one straight to the bowels of Hell."

"Ah. There's a tiny spark still inside you that wants to live."

"I do not deserve a life," she said flatly. "This is my deserved chastisement. I heard you say that you would not couple with me. I will not fight if you decide to."

"I know."

"I have earned punishment."

"So, my skills as lover would be punishment?"

"I didn't say—." She stopped. The remark would not be dignified with response. "Sire, why do you wish for me to be your guide about the valley?"

"I hold no title. Call me Quinn, call me mister, call me son-of-bitch," he replied. "To answer your question, you know the valley. You grew up here after all. I believe you shall be adequate guide for my needs, and until now, I thought you'd be quiet for the most part."

"Apologies. I am a talker. That I will not deny. But since the death of Father Genovesi, I have had no one to talk to. You have seen with your own eyes how they treat me. Most will not even look at me."

"Aye. That's another reason I want you as my guide. With you riding beside me, the valley citizens will keep their distance and not talk to *me*. I will like that." He paused for a moment then continued. "Tomorrow you will take me to a good pond or stream. One where the waters are not too cold."

"Why?"

"How long have you been jailed here?"

"Not certain. The days swirl together for me. 'Tis been a month since Father Genovesi died. Mayhap a month and a half."

"I once rode with a man who didn't ever bathe. Said it would wash away the body's natural shielding. When he died, the vultures wouldn't go near his corpse. You, lass, are riper than he ever was. You need a bath."

"I requested bath, but the women of the valley were too frightened to escort me. So, I haven't been allowed."

"Well, I'm not afraid."

"You are confusing, sire...uh, Mister Quinn. You say you have no honor, but I believe you do."

He sighed. "Nay. But believe as you will. Now I want you to tell me what occurred after the cursing. Tell me what happened to your loved ones."

Bree frowned. "I am unsure if I can. I only spoke with Father Genovesi about the deaths of Mama and Papa and Ian. I have not talked about the deaths of the good priest and Trish. There has been no one to speak with."

"Now you have me."

"You are not priest. You have not taken their vows for confession."

Quinn chuckled. "No, I'm not a priest but know this," he said, "my code of honor is written in smoke, not stone. I adapt when it's called for. So, this is me. I am what I am, and I am what I am not. I do not step aside for any man. I have never known the touch of a woman that I haven't paid for. I have never had a comrade-in-arms that I would've risked my person to protect or save. I will break my given word if need arises." He paused, seeming to organize his following words. "I have never prayed to any god even when I believed I was about to die. There is no tallying of good deeds and mortal sins when one's life ends to determine whether the soul goes to Heaven or Hell. After death, there is nothing, a person is just food for vultures and worms."

Bree bit her lower lip, thinking.

"But I will listen—," he started.

"I believe," she said, interrupting him. "I have met people before who think as you do. Papa and Father Genovesi would have known the right words to say to you. I do not. But I believe in the all-knowing, all-seeing, and all-forgiving Lord Almighty and his loving Son. I believe life is a testing and, in the hereafter, one earns their just reward."

"So, life is a test. If true, lass, you're failing it. Mayhap tomorrow we shall talk more about this. But for now, I want to hear about after the cursing."

She watched Mister Quinn rise, walk over to the table and snuff out the lit candles. Before they were cloaked in the darkness, she saw the razor on cord sway across his strong chest.

"I think, in the dark, you will be able to speak more easily," Mister Quinn said to her.

Bree remained seated where she was, inhaling and exhaling, as his shadow moved back and onto his bed. Could she do what he wanted? Would she say aloud the events that haunted her. Mayhap if she did, 'twould aid her in understanding what she had done to cause this punishment.

"Tell me, lass," he ordered gruffly.

"After the cursing and Loki's suicide," she said slowly, "I recall hugging Mama, Papa, Ian, and Father Genovesi and telling each how much I loved them. The words of the curse had not yet become firm in my mind, and Father recited a prayer of protection over us. When we returned to our estate, Mama suggested that a ride might aid me in relaxing and give me peace and calm. My favorite pony was saddled. The ride did not last long. The pony seemed distressed and weak. Before giving her back to the grooms, I stroked her neck and said I loved her. The following morning, my pony was found dead in her stall. No injuries nor wounds were on her."

"Sounds like your pony was already at her end days."

"Papa told me the same."

"Go on."

"Two days later, Ian was hawk-hunting with the MacLeod brothers. He suddenly grunted in agony, grabbed his chest, and swayed dizzily with sweat cloaking his face. He fell dead to the ground before his cousins could reach him." She paused, gathering her thoughts, then continued. "I took to my bed, weeping and praying. I am sure not how long of time passed when Father Genovesi came to me with sad face. A sudden storm had come to our valley, he told me. Mama and Papa were crossing a stream in their pram carriage. A flash flood caught them, and their broken bodies were found far downstream."

"That must've been overwhelming," Quinn said.

"I clung to my bed, lost in a most black haze. I don't know how many days passed when I woke and knew I had to go to the church and light candles for the souls of Mama, Papa, and Ian. That was my only goal. I rang the bell for maid assistance. No one came. I rang again and again but 'twas in vain—no one appeared. Determined to do the proper for my loved ones, I struggled into a robe. I went downstairs but saw no servants and heard no talking nor noises."

"They'd left?"

"Not all. Father Genovesi walked out from Papa's study. He informed me all the estate staff, household and grounds, had departed. Even Matron Harriet had left. They were so afraid to stay that none asked for final wages. I learned our priest had been at the estate for several days, tending to me and searching his ancient records and Papa's books for a church solution to the cursing. He'd posted letters to the First Church Basilica asking for aid. I said I would dress and ready myself for the funeral services. The last rites and burials had been ministered five days before, Father Genovesi informed me, but when I was ready, he'd escort me to Mama's and Papa's crypt. He did. I gave heartfelt prayer over each. Ian's remains had been taken to the MacLeod estate at the capital. But I said prayer for my beloved also. Father Genovesi advised me later that my aunt and uncle had come to offer their support. But when they learned of the curse, they left the same day. I was now alone. Save for Father Genovesi."

"Sounds like Genovesi was a good man to you."

"He was." Bree inhaled deeply. "Late that night, a fire started in the study. I believe Father Genovesi was at Papa's desk reviewing again his church documents, looking for a way to save me. He must've fallen asleep and knocked over a candle. The flames engulfed the room and him, then spread out. Not from conscious thought and action, I escaped the inferno. I stood outside watching my home become burning ruin. No neighbors came, not a single person."

Quinn snorted. "That tells me a lot about the people here."

"Do not judge them harshly. They are afraid."

"You're too forgiving. Continue with your tale."

"I do not know whether 'twas that coming day or the next when I walked, barefoot, down the roadway to the township. I was taken to the church. Soon the valley nobles and elders were gathered around me. Most of their loud talk and shouts were confusing. I wanted someone to hug me. Then I saw, at the back of the crowd, near the door, Trish. We made eye contact and I raised a pleading hand to my best friend. I was told I mouthed the words "I love you" to her. Trish screamed and collapsed as if she'd turned to rags. She was dead, dead from fright they said. I was escorted to the gaol, and I have been here since that day."

"Now I know," Mister Quinn said from the dark across the room.

"I have forgiven Loki," she added.

"You what?"

"I gave this much thought. Prayed about it, with Father Genovesi's aid and advice. To forgive her was right."

"Explain."

"How terrible it must have been for her to love someone who did not love her in return. She saw Ian every day and he did not see her love for him. She truly believed I had stolen the life that should've been hers. I always had loved ones to aid me in troubling times when I was tested. Loki had no one. Demons took advantage of her sad, lost soul and confused her thoughts. If there had been a single person to guide her back to the righteous path, all might have been different. I have forgiven her, and I pray that it gives her a little comfort in the afterlife."

Bree heard him sigh in disbelief.

"Lass, you are a wonderment," he said. "Now go to sleep. We have much to do on the morrow."

Quinn selected a little dun-colored pony for her from among the eight brought to him at dawn.

After saddling the mounts, before riding from the township, Baltimore uttered warning to him. He'd been surprised, the man had not seemed concerned about Quinn's welfare earlier in the least. 'Twas the lass's birthing day, the magistrate had said. The curse could be at its most powerful this day. Quinn hadn't responded to Baltimore. The magistrate's words of caution were shite.

He noted immediately as they rode away from the gaol, being outside her confinement for this journey had lifted the lass's spirits. But only a tad. He saw that when a smile started to come to her face, she quickly ended it. Being happy, even for a moment, was shameful to her and would not be allowed.

They first rode to the northernmost point of the valley. Bree only spoke for the most part when she told him the name of the family inhabiting the manor or farmhold they were approaching. Many people saw them but none, as he'd predicted, spoke to them. Bree showed him two fire-destroyed homeholds and several graves. The Watchdogs had come to these homes, and this was the consequence of not paying them the demanded tax.

Bree asked him only one question that morning. She enquired what his Christian name was. He replied that he'd been abandoned as a babe and didn't like the *Christian* name he'd been given so he only went by Quinn. She said that was sad. He wished she'd stop feeling sorry for him. What was, was.

During the warmest part of the first scouting day, past noon pinnacle, they stopped the horses at a secluded cove beside a meandering river.

Quinn heard her whisper the word 'oasis' but didn't know what it meant.

At the cove, he hobbled their mounts.

"Bathe," he ordered her.

Bree stared at a moss patch. Appeared to be in a fogged daze, he thought. Or in another mind world. The lass, without any pretense or modesty, disrobed and walked into the rippling water.

Quinn always noticed fair women within his eyesight, he was a man after all. But he did not gawk. Yet he found himself watching Bree for a long stretch this noon. She was lovely. He recalled a story he'd heard when he was a lad in Rivenran. The tale was of course a warning. 'Twas said there were beautiful mountain nymphs who would appear near naked, with their feminine charms teased but not visible to the eye, out of the mist. If a lad stared at one, he would become entranced, unable to look away, and he would follow the nymph until he perished from thirst and hungry. Bree could be one of those mountain nymphs, he decided. From her shoulders and well-endowed bosom to her tiniest of waists and sleek legs and feet, her flesh was smooth and flawless. Her small round buttock was perfect for a man's hands to hold and her trim, female triangle had the same reddish-brown color as the hair at her head. He, at last, looked away. The fate of the gawkers in the old tale would not be his. But he still wondered what 'twould be like to have those legs wrapped around one's body and how enthusiastic her partaking would be.

He gathered her dropped dress and shift undergarment into a bundle.

Bree kneeled, with the cove water lapping at her breasts and shoulders. She washed herself with her hands.

Quinn tossed the bundle beside her.

"Washing your body will not relieve your rank stench if you don't clean your garments, too," he said.

Bree began rubbing wet cloth against cloth to attempt a cleaning.

Quinn studied the cove and surroundings. 'Twas a secluded spot as Bree had said 'twould be. To him however, it did not matter one way or t'other. He removed his boots and clothing then dove into the water near Bree. After dunking his head, he started shaving with his straight razor. He preferred face soap, but he'd done without it often.

He was shaving the beard from the curve of his chin when he caught movement from the corner of his eye. Pausing, he studied the water. Saw nothing.

Then.

The creature skimming under the surface had to be ten feet in curling length.

He moved quickly toward Bree. As the creature was doing.

"Lass, to shore!" he commanded.

Bree looked at him, uncomprehending. Then, too late, she saw it. She screamed, flailing backward, tossing her garments at the movement as if they were shield.

The spiked-skinned eel, its maw wide in intent, launched from the water at her.

Quinn caught the eel by its throat, under its head, with one hand and a mere inch from Bree's terrified face. He slashed hard four times with the razor before he decapitated the creature and slung the body aside. The garments floated in the current toward the river. He managed to grab the dress, but shift undergarment went into the river and was gone.

He led Bree onto shore.

The moment they were on land, the lass seized him in tight hug. With their bodies pressed together he noted she was trembling…and his cock was rising. Her face was hidden against his chest, but he realized she was weeping.

He stroked the back of her hair tenderly. "You nearly had your desire, lass. To be dead. Yet you fought and tried to escape. Part of you wants to live."

Bree edged her face from his chest and gazed up at him. Her eyes, yes, they were tear wet, appeared to him to have a thunderstruck hue to them.

"You are my guardian angel," she whispered.

Quinn was taken aback. No one, not ever, had called him an *angel*. Mayhap the damned Angel of Death a few times but not the other.

"My Christian name is Youngblood," he told her.

Bree sat in the low grass where Mister Youngblood Quinn had put her. She let the sun dry her and the dress spread out at her toes. But she would not allow any pleasure, no matter how tiny, to come over her from the warming sun as it had in the past. That she didn't deserve.

Her mind was a swirl, flitting from memory to pondering to questioning prayer.

This cove was where Trish and she had come after they determined they could no longer swim with the boys. As far as Bree knew, no one, no lad nor man, had found and spied on them. If someone had, they would've discovered two lasses swimming and splashing happily in the cove waters. They would have seen two lasses practicing their dance steps. Bree had always taken the lead; Trish couldn't do even the simplest dance in what she called the backward role. This had caused, before Ian MacLeod, for Bree to be leader in ballroom dances with lads. The lads didn't like that, at least the ones who understood what was happening didn't. Once, mayhap twice, Trish and she had considered kissing to improve their skills, but they'd never followed through. Yes, they held hands often and hugged in greeting, farewell, and after delighted happenstances but no kisses to mouth occurred. She remembered Trish saying that Bree's pillows were wonderment today but when they grew old, Bree's teats would be saggy bags hanging down to her knees and Trish's small teats would still be where they were now. *Grew old.* That day would no longer come for her best friend. And not for her either.

She looked at the spot where she'd lain with Ian. On that ground, her betrothed and she had loving coupled.

"Lass," Quinn called.

Bree glanced to her right. The man sat nearby, cross-legged, sharpening his razor on a wet stone. He had dressed after sitting her down.

"If I say to you—run, drop, hide, you will do so immediately and without question. Do you understand this?"

"Yes, Mister Quinn. I shall try."

"No trying. Just do."

She furrowed her brow. If anyone had ever told her on her birthing day, or on any day for that matter, she'd be at her favorite cove, unclothed, with a man, who had been unclothed too, a man she had known for less than a full day, she would've deemed the teller mad as could be. Mister Quinn was a man. That could not be disputed. She had noted, in only the briefest of a glance, that he had a larger erection than her beloved Ian had had. Yet, she realized now, Mister Quinn was more than mortal male. She had envisioned her guardian angel as beautiful female with glorious wings and halo and donning the whitest of white gowns. The angel would speak to her in loving and kind words, and she would be at peace with the guardian. She had not imagined her guardian angel would appear in the guise of a hard, curt nonbeliever whose words would challenge her core beliefs, one who would cause disquiet within her. Now it made sense. Her faith was being tested as Job's had been in the Holy Book. Mister Quinn made her stand her ground. And she would not fail. When her earthly life ended, she prayed she would have merited Heaven's welcome and the embrace of her loved ones who had gone ahead of her. She knew she had earned sins in her life ledger when Ian and she had coupled outside the bonding of marriage, but it had been done in love, not in wish to be wicked. 'Twas sin but understandable one. She hoped.

Suddenly a thought popped into her mind. If she were slain by a nonbeliever, would that personage *not* inherit the curse from her?

"I have questions for you," Quinn said.

'Twas a full moment before she realized he was talking to her again. She saw him run his hand over his face to see what spots he had missed when his shaving was interrupted.

"You believe your loved ones are in heaven and watching over you?"

"Most certain." There was no doubt in her mind.

He scraped the razor once more under his chin. "Would they wish for you to be in misery for the remainder of your life? Would they want you to never know a single happy moment ever again? Would they wish, demand, your mortal life be ended so soon?"

She frowned. This was bewildering as all had been since the cursing. Nay, they would not wish her ill, as she had not wished it for them.

Mister Quinn walked to her and picked up the dress. He motioned for her to rise.

Bree stood. She knew he would take advantage of her nakedness and stiffened her spine for what was coming.

He slipped the dress over her body. Straightened it at the shoulders. His hands only touched cloth. There was not a solitary brush to her flesh. Yet a warmth blossomed along the folds of her intimate. A small sin crept into her mind. She wanted him to touch her. Needed the kind touch of another person.

Then it came to her like candlelight in a pitch-black dark. I now understand, she nearly cried out. She had task before her life ended, knew why she had been spared thus far. She had to guide the nonbeliever within this man to the righteous path, to save her guardian angel from himself.

She vowed she wouldn't fail.

The more time Quinn spent with Bree, the more annoyed he grew. Exasperated quite often but not angry. Bree had found her voice and, from late the first day onward, kept saying homilies from the Holy Book to him. In the beginning, he hadn't understood why she was doing this, then he did. He nearly told her stop wasting her time ministering to him, but she was so sincere he found he couldn't. He'd just swear, under his breath—didn't want her to hear him—and let it roll off.

Each day at some point, and each night, she would repeat one verse:

"All persons are welcome on the lighted path of the good and righteous."

The only thing of actual import for Quinn was that he knew the lay of the valley land so he could use the landscape to his advantage to slay Seton Martell when the once-knight came here. Quinn would see to it that he did. His plan would get Martell to come to him instead of him hunting Martell down.

Each day followed the same routine. They would ride from the gaol in the morning and Bree would show him a different section of the valley. They would return to the gaol at darkfall for supper and night's rest. He noted during these days that Bree had taken to staying within arm's reach of him. Did not matter whether they were riding or afoot. The only times they were separated was when one or t'other needed body relief.

On the second day, when he saw the manor houses of Blackwell and MacLeod, he wondered if any person or family, save a king mayhap and that was in doubt, needed so much coin in their fortune. He'd seen content people who didn't own a cooking pot. He admitted however he was impressed with their rich growing fields and large herds of cattle.

At the O'Darrow estate, during the third day, he left Bree behind a high hedge so she wouldn't have to look upon the ruins of her homehold. He studied the manor, found no difference to the ash and burnt timbers than any other fire-gutted structure he'd seen in the past. He wondered why he had stopped here. This tragedy, and the little lass, would not aid him in his King's task. So, why? Damn. He found himself being more reflective in the current than he ever had before. And there was no point to these thoughts. As he'd told the lass, he was what he was—he was what he was not. He took each day as it came and saw no meaning beyond what he could see, smell, and touch. That worked. Always had. So, why was this lass causing disquiet within him? Why? That question kept repeating itself to him. Shite. Now he was thinking about thinking.

That night, back at the gaol, he noted that she was quiet for a change but had started looking at him with this mooning expression. Damn. What daft thoughts were flitting across her mind now?

Then.

Quinn had removed his boots and tunic, preparing for bed. He turned to find the lass standing beside him. Bree had her eyes closed and tilted her face up with her lips aquiver. He turned her about by the shoulders and nudged her toward her bedstead.

"Sleep," he said.

She looked back at him with that dreamy expression she had adopted but went to her bed.

He put out the candle. Shite. All women that had offered their bodies to him before also had their hands out for coin. The lass did not understand what a kiss could lead to. He paused. Or did she? Bree O'Darrow and Ian MacLeod had courted for several months. She was in love with him. Had MacLeod seduced her? Damn. Didn't matter. He would stay the path he'd chosen with her.

On the fourth day, they rode toward the Fitzgerald estate in the southernmost part of the valley. He wondered whether that manor house would be stately or garish. Would it match the personality of its lord?

They neared the border of the House of Fitzgerald estate and passed another fire-scorched homehold, another dire warning for those in the valley. Bree said this had been the last attack. After this one, the valley began paying the Watchdogs' demand.

Quinn saw a man riding swift toward them.

"Do you know this rider?" he asked Bree.

"'Tis Hew MacLeod," she answered.

MacLeod spoke directly to him, didn't look for even a half-moment at Bree. It was plain that he despised the lass.

Hew MacLeod said, "The Watchdogs are coming. They sent word to prepare their payment and meet them at the meadow."

Quinn nodded. Now his task began in earnest.

Quinn ordered Hew MacLeod to escort Bree to the gaol.

As he started eastbound, he heard her call out, "Godspeed and Heaven's shield, Mister Quinn."

Didn't need it.

Thanks to Bree's shepherding him around the valley, he reached the meeting place in swift measure. The tax extortion was mostly—with a few exceptions—delivered to the brigands in a wide meadow grove on the eastern side of the valley within the border of the MacLeod estate. He'd been told this by Fitzgerald and Baltimore. The meadow was the closest place in the valley to the Frontier where the Watchdogs could hide and camp in the unmapped terrain. That made sense. He knew 'twould be utter luck if Seton Martell was among the outlaws this day. But Quinn had always been charmed in battle. So, 'twas possible. Not likely but a mayhap. If Martell was not with this knot of brigands, Quinn's plan would work and would bring the once-knight to him. Similar had worked in the past. 'Twould work *if* the brigands didn't kill him as soon as they saw no bags of coin and no cart loaded with food supplies. There was that risk. He knew however, they would pay severely if they tried.

He hobbled his horse and took position on the western edge of the meadow grove.

Then any luck he had was gone like a heavy sack ripped open at the bottom.

As Quinn saw the Watchdogs advancing from the east, and counted eleven in their number, he heard the nicker of the little dun-colored pony and a tiny cry of pain in the thicket of bushes at his back.

Damn.

"Stay hidden and silent," he ordered, growling, without looking behind him. "No matter what happens. No matter!"

The lass did not respond. Mayhap she understood *this* command. He could hope. Hope wasn't good in a fight.

Quinn studied the brigands approaching. They were a ragtag bunch and not in any kind of formation. Their weapons were mostly swords and clubs. Three had crossbows. Had to keep close eye on that trio. There weren't any outriders in the thick woods and bushes around the meadow grove. So, they weren't scouting him and determining if he was alone or not. It appeared they accepted what their eyes saw—one solitary stranger with hobbled horse and no bags of coin, no cart of food supplies. There was confusion among them. This was not what they were supposed to find here.

Two misfits had the lead. One had long red hair and wore a shaggy greatcoat. The other had a ruined face with scarred, half-missing nose and broken front teeth. As they neared him, Red put his hand to the hilt of his sword, showing a tad of common sense, Quinn thought, but Half-Nose didn't reach for his blade. Quinn would brace the red-haired brigand.

The two men reined their horses to a stop in front of him. The other outlaws halted behind them. Again, he saw no structure to their assembly.

"Where's the food an' coin?" Red asked.

"I have it," he replied.

"Bring it out," ordered Red.

"Later."

"Now! We make the rules."

"Used to, you mean."

Half-Nose snarled. And drew his sword.

Red raised his sword partway from its sheath to show he was to be taken seriously, and was deadly, and Quinn contained his urge to kill the man without hesitation.

""Ye a'gin all of us?" Red asked.

Before Quinn could reply to the outlaw, he heard the pony nicker a second time.

"What makes you think I'm alone?" Quinn asked quickly.

The brigands immediately began looking toward the trees and bushes. The ones behind the two leaders shifted uneasily in their saddles. Befuddled, unsure. Only one, in the back, slid arrow in his crossbow.

Quinn knew they were used to Martell making their decisions, and he wasn't here.

He added, "I only have to concern myself with you two and you're no worry at all to me. My fellows will tend to the rest of you."

"None of us is afeared of dyin'," replied Red.

"So."

Red started to lift his free hand.

Quinn shook his head. "Don't. Before your men raise their crossbows at me, you and Half-Nose shall be dead."

Red studied him more closely. It was plain to Quinn that he hadn't planned this. Was unsure on how to proceed.

The brigand lowered his hand. "Martell won't let this go, won't allow ye to take *our* plunder."

"Don't expect him to. Tell him to meet me face-to-face. The King is upset that he hasn't received his proper share of the tax. Martell and I will negotiate on this. You know what 'negotiate' means, don't you?"

Quinn realized he'd said too much at once to the red-haired outlaw and had flummoxed the man.

"The King?" Red said, at last.

"Aye. King Richard sent me to meet with Martell. I am his enforcer."

Red hesitated, pondering this news.

"Anyone could say they was the King's enforcer," Red said. "He is not known by sight around here."

"Take the gamble that I am. 'Twould be a wise bet."

Red nodded slowly. "I'll tell Martell what ye said. We will return, an' there'll be more of us."

"How soon?"

"Soon. Martell finds us, we never know his whereabouts 'til he shows up."

"Ah," Quinn said. "One more thing. We're good horse trackers. Before Martell and I meet, if a single homehold in the valley is burned, if people are murdered, we will hunt down those responsible and kill them without mercy."

Red's jaw tightened.

"Tell 'im," Half-Nose said.

"Later."

"Nay, tell 'im now aboot the new tax."

Red frowned, thinking for another long moment.

"Besides the coin an' food supplies," he then said, "the valley folk will send women to service the Watchdogs doin' the collectin'."

Quinn smiled. "Will be done, and I'll make certain the women are thoroughly dosed with crotch rot."

Half-Nose grimaced. "Do he—?"

Red stopped his partner from talking with a hard swipe of his hand. "I wonder, enforcer, how tough ye will be when yer guts is hangin' in the mud."

Quinn half-bowed to the red-haired man. "Step down from your horse. Have your partner join you. Hell, bring up a couple more. Let's do it right now. Then we'll know for certain whose guts will be in the mud."

Without a further word, Red hard-reined his mount around. Half-Nose followed.

Quinn watched the outlaws ride out of eyesight. Then he waited to see if any circled back. None did.

He sighed and turned.

"Get out here, lass."

He was angry, and there would be punishment for her following him. Why hadn't someone in the township stopped her? He knew that answer before the thought finished in his mind.

Bree lowered her chin and walked toward Mister Quinn, guiding the pony by the reins. She understood he was upset with her. But she hadn't been able to wait in the township to see if he returned or not—had to know his fate immediately.

She stopped beside Mister Quinn and slowly looked up at him. And she blanched. He was not irritated with her, he was furious.

"Why aren't you at—?" he started.

Then he saw the kerchief she had wrapped around her left forearm. The cloth was tinged with blood and was growing darker.

He sighed as if releasing the black thoughts within him, and she felt her body warm.

"How did you injure yourself?" he asked.

"Didn't see the thorn bush," she replied. "I tried to stay quiet as you told me to."

Without warning, he put his thumb to her lower lip and edged it down. "You bit yourself to keep from crying out."

Bree had the sudden urge to take his thumb between her lips.

Before she could, before she could react in any way, he released her lip and lifted the kerchief. The slash wasn't deep but was about three-fingers in length and across a vein. Blood seeped from her flesh.

"How much does it hurt, lass?"

"O-only a tad."

"We don't have any cloth to use as binding. My clothes are too dirty, and you don't have your undergarment to tear piece from anymore. Wait here. I'll be back shortly."

She didn't want him to go.

Not even a few yards away.

She liked being beside him. Felt safe. Most of the time.

Mister Quinn looked at the pony. "No water bags. You should never be allowed to go anywhere alone. Get the water bag from my horse and wash your injury." He paused. "Did Hew MacLeod take you to the gaol?"

"Nay. He said I knew the way and he left me."

He shook his head. "And you decided to follow me?"

"I thought I would catch you before you got here. Your horse is much faster than my pony."

"Do you know what those brigands would've done to you if they'd caught you?"

"I knew I would be safe with you."

"Dammit, lass," he muttered.

Then he was gone, into the bush.

Bree dashed to his horse, gathered the water bag, and rushed back to the pony. She looked about, in all directions, expecting to see Satan himself watching her. A sin, a small one, had come over her. She had pictured Mister Quinn and her embracing. Could her guiding him along the righteous path be peppered with improper deeds? Tiny ones, but most certain wicked.

Suddenly she wondered what his kiss would be like.

No, no, no! She chastised the thought.

She had rinsed her injury twice by the time he returned.

Furrowing her brow, she watched his approach. He walked with his hands at chest-height and about one-hand length apart.

When he reached her, she saw that he had a spider's web between his fingers.

He pointed his right hip at her. "In my pocket are aloe leaves. Tear them open and rub their balm on the wound."

Blush crossed her cheeks as she slipped her fingers into his breeches pocket. Before she found the leaves, she felt the hard muscle beneath his clothing.

She spread the aloe over the thorn injury.

Then he wrapped the web over and into the cut on her forearm.

"Spider silk is strong and will stop the bleeding," he told her. "Vinegar and honey are best to halt infection, but aloe is fine substitute."

"Thank you," she whispered.

"Mount up. We're going back to the gaol. We will scout Lord Fitzgerald's estate another day."

As they rode, side by side, she kept glancing at his mouth and hands, and once a quick glimpse at the crotch of his breeches. Heat touched her cheeks. Prayers of contrition would be said that night.

Could she lead him onto the righteous path?

Or…

Would he take her onto his road? A pathway more dangerous than threat to one's life.

5

IN THE NIGHT IN THE GAOL ROOM, WITH NO candles lit, Bree rose from her bedstead and stepped timidly toward his. This would be wicked on her part. No doubt in that. Yet she would do it.

"What?" he said sternly as she neared.

"I have no one left. No one to hold me."

"I'm sorry, lass."

"May I lay beside you? I shall be quiet."

"Won't that be a sin?"

"Mayhap. But."

Mister Quinn grunted. "No talking. Sleep."

Bree slipped onto the bed against him. She rested her head at the joining of his arm and shoulder. She placed one hand on his bare chest below the straight razor and extended her legs along his leg. Her feet did not skim his. He was too tall.

She inhaled. Liked his musky scent.

"When Ian and I laid together," she whispered to him, "Ian would kiss me and cuddle my pillows. I shall not fight if you wish to."

Where did that declaration come from? Was she truly seeking more of his touch?

"Hush. Sleep," he said. "Or I'll boot you onto the floor."

She nodded against his shoulder that she understood he meant his words. She knew she shouldn't be doing this. But the embrace of another person was wonderful. Even the touch of this nonbeliever, this King's killer. She didn't think she would sleep a tad as she basked in his closeness. So, she would just lay there, and not talk as he commanded. If there was no more than this, 'twould be all right.

This was the last thought she remembered.

Until.

Bree woke.

She was wide awake, frightened, shaking, with Mister Quinn's hand clamped over her mouth and his lips to her ear. *Oh, my heavens! Please, do not harm me, sir.* Quivering tears were close.

"Get under your bed," he whispered.

What? She didn't understand.

"Stay there," he continued. "Count to five then scream loud enough to wake everyone in the damn valley."

She nodded her mouth against his palm. What was happening?

He released her.

Dashing to her bed, she slipped underneath. One, two. She watched Mister Quinn's shadow ease past the door to the side with the hinges. Three. It appeared the enforcer had his dagger in one hand and short sword in the other. Four. She heard a horse outside. Then torch flame outlined the door.

Five.

She screamed as loud as she could with all the strength she could muster.

The door booted open.

She saw Red leap inside with burning torch in one hand and sword in the other. The brigand threw the torch at her bed. It hit the bedpost and ricocheted into the necessity shielding, its cloth catching immediate flame. Half-Nose, gripping sword, rushed inside, following Red.

Yes, she saw it all in the growing firelight. Mister Quinn hard slammed into the door, catching Half-Nose between door and frame and crushing him. Then he thrust his shortsword into Red's back before the outlaw could turn. Whipping around, Mister Quinn kicked the door wide and slit Half-Nose's throat with his dagger.

A half-moment later, he was outside. Out of her eyesight.

Unable to look away, she watched Red spasm, with desperation and pain on his twisted features. Then die. Half-Nose, sitting upright against the doorframe, held a broken hand to his throat and struggled to stop the blood flowing from the dagger cut.

Outside, she heard a battle cry, sword striking sword, a pained groan, then the galloping of horses.

"Tell Martell I wait for him!" Mister Quinn yelled.

He came back inside, cleaning then sheathing his shortsword and dagger. He gathered his other shortsword from the floor, sheathed it. Grabbing the water pitcher from the table, he hurled into the fire in the corner.

Mister Quinn squatted beside her bed.

"Come to me," he said most gently.

She crawled out and hugged him.

"I did what you told me," she said into his chest.

"You did fine, lass."

"I saw Trish die after I told her 'I love you.' But I have never seen persons slain like…this. 'Twas horrible."

"Don't look."

He guided her to his bed. After easing her hands and arms from his body, he sat her on the side of the bedstead. Then he stepped to the doorway, grabbed Half-Nose by the tunic and dragged the corpse outside.

She rose and moved to the wall beside the wide-open door. Peeked out. Two more Watchdog bodies lay sprawled on the ground. A rider-less horse dashed about in terrified panic. Three discarded torches still burned. The gaol roof was tile covered, she thought. If it had been thatched or wood-shingled, they would've set the structure on fire before attacking.

She watched Baltimore, in his robe and nightclothes, run to Mister Quinn. While the gaol was across the roadway from the rest of the township, 'twas not that far away. Still, the magistrate was panting and wheezing as if he had been running for a full kilometer. Several township people followed him. The tavern owner caught the horse and calmed the animal.

"Get the damned corpse out of the gaol," Mister Quinn ordered. "And the burnt shielding screen."

Four men came into the goal. None spoke but she saw that one did look at her and nod his head in sympathy. Three took the charred wood and cloth outside. The burning lingered in the air. The fourth man lugged Red's corpse from the room.

"I saw the battle," a young, excited voice announced.

She peeped out again.

'Twas the smith's lad talking to Mister Quinn.

"Never seen anyone move as quick as ye, sire," he said, in awe. "Ye were dervish. One of those that rode away was wounded."

"Wounded, you say. I'm getting shoddy in my fighting."

The lad laughed, and the smith guided his son away from Mister Quinn.

"What will you have us do?" asked Baltimore. "Stand a guard?"

"They won't be back tonight," Quinn replied. "Take the bodies to the meadow where the tax is delivered. Take the horse, too." He paused. "Do not defile the corpses."

"It shall be done," the magistrate replied.

"And ask about. The Watchdogs weren't told where I was staying in township. They had to have sent scouts. Find out if one was seen. If none, then Martell has a spy in the valley."

"No one would—." Baltimore paused. "It shall be done."

"Now. I intend to sleep."

Mister Quinn walked inside. He set the door ajar, to air out the burning stench. But he placed the chair, with several objects upon it, against the door. Why was he doing that? she wondered. Oh. If the door were opened even a mere inch, she realized, 'twould strike the chair and the objects would fall and din would sound in alarm.

Leaning her back against the wall, she studied him in the

moonlight as he set the shortswords and sheath belt on the ground beside the bed then placed the dagger under the pillow. A thin sheen of sweat cloaked his face and bared chest. He had fought them wearing only his breeches. While he wiped his person dry with a cloth, she looked through the space between the door and frame. The township people were gone. She glanced up at the moon and stars painted across the night sky. Her mind was a swirl. Some were righteous thoughts, others most wicked.

Mister Quinn stretched out on the bed.

"Lass," he said. "Go to your bed, lay beside me, or stand where you are. Your choice. I intend to sleep."

"How did you know they were out there?"

"Birds."

"W-What?"

"Only loners fly after dark. Most birds, except during migration, rest at night unless something frightens them. Birds woke me taking to wing."

"I am in your debt, sir," she responded softly.

"You're not."

"You rescued me from the eel, tended my thorn-bush wound, and now you have saved me from the brigands."

"They were after me."

"They would have savaged me if you had not prevailed."

"You do not owe me."

"Papa said one must always repay one's debts. As soon as possible with whatever means you have."

"Stop talking."

"I only have me."

Bree accepted that her time in the world was numbered, and all the people of the valley wanted it so. Sooner than later. She had also. Had. Did she still? The king's enforcer, laying within reach, could be the one ordered to execute her. But would he? She had seen and heard him refuse Lord Fitzgerald's commands. Would he disobey the King's order?

While she knew her dreams of being wedded wife with loving husband, overseeing her own blissful home, and raising happy babies would never come to be, she found she longed for a little joy in her last hours. Was that so wrong? She understood there were few choices for her. Few? That was exaggeration. The one she could pursue was wicked. No doubt in that. Would this man be guardian angel for her again, or devil's disciple? She decided. A handful of minutes filled with pleasure and joy was worth the dark mark.

Suddenly one cringing factor filled her mind. She had not been able to do her usual grooming since being brought to the gaol. Her body bath without soap at the Oasis cove had been her sole all-over soaking since the cursing. The most she had been able to do here was wash with wet cloth and on some low days she had not done that much. And she had been unable to groom her body as she had for the last year. What if she revolted him? That was possible.

Still…

She saw his eyes were closed as she removed her dress. She laid down on the bed, pressing herself firmly against him.

His body tensed into rigid muscle.

"Damn," he grunted. "Lass, I am not stone nor ice."

"I am not v-virgin," she said, her words barely a whisper. "But I am not well versed in coupling."

She traced her hand across the fine hairs on his strong chest and toyed with the closed razor blade.

He shifted onto his side to face her. For a moment, she believed he *was* going to boot her onto the floor as he had threatened to earlier. But he gentled her onto her back and moved above her. She couldn't breathe. She'd invited him. She had. No misunderstanding there. However, part of her didn't believe he would accept. Another part, a wicked piece of her, truly hoped he would.

Now…

…the moment of truth.

For both.

Mister Quinn swept his lips gently across hers. Her heart began pounding so hard at his touch she thought it would erupt from her body. His lips were firm yet soft. Like the finest silk. But with blade steel underneath. *Oh, my goodness.* This brief stroke 'twas wondrous.

Kissing, the sharing between two who wanted it, was a glorious act.

In her mind, images of Ian's and Mister Quinn's faces merged together. Ian was giving her his consent. She responded as her betrothed had taught her. She opened her mouth. Wanted more. Wanted to be lost in kiss and embrace. With no other thoughts. His tongue slid inside, across hers. Suddenly, she envisioned Death with its skull face kissing her. Then Death stepped back and pointed its accusing, skeletal finger at her. She froze still, rigid. Didn't respond further to his kiss. She laid there motionless, not moving a tad. 'Twas she that had turned to icy stone, not him.

Mister Quinn groaned, exasperated. Muttered a vile curse. Raised his mouth from hers.

Nay, nay, nay! Do not retreat, sir.

Finally, before he had moved too far away, she willed herself to stir, and grabbed the back of his head with both hands clutching his hair. She pressed her lips desperately to his and plunged her tongue deep into him. She circled his tongue with hers. Again, and again she repeated her entwining. He had a spicy, pleasing taste. Ah, he did.

Oh, my glory, she rejoiced.

The sensations at her mouth overwhelmed her.

The numbness within her, that had been slowly, so ever slowly, easing into the background since Mister Quinn's arrival, inched further aback. She saw, in her mind's eye, Mama and Papa giving her approval to have a joyful time. *The best honor you can bestow on us, daughter,* Mama said, *is to live a fulfilling life.* Papa added, *we do not wish you to be miserable and sad for the rest of your days.* Trish appeared, nodding her agreement with the words. Was she deceiving herself? If so, 'twas grand deception. She allowed his tongue to savor her and she savored him. 'Twas as if their mouths were becoming one with t'other.

Aye, she wanted this.

Still, tears crept into her eyes.

Mister Quinn's tongue embraced hers. At moments, he darted as if teasing. Other ticks, his strokes were long and overpowering.

She relished his mouth. Nay, *cherished*.

Then she felt his hand cup her pillow. Fingers feathered her warm flesh, and nipple grew to taut. Thoughts swirled in her mind. But mostly, there was only luxuriating in touch and caress. She pushed her tongue as far as she could into his mouth as he kneaded her pillow. *Yes, oh yes! Hold me, sir. Do not let me go. Please. I beg you.*

He continued kissing her, and that was the only reason she couldn't cry 'no' when his hand fled from her pillow.

She felt his body shifting away from her and didn't understand what he was doing.

Then, most swiftly but also seeming like forever, his hand went to her other pillow. Brushing, ringing her, nipple already standing erect like the other. And he eased his body against her side. Now she understood, his body shifting moments ago had been him removing his breeches. She felt the flesh of his legs against hers and his cock firm against her hip.

She gasped into his mouth. A wondrous warmth now tingled between her legs along her intimate folds and at her center. 'Twas as if he intuited this, and his hand went from her pillows to her thighs. He stroked her flesh slowly, gently. He moved closer and closer to her intimate.

Wonderful.

Bree gripped his dark mane tighter in her fists, if that was possible, and she fiercely kissed him. This could not be. Ian would always ensure, with his hand stroking, that she was ready when they joined in coupling. Never dry, unprepared. She had desired and wanted to be at-one with her betrothed with all her mind and body, but he had to caress her feminine folds to ready her. Mister Quinn had not yet touched her there. Not even with skim. Her body shivered from crown to quivering toe. This could not be, she repeated.

Her intimate's lips were swelling, and she was moist from upper tip to lowermost. Her entry, she would've sworn, was blossoming open to welcome him.

Urging her, with only tap of his fingertip, she eased her legs farther apart. He probed his fingers through the fine hairs above the hood of her cleaving then, at last, against the tenderest flesh underneath her triangle.

Mister Quinn, not breaking kiss, continuing to stroke her tongue, moved above her with his legs between hers. Bree understood he could pin her against the bed with his naked body, even crush her. She'd be helpless and at his complete mercy. He did not. She felt his warmth, the brush of his flesh at her bosom and thighs, but not his weight. The closed razor hanging from his neck tapped one pillow and settled against the other. She grew overwhelmed as his cock, hard and full, skimmed her now wet folds and became cloaked in her essence. Her feet and legs quivered.

He stopped his stroking of her tongue.

Suddenly she was afraid he'd misunderstand her shuddering.

She broke the kiss and, immediately, in the same moment, gripped his head with both arms, buried her face into the side of his neck, and curled her unsteady legs and feet around his waist. Then she arched her body up to his and glided her cleaving against his cock. *Take me, sir. Make me feel only pleasure.*

Mister Quinn eased the thick head of his member inside her.

Bree moaned into the flesh at his neck as the sensation increased the shudder to legs and feet. Wanted more, wanted to know only pleasure. He guided his cock, as if timid and reluctant, within her. Deeper and deeper until he fully filled her. And he paused. She nearly cried 'nay' aloud. Knew, without doubt, if she did not crest soon that she'd perish. She rocked her intimate back and forth against him. He remained still. She shifted her face and bit her teeth into his muscle running at curve of shoulder to arm. And would've sworn she heard him chuckle.

"P-Please," she pleaded.

"Say take me to glory, lass."

She whimpered. 'Twas all she could further voice.

But he understood and complied. His rhythm was steady within her. Pinnacle, all glorious, edged closer and closer yet did not arrive. Her entire body was now quivering. Moisture rose and shined on all of her from crown to toe. She needed to peak, and she beat her tiny fists against his shoulder blades.

He increased his pace. Pumping, stroking her faster and faster.

Almost…almost…

The cresting arrived, at last, in magnificent wave after wave, rippling from her intimate core throughout all of her. 'Twas wondrous and most grand, 'twas heaven sent.

He stopped.

With pinnacle still glorying within her, she knew he had not peaked, had not seeded. Why had he halted? Did he not need satisfaction, too? Was she displeasing? As she had wondered with Ian, was she too country and boring, too simple and unworldly? Was her lovemaking too timid and unadventurous?

Mister Quinn slipped his hands under her as he pressed his body to hers and rolled over. She found herself suddenly on top with her bent knees and legs against the outside of his hips. She felt his thick cock, still inside her, pulsing as if his member was matching the hammer of her heartbeat. He took her by the shoulders and eased her from his chest until she was upright upon him. She didn't understand. Ian and she had never done this. Always it had been with her betrothed atop as coupling was meant to be. She knew, of course, animals mated with male on top of female from behind, but man and woman joined in the expected and natural bonding. Not like this.

He shifted slightly to ensure his cock was fully within her. Then he tapped her buttock cheek with two fingers.

"Your turn," he said gruffly.

She was confused, at a loss. Her turn for what?

He intuited her thoughts.

"To take the lead."

She did not understand. Then she recalled dance practice with Trish. She had taken the male role in their steps together. Is that what he meant?

Again, intuiting her thoughts, he took hold of her hips with his hands. He lifted her a tad upward on his cock and back down then slightly higher and down once more.

Bree flattened her hands on his chest and positioned her lower body. And raised her intimate on his cock. At first, she was awkward but quickly had the motion mastered. She glided up and down, each time going slightly higher.

It did not take long.

She heard him grunt. 'Twas satisfied sound.

She intended to stop but she felt fresh pinnacle storming toward her. Her arms and legs were again aquiver, and her cleaving too began throbbing. This was…was…She glided along the length of his cock, going higher each time before lowering. *Oh, me!* She pumped faster and faster.

This-this…

…oh, my goodness!

The cresting exploded within her and she cried out aloud. She shattered and the entire world around her vanished as the pinnacle, so magnificent and grand, overwhelmed her. *OH…heaven!* Its engulfing continued and continued. Then. It began to fade. *No!* She wanted the cresting to stay. She did. Most truly. Yet it slowly faded, and she did not have remaining strength to glide upon him again. She lowered onto his chest. His cock slipped from inside her and a tiny sadness that they were no longer joined came over her. She pressed her face to his comforting breast and lingered in the sensations still glorying within her.

As she smiled against his breast, another glory rose within her. They had shared their bodies with one another, and *lovers* remained together after that. Whether she had hours or years left, Mister Quinn would stay at her side and she at his. That was the way of the world. Lovers always stayed together unless Death parted them. And she would have the time needed to guide the nonbeliever within him to the lighted, righteous path.

He stroked her hair with gentle sweep.

"That was fine, lass."

Quinn cursed himself with a harsh damning. There were a hundred things he could have said to her. Phrases with some poetry that would have pleased the tiny lass, made her feel good about herself and their coupling. Many came to him now. But what did he say? 'That was fine.' He was an utter arse. At least he said something to her. Never had considered it in the past. His usual, after swagging, was give the coin he'd agreed to. Shite. Now he was trying to justify not only his lame words but that he'd said anything at all.

Except he hadn't swagged, he had made love to Bree. When had he ever done that before? With the others, he'd only cared about satisfying his own body needs. Didn't care about the woman's. He was a miserable son of a bitch. And that said it all.

Sitting on the edge of the bed with his feet on the ground and his arms on his knees, he looked at her. The lass now lay curled on her side, facing him, asleep. He leaned closer. She had a wee smile on her lips. His heart cinched and he damned himself again. He had taken advantage. Yes, she had come to him and, yes, she had a lush woman's body. But her thoughts and mind were confused, atangled. The lass had not been a virgin as she'd told him, but she was very inexperienced in the act of coupling. Had only known the one position and continued to believe in tales of angels and such as most young, sheltered maidens did. Hell, she'd said that he was her guardian angel. He had not acted as guardian and most certainly not as angel.

He forced himself to turn away from her. Just gazing at her fine body was causing his cock to rise once more. The lust for her he recognized but the other reactions he did not. When she'd laid, fully clothed, beside him and nestled her lovely face against him and stroked her tender hands upon his body, he had nearly jumped out of his skin. What had caused that? Later, when they laid together naked, he found her soft flesh and kisses intoxicating. Dammit, her sweet cries as she came in orgasm had caused him to thank God and say 'twas a blessing. He'd never muttered that before. Why did *this* lass intrigue him? Why did she stir him so? She caused feelings to arise within him that no woman had ever caused before. This should not be. Especially in the short span of time they'd been together. He knew already they were as mismatched as two could be and their relationship would only last until he finished King's task and left the valley. Bree O'Darrow did not see him as he truly was. She was besotted in her fantasy of him. And he had taken advantage of her enamor.

Quinn knew, without single doubt, he was a callous son of a bitch. Yes, this coupling seemed inevitable, as if guided by a force of nature since their first meeting. Certain. But he knew he was lying. Both had free will. This did not have to be. It happened because they wanted it to. Shite. If there was a Heaven and Hell, as Bree truly believed, this one night alone had earned him the afterlife's fiery pit.

He glanced at the round of his shoulder. Frowned. He had never been wounded or scarred in fight. Even bruises were rare. He was that good in battle. He studied the outline of teeth on his muscle. Dried, dark red rimmed every indention. Now he had his first scar, and it had come from a lass who he could put down with a firm poke of his finger. Yes, her bite would leave a mark on him. She had placed her brand upon his person.

He would be her shield.

From this minute onward, he gave his oath to protect her from harm intended by any person, by any creature. He would keep his word this time no matter the consequences even if he had to disobey King's command or put himself in perilous path. His rigid cock throbbed. His mind whispered to him to roll her onto her back, to wake her from her dreams by taking her reddish-brown trimmed femaleness with his mouth. He knew her pink would taste sweet and honeyed. Slowly, with concentrated deliberateness, he would use his lips and tongue to guide her to blissful orgasm. He could already feel her fists clutching his hair and her thighs locking his face betwixt them when she cried out in pleasure. His hard bollocks ached. He suddenly pictured her mouth—with the tiny mole beside the left corner of her full lips—kissing and sucking the length of his cock. When he came, he'd melt into the bed. He intuited that while she, more than likely, did not know about this act, she would, as she had with mounting atop him, swiftly become a master.

He doubled over at the agony overwhelming his crotch.

Damn, damn, damn.

Then he heard the creak of boot.

His painful erection began to recede as he sat upright. He slipped his hand under the bed pillow and around his dagger.

"Whoever you are," he said, "why haven't you made your presence known?"

"Ye were occupied," a man replied from outside the doorway, remaining beyond eyesight. "So, I waited. Longer than I anticipated. It is strange that the lass is satisfied and much sated, but ye are miserable. Why is this?"

"Is that you, Beaudry?"

The knight, who he only knew from Blackwater gambling rooms, stepped into the doorway.

"You are riding with Lakesnow?" Quinn asked.

"Aye."

"Where's the troop?"

"Will arrive on the morrow. I came ahead as scout and give you message."

"I take it that the Watchdogs are coming to the valley."

"Aye. They have banded their groups together and are riding here."

"How many?"

"Thirty-five."

"Is Seton Martell with them?"

"He is."

"They're coming for me. I've pissed them off. Didn't give them their plunder demand."

"And ye slayed four this eve outright. Wounded one more. He did not survive ride back. I have always admired that ye do not waste single movement in battle."

"Tell Lakesnow not to come into the valley. To stay back and hidden. The Watchdogs may have a spy here. If so, they will report the troop's arrival and the brigands won't come. Tell Lakesnow to use me as Judas goat."

"Judas goat?"

"An animal trained to lead the herd to slaughter. I'll be the bait for the Watchdogs."

"I will tell Sir Bryce."

The knight turned and departed.

Quinn nodded. His King's task was at hand.

He would cover Bree with quilt, letting her to continue to sleep. He'd dress and find a good waiting spot outside, one not far from the gaol.

He felt her move before she traced her fingers along his spine.

Turning, he saw her eyes were open. She was smiling as she lifted her wanting arms to him.

Moments later, they were kissing. Long, deep.

Then he was above her, between her open legs.

The besotted lass matched his pace as he edged her again toward pinnacle.

He slowed, intended for their *last* joining to be magnificent.

For her.

She crested, moaned, and started whisper to him.

Then she stopped, turning stone rigid after saying only two words.

Bree had said in her whisper:

"I love…"

6

I LOVE YOU.
    Bree *had not* said all the words of the curse to Mister Quinn. But she had intended to. The words had tumbled from her mouth without consideration beforehand. In the midst of pinnacle that her guardian had created, as wave after grand wave rippled within her, she'd started to say them. When she realized what she was saying, the cresting within her ceased abruptly before she completed the sentence. She had spoken the words out loud to Mama, Papa, Ian, Trish and Father Genovesi before their deaths. Had she now given Mister Quinn his death sentence?

    Last night, after the battle that left four men dead—two killed right before her eyes!—that could have led to Mister Quinn's demise and her own savaging death, she had offered again her body to him. He accepted this time. Her giving and receiving of bodily joy had overwhelmed all other thoughts. She blessed him for it. Was that what her words were actually for? For the blissful coupling? And not for the man himself? She could not see herself bonded to him. They were too different. In almost every way. But she had witnessed acts of honor that he proclaimed not to have. Had she influenced the good within him? She would like to believe she had. A little mayhap. Nay, she was not *in* love with him. She relished the joy he brought to her but no more. She would tell him that upon his return. She would. Because lovers always remained together. Forever. That was so.

She could not picture Mister Quinn and her forever.

Or could she?

She was most conflicted.

Mayhap if, perchance if…

Before the cursing, she would never have been alone with the King's enforcer. If in his presence, she would have been hiding behind Mama and Papa or Ian and barely peeking at him. He was a bad man, a nonbeliever. *Yet* he was the only one who would stay in her company and talk with her. He gave her comfort.

Was that enough?

Were the angels telling her that his comfort was the first building stone for a lasting relationship?

A life with him. He was her guardian angel, he kept proving that. He had stopped questioning her belief in the heavenly kingdom. She believed she had shown him the path of the good and righteous. Could she induce him to walk the path beside her? Might take a lifetime to do so, the angels whispered. Are you willing to do that? Was she? Would she?

'Twas mid-morn. Bree stood in the open doorway of the gaol and gazed at the sky's drifting, white clouds and let the sun warm her face. Last night with Mister Quinn, she had been naughty. That was a mild word for what they had done. Still she could picture Mama, Papa, Ian, and even Matron Harriet smiling in approval. Trish, of course, would have the grandest smile. She could have, was allowed to have, some pleasant times. That was another tame word for last night.

Mister Quinn had ridden from the township an hour earlier with Magistrate Baltimore. The men's attendance had been commanded by Lord Fitzgerald. They were to meet with him at his manor house. The magistrate said they had enough time for meeting before the Watchdogs arrived. Mister Quinn had chuckled and told her that one goes to power, that power does not come to one. Lord Fitzgerald had high importance in the valley and in their previous gathering he had been intimidated by the King's enforcer. Now the Queen's brother was attempting to reestablish his position with this command. Papa had tried to explain the world of men to her. Tried. She did not understand the games that men and boys played.

Bree could not stop her smile as another naughty thought rose with her. She would talk to Mister Quinn if given the chance. Immediately upon his return, they could be kissing and joining. She giggled at the notion and surprised herself. She had turned brazen. Ian and she had loving coupled in early morning light. Never in the middle of the day. That was scandalous for even wife and husband. But now that the thought had come to her, she doubted she would think about anything else.

I love you. She once again pondered if comfort and wondrous coupling was enough for long-lasting bond? 'Twas a beginning, she decided. That was what the angels were telling her.

She turned her attention to the center of the township. A very tall man, wearing a long black cloak, sat on a very large stallion talking to three township men standing on the porch of the tavern-inn. She saw one of the men, who she knew was quite often under the influence of whisky, make the sign the cross upon himself while the second hastily retreated inside the building.

The third townsman pointed directly at her.

The tall man nudged his stallion toward the gaol.

Bree stood anchored in the doorway. She could not look away from the tall man as he rode to the gaol. He wore no hat and was mostly bald with what remained of his gray hair neatly trimmed and was clean shaven. At first, she wanted Mister Quinn beside her. Then, deep inside, part of her said she could trust this man. She did not know why she thought that. As he came closer, she saw he had a kind, congenial face and seemed to be at peace within himself. But the wilt in his broad shoulders added that he'd seen too much during his time in the world.

The tall man reined the stallion to a halt near her.

"Good day, lass," he said, his voice gentle.

"Good day to you, sir."

"I am seeking Genovesi, the township priest."

She frowned, sad. "He perished in a fire. Lord be with him."

"Ah. I shall say a rosary for his soul. Genovesi wrote a missive to the Basilica in Camd'n Rin."

"Where his High Pontiff lives?"

"Aye. What is your name, child?"

"Bree, House of O'Darrow."

"I am LaBach." He stepped down from the stallion. "Your priest's missive was compelling and persuasive. I was sent to assist him in vanquishing a curse. Well, to be more correct, to aid *you*."

"You are priest?"

"Aye."

LaBach moved beside Bree and looked inside the gaol.

She suddenly felt comforted and uneasy. Both in equal measure.

"I sense an evil here," the tall man said. "From Genovesi's description, I believe I know what it is. 'Tis very ancient and seldom called into our mortal world. That is why Genovesi could not uncover anything about it."

"Father Genovesi and I prayed often together. The curse remained."

"I am aware."

Mayhap…could this priest lift the curse? Bree was afraid to move. Fearing if she did the tall man would prove to be mirage and would vanish.

He returned to the stallion, began removing his bags. "I must prepare. I had thought Genovesi and I would work together. Now, I shall do so on my own. We begin soon."

"Father LaBach," she said slowly, "I have been told the curse will be with me for the rest of my days. Was told this many times."

"That may not be true. There are no absolutes in this—I have been unsuccessful once in the past, the lad died during the rites and the demon laughed at me—but I shall try to exile the curse from you."

"I am humbly grateful. Much so, and I bless you for coming. I mean no disrespect with my words, sir. What can you do that Father Genovesi could not?"

"Lass, I am the Church's exorcist."

Hope washed over her with his words. Could the curse be vanquished? If so, would her words last night to Mister Quinn be dispelled? She said prayer for both.

"Ye have been ordered by our King to act as executioner for us and wield death sentence upon Bree, House of O'Darrow," Lord Fitzgerald said smugly.

Quinn appraised the folded missive Fitzgerald handed him. He did not respond to the lord's pronouncement, he remained cold and expressionless.

This isn't how it is done, he thought. The established protocol was that he received his tasks from Duncan. Always. Usually face-to-face, occasionally in written missive. Never had he been given assignment directly by the King. But then, Lord Fitzgerald was the Queen's brother. Was that the reason for this breach in practice? The majority of his tasks were given and done in secret. But some had been done in public to establish his position and reputation. He had slain three villains who had commandeered and were operating their crimes out of a small Blackwater church. He had stood on the gallows when one of the traitorous nobles had been hanged. Quickly, the people of the capital knew who he was and what his duty for the King was. Today he knew, even if he slayed Seton Martell as commanded, if he refused to execute the lass it would end his days as King's enforcer. Duncan had said, in their first meeting, that the chosen enforcer would have to swear fealty to the King, always be available for any task, willing to travel anywhere. At no time had it been implied he had the right of refusal. And despite giving his pledge of fealty to the King, he could walk away, could just say the hell with it. Had that time, at last, arrived?

Quinn stood in the front entry of the manor house with Fitzgerald and Baltimore. No need for formalities for this meeting— he had not been escorted to the lord's private study or to a downstairs parlor. He was not a guest. To further emphasize his power and Quinn's lower station, Fitzgerald had them wait for a quarter hour before he appeared. The lord did this despite that he was brimming with elation. And one might say, with glee.

Baltimore stood beside Quinn and was nearly as pleased as Fitzgerald with the news.

Could this be forgery? Quinn wondered. That was desperate thought. When had he ever hoped for a task to be sham? Never. He hadn't cared one or t'other in the past.

Quinn looked first at the broken seal. It had what appeared to be a smeared King's shield stamped into the wax. Opening the missive, he read the brief message. As Fitzgerald had said, it instructed him to act as executioner for the valley people and put an end to the life of Bree O'Darrow. Very distinct in command. No misinterpretation in the words. His name had been misspelled—no 'u' and only one 'n.' That didn't really mean anything. Below the command was King Richard's signature. He didn't know whether the king's hand signed it or not. Never seen the royal signature before.

Finishing, he handed the missive to Baltimore.

"The execution shall be done posthaste," Fitzgerald said. "Then we can give our full attentions to the dire situation with the Watchdogs as we need to."

"Did the messenger give the missive to you personally, your lordship, or to one of your people?" he asked, giving himself time to reason his options.

The lord furrowed his brow. "You will do as instructed, enforcer. Straight away."

Quinn eased closer to him and Fitzgerald backstepped.

"Had you ever seen the messenger before?"

"W-wha...?" the lord stammered. "The messenger has no import. Only the message does. One does not appraise the courier as one does not study a houseman or field worker."

"Seen him before?" he repeated.

"Aye. He was a local lad from our township."

Quinn crossed his arms over his chest. Why was the missive not delivered straightaway to the lord? Why the roundabout route? Why was the missive not delivered to him and written by Duncan? He was grasping at straws. That he knew plainly.

"Now...I fathom. Ah, yes," Fitzgerald said, calming. "You have been keeping company with lass since you arrived and do not wish to put an end to her. A *fondness* has arisen. You will however fulfill your duty, enforcer, as our King has commanded you to."

"Mayhap," Baltimore added, "there is more than fondness between you and the lass. Still, as his lordship stated, you must do as ordered."

"Nay," Quinn replied. "I will not execute the lass."

There, he's said it. And his decision was firm.

Fitzgerald jabbed Quinn in the chest with his finger.

"You will—," he began then stopped when the enforcer's eyes narrowed at the touch.

Quinn leaned even closer to the lord. "This is forgery."

He decided to push this whether it was true or fake.

"'Tis not," Baltimore said. "It has royal shield and King's signature upon it."

He kept his focus on Fitzgerald. "I only receive my tasks from royal counsel. Never from our King himself. The forger is more than likely the same person who is the valley spy for the Watchdogs. One who knows how to write and has seen royal documents. Such as one of the two of you."

The lord's face paled.

"Tell me," Quinn said in hard words, "why has your estate never been assaulted by the brigands?"

"I did not pen the missive, enforcer," spat his lordship. "And I am not a spy!"

Quinn turned to the magistrate beside him. "You told me at the gaol that we had time for this meeting because the Watchdogs had not arrived yet. How did you know that?"

Baltimore swallowed at the lump in his throat. "We have persons looking for them. Word would have come to me if they had crossed from the Frontier into Thuria."

He looked back at the lord. "You are many things, your lordship. I would not count stupid among them. If you'd done this forgery, you would not have claimed you'd received it by messenger. You'd have had it delivered to another who would have believed it true."

Baltimore dropped the missive as if it the parchment had bit him.

Quinn put his hands on his sword hilts. It appeared to him that the magistrate was about to run and the lord about to collapse to his knees.

"I'm Queen's b-brother," Fitzgerald stammered.

"So."

The lord did not respond.

"Once, if I couldn't determine between two who was guilty party, I would've slain both," Quinn said.

He waited for a long moment. Was sure that both men grasped that their deaths were at hand and certain. He knew that neither, separately nor together, were the spy in the valley for the Watchdogs and the missive was more than likely not a forgery. 'Twas the King's directive to him. It came down simply to the fact that he disliked these two men and their repeated insistence that a sad lass, who had lost all those she loved, be put to death. Disliked? Nay, despised was better word. He would've had some respect for either if they had done the execution.

"I have not betrayed the valley people," whispered Baltimore.

He ignored the magistrate.

"We have not," Fitzgerald added.

He departed without further comment.

Had first task to attend to. Then he would take the lass out of the valley.

Slowly, ever so, Bree woke. The befuddled haze in her mind faded bit by bit, and she began to comprehend her surroundings and the event that had occurred.

She lay on the gaol bed, her entire being spent. Every tad of her. Her Holy Book was beside her head on the pillow and she wore a white night dress, blessed with holy water, that Father LaBach had given her. Her person was cloaked in heavy sweat. A tiny cross on neck chain, that the priest-exorcist had also given her from the Church's archives, was beneath her bosom. It rested in a pool of wetness. Her back pounded. She knew, without remembering the actual moment, that she had arced her back so high that she'd nearly snapped her spine in half. Only the bindings at her arms and legs to the bedposts had kept her from going higher and doing so. Her wrists and ankles throbbed and there had to be deep bruising. There was a gag in her mouth to keep her from biting her tongue off and gritting her teeth so hard that she shattered them.

She smelled the frankincense Father LaBach had used in a gold thurible to purify the room.

The priest stood in prayer at the end of the bed. At some point during the exorcism, he had removed his tunic. He was veiled in sweat as she was. On his back, she saw, from his shoulder down, six claw marks. The wounds still seeped blood. A bruise decorated his cheek under his right eye. He finished his invocation and gathered his tunic. As he eased into the covering, she was surprised to witness the claw wounds and cheek bruise vanish as if they had never been.

Father LaBach removed the gag then untied the binding at her left hand.

"We have won, child," he announced.

Bree gave sincere thanks.

"The curse was from the demon I believed it was," the priest continued, releasing her right hand. "We did not destroy it, but, badly wounded, we compelled it to return to Hell. It shall not return to you. You are protected from that."

She remained motionless after he untied her feet. Even taking a small breath hurt.

"What do you remember?"

"I recall, after you bound me, you lighting the incense and speaking words in the original language," she said. "Nothing else until a little while ago."

"Good. You may receive glimpses of what occurred but no more. And those shall be gone soon. Forever."

"I hurt."

"Within the hour, your aches and pains will heal. You will feel renewed and strong."

"Bless you, Father LaBach."

The priest sighed, sadly. "During the battle, you cried behind the gag."

"I did?"

"Aye. You called out for a mortal man named Quinn to rescue you. You cried out for him to come to you more than you did for Heaven to save you."

Bree looked away from the priest.

"The angels spoke to me. Youngblood Quinn is a dark man. Your vow to guide him to the righteous is admirable. But he could lead you into his world instead. I was told that a shimmer of light now marks him and that was credited to you, my child. I keep calling you 'child', but you are woman." He nodded. "Your vow is fraught with many perils. You have already succumbed fleshly sins with him."

She tightened her closed eyes.

"The angels understood your need. But you must know this. Quinn has a strong wall surrounding his heart. No one has ever touched him there. You may. However, the odds are against you."

Bree opened her eyes to the priest. "I believe I love him."

"There is some doubt in your voice," LaBach replied, patting her perspiring brow with a cloth.

"I-I..." She hesitated.

"We shall part shortly, but I will leave you with this advice," he said. "What one sincerely believes is what one earns in the afterlife. You know there is Heaven and your loved ones wait to welcome you when your life is completed. This is truth. Your life's journey is not done. Mayhap it will end in a few minutes and mayhap in several decades. One does not know. But one must be prepared. I have met others like Quinn and, when they passed, their souls turned to dust because that is what they expected. You may stay with Quinn, you may not. The choice is not fully with you. From this moment on, you must consider each step you take on life's path. Your reward in the afterlife is not yet determined. You could stumble. Travel, my child, with humble care. And always with love in your heart."

7

AS QUINN REACHED THE OUTSKIRT OF THE township, he spotted people gathered outside the buildings. They were listening to a very tall man, wearing a long black cloak, on a very large stallion. A few made the sign of the cross as he talked.

Quinn neared the gathering. He knew now, from his clothing, that the tall man was First Church layman.

When they breasted one another, the man spoke to him directly:

"Do what is best for the lass."

Quinn knew immediately that something had happened while he was gone. Suddenly uneasy, he spurred his mount toward the gaol.

He saw Bree.

And smiled.

The lass was dancing with her face tilted to the sun and her arms outstretched. Her glorious smile turned to delighted laugh. She twirled and twirled, the hem of her wrinkled dress rising to show off her sleek legs.

Well, I'll be damned, he muttered.

He dismounted at the gaol beside the little dun-colored pony.

Turning, he was prepared when Bree leapt up onto him, hugging her arms around his neck and pressing her face to his flesh. He held her tight. He could feel her body through his tunic.

"The curse is gone," she announced. "Father LaBach forced it away. I am no longer blasphemed. Bless Heaven."

"Good." That would mean execution was no longer required.

Quinn said no more. The lass and the valley people believed the curse was true. So, it was for them. Now they trusted that the priest had vanquished it. Again, so it was. He knew the Church was a fraud. The biggest one in the history of the world. But he wouldn't say that to the lass. 'Twould devastate her.

Then he heard her voice in his mind:

"You are wrong, and you know you are."

He lowered her to the ground. She planted her bare feet atop his booted feet and a mere breath now separated their bodies.

Bree gripped his tunic in her tiny fists to secure her position.

His first impulse, seconded by the rising at his crotch, was to carry her straight to the bed.

"Do what is best for the lass."

The rising faded.

She lifted her face toward his.

"May I speak with you, Mister Quinn?" she said timidly.

He didn't like the look she had. She was plainly happy, and thankful. That was fine. She deserved that. But he saw a wish—or was it more of a determination?—in her eyes. This would not go well. He knew that without a shred of doubting.

She paused for a long moment.

"I love this valley, but I cannot stay here," she said at last. "The bad memories loom over the many good ones. And the people here will never forget. I shall be outcast and alone. There is no family I can go to. I thought I was lost…"

She stopped.

Shite, he swore. *Don't say it. Do not.* He knew what he'd decided but he no longer needed to take her from the valley. He could continue in his position.

Bree smiled at him.

"I know what I must do."

Dammit, lass, don't do this.

"I shall go with you, Mister Quinn."

He furrowed his brow and saw her smile wilt.

"Enforcer!"

Turning, he saw Hew MacLeod racing his stallion toward them. He knew the message MacLeod brought. The one Beaudry had apprised him of.

"Watchdogs are here," MacLeod stated, his mount skidding to a stop.

"Where?"

"Coming from the east. Headed toward that meadow grove where you met them the other day."

Quinn nodded. "Stay with the lass. Protect her. The curse is no more. Priest vanquished it. The township people will confirm this."

Hew MacLeod stepped down from his stallion. "I shall do as you request."

Quinn hugged Bree gently.

She was shivering.

"Do not follow," he said, sternly.

Tears seeped down her cheeks.

He looked deep into her eyes.

She nodded, her chin trembling, that she understood.

Bree, with her folded hands pressed to her bosom, watched Mister Quinn mount his horse. Without looking back, not even a glance, the enforcer rode around the corner of the goal, heading out to confront the Watchdogs, to do his duty for the king.

She prayed for him to remain safe and unharmed. But there were too many brigands.

Rushing to the corner of the gaol, she stopped short. Looked quickly left, then right. He had already ridden out of eyesight. One moment he was there, and the next he was gone. He had become ghost.

Above her, from the roof of the gaol, several crows took to the air.

She watched them fly away. What had Mister Quinn said about birds taking sudden flight? *Oh, yes.* But that happened at night not during daylight.

Hew MacLeod grabbed her by the arm.

She cried out as he dragged her to the horses.

She fought against his bruising grip, hit him with her free hand. What was happening? Why was he doing this? She slugged him as hard as she could. He clutched her tighter.

"Release me!" she shouted.

He gagged her.

From the twisted anger of his expression, she knew Hew MacLeod hated her, blamed her for the death of his cousin. It did not matter to him that the curse had been taken away.

MacLeod lifted her rough into the dun pony's sidesaddle. She thrashed and writhed as he lashed her hands and wrists to the saddle's horn.

She kicked her bare feet at his face. Missed.

"Martell wants you," he growled.

What? She did not understand this. Hew MacLeod was heir to a fortune. He wanted for nothing. Could have almost anything he desired. Why would he be in league with the Watchdogs? And why was he kidnapping her? *Oh, dear Lord.* She realized the Watchdogs would use her to draw Mister Quinn into the open to slay him. She looked around, in all directions. Saw no one who could help her.

Bree struggled again, with all her strength, against her binding. There was no give. None. *Dear Heaven, aid me. Please I pray.*

Then.

She saw MacLeod's angry features turn grimmer.

He turned his back to her and drew his sword.

Bree looked in the direction Hew MacLeod was staring.

From the other corner of the gaol…

…Mister Quinn marched toward them…

…with his shortswords in his fists.

Plainly he'd ridden around the gaol, and once out of their sight, had dismounted.

She watched, horrified, as MacLeod took fighting stance and Mister Quinn moved closer. She knew Hew MacLeod had trained most of his life with blades and his skill was highly touted in the valley. He was in battle posture while Mister Quinn carried his shortswords, as if forgotten, at his sides.

"What gave me away?" asked MacLeod.

"You agreed too quickly to watch over the lass. Didn't sit well with me. You left her on her own last time," replied Mister Quinn. "You're the spy in the valley for the Watchdogs."

"I have to protect my family and estate. Others would have done the same if they had thought of it first."

Mister Quinn nodded.

"My thoughts are one, enforcer," MacLeod said. "To slay you. I have advantage. Because yer thoughts are divided."

With his free hand, MacLeod reached behind him and patted Bree's leg.

Bree leaned back in the saddle, mortified. Yes, Mister Quinn would be worried for her and not centered on the fight. She started to pray. But stopped. What would Mister Quinn do?

She kicked the heels of both bare feet straight in the back of Hew MacLeod's head.

MacLeod went forward, with grunt, and Mister Quinn leapt toward him. The enforcer blocked MacLeod's awkward sword swing then cross-slashed his blades across MacLeod's body. He sheathed his shortswords before Hew MacLeod dropped his sword and fell to his knees.

MacLeod clutched his arms around his body and looked up at the enforcer.

"Ye c-cheated."

"Always."

As Hew MacLeod toppled to the ground, Mister Quinn moved

to her and untied her binding. Gently, he took her into his arms. She laid her face against his chest and hugged him around the neck. He carried her inside the gaol.

Setting her on the bed, prying her arms from around him, Mister Quinn cupped her face between his hands.

"Wait here," he said. "If you follow me, I shall not take you with me when I leave the valley."

Bree's heart clenched. "There are too many."

"I only fight one."

"That is worse."

"One is worse?"

"You intend to murder the man."

"He deserves death."

"You are the one I fear for, not him."

"I can defend myself."

"Not against your heavenly fate. You cannot continue as you have in the past. Hew MacLeod gave you no choice, but you must change your life path. I pray that you get a second chance."

He rose. "You can preach at me after," he said. "Stay here, lass."

Mister Quinn headed outside.

Bree waited, counting to ten, before rushing to the doorway. She started to step further but stopped. Stay here, he had commanded. He had not been ambivalent in his words. She edged her foot into the sunlight then yanked her toes back.

She saw that Mister Quinn, and the corpse of Hew MacLeod and their horses were already gone. Once again, the enforcer was ghost.

Bree lowered to the ground and leaned against the frame of the door. Tears seeped down her face. She would wait this time. If she followed, he would be furious. And she would be distraction that could cost him his life. He'd also told her that he would not take her with him when he left the valley.

Had she decided that was what she wanted? Yes, she had. They were each other's deliverance and salvation.

So, she would wait here, as he said to, and pray for his soul.

For forever and an hour if need be.

Quinn found them at the grove meadow as Hew MacLeod said they'd be. He'd hobbled his horse a kilometer back and walked the remainder of the way. This time there were outriders and sentries scattered in the woods for him to avoid. The Watchdogs believed they were ready. But he'd found two slain sentries during his approach. Their deaths meant Lakesnow and the troop were here, too. In hiding. Lakesnow had followed his plan. It would work. Martell had become so consumed with the enforcer in the valley that he had lost track of the knights. The end of the Watchdogs was at hand.

Now he squatted among the trees bordering the meadow, watching, and twisting in his fists the extra tunic he'd brought with him.

Seton Martell stood at the outskirt of his dismounted band speaking to a bearded, wide-shouldered man. The leader of the Watchdogs kept glancing at the position of the sun in the sky. Quinn understood. The once-knight was waiting for Hew MacLeod to arrive with the lass. That would not happen. Bree wouldn't be here to lure the enforcer into the open.

As he waited, he cursed himself. He'd wanted Bree to realize that she could not follow him this time, wanted that to be very clear. But why had he added if she did follow, he wouldn't take her with him when he departed the valley? That implied he would allow her to accompany him if she obeyed his command. He couldn't. The little lass did not belong in his world. She would be miserable and that he didn't want for her. She would be alone often when he was sent on king's tasks and the lengths of time gone would be unknown, and she'd always worry, that was her way, if his latest task would his last. Someday he would face an opponent who had better skills than he did. That eventuality was in stone. And she'd be an outcast in the capital, no one would befriend the woman of the King's enforcer except for nefarious aims. With him, she would be in a lifelong purgatory. Dammit, he was planning all reasons to tell her why she could *not* go with him. Which meant he'd considered taking her.

That should not have ever crossed his mind.

Not ever.

To his left, a rider-less Watchdog horse suddenly galloped, terrified, from the woods and across the meadow. The outlaws watched the horse, befuddled and unmoving.

Seton Martell, however, and the bearded brigand leapt immediately onto their mounts and drew blades.

The voice from the woods sounded loud and plain, no quarter in the words:

"You are all under arrest in the name of our King."

Panic grabbed the Watchdogs and the brigands scrambled about, unsure and confused. Three jumped onto their horses.

Lakesnow and three knights advanced in a single line, side by side, out of the woods. To his right, Quinn saw four more knights ride into view. The last two knights appeared at the rear of the meadow. He did not see Beaudry among them.

"Throw down your weapons," Lakesnow ordered. "Do so now."

The Watchdogs were surrounded on three sides. The only escape route appeared to be toward Quinn.

Martell and the bearded brigand raced their steeds toward his position.

Quinn moved quickly, gripping the tunic in one hand and his shortsword in the other. The brigand was in the lead and he was sure Martell intended for the man to be so. He allowed the brigand to go past unharmed.

Then, as Seton Martell came abreast of him, Quinn threw the tunic into the horse's eyes.

The mount cried out and reared onto its hind legs. Martell flew from the saddle, slammed hard into a thick tree, losing his blade and collapsed to the ground.

Behind him, Quinn heard the bearded man grunt. Now he knew where Beaudry was.

He advanced toward Martell.

The once-knight struggled to his feet. He looked at Quinn and raised an open hand above his head.

"The other's broke," he said, wincing. "I surrender. I am unarmed."

Quinn didn't respond. The Watchdog leader should have surrendered to Bryce Lakesnow when he had the chance. The knight would have accepted. His code of honor would have demanded it.

Martell grasped his fate.

Quinn hesitated. But only for a slight tad.

Before Seton Martell could attempt a final action, the enforcer thrust his blade between the man's ribs and into his heart.

Quinn remained where he stood as Beaudry marched the bearded brigand, wounded, past him. They nodded to each other. He scanned the meadow. A few corpses—he didn't count—were scattered about. Most of the brigands had surrendered to Lakesnow and his knights. The terror of the Watchdogs was over.

He glanced once more at the corpse of Seton Martell.

"Damn," he muttered aloud. "I hesitated."

As evening fell, Bree believed her heart would burst with joy when she saw Mister Quinn return unharmed from his battle with the Watchdogs. But now her heart was breaking.

With her fingertips, she wiped the tears from her eyes. Mister Quinn had said she couldn't be with him. He was firm and resolute with his words.

"I cannot remain in the valley," she repeated. Her legs trembled and she dropped onto the side of the bed.

"I'm not your answer. I will help you find a place that will be safe."

"I am safe with you."

"You need a good man. One who believes as you do, one who will care and protect you."

"I am confused. You wish for another man to kiss and lay with me?"

Mister Quinn didn't respond. But she saw his hands curl into fists and pulsating veins rise at his temples.

What did that reaction mean? she wondered. He appeared as if he was about to strike out in anger. She knew however he would never harm her.

She pressed her folded hands to her bosom.

"I would be fine wife for you." She paused, suddenly she believed she understood. "If you do not wish to marry, I would accept and still be fine wife for you. In all ways."

He sighed. "How many reasons, lass, do you need to hear to understand that you and I should not be together? Ten? One hundred? A thousand?"

"I have only one question for you. Your answer will decide all."

"Tell me it."

"Do you love me? I love you."

The Queen
and the Oracle

"A FORTNIGHT AGO," QUEEN IGRAINE SAID, "Matthias Duncan found a signed parchment on his study desk. The missive was from the enforcer. He thanked the King and wrote that he was leaving. There was no more in the message."

The oracle nodded. "The high counsel ordered soldiers to find the enforcer and bring the man to him. But there was no trace of him within the city. He was gone. No one knows where."

"What happened to the O'Darrow lass and Youngblood Quinn?" Igraine frowned. "I must know more."

The ancient woman waved her hands over the teacup, laced mat and circle of crystals. She closed her eyes and stroked her fingers over her bald head, concentrating.

The Queen waited.

"The future is always in fogged vision," the oracle said. "So many things can alter what is seen."

"Then tell me what appears to be."

The oracle opened her eyes.

"I see a farmhold in the Frontier," she said, "near a lake that maps will one day call Bella Bleu. 'Tis a holding with solid house, well-tended and prospering small fields of wheat and barley, and a corral of fine horses."

"Do you see a family there?"

"Aye. The husband is a somber taciturn man and will negotiate truces with the neighboring barbarian clans that appear to be honored by all. The clan elders will warn their young men not to brace the westerner to prove they are warriors. There shall be graves of those who did not heed the counsel. The husband is not a jovial individual, there shall be no man he calls friend. But visitors will say he is content, that a genuine smile appears on him when he gazes at the females of the family."

"Females."

"The wife is a cheerful, charming and Godfearing woman who welcomes all into their home. She calls her husband 'Mister' and always with joy in her heart and voice. Outsiders shall say they are a very ill-suited pair, but their bond is true and strong. They shall begat two loved and loving daughters."

"Good. I like that vision of the future for the lass and the enforcer."

The oracle picked up the teacup and looked at the leaves.

"My next tale took place a week back, over a three-day span of time. Yer Majesty does not know the lady but yer proclamation, yer order to the kingdom people, changed this lady's life forever…"

Mariah Avalon:
Her Bound Knight

8

TODAY THE KINGDOM'S WAR WIDOWS COULD choose a new husband and the man was forbidden to decline.

Until Mariah had heard the Queen's royal decree yesterday afternoon, she'd believed she had few choices left in her life. But between this dawn and this dusk, she had been given a choice other than nunnery or brothel; other than being murdered, or worse, on the street.

Sunrise was soon but 'twas still dark for now. Above her, she saw in the cloudless sky a red-ringed moon and a glistening sweep of stars.

She felt so insignificant within this world, as if nit buffeted about in a directionless wind.

She followed the other women along the unpaved roadway with the hood of her gray cloak covering her head and a matching scarf across her lower face, wearing the last gown she possessed—an indigo-blue surcoat over white blouse, and carrying one small bag of belongings.

Each woman in the procession, like her, was walking swiftly.

Without looking back, Mariah heard more women coming up behind her. She understood that the rebellion of the Usurper had cost many, many lives in the kingdom, but she had not realized how numerous, like herself, were soldiers' widows. The Queen's decree said the chosen unmarried man had to be equal to, or less, than husband's rank. She was only acquainted with a few of her late husband's fellow knights and only two or three had been unmarried. She repeated to herself that she would not choose a total stranger but then again, all that had come to their home she had not known well. So, in fact, she would be taking a stranger as husband.

"When we find them, long Adam's mine," announced the taller of the two lanky women ahead of her. "Remember I'm stronger than ye."

"But I'm quicker," replied the other. "Ye can have short Seth."

"I heard that a noble widow was traveling to the estate of the House of MacLeod. At least one of the brothers there is unmarried, and she intends to take him for husband."

"Adam and Seth will do for us."

Would this husband choosing truly do? Mariah wondered if her heart could rise any higher in her throat and if her hands could become damper than they already were. She switched her bag from one hand to the other as she wiped each bared palm on her cloak. They didn't stay dry for long.

The soldiers' widows rounded the last curve of the road leading to the fifteen-thousand-man army encampment at the outskirts of the capital city.

She stopped, taken aback. A woman close behind bumped into her, adding another rattle to her person. The woman said what did not sound like apology and moved onward.

Mariah stared ahead. At the camp's entry, despite there being no fencing around the encampment, she guessed that a hundred and fifty, mayhap two hundred, women were already gathered at the entrance. And more were arriving at every minute. Most were alone like her, some however, had children with them. 'Twas hard to tell in the fading darkness but the women appeared to be all ages from young to elder. She saw a female attempting to sneak into the encampment early and the woman was apprehended by well-positioned guards. The woman was told, in a commanding voice, loud enough for all on the roadway to hear, that she would be incarcerated until dusk and her day of choosing was no more.

Inhaling deeply, Mariah continued forward. She had to do this.

"I heard," a woman near Mariah said to a friend, "that all the married men were placed in a second camp. So, all we see are available for choosing."

There had never been a day such as this in the history of Thuria and, Mariah understood, might never be again. Her Royal Highness, Queen Igraine, had said 'twas to their kingdom's disgrace that so many women had lost their husbands in the war and, adding to that dreadful event, too many suddenly found themselves, and their children if they had any, without income nor basic living support. Soldiers' families only received minor death stipend, and not all women had family to assist them in this dire time.

She had memorized the four provisos in the Queen's proclamation: the woman had to be widow; the man had to be unmarried of course and not formally betrothed; he had to be equal to or lesser than late husband's station; and if the man refused the choosing, he would be stripped of his rank or title then sent to the labor mines. The Queen, her meaning plain, was serious about the decree.

Mariah believed she had the skills that would be favorable to a marriage. She could, and would as she had, keep a clean homehold with all things in their proper place. When at home from his soldier duties, husband's favorite foods would be prepared. She would mend his clothing and forego new garment for herself if he had need. She would listen to all his words, heed his instructions for the man was the head of the homehold and she would not nag, she would rarely make request. When husband was at home, and *only* when he was home, she would welcome his friends and companions no matter the day or time.

Her main worry was coupling. Late husband and she had followed the intent of First Church's Diocese rules for proper martial relations. Husband and wife would only mate to produce child. *Never* was the act to be pleasurable for either one. Sinful troubadours sang about courtly love but that was the Devil's ploy to entice the weak to his kingdom. Coupling was not allowed on Sundays, the thirty days before their Christ's birthing day, the six weeks of Lent, or during the Feasts of the Saints. The solitary acceptable position was man on top and would only last long enough for husband to put seed into wife. She was concerned for herself and had been glad that knight-husband was away for long periods serving the kingdom. During coupling, she had found her body starting to respond *in pleasure*, but late husband always finished before it went too far, thank the Lord. Knowing that sin in heart and mind was equal to enacted one, and chastising herself for her impure thoughts, she wondered much more than she should have—how would her body answer if she had pagan lover?

She prayed that new husband's intimate wants were like late husband's.

Occasional, and over quickly.

And he would be gone for long periods of time fulfilling his duty to the King.

More widows arrived at the encampment entry.

The number now, she estimated, had to be double the amount when she first arrived. While she knew the capital city was the largest and most populace in the realm, she never thought this many would be in need. She wondered if any of the women among them had never been married. Did they see the Queen's decree as their only chance to end their life as spinster? What would be their punishment if their deception were uncovered?

Had it only been five months ago, she reflected, when word came that the King's army had defeated the Usurper and his troops? And two months since the traitorous lord and most of the nobles that had joined with him had been executed on the gallows?

Celebrations had crisscrossed the capital city during that time and reigned across the kingdom.

The war was over. Victory was theirs. The kingdom was once again safe and secure.

But with the joy came grief. But her grief was not as deep as others expected it to be.

A squire, looking more like vagrant than knight's apprentice, had come to her homehold and informed Mariah that her husband, Sir Malcolm Avalon, had died in his service to the kingdom. No other details were forthcoming. Not that it mattered. All that did was that he was dead. The squire added that Sir Avalon's remains had not been recovered and therefore could not be brought to the capital for funeral. Then the squire had presented her with a kaleidoscope that Sir Avalon had acquired as a gift for her. He added that her husband had said the scope was valuable and should be guarded from loss or theft. She was surprised at this token because Avalon had never brought her gifts from his previous military travels. Still she accepted the red-gilded cylinder and thanked the squire for his devotion to his knight master.

She stood blocked by other women from getting closer to the entry. And soon she was crushed by those amassing about her. At barely five feet in height and weighing less than forty-five kilos, most females in the kingdom were taller than and weighed more than her. The crowd would have its way with her and there was naught she could do about it.

Guards, solemn-faced, stood shoulder-to-shoulder in front of the roadway entrance. They would open the camp soon as the order was given.

Her attention was drawn to her right and she was puzzled by the sight. At the entry, standing alone but watching all, was an elderly bald-headed woman with brass coils around her neck. Could this woman be seeking husband?

Nearby, the two lanky women began to scuffle with others over position. The soldiers did not interfere.

Mariah glanced at the eastern horizon. Very soon now. She'd heard that several noble officers and knights had volunteered for immediate patrols in the unmapped Frontier. They had all been declined with disciplinary action promised for any not at the encampment this day. But she also overheard, in her walk this morn with the other women, that many of the unmarried men intended to hide.

The last few days been a blur in time for Mariah. She'd learned, again, that one's life could change drastically without warning, that safety and security were guaranteed to no one. Within a day of the news of Avalon's death, she had been sought out. Her friend, Lucille, came to offer condolences. But most did not. The abbess of the neighboring rectory told her that devoted sisters were needed to tend the unfortunates at the leper colony at *faraway* Xadag. An odious man informed her that she could be rich in a year's time with her quarter share of the monies collected if she took a coupling bed in his establishment. An artist, who had done portraits of Queen Igraine and King Richard, suggested she sit for him unclothed and they would split equally the monies received when painting sold. A local goldsmith had come and offered his name and home to her. During his entire rambling and mostly incoherent speech, he drooled, tugged at the dark-stained rear of his breeches and sipped from a small flask he attempted to keep hidden. She blocked from her mind what a neighbor knight and wife had proposed to ease her mourning sorrows.

The sheriff came the day after.

She learned Avalon had many outstanding debts. The arrears included gambling debts she had not known about. Her homehold and its contents would be auctioned to partially pay for the debts. She was put onto the street.

Shortly before she left the homehold for the last time, a strange woman carrying babe on hip came to her. Said that Avalon was the father of the child and demanded coin for the caring of the babe. Mariah told her the crown had taken all for unpaid debts. The woman cursed then left immediately and did not look back once. Mariah knew, in her heart, without any proof, that the woman had spoken the truth.

She went to Lucille.

Mariah found her good and dear friend in tears. Lucille, two and forty in years, wedded wife of Sir Thomas Ianeillo, said an army lieutenant had come to her followed by the sheriff. The lieutenant informed her that her knight husband had succumbed to dysentery and died. Mariah later heard that the disease, also known as bloody shite and barbarian's fever, had slain more kingdom officers and soldiers than the traitor's army in battle. The sheriff, waiting only a short time after the lieutenant departed, said the Ianeillo homehold and its contents would be auctioned to partially pay for the family arrears. Lucille, with a paltry bag of belongings, was also put on the street.

Mariah and Lucille went to Lucille's cousin's home and were given shelter for the night. The next day, Mariah was told she could not stay—there was not enough food for all. She understood there was another reason for her expulsion. She'd seen the cousin's husband leering at her as he pulled at the lacing of his breeches.

"I shall accompany ye," Lucille had said.

"Nay," she replied. "I give heartfelt thanks to you but stay here with family where you are safe."

Mariah went to the homehold of a woman she *had* believed was a good friend. The woman turned her away stating flatly that Mariah's mere presence would cause her husband and sons to sin in their minds and that could lead to actual sinning.

That night was the first time ever she'd been alone on the street. She had been terrified to the core of her being. Alarming near encounters had occurred but only one, a drunken seaman had managed to place his hands momentarily upon her person before she escaped.

'Twas shortly after midnight when she discovered, by mere chance, that the church at the end of Market Road kept its doors open all night. Inside, among the others who appeared to be lost and struggling souls, an elder priest ministered to all. With a tad of the evening chill leaving her body, she sat in a middle pew, not close to any of the others, and prayed. The priest aided her with one prayer.

She knew she was a sinner, in mind but not actual deed, but she still asked for divine guidance.

She knew she would not survive many more nights under these circumstances.

The following day, Mariah received sign. She heard the town crier announcing the Queen's decree and had another woman read the posting he left behind.

She couldn't read. Father had attempted to teach her, but both gave up in frustration after several lessons. When she looked at written words, whether penned or printed, she saw the letters in reverse and, sometimes, with Father pointing it out to her, different letters appeared to her than the one authored. If she stared too long at a page, the words became a swimming haze and soon a head throb. This failure told her, adding to other failings, that she was unworthy, stupid person.

After hearing the royal decree, she decided what she must do. Recalling a few unattached men, one kept rising high in her thoughts. Why him? He frightened her she admitted. So why did her thoughts keep returning to him? Why? She did not understand her fixation on this knight.

As they waited at the camp entrance, most of the women around Mariah were quiet as she was. But a few voices—bits of conversation—cut the silence.

"…need man who is carpenter to add to my shop…"

"…always had my eye on his brother…"

"…Lord bless our Queen for this…"

"…beggin' on street I will be…"

At last, slants of dawn light seeped onto the horizon.

She saw a crowd of men hiking down the camp's main roadway toward the entrance. These soldiers were presenting themselves for husband choosing. Well, it seemed that not all unmarried men objected to the Queen's decree.

An army captain shouted order to open the entry.

And the guards stood aside.

Mariah nearly went down in the rush into the encampment.

One woman, she saw, took a single step inside the camp. This widow approached a flabbergasted guard and said the required words: "I choose ye."

Moving quickly to the side, Mariah saw the ancient woman had fallen, or had been knocked, to the ground during the rush to enter the camp.

She hurried to the woman. And aided the elder to her feet.

The woman looked straight into Mariah's eyes, and Mariah felt a cool shiver down her spine.

"Thank ye, kind lady," the woman said, taking Mariah's hands into hers. Then she smiled. "Ye shall find yer heart in the camp. If ye do not take the chance, yer days in this world shall not be many more."

The ancient woman released Mariah's hands and walked toward the roadway.

"Good fortune, Mariah Avalon," she called back.

Mariah stood where she was. How did the ancient woman know her name? Why had she given encouraging prophecy then added ominous words?

Slowly, Mariah studied the encampment. To her right were the soldiers, to the left were the officers. At the rear of the encampment were the knights. And there she would find the man she was seeking.

You can do this, she repeated to herself again and again. *You* must *do this.*

At last, she began walking the path toward the rear of the camp. Even with her head down, she still observed a number of situations. Some gave her hope, some dismay, and one was most bewildering. She noted that less than a quarter hour had passed and already several twosomes were headed toward the tents of the priests and magistrates to be married. Several pairs seemed happy. One couple, a bone-thin man holding the hand of a woman thrice his weight, were, without error in her observation, truly joyful. A handful of men, and surprisingly one woman, appeared miserable as they proceeded to the marriage tents. She saw a cook, wearing his stained apron, watch two women in front of him brawling in a flurry of punches, kicks, and clawing; she saw a widow pat a soldier's chest and arms, check his teeth, then grab him at the crotch; she saw a young officer stop his pleading for release when the youthful woman choosing him opened the top of her frock and bared her bosom to him. One knight proclaimed he was betrothed and when the widow responded that he had to provide proof of words, he blanched. She was most confused and baffled when she saw a handsome woman—plainly a lady-of-means by her dress and deportment—strolling toward the tents with a stalwart man on *each* arm. That would not be allowed. Would it? 'Twas against church and kingdom laws. Then again, this was a unique day in the kingdom. So mayhap.

Mariah paused at the edge of the knight's encampment. The area appeared deserted. Of men. Several women were hurrying about and peering into the tents. Near her, she saw the two lanky women from before. They stood flatfooted and open-mouth agape. The two knights they watched were walking toward the marriage tents holding the arms of two women, smaller than Mariah, appearing by physical features to be sisters.

The taller of the lanky women uttered a blasphemous oath. The other said they should fight the two women for the men's hands in marriage. The first suggested cousins that they knew, and they scurried away.

Another woman hurried her two children past one tent. A snoring knight lay half in and half out his shelter. A jug was next to him and vomit decorated his beard and tunic. Then, when the woman and children were away and her presence unnoticed, Mariah watched the knight's chest move in what appeared to be laughter. His positioning was ruse. It reminded her that not all was what it first seemed to be. Then again, some things were exactly what they appeared to be at initial sight.

To her far right, Mariah spotted Sir Gawain Beaudry. He sat outside his tent in a chair beside a ringed fire without any attempt to hide himself. At thirty years of age he was a strikingly handsome man with a honed muscular body, beardless face, and curly dark blond hair. His eyes were a rich brown in coloring. 'Twas said he was distant relation—second or third cousin—to their King and to both the high esteemed families of Duncan and Blackwell.

A man handed the knight a mug. The fellow was about fifty years of age and weighed near eighteen stone, had graying hair and beard and his left foot from ankle down was missing.

Between the men, on a perch, was a hooded white-breasted hunting falcon.

She hesitated, gathering her strength of will.

Five years ago, Sir Malcolm Avalon and she had wed. She had been six and ten. 'Twas a marriage endorsed by her father.

Father had been a widower of the lower-class gentry, a farmer who owned the land he worked. With no memory of her dear mother who'd passed while giving birth to her, Father had kept her safe and protected. He was a genial, sweet-natured man who could never say no to any neighbor in need. She noted as she grew older that few repaid the coin loans and fewer still came to help when they were in need. And Father never pressed a single one for repayment.

She'd been told from an early age that she was a beauty. The face of Aphrodite she'd heard beyond count, with her light ash-brown hair, deep hazel eyes, and full lips adding to her beauteous features. Then, if that curse was not enough, when she bloomed into womanhood her bosom grew, her hips remained slim and her legs sleek. Father said she was mirror image of her maternal grandmother. She'd always dressed to conceal but the stares of strangers still came, along with obscene catcalls and disquiet followings when she was in town. While they had always had difficulties in finding good help, Father had fired several male farmhands over the years for looking at his daughter in what he deemed inappropriate manner. She'd intended to spend her life in the shelter of her father's homehold, and care for him as he grew elder as he had cared for her as a child. Then he became ill. Physician was unable to determine cause of the ravaging malady, but it came, swift and harsh. One of the last requests Father made was for her to wed Avalon, old family friend. He was, Father told her, an honorable knight who would keep her safe and shielded. Standing beside Father, who was too weak to leave his bed, Avalon proposed to her. She accepted.

She had still barely known her husband after five years of marriage. Following Father's passing, Avalon sold the family manor and land, then found them a homehold dwelling in capital city in a neighborhood housing several army families, but 'twas rare for him to be there. Most of the years, he was gone on military duties. However, she kept their abode clean and neat as if he would walk through the doorway at any moment. One reason she hardly knew her husband was that he was not a talker like Father had been. He did not talk much even when he invited his knight companions and fellows for meal and sharing of ale.

Avalon initiated their couplings, she never did. Most of their rare marital joinings were a repeat of their first night. Before Avalon led her to the bed, to consummate their marriage, he slapped her once across the face and said she would be an obedient and faithful wife—if she was not, in all ways, then she would be soundly punished. The couplings were always at night and with no lit candle. She would lay on her back in their bedstead and raise the hem of her night dress to her waist. Avalon would position himself above her and, without any preludes, enter her. He would stutter a few times, then release. She gave blessing, despite her body attempting to go rouge in pleasure, that the act was quick. Sad she was that the couplings never resulted in her being with child. Another failure in her. She also thanked the heavens that her husband was not fond of kissing. The few times they had, she thought his mouth tasted like old fish and she restrained the urge to gag during the brief act. She'd heard about flesh enticements other than kissing and man-atop coupling but, and she was blessed by this—Avalon never pursued any. Still, when alone in bed at night, she often wondered about those stories of body pleasures.

She'd discovered that if she stayed within the few streets around their homehold she was not usually bothered, for the people there knew who her husband was. When she *had* to go about town, she dressed dowdily with cloak hood raised and scarf covering lower face. Notwithstanding, 'twas always a nervous outing.

Before she knew of the Queen's decree, she believed her life would end, in desperation and pain, on a back street in their city; that her corpse would be part of the curb refuse.

Mariah studied the knight sitting outside his tent. 'Twas plain to her that he hadn't taken note of her arrival. Again, she wiped her damp palms on her cloak.

Of Avalon's fellow knights who had come to their homehold, Sir Gawain Beaudry stood out from the others. When her husband introduced her to this fellow knight, she had trembled which was not unusual when she met strangers but this shiver was different than most as she looked up, only for a half-moment, into the knight's intense gaze. His presence filled their homehold when he visited, more than other visitors—no matter how many. She always knew where he was inside their home: his movements, his stillness, and his spoken words. Since first meeting, she avoided him. Gawain had a black reputation. He was feared not only by the king's enemies but by many of his companions as well. While he never left a wounded fellow behind, he would advance into enemy positions that were considered death traps by seasoned warriors and survive with victory. His skill with the sword was often compared to the legendary King D'Arth of old Thurian history. One repeated and dreadful story said that he'd slain a fierce enemy knight by cutting the foe in half with his blade—not from side-to-side but down from shoulder to crotch. She'd heard female gossip that he was also a notorious rake among the ladies. Lucille told her that Gawain had sweet-talked a *nun* into intimacy and that two—*possibly more!*—women had to be carried from Gawain's bed the morning after a coupling. Lucille insisted that the stories were true, she'd heard them from different trusted parties.

Gawain hadn't abused the carried women, Lucille continued. His lovemaking had caused his partners to achieve pinnacle so superb that they had passed out in bliss, and their nether regions and legs were so weak afterward they couldn't walk unassisted. This Mariah knew, without insulting her friend, was not possible.

She clearly remembered one dreadful day when she was preparing mid-day meal for husband, Gawain, and three other knights. One knight had brought along his wife and newborn son. She became so enchanted with the babe that she left the suckling pig unattended. The roast caught fire and burned to char. Avalon spoke that day with angry words, called her stupid more than once. If the others had not been present, he would have punished her. As she wept, at a loss of how to replace the suckling, Gawain suddenly appeared beside her. Clearly, he had left the homehold for a period. He gave her already-roasted flank of mutton. Then the terrifying knight touched her wet cheek with his fingers. He asked, "Did you burn the suckling on purpose?" "N-N-Nay," she stammered. "It was an accident," he said, "and you should forgive yourself."

At the now, Mariah's heart skipped a beat as she saw a stout woman walking toward Gawain. The knight fixed a stare upon the approaching female and the woman turned back. The older man chuckled.

She inhaled deeply. She could do this, she had to do this. Forcing herself, she put one foot in front of the other and walked toward him. Suddenly, the two lanky women were beside her. Then they saw who she was advancing toward, uttered more curses, and were gone.

At last Gawain looked at her, his eyes narrowing and his unshaven face growing tight. Her heart felt as if it had been stabbed with ice blade. Still, she walked to within a few feet of him and set her bag on the ground. As when she'd first met him, her body from crown to toe trembled.

"Milady Avalon," Gawain said gruffly, not rising. "My condolences to you. Malcolm was a brave man. I would've come to your home to extend sympathies, but we only arrived in the city yesterday."

Mariah didn't reply. Her voice had vanished.

He drank from his mug then leaned toward her.

"*Boo!*"

She nearly leapt out of her shoes.

Gawain shook his head, leaned back in his chair, then announced: "I know what our queen has decreed. But I do not wish to marry. Ever. And if I did, 'twould not be to one as timid as you."

She didn't respond.

"Did you understand me, milady?"

Mariah braced her shoulders, found her words and whispered, "You are a man of honor."

"Speak up, woman. You always talk too softly."

"You are a man of honor," she repeated, a little louder.

"Am I, Jae-Sifuentes?" he asked over his shoulder.

"Not in battle," the elder man replied. Then he guffawed. "Nor in bed."

Part of her wanted to retreat but most of her was determined to remain where she was. She had come this far, and she would see this to conclusion.

"You would never disobey our Queen," she said.

Gawain frowned and set his mug angrily down on a stone of the fire ring. "I beat my women."

"That is untruth," she said, praying that it was. "You would not abuse those weaker than you and unable to defend themselves from your wrath. You are not craven."

"You wouldn't know." He crossed his arms across his powerful chest and looked at his companion. "Blue hell. If it had taken a few days longer to capture the damn Watchdogs, I wouldn't be back in the capital for this miserable day."

"So, ye have said several times," responded Jae- Sifuentes.

"You heard the rumor I did. That Quinn resigned his position as enforcer and has vanished."

"Ye have repeated that, too. Said ye would go to High Counsel Duncan and offer yerself as replacement and immediately accept task outside the kingdom. But alas, the high counsel is not in the capital—has gone to Quantero a fortnight ago to act as King's voice in some treaty or negotiations. In the last day, ye have been echoing yerself a lot. And none of it has been worth remembering."

"So, here I am." Gawain returned his gaze to Mariah. "I frighten you. Always have. So why in the blue hell would you want to marry me?"

"I am accustomed to the life of knight's wife. You will be gone for great periods of time in service to our kingdom." She swallowed at the lump in her throat. She would tell him the truth. "By taking your n-name, I shall be safe and…shielded."

"Safe? From others, mayhap. And what would I gain from our bonding? I don't need a maid or cook. Hell, I've never even seen your face. You always wore covering when I visited your homehold as you do now. Remove hood and scarf so I may look upon you."

She raised her hands to her hood and scarf but hesitated.

"Come now, woman," he said, growling. "No one would accept a brood mare sight unseen."

Jae-Sifuentes snorted a chuckle. "Unseen brood mare. Those are the best words ye can say to her? I am amazed that ye ever entice any woman into yer bed."

"I'm trying to talk her *out* of my bed not into," he replied. "I have no experience in this line of speech."

"Mayhap if ye take her into yer bed, she shall change her mind about the choosing."

"Nay. Never received any complaints about my dockings."

Mariah knew he was being rude and unpleasant in attempt to drive her away. Still, on the other hand, this might be his genuine character. Despite the cross decorating his knight's shield, she already knew one truth about him. He was pagan in bed.

Slowly, she lowered the hood and scarf.

Gawain didn't speak.

But Jae-Sifuentes muttered, "Shite on me. We have seen many, many lovelies in our time but have ye ever seen any as beautiful as this one?"

"Once, twice."

"Who?"

Mariah felt her face flush with heat.

"Remember when we were at the palace of the king of Zar. There was that sculpture by Omusa of the goddess Athena. Or was it, Aphrodite?"

"No, no, not a statue, or painting. In the flesh with yer own eyes? Damn. She's even more beautiful when she blushes."

"Uhhh…" Gawain shifted in his chair then stilled. "I do not wish to marry," he repeated sternly. "Especially to a woman as timid as you. I have no interest whatsoever in a tiny mouse of a woman."

Mariah inhaled and stared down at her feet. "I understand a man's physical inclinations and I would never decline you." She paused. Believing her next words. "I would stay faithful to our union, but I would not expect you to honor your vow of fidelity."

"That's most generous. Blue hell. Come with me. I can think of two knights this very moment who would fall to their knees in bliss if you picked them. We'll find these men."

Gawain stood. He didn't offer his arm to her.

She felt that her heart was about to explode from her body, and she asked herself again. Why him?

He scowled. "Our Queen's proclamation is ludicrous. I won't do it."

"If ye intend to tell her Majesty that," said Jae-Sifuentes, "give me a day's start to hide out in the Frontier."

Gawain looked directly at Mariah. She felt his eyes burning into her.

"If you do this," he said, "it won't end well."

She wiped her palms against her cloak.

And spoke the fateful words:

"I...c-choose...you."

The sun had risen fully above the eastern horizon when they returned to the tent.

As wife and husband.

Clutching her bag, Mariah had trailed after Gawain during the walk to the priest and magistrate tents. He never offered his arm to her and she'd had to run to keep up with his long angry strides.

A couple passed by her and she heard the soldier reciting poetry to his enthralled bride. Her heart warmed. Would Gawain? No. The knight did not give impression that he said verse when seducing his conquests. He had other maneuvers. None of which he would use upon the woman he was forced to wed.

She spotted, and quickly looked away, a couple who could not wait to reach their tent and were, standing upright, consummating their vows.

As they neared the lines in front of the tents, she saw a couple exit the nearest one. The man—an officer—was sullen. She heard him say to his new wife, "Now ye have my name and that is all ye shall ever receive from me." He marched away without looking back. The woman collapsed to the ground on her knees, sobbing.

Mariah swallowed at the lump in her throat. Would that be her fate?

Close by, she saw the two lanky women again. They were alone and looking about in obvious desperation.

The couples in line, without command, stepped aside for Mariah and Gawain. The men were surprised that he was among them, and the women appeared to disbelieve her choice. She pondered again: why him among the unmarried knights she knew of? Why? She still had no answer for herself.

Standing before a priest, still clutching her bag, she whispered her vows. He grunted his. There'd been no kiss at the conclusion.

She followed him, again at a fast sprint, back to his—now their—lodging.

Nervously, she stepped into the tent. 'Twas larger than it appeared from the outside and, she was amazed at how clean and tidy it was. 'Twas not a man sty. She saw the bed—an actual bed not a cot nor blankets on the ground—and became rooted to the ground. She pondered how many women he had entertained upon it.

Gawain turned to Jae-Sifuentes. "See that we're not disturbed."

Mariah felt the hairs on her arms rise.

Without a word, the elder man lashed the opening closed.

Gawain moved to the bed and pulled the sheet and blanket down to the foot. Then he removed his tunic.

She gazed at his bare, chiseled chest and arms. And at his scars. Avalon had never been fully or even half disrobed in front of her.

"This is as good an hour as any to consummate the marriage," he said.

Mariah trembled, mortified. "It is…d-daytime."

"Aye."

"Should be after nightfall. To do otherwise is wicked."

Gawain smiled, pleased.

"Very well," he replied. "We shall go back to the magistrate, inform him that you refuse to engage in your wifely duty, and have the marriage annulled."

She hesitated, attempting to calm. She half did. "If you will give me a few minutes of privacy, sire, I will don my nightdress."

"Nay." He sat on a bench and yanked off his boots. He tossed them aside. "Throw your nightdress into the rag heap. You will no longer need it."

"You wish me…*unclothed*?"

"We shall, whether docking or only sleeping in our bed, be flesh to flesh with no clothing barriers between us."

"That is sinful."

"You are beginning to understand me," he announced, removing his stockings. "I'm not noble. I am a wicked, dreadful man."

Her hands went to the ties of her blouse and gripped them. No, this was not right. He was attempting again to frighten her. And he was succeeding.

He stood and hooked his thumbs behind his breeches belt. "Back to the magistrate?"

Slowly, truly reluctantly, she began to undress. Did not look at Gawain again. She knew he was now fully unclothed. This event she had not considered. What decent woman would? Compliance or annulment. Were these her only choices? Was she back to the choosing she had before she heard the Queen's decree?

When Gawain stepped beside her, towering above her, she was cloaked only in her undergarments. She tightened her closed eyes. Didn't want to see his naked body. Tears burned her eyes and seeped down her cheeks. He eased the undergarments off her, then took the combs from her hair. Her ash-brown tresses tumbled down her back to mid-buttocks.

"Blue hell," he said. "You are very pleasing to the eye. I may have you always be *unclothed* when in my presence."

She shook more, so hard she knew, that at any moment, she'd go to the ground and, more than likely, do so in a faint. If he didn't take note and consummated their marriage with her during that time, 'twould be blessing.

Gawain cursed again then he did a most unexpected act and caught her completely off guard.

She had prepared herself for slap to the face.

But that did not happen.

He brushed the tears from her closed eyes and flushed cheeks with a gentle thumb then enfolded her in his arms and held her against him. As her face pressed against his warm chest, he kissed, most tenderly, the top of her head. She didn't know how long, or how short, the embrace lasted but she suddenly found herself lifted into his strong arms.

He carried her to the bed.

The time of consummation had come.

He laid her on her back in the center and tucked a feather pillow beneath her head. She kept her eyes shut and parted her legs as she'd done with the mountings from Avalon. What did Gawain call his couplings? Dockings.

"Lay easy, milady," Gawain said into her ear. "I have many sins marked in my life book, but I have never forced any woman to couple with me. We shall complete our union when you wish it so."

"N-n-now," she stammered. She wanted this over and done.

"Later," he replied.

"Now!" she repeated, nearly barking the word at him.

Silence grew heavy within the tent, and she felt his weight ease onto the bed beside her.

But he moved no further.

She sensed his heat from her shoulder to her side and waist, and down along her leg to her foot. Why did he not continue?

After a long moment, she eased her eyes open a tad.

Gawain, above her, gazed upon her face. He appeared curious.

What did that mean? she wondered.

At last, he moved. He skimmed his lips across the delicate brows above her eyes then marked the tip of her nose. Oh, heavens, he intended to kiss her. She pleaded for the act to be brief. He brushed his lips against hers and she opened her mouth as she knew he expected her to. She tasted...*mint*, not fish as she had when Avalon kissed her. That was pleasant. She was prepared, her body tense, but he didn't plunge his tongue inside her mouth. He brushed her chin with his lips and whiskered cheek. And, in the moment following, sketched one fingertip around the areola of her right breast then over the left. She was surprised. Her nipples grew erect. What was happening here? Why was her body reacting this way to his touch? *Nay,* she wanted to cry out. *Mount me and be done.* He shifted his face and body, and gently, ever so gently, traced his tongue from her ear lobe down her flesh. As he pleasured her neck with his mouth, his hand caressed her breasts. Time seemed to stop, and his strokes consumed her mind and body. He eased his mouth to her teat and kissed her stiff nipple. She arched her back. My heavens, was she asking, without word, that he take more of her breast into his mouth? In a matter of minutes, had this man turned her into wanton? He caressed with his fingers along her hip then across the fine hair and tender flesh above her cleaving.

She closed her legs.

He chuckled.

"We shall continue this later, milady," he said. "Mayhap after dark so it is not so wicked. And I will expect, nay, demand, that you participate and not just lay there."

Mariah, astonishing herself, turned on her side toward him. She pressed her hands against his chest and nuzzled her face against him. Then she hooked one leg over his. He enfolded her in his arms. She gasped. Below her cleaving, against the flesh of her inner thighs she felt the thick column of his cock. His body sword was plainly more endowed than Avalon's had been.

He tightened his embrace.

Her tension began to melt, and sleep, held at bay the entire daunting night, began to take her.

She was safe.

Mayhap. From all others, at least, as he had said.

Mariah woke to voices outside the tent.

Gawain was no longer with her.

She was still naked but her new husband had tucked the sheet and blanket around her before departing. And he had been true to his word—they had not consummated their bonding. However, and this amazed her, his touch lingered on her lips and bosom.

Mariah looked about the tent interior. And panicked. Had he also meant his words that he intended to keep her always unclothed? Then she relaxed. Her clothing, folded, had been placed on the bench beside her belongings from her small bag.

First, she found the chamber pot and swiftly relieved herself. As she moved to the bench and quickly dressed in her undergarments, she was astonished. She saw that all her meager possessions were accounted for. Even her nightgown was there. But it had not been folded, she noted. She drew on her blouse, surcoat, and shoes then gazed at her belongings. Besides the clothing she wore, she had hooded cloak, two silk scarves, hair combs, brush, ribbon, teeth cleaning cloth, sewing sachet, three copper penny coins, and the kaleidoscope. Why had she retained that? Simple—because Avalon's last directive to her was to keep the cylinder.

She tied her hair back with the ribbon then donned her cloak. As it was her routine, she gave no thought to the act as she placed a scarf over her lower face.

Moving to the tent opening, but not going outside, she listened.

There were three voices.

She recognized Gawain and Jae-Sifuentes but not the other. Then she glanced back at the kaleidoscope and knew the third. 'Twas Avalon's squire who had come to the old homehold and informed her of first husband's death. His name was…Tywin…Tyrone. No, 'twas Tybalt. Aye, that was his name. Why was he here?

She peeked outside.

"…a pack horse lost a shoe and I stayed behind to fix it," Tybalt was saying. "When I caught up with the guard, they'd been ambushed by brigands. Most were dead, along with some ambushers. Only my master and one officer escaped into the forest. They took the chest of gold and jewels with them that we were escorting to the King's encampment. I followed. I am not a good tracker. By mere chance I must admit, I came upon them a few hours later. The captain was dead. Sir Avalon was seated on the ground with his back against a tree. He had a bad head wound…"

Tybalt paused, inhaling deeply.

Then he continued: "When Sir Avalon turned his head, I could see brain peeking out from under his scalp. I was stunned that he was still alive. He could not recall my name, or that of our king. His speech was slurred. He did know I was his squire and he ordered me to ride to the King's encampment for help."

He stopped again for a moment.

"Before my departing, the sire did a most strange thing, he handed me a kaleidoscope and ordered me to give it to his wife. Gave instructions to tell milady. I rode hell-for-leather to our camp. When I returned with troop, the body of the captain was still there but my sire had disappeared. There were now fresh tracks of three unshod horses among the other two in the clearing."

"Three ambushers had found him," Gawain said.

"Our troop commander thought the same. We searched but neither my master nor the brigands were found. We did not come across the chest of gold and jewels either."

"Did you see the chest when you found Avalon?" asked Gawain.

"I do not recall, sir. I think I did but my attention was centered on my master. We did find my sire's sword. From the amount of blood at the tree and that no knight would leave behind his blade, the troop commander said Sir Avalon had to be dead. Later, back at camp, the commander ordered me to seek out Milady Avalon and give her the news. I did so, also giving her the kaleidoscope as my lord had instructed. After, I didn't know what to do or where to go. I heard that Milady Avalon came to ye, sire, so I decided to do the same."

"How did you hear that?"

"For days, all the talk in the capital has been about the Queen's proclamation. This morning the people are already talking about what happened here at the camp. I heard more than once that the Widow Avalon chose ye."

Jae-Sifuentes laughed. "I can picture the next time we go to a tavern. The boorish words said to ye shall result in the most entertaining fights."

"Oh, blue hell," muttered Gawain.

Tybalt shifted to an at-attention stance. "I offer to be yer squire," he said solemnly. "I accept when I displease or make error to be struck by fist."

"I have a squire," Gawain replied.

Jae-Sifuentes frowned. "Where have ye been keeping this squire hidden? Or, I have been given a magnanimous promotion?"

Gawain ignored him.

"*My man* is going to town to get supplies," he said to Tybalt. "Assist him and I will think on your offer."

"Thank ye, sire."

Then.

Gawain snapped command.

"Woman, get out here!"

Mariah stepped from the tent. She saw the fierce expression on Gawain's face and looked directly at her shoes. She trembled from crown to toe.

He moved to her side, looming above her.

"You do not need permission nor invite to join us. And I hate skulks and eavesdrops. You did that often at your homehold when I visited. No more!"

"A-Apologies, my husband," she whispered.

"I must speak with my commander then tend to some other tasks," he said. "Go with Jae-Sifuentes and the lad to town. You need boots. Your little shoes will not last long."

She straightened her shoulders but didn't look up at him. "May I also get a dressing robe and a small mirror for grooming?"

Gawain sighed, accepting.

"Here is coin," he said, placing pouch in her hands. "Get all the female accoutrements you need. All. But remember, the more you spend, the less there is for *food and drink*. Now go. They don't need to be waiting for you."

She didn't advance but saw Jae-Sifuentes and Tybalt approaching a readied mule and cart.

Suddenly…

…without word of warning…

…Gawain swatted her buttocks with the flat of his hand.

"Move it, woman!"

Mariah hurried toward the cart with a quick step.

She quaked as she walked, her face a hot flush. No one, not even Father when he'd reprimanded her, which was rare, had ever put spanking hand to her bottom before. Gawain had not hurt her. She knew there'd be no bruise or mark. But there was much more than surprise from his action. Aye, there was. Her buttocks were now warm and tingled. Most pleasurably. A tiny voice in her mind called out for her to remain where she'd been. If she did, mayhap he would swat her bottom again. What was wrong with her? Why was her body turning traitorous and wanton when she was with Gawain? They had been joined less than a full day—*the dreaded wedding night still to come*—and her flesh was craving his touches. Nay, this should not be.

She looked back, over her shoulder, at her new husband and stumbled. To her horror, without examination, she knew her cleaving was growing moist. This was most wicked.

Jae-Sifuentes assisted her up onto the large wheel and Tybalt helped her into the rear of the cart.

"Are you injured, milady?" Tybalt asked. "Your forehead is all red."

Jae-Sifuentes chuckled.

Mariah pulled the cloak hood more fully over her head to aid in shielding her face.

Jae-Sifuentes chortled again as he climbed onto the cart bench and gathered the reins to the mule.

Tybalt appeared confused by Mariah's silent response and Jae-Sifuentes's loud amusement.

There would be no clarification to the young squire from either.

At the township market, Jae-Sifuentes purchased one bag each of rice, milled oat, and dried beans. He also bought a small ration of fresh potatoes and carrots, and a slab of salted pork along with three large jugs of ale and one small decanter of sweet wine.

Mariah looked at, for a long moment, a box of harvested peaches and Jae-Sifuentes purchased four.

Tybalt guarded the supplies in the cart, and Gawain's man accompanied Mariah to the bootmaker to aid her in selecting a pair. The calf-high boots with heels were a good fit but much heavier than the shoes she was accustomed to wearing.

Jae-Sifuentes followed at a discreet distance as she went into a lady's shop, then into a second one and into a third.

With the coin amount given, she bought a plain cotton-woven robe, small mirror with stand, teeth cleaning powder, two bars of scented body washing soap, and, on impulse, a tiny bottle of jasmine-scented perfume. She looked at the empty coin purse. She'd spent all, had not saved a single coin for food. Gawain would punish her for this. She was surprised at the warm tingling that bloomed across her bottom.

As they walked back to the cart, with Jae-Sifuentes insisting on carrying her purchases, Mariah spotted Lucille on a cobbled walkway outside a three-story building. Her dear friend stood, arm in arm, with a very young woman of southern Memphi descent who was well swollen with babe. It appeared that the women were about to knock on the front door of the building.

She gasped aloud. The building the women stood outside was a notorious brothel.

She hurried to them.

Lucille embraced her tightly.

"This is Kynekka," her good friend introduced. "Her deceased husband was army sergeant-of-arms."

Mariah smiled at the young woman and said greetings, then she cupped Lucille's face between her hands.

"Why are you not at your cousin's home?" she asked.

Lucille looked away.

"Cousin took my belongings as shelter payment, then put me out," she replied. "Said there was not enough food for all in her home as she told you. Family should aid family...never mind, no longer matters. Kynekka and I have been acquainted for a while, and we found each other. Neither of us has place to go."

"Do you know what the business is of this building?"

"Aye."

"We have little choice," added Kynekka. "Except harm from street villains."

"Nay!" Mariah retorted.

"What else are we to do?" Lucille asked, most sadly.

"Have you not heard the Queen's decree?" replied Mariah.

Lucille and Kynekka both shook their heads.

"'Tis not yet dusk. There is still time." Mariah told them.

"Still time for what?" asked Lucille.

"I shall explain all as we go to the army encampment." Mariah paused. "I was wedded this morn to Sir Gawain Beaudry."

Lucille's eye grew round. "The scandalous knight?"

She took Lucille and Kynekka each by the hand. "Come with me. I shall see you both safe and shielded."

9

DARKFALL.
Mariah was disappointed. Earlier, when she'd explained the Queen's decree to Lucille and Kynekka, the two women understood immediately. They were prepared, they said. Each seemed determined to find a good man. Then they walked the camp. Mariah spied the two lanky women still wandering about in their search. The first men they saw, upon seeing them, literally ran in opposite direction. After that, the choosings, despite the size of the encampment, seemed sparse and dismal. The best already chosen. Lucille and Kynekka soon lost purpose and did not approach any. At eventide, the Queen's decree done, she escorted the unwedded women to their camp. She did note that Tybalt kept watchful eye on Kynekka and jumped to assist her even if task was insignificant. Jae-Sifuentes found much amusement during the evening supper, and after.

She now waited, inside the tent, dressed in her robe, for Gawain. He hadn't returned yet from his meeting with commander and unnamed tasks. She had considered staying outside with the others but decided she needed a brief period alone before new husband's arrival. During her five years with Avalon, she had become accustomed to, much of the time, having only herself for company. 'Twas comfortable. She had noted the sad looks she received from Lucille and Kynekka when she bid all a good night. While she had husband, they knew Gawain's reputation and, mayhap she had confessed too many of her worries to them. At least, she had not admitted all. A few she kept sealed in her heart.

She tucked her lower lip between her teeth. Wedding night had come with all its implications. Her stomach was much aflutter. Had been since well before dusk. She'd been unable to eat any of the meal Jae-Sifuentes had prepared. A tight band coiled around her chest and, without conscious thought, at different intervals, her feet nervously tapped at the ground. At least, her palms were staying dry. What there was for her to do in her night preparations, she had done. More than once.

With two lit candles on each side of her mirror on stand, she sat on the bench at the small table and brushed her hair with long steady strokes. It already shined but she continued. She doublechecked that there were no more rogue hairs on her chin other than the one she'd plucked. Twice she'd cleaned her teeth. Lovers' kissing would be anticipated and not only to his mouth. Earlier Gawain had caressed his lips and tongue to her lips, brows, nose, ear and neck as he stroked her breasts. She was expected to do similar. He'd commanded that she participate in the pleasuring. That she recalled. She was unsure if she could. Had never done so in the past. Avalon, when they husband-and-wife coupled, only required she just lay there in the dark with hem of gown raised to waist. Yes, she knew what new husband expected this night—he had made that clear. She knew she had to oblige. What she did not know was whether she was blessed or cursed, whether angel or demon was watching over her. A few times when she did her wife's duty with Avalon, her body had started to rise in uncommon pleasure before late husband finished. Her enjoyment never went further than rising. Was there more? Or was that all females could experience? Over the years, she heard women gossiping about coupling. Some thoroughly delighted in it, others despised the act. Lucille had bragged, with smile, that her husband had often brought her body to glorious pinnacle. Were any of these tales true? Many sounded sinful and wicked. But she had pondered on more occasions than she was willing to admit that she desired to try pagan love, wanted to see first-hand if there was more than she knew.

Outside, Mariah heard Jae-Sifuentes ask Lucille and Kynekka if they wanted another blanket for their beds and shame cloaked her. She hadn't invited Lucille and Kynekka into the tent for overnight shelter. She knew, just knew without being told, that Gawain would consummate their union even with audience. So, the women would sleep outside, near the fire ring that Tybalt kept ablaze, and under the blankets Jae-Sifuentes had supplied.

Where was husband?

She immediately told herself that her eagerness was unseemly. She placed the brush in front of the mirror and picked up the kaleidoscope. She put the cylinder to eye and turned its housing wheel. Its lace-style patterns were bright reds and oranges, browns and purples. Then, at the bottom of the sphere, she saw a black triangle spoiling the design. She rotated the wheel again and the triangle grew larger, blocking more. *Was it broken?* she wondered. If so, there was no reason to keep it any longer. She twisted the top of the cylinder off.

And.

She heard, at last, Gawain's voice outside. She set the kaleidoscope aside and turned toward the tent opening. A warm shiver coursed through her body. Nay, she told herself. Couldn't be. She opened the top of her robe. Her nipples were rising taut at the mere sound of his voice. She then slipped her hand beneath her robe between her legs. *My stars!* Her fingers found that her cleaving was moist.

Husband stepped inside, moving directly to her side. His aura filled the tent.

Quickly, she removed her hand from under her robe. Her heart pounded; her mouth grew dry.

"Our campsite has increased in population," he said to her.

"They are friends, and soldiers' widows," she replied, attempting to gather the strength to stand. "With no family to go to, I offered them our protection."

"*My* protection," he corrected. Then he shook his head. "Ah, blue hell. What's two more?"

Slowly, ever so slowly, she rose. She felt her legs quivering.

He put his forefinger and thumb to tongue then snuffed out one candleflame.

"Your pardon, milady. I haven't yet become accustom to the courtesies of a wife-and-husband relationship." He bowed with his shoulders. "Good evening, woman. I was successful in my first task. I got leave from the commander. We depart at dawn. It's a day-and-a-half journey north along the coast to my family's estate. You will need homehold while I soldier."

"Your f-family?"

"Have no worries. My mother and father, sisters and brothers will welcome you with open arms. I told you this morning that I didn't want to marry, and I never intended to. This was well-known among my blood. The family will find it most amusing that I have wife because our Queen ordered it."

She nodded at his words, praying 'twas truth, that his family would welcome her.But would he ever think of her more than his Queen's command?

He looked at her in the last candle's wavering light. Appeared to be deep in thought. As if he was pondering the very nature of her character and the bonding he'd been forced to accept. Then she realized the erect nipples of her bosom were plainly outlined against the material of her robe. Was that where his thoughts were centered?

Once again, she shuddered. She wondered if Gawain could hear her knees bumping. She gazed at her bare feet, not believing the words she was about to speak to him. Did she dare? And why was she asking this first? She'd learned many new things about herself this day. A few, as was this one, were very disconcerting.

"Sire," she whispered. "I must make confession."

Gawain tucked his fingers beneath her chin and raised her face until their eyes met. His eyes narrowed, and she felt ice chill as she had this morning.

"You shall look at me when we speak." He tapped her nose. "And speak up. Sometimes I see your lips moving but hear no words." He paused. "Confession, huh? What have you done now that I don't already know about?"

"I was irresponsible and spendthrift."

"Tell me how."

"I spent all the coin you gave to me on myself. I need to be punished."

"Is that so? Very well. Have you decided on the method for this reprimand?"

He appeared very amused. This was not joking matter.

Mariah walked stiff-legged to the side of the bed and placed her feet shoulder-width apart. She *could* do this. And she would.

Bending over, trembling more, she raised the hem of her robe to her waist and bared her bottom. "By your h-hand, sire."

She knew Gawain had stepped behind her. But he did nothing— no swat, not even touch.

Looking over her shoulder, she saw he was smiling. "I must be punished, sire," she said. "I am serious."

"I know you are, and I'm willing to oblige."

She was ready. Mayhap. She studied the weave of the bed blanket and waited.

And he began.

But not as she had expected him to.

He glided his hand down her right buttock cheek to inner thigh. A moment later, he floated his other across her left cheek and goosebumps rose delightfully around her wee faint hairs. Then she nearly jumped forward, across the bed, when he placed the flat of his hand at the base of her spine and his other fingers against the lower peak of her cleaving and stroked her. *Oh, glorious heaven,* she almost said aloud. Her heart pounded like drum announcing charge, her cleaving lips swelled larger under his touch. He continued until she thought she would shatter. But he paused as if he knew she was about to crest. He traced his fingertip up her buttocks cleavage and lingered, caressing, her anus ring. She put fist to mouth to keep from calling out. He pinched a bit of flesh on each cheek between thumb and finger. Her entire body shivered from crown to toe.

She suddenly realized he'd stopped. For how long or short a time she did not know but she would've sworn 'twas for an eternity. But she knew that at times one moment could seem like forever. Only his unmoving hand at her spine still touched her flesh. Before she could beg for him to continue, to plead for him to resume, his hand swatted her right cheek and followed with one to her left. *Oh, yes!* As her bottom tingled in warmth, he caressed her cleaving. Then he spanked each cheek again, only a tad harder, and followed with more cleaving strokes. *Oh, my goodness!* After a brief pause, he once more swatted and caressed.

She rose onto her toes and her leg muscles tightened.

My stars, my stars, my stars!

Sensation, as she'd never known during coupling with first husband, was building within her. Then liquid fire heated her flesh, beginning at her cleaving and spreading into the rest of her body. There'd never before been hint such as this within her. *More,* she wanted to cry out, *please more!*

And, during the following swats and strokings, to her amazement, a wondrous spasm swept over her.

She became still. Not moving a twitch, not breathing. What had just happened within her? Never had before. 'Twas marvelous and overwhelming. She folded onto the bed.

Glory be. Oh, my yes! Glory, glory.

Gawain collected her into his embrace. She slipped her arms around his neck, breathing again, and pressed her face to his flesh. Tears, not from pain but from joy, seeped from her eyes. He pulled aside the blanket and sheet and placed her face-down in the center of the bed. Slipped the robe from her body. Tossed it to the foot of the bed. She eased onto her side. He guided her firmly back face-down.

"Remain as you are," he commanded. "I may decide you need further reprimand."

He quick-spanked her buttocks cleavage.

Smiling, unable to stop herself, she nestled her face into the pillow and closed her eyes. She'd turned wanton shameless with new husband. *My stars, glory be.*

He cleared his throat. "Look at me, woman!"

She opened her eyes immediately.

He stood beside the bed and finished removing his boots.

"You shall look at me when we talk," he repeated, tugging off his stockings. "I will not tell you again. You shall look at me when I dress and undress. You shall look at me when I am unclothed. You shall initiate couplings, not always waiting for me to do so. Do you understand this?"

"Aye," she whispered. She marveled that her cleaving and bottom remained graced in warm pleasure.

"When we make love," he continued, stripping off his tunic, "you shall join in. You shall not just lie there unmoving. You shall use your mouth, hands, and body to pleasure me as I do you."

She swallowed at the lump in her throat. "I-I do not know how, sire."

"You have sharp mind, milady. I have seen that in what you say and do, and in what you don't say and don't do. I believe you shall master our together time in short order. The timid mouse I saw this morning holds no interest for me. That fainthearted creature would soon be *discarded*. The much different woman tonight intrigues me."

"I am not deceiver."

Gawain frowned and stopped the unbuckling of his belt. "I understand much has happened in your life that causes you to be frightened of the world around us. I don't belittle nor dismiss any of it. No matter how it came to be, you now have my shield and protection. You are safe. Do you understand this?"

She smiled. "We have been husband and wife less than a day and I already feel safer."

"*Safer.* That means you still retain some frights. I shall do my best to relieve you of those in the coming days ahead."

She was pleased with his words. No, she treasured them.

He removed his breeches and small undergarment, dropping them onto the ground. She wanted to shut her eyes, and not gaze at his unclothed body, but she did as he had instructed. Still, she hoped, in the few feet that separated them, he couldn't see the embarrassed blush heating her face. He stood naked in the drifting candlelight that washed over him. *Oh, my yes, even unshaven, he was a most handsome man.* He was, without debate, beautiful. She'd found that she always took note of his brown eyes first and the way they could cut through her with a mere glance. Tonight, she studied his strong mouth and prayed she'd learn to properly kiss him. She knew he would like that. His shoulders were wide and solid, his arms thick with much-honed muscle. She was amazed at how his callused, powerful hands could arouse her body to such magnificent heights. His chest was all brawn and his waist narrow with muscles rippling down from his well-hewn breasts past his iron-flat stomach. She spotted again the scars on his upper torso, including one that appeared to cross the flesh down over all his right ribs, but the candlelight was not bright enough to reveal them fully.

She started to peruse his hips and legs and gasped aloud. *Oh, my stars!* From a nest of dark-blond curls, his erect cock rose. She realized she was being wicked, but she couldn't avert her eyes from the sight of his body sword. She'd seen very few male cocks in her life—she had only glimpsed Avalon's manhood a couple times and it had been flaccid each instance—but she understood, without personal knowledge, that Gawain's was exceptional. Yes, she'd known, since this morn, when his member pressed against the flesh of her thighs, that he was well-endowed but seeing him unencumbered was breathtaking. His cock had to be as thick as her wrist. Even in the faint candlelight, she took note that the head was plump and round; the column long and lined with thick veins; and the flesh shined as if made of satin.

Suddenly, in her mind, she heard Lucille's words again. *His talented lovemaking has caused two partners to achieve pinnacle so superb that they passed out in pleasured bliss, and their nether regions and legs were so weak afterward they couldn't walk unassisted.*

Her face flushed hotter as she realized that his erection was for her!

He would entirely fill her, without doubt.

Oh, my! She shivered. What sensation would that cause within her? Would it be grander than the one he caused with his hand? Couldn't be.

Gawain moved beside her, the bed sagging under his weight. He collected her in his arms and eased her upper torso onto his. She looked deep into his eyes. They appeared kind and threatening at the same time. Her breasts, brushing against his chest, tingled pleasingly. *You shall join in,* he'd said. *You shall pleasure me as I do you.* She hesitated. What should she do? Then she knew—*as I do you.* She did as he had done to her this morning—she feathered her lips across his eyebrows; she glided over his nose. He smiled, and she gazed at his strong mouth.

Shyly, the mouse in her had returned, but she overcame, and she touched her lips to his. They were soft and silky, yet strong. Tasting of hint of sweet mint. She slipped her tongue between his lips and teeth and grazed his tongue.

For a moment. Then retreated.

She did not get far. He cupped the back of her head in his hand, lacing his fingers in her hair. She couldn't escape his hold, but she didn't feel restrained nor forced. He pressed his mouth fully against hers, first stroking his lips against her lips. She opened her mouth as was expected. He caressed her tongue with his. Then, groaning, he plundered her mouth—probing, sliding, sweeping. *Oh, glory!* She'd never believed a kiss could be like this. 'Twas wondrous. Her heart pounded; sensation overwhelmed her in heated, quivering waves. *Yes! Oh, yes!* As he continued loving her mouth, she brushed her throbbing breasts against his chest. *More*, she almost called out aloud. *Please, more!*

Without consideration of consequence, without any thought, she slid astride his left leg. She hesitated, only for a mere moment, then stroked her cleaving—from side to side—against the muscled flesh of his thigh. Her tender cleaving lips found a rough, raised scar. *Oh, my heavens. Glorious.* She stroked faster against the old wound. And faster.

Once more, as if he knew she was near cresting, without breaking their kiss, he rolled her onto her back and moved atop her with his hands flat against the bed above her shoulders. She spread her legs and he moved between them.

And she tensed, shutting her eyes. All the sensations within her body evaporated. The joining was coming. The wonders he'd gifted upon her would be no more. At least, she noted, he wasn't crushing her with his weight as Avalon often had. She could still feel his heat but not his bulk. *Please, be quick.*

He was not.

Not a tad.

As he continued his kiss, he guided his cock to her cleaving.

She was ready. However, he didn't plunge into her. Nay. He stroked his column up and down her feminine lips until his member was cloaked in her wetness. Then he eased the head of his cock to her opening and she would've sworn oath that her channel was spreading wide to accept him. This was…no words came to her. He slid the thick head of his cock into her and breath was pulled from her body.

Oh, my dear stars! But he went no further. He raised his mouth from hers and she knew, without opening her eyes, that he was gazing at her face. Her fingers tightened upon his shoulders. He moved, millimeter by millimeter, deeper within her. Then drew back. She knew her channel was tightening around his column, attempting and failing to halt his retreat. Wondrous sensation she'd never known before quivered inside her. Again, he understood that pinnacle was rising within her and, without wholly withdrawing, the head of his cock still in her channel opening, he paused. This was not possible. First husband had never caused, in five years' time, cresting within her and tonight new husband of less than a day had brought her to unexpected pinnacle with his hand, and now seemed about to bring forth second glory. Not possible.

Raising her hands to the back of his head and gripping his hair with her fingers, she pressed her legs against his. She moved her lips back against his; and whimpered, begging, without solitary word, into his mouth. He understood. Slowly, ever so slowly, he edged deeper and deeper within her until he filled her channel. Completely he did. He paused once more. *Nay! Please continue.* Her body, from cleaving outward, quivered. He sensed this and moved his member back and forth, forth and back, with increasing rhythm. Faster, and faster.

She shattered.

And cried his name aloud!

"*Gawain!*"

Every inch of her body, inside and out, joyously trembled with spasm after spasm.

Her head went back onto the pillow; her hands fell from him onto the bed; and her legs dropped limply away from his.

She would've sworn that a blessed blackness engulfed her. As if waking from the most magnificent dream, she realized that he was still fully within her and again no longer moving. She managed to half-open her eyes and saw him gazing at her. He had a plainly satisfied smile upon his mouth.

Once more he began his rhythm within her.

Another climax quickly began to rise.

Nay! she struggled to call out. But no words came. *Nay, I shall perish if I pinnacle a third time,* she wanted to tell him. 'Twould be beyond wondrous but perish she would.

His stroking within increased.

With a strength unknown to her, she grabbed the back of his head in her fists and captured his mouth against hers. Her mouth plundered his lips and tongue.

He tensed and crested, sighing as he did.

A half-moment following, the third peaking—wave after wave—rippled within her.

"Glory," she whispered into his mouth.

Yes, glory be.

10

GAWAIN, ALREADY DRESSED, WOKE HER shortly before dawn as he pulled the sheet and blanket from her body.

Mariah attempted to nestle facedown into the warmth of their bed to escape the chill of the morning air. She failed.

"Be quick dressing," husband said gruffly. "The tent needs to come down. If you're still naked when I start, then so be it."

Gawain swift-spanked her buttocks cleavage and she bolted upright. Once again, the look in his eyes appeared kind and threatening in the same moment.

He left.

She smiled, luxuriating in the moment, her bottom atingle, and smiled wider.

Then she rose.

Mariah dressed and groomed herself. She felt marvelous, more invigorated than she could recall being in a long time, and wickedly wondered if they would have enough privacy on the roadway up the coast to repeat last night's coupling. Could it be reprised? She prayed it could be and would be. Without doubt, she had to do more on her part. If the mouse returned, he would be true to his word and discard her. She knew he'd bedded women much more skilled in the art of joining than she, and still he had said to them that he did not intend to marry ever. She would attempt to recall body pleasures she'd heard other women speak about. A flutter rolled inside her stomach as she remembered what some said they did for their man with their mouth. Did she dare that? Did she? Would husband enjoy it? All men did, she'd heard stated.

She finished her dressing with slipping on the new boots. She placed her shoes and other possessions into her small bag.

The last item she picked up was the opened kaleidoscope. The corner of a sheet of parchment struck out. Was that what was blocking the designs?

Outside, she heard movement. All, except her, were preparing to break camp. She shoved the kaleidoscope into her bag. She'd deal with it later. More than likely, she would discard it—was a reminder of a life that was no more. One she was finding she did not miss.

As Mariah walked from the tent with her uncovered head held high, she noted that her legs did have a touch of wobble. But she was walking unassisted. *Glory be,* she pondered. Was there even more Gawain could do to her body than he'd shown her last night?

She was only a few steps from the shelter when Lucille and Kynekka hurried to her, surrounding her, all rattle.

Kynekka spoke first, concern etched on her face. "How bad did he hurt ye, milady?"

She was confused. "Husband didn't—," she started to reply.

"We heard," said Lucille, cutting her off. "Most of the camp did when you cried out his name. Except during difficult birthing, I've never heard any woman call out that loud. Dear heaven above, what did that beast do to you?"

Mariah stood unmoving as if rooted to the ground. Blush raced across her face. *Oh, my stars.* The entire camp had heard her call out his name when she pinnacled? From the corner of her eye, she saw Jae-Sifuentes and Tybalt mounting the falcon and its stand on the cart. The big man was looking directly at her, clearly amused. He knew that her outcry was *not* from being abused. Her flesh, face and now body, bloomed hotter. How could she face anyone here? She tied the scarf over her chin and up to bridge of nose. Then she pulled the cloak hood over her head.

"You never talk aloud," Lucille added. "Your voice is always low and soft. Remember that time we were shopping, and those men knocked down that wall and thousands of rats stormed onto the street? People were running in every direction and screaming. I was shrieking louder than anyone. You never spoke above a whisper even when that giant rat was crawling up your skirt. What did your *husband* do to make you call out like that? He is a son of a bitch."

"N-Nay," whispered Mariah.

Lucille frowned. "What did you say?"

"We can't hear yer words," Kynekka said.

"I-I cannot speak about this now," she answered slowly. "Mayhap later. Mayhap never."

Lucille and Kynekka nodded they understood. The women curled their arms protectively around her and they moved toward the cart.

Mariah saw a shaggy, brown she-donkey tied beside Gawain's strong dark stallion. Both equines were saddled.

"Yers, milady," Tybalt said to her as Jae-Sifuentes and he walked past the women. "Sire bought it for you to ride."

Mariah started to reply, to say she didn't know how to ride, but there was no point in telling them. Confession of another lacking in her skills would need to be told to husband. She studied the animal. It appeared to be gentle. She prayed it was so. Father had not taught her to ride. He'd seen too many injuries from being thrown from and kicked by horses. He would not place her at risk. She wasn't even allowed to ride with him. They always traveled in small two-wheeled carriage.

She watched Jae-Sifuentes and Tybalt join Gawain at the tent. Gawain and Jae-Sifuentes moved quickly. The breaking of camp was plainly a well-practiced routine for them. The young squire attempted to keep up. The tent and furnishings were packed snugly into the cart with the food supplies. Every item had its specific place.

Lucille and Kynekka still held her, stroking her with sympathy and shooting glares at Gawain. She couldn't allow this to continue, to no longer speak up for him.

She inhaled deeply. "My friends, husband did not harm me last night."

"No need to shield the swine with us," Lucille replied.

Kynekka nodded in agreement.

"I am not," she said as firmly as she could. How much did she dare to confide? She had to correct their misconceptions. That she understood. "I- I did my...wife obligations with Avalon. We followed Diocese guidelines always." She looked at Lucille. "You shared with me that Sir Ianeillo pleased you in marriage bed."

"Aye."

"'Twas never like that for me with Avalon."

"Never?" said Kynekka.

"Not ever," she continued. "I did not understand the body glory you talked about, Lucille."

"But you had to know what was possible from when you satisfied yourself with hand."

The heat from her flush grew. "'Twas stressed to me, since I was still in Father's homehold, that was wicked. I didn't do the act, ever."

Lucille and Kynekka glanced at one another, incredulous at the admission.

"I believed," Mariah continued, "that my coupling with Avalon was the way it was supposed to be, so I was satisfied. Mostly. I will confess I had wonderings upon occasion." She inhaled again. She had to finish. "Then, last night, new husband showed me body...*glories*...I had never dreamt of."

The women looked at Gawain again. This time their features were etched in astonishment. And a tad of envy.

Lucille turned back to her. "Your outcry last night was from coupling pinnacle?"

"A-A-Aye."

"Then the tales about Sir Beaudry's bed skills are true?"

"All I know is that he very much pleased me."

The men finished packing up the camp.

As Jae-Sifuentes approached, Lucille whispered into Mariah's ear. "You shall tell us more, later."

Mariah nodded slowly. But she did not intend to. She'd said enough.

Jae-Sifuentes guided Lucille onto the cart bench. The big man, Mariah noted, gathered the reins to the mule harnessed to the cart and settled beside Lucille on the seat leaving her friend with proper, respectful distance between them. Plainly, no longer pondering her and Gawain's coupling, Lucille kept glancing from Jae-Sifuentes to the hooded falcon and back. Tybalt aided Kynekka to a spot in the rear of the cart that appeared to have been designed for the with-child woman to ride comfortably upon. The squire took position beside the cart. He would walk.

Gawain stepped to her and waved his hand at their animals.

Mariah turned, looking at him as he had ordered last night. "Confession."

"Another? I believe this will be an oft-conversation between us. Well, speak, woman."

"I do not know how to ride," she said, then she tucked her lower lip between her teeth.

"Ladies ride sidesaddle not astride like a man does," he replied. "If you have trouble mastering it, I can lash you to the saddle." He smiled. "Then again, if you fall and break your neck, our marriage would be at an end."

She stared up at him. "You are teasing me...*aren't you?*"

"That you shall have to decide."

Gawain started to lead her to the donkey. But she became a tad bold. She did not move. Husband glanced at her not understanding. She swayed her hips. He chuckled and swatted her playfully on her bottom.

Then Gawain lead Mariah to the she-donkey and, without word, taking her by the waist, lifted her into the saddle. He guided her right leg, with a familiarity she was unaccustomed to, around the upright pommel, securing her thigh against it then placed her lower leg down the animal's shoulder. After adjusting the length of the saddle's single stirrup, he put her booted left foot into it and pressed her leg against the she-donkey's body. He handed her the reins.

"Watch the animal's head," he said. "If she turns back toward you, she intends to bite. Just snap the reins on her snout and that should curtail the act. It won't hurt her."

Glancing at the donkey's head then back at husband, she nodded that she understood. But could she do it?

He smiled, and she felt a warming in her chest and around her heart.

"Thank you for your guidance," she responded.

He tapped his fingers on the side of her bottom. More unaccustomed familiarity.

"When we make night camp, milady, your ass shall more than likely ache and be chafed. I will rub butter on you to soothe the discomfort."

She blushed.

He chuckled. "Then again, you might like the throbbing. If so, I will add to your enjoyment."

"You are teasing once more," she replied quickly.

Gawain shrugged his shoulders, not answering. He moved to his stallion and mounted.

Mariah smiled, pleased. Husband was playing with her. 'Twas delightful.

Then the delight ended. She stared at the reins, held loosely in her hands. The she-donkey lowered its head and snorted. What did that mean? She felt the animal's body beneath her turn rigid and tense.

"Oh, my stars," she whispered, not knowing what to expect next.

Beside her, she heard husband sigh. He leaned toward her, gathering the reins from her. And he flicked the reins lightly on the side of the she-donkey's neck. Immediately, the animal raised its head and its ears pricked slightly forward. It seemed to relax under her. However, she gripped the pommel with both hands.

Gawain spurred his stallion. Side-by-side, they took position in front of the cart and all headed down the pathway. She noted the she-donkey had turned compliant, responding straightaway to husband's directives. He hadn't been cruel to the animal, but plainly firm. That was the same manner that he directed her.

Mariah wondered if she would ever understand her husband's character. His moods and temperaments? Likes, dislikes? Would she ever grasp when he was teasing? Did it matter? He was soldier and would be gone often. She'd achieved one goal, however. She had his name, and soon would be with his family. Aye, she was now safe and shielded. But, and these thoughts surprised her, what if in the coming days, she became fond, very much so, of him and of his pleasuring of her body? After last night, that was true possibility. 'Twas. Could she be content with going back to her days sleeping in bed alone? And when he was away on his soldier duties, would she continuously fret that he was coupling with other women? That had never been a twinkling of a worry with Avalon. It appeared, from the woman with babe who had come to their homehold, that he had, and she realized she didn't care if first husband had broken his vow of fidelity. But Gawain's faithfulness weighed heavy on her. Alas, there was nothing she could do about it. However, she knew it would continue to plague her thoughts.

When they reached the camp entrance, Mariah had already shifted in the saddle several times to find most comfortable position. None were.

Outside the encampment, a flat-nosed, skeletal man on horseback waited. A tiny woman—of Eastern Sun descent, it appeared to Mariah—sat on a swaybacked pony behind him. He had a string of three mules. One carried camp equipment and food, and the other two were draped with copper pots, skillets, and kettles.

Mariah saw the man raise his hand to them. She knew, of course, that the upraised palm was only for Gawain.

"Greetings, Knight Beaudry," the man called out, exposing his blackened gums and brown teeth. "Called Oakes I am. Copper smithy—sellin' and repairin' copperwares as ye can see. No shop. I call my woman Rain—her given name is too twisty to say. Heard that yer caravan is headed northbound up the coast. I am goin' to the villages around yer namesake manor. Never been that way 'fore. May we be allowed to join ye?"

Gawain didn't reply, still studying the man.

"We won't ask for share of yer food and drink," Oakes continued. "Have our own. Won't ask to join yer night fire but, as ye can tell, I like to talk. Rain talks a lot, too, but mainly in her native tongue, but few, including me self, understand her. If yer cart becomes bogged down in road mire, or wheel is damaged, I can assist. If you brace brigands, I am fair hand with my axe. Rain knows healin' and has heaven-gifted singin' voice. May we join with ye?"

After a long moment, she saw Gawain shrug his shoulders.

"The road is free to all," he answered.

"Thank ye much, sire knight."

She noted that Gawain spurred his stallion at the same time as he gave a gentle flick with the she-donkey's reins. They rode forward in unison. Behind them, she heard Jae-Sifuentes mutter command to mule then the creak of the cart's wheels.

Gawain glanced at her. "Ah, blue hell. What's two more."

Mariah, uncomfortable, shifted her bottom again in the saddle, then looked back. They were eight now. Jae-Sifuentes and Lucille sat on the cart seat not talking, not touching. Lucille kept glancing nervously at the hooded falcon on its perch. Tybalt walked beside the cart reciting a tale to Kynekka. She held her hands to her swollen belly and appeared enthralled—or was it amused?—by the squire. The coppersmith followed, coaxing his string of mules to pick up their pace. The woman assisted, holding a small leafed-bush branch and waving it at the lead mule's head encouraging the animal forward.

Mariah saw two carts ahead of them at the side of the roadway.

The first was a horse-pulled, low-sided dray with two hogs

tethered to the rear. It held weathered homehold pieces and fishing nets. A man and woman stood beside it. With the couple were three boys, all of walking age, and a fourth babe suckling at woman's breast. The man removed his three-cornered hat and bowed to Gawain. He appeared fretful.

Without speaking a word, Gawain jabbed a thumb toward the rear of their group.

The man and woman smiled, and both bowed to husband.

The second was an ox-pulled, bullock cart filled to overflowing with bolts of colorful cloth—cotton, wool, and a few of silk. Two older women stood in the road. As they came beside them, the elder woman held out her hand to Gawain, showing him a few coins in her palm. Husband refused the coin then pointed at the rear of their caravan.

"If these women," he said as they rode forward, "have cloth you find to your liking, I shall purchase some. You need more dresses than the one you are wearing."

She smiled, pleased again. Husband had noted her minimal belongings. It appeared to her that Sir Gawain Beaudry was not the rogue his reputation said he was, just as Sir Malcolm Avalon was not the gallant man he was said to have been.

Mariah looked back at the line of their caravan. She wondered how many more she would have to share her husband's shield of safety and protection with before the two-day journey concluded?

She did not mind. Not a tad.

"Blue hell," muttered Gawain. "This is your fault, woman."

"M-My fault?" she stuttered. "What is?"

"Yesterday, several females approached me and with a mere glance I caused them to retreat in haste. Today, I am bound to you and half the populace wants to accompany us up the coast. This is your doing. Stop appearing so friendly and charitable."

Mariah was speechless, did not know how to respond to husband's words. Was he teasing her again? Would she ever know when he was joshing her or when he was serious?

Then she heard Jae-Sifuentes laugh.

"Milady," the big man called, "have him tell ye about King Richard's crusade to the Sacred Lands. We became separated from our army troop but received word to return home. By the time we crossed our kingdom's border, we were leading a cavalcade of two hundred pilgrims."

Gawain did not look back. "Your telling of that tale grows in leaps every time you repeat it."

"A smidgen mayhap. I do recall most clearly the grateful, buxom widow who kept me warm and satisfied each night, and the several lasses who offered to bestow their gratitude upon ye."

Gawain grunted. Jae-Sifuentes laughed again.

Mariah had started to like this tale until the turn of events at its end. How could she be jealous of women husband had known before they'd met? Yet she was.

The encampment was at the outskirts of the city. Within an hour of traveling, covering about six kilometers, all Mariah could see when she looked back was the highest tower of the royal Citadelcourt castle. Soon that was out of her sight also. She trembled, shifting her bottom in the saddle for the hundredth time. She had grown up near city and rarely had been in the out-country. Even with Gawain riding beside her, she was nervous, out of her element. She listened to the cries of unrecognized birds and animals. Her husband was silent. She was quickly growing accustomed to his silences as she had with Avalon's. Seemed natural to her. She heard Tybalt telling Kynekka another tall tale and occasional chuckling from Jae-Sifuentes. Oakes and Rain were not far behind. She heard Rain singing a ballad. The words were in her Eastern Sun language that Mariah did not understand but her voice was beautiful. Following the coppersmith and his woman were the fisherman family and the two older women.

At mid-morning, they rested the animals, then continued onward. She'd remained in the saddle the entire time. Did not dismount, even to relieve herself. Afraid if she did, her legs would crumple beneath her and she'd be put in the cart. She wanted to remain riding beside husband.

Two hours later, nearing day's high noon, she looked back and was surprised. Lucille had curled prone upon the cart seat, napping. She was resting her head upon Jae-Sifuentes's thigh. Kynekka was also asleep. Tybalt ensured that if Kynekka stirred during her nap, she did not tumble from the cart. Furthermore, she spotted a man afoot, shaved head, no hat, with large bundle on his back, walking behind the women's cloth-laden cart. Their caravan had grown to seventeen.

As they rode, she found herself looking often at Gawain. Studying the curl of his dark-blond hair, the set of his jawline, and at his most powerful hands. She didn't see him glance at her even once. Yet she knew he was aware of her every movement and act. She wished he would talk to her, would tell her about himself. She wanted to know more. Thus far, what she'd learned was confusing and contradictory. She knew he was the son of a noble family, had dedicated his life service to king and country, was fierce warrior and wondrous lover. He had never intended to marry but had followed the Queen's decree to do so. After he presented her to his kin, he would ride away. That thought cloaked her in a web of sadness. But isn't that what she had originally wanted—his name and shield and for him to be gone for long periods. Wasn't it?

Inhaling deeply, she decided she would make him talk to her.

"You are a kind man," she said.

"I believe you spoke to me. If you did, you need to speak up."

She cleared her throat. "You are a kind man to aid all these fellow travelers."

"A flaw in my character that thankfully does not happen often. When it does, I only allow it if it doesn't inconvenience me."

"How long has it been since you were last at home?"

"Now I can hear you plainly. Home is where my horse is."

"With your family."

"My youngest sister's wedding. Four years back."

Four years? An ice blade spiked her heart.

"W-Will ye come more often now?"

"When duty permits," he replied. "If I'm inclined to."

"You're teasing me again."

"Am I? Hmmm…"

Mariah saw a pebble strike Gawain's left shoulder blade. She started to turn around.

"Do not look back," he whispered sternly.

She stopped.

"Jae-Sifuentes is warning me that there is a rider up ahead. The others, wishing to join us, stood in plain sight. This one is hiding in the trees on the right. *Don't look there!*"

Mariah concentrated on her hands gripping the saddle pommel and attempted to breathe normally. As they passed the spot Gawain had indicated, she side-glanced and saw no one. How could she miss a rider and horse? Gawain flicked his reins against her bottom, and she focused immediately on the pommel again.

They continued down the roadway until they came to a bend. Gawain guided his stallion and her she-donkey into the trees.

"Do not speak, woman," he ordered. "You must remain quiet."

She nodded that she understood. Her entire body trembled.

Their caravan passed, only Jae-Sifuentes knowing they were there, and mayhap a quarter hour later, she saw the rider coming toward them.

She was surprised. 'Twas a…*woman*. A lean woman—much taller than Mariah—with a shallow oblong face, heavy-lidded eyes and fine dark hairs across her upper lip. She was dressed in man's clothing, all black. Her attire, including cloak and knee-high boots, were decorated with heavy road dust. A thin rapier was sheathed at her side and a curved dagger at her belt buckle.

As the woman moved parallel to Gawain and her, she reined her horse to a halt. Then she looked directly through the trees at them.

"Knight," she said, "ye need to teach your woman not to breathe so loud. Spoils the ambush."

A lump rose in Mariah's throat as Gawain guided them onto the roadway.

He and the woman studied each other for a long moment.

"Why are you following us?" he asked finally.

"Happenstance."

"Nay. I saw you back at the encampment when we were departing. Why do you follow us?"

"My error. I believed this roadway was free to anyone wishing to use it. I was unaware that ye were the keeper of the road."

"Last time. Why are you following us?"

"Most sincerely, Sir Knight, go couple my dead dog's ass."

Mariah expected Gawain to draw his sword or, at least, for his body to turn tense. Neither happened.

Gawain turned their mounts and moved northward on the road.

Without looking back, he called, "If I come to believe that you are threat to anyone under my shield, I will brace you."

"Barbarian's revenge on ye," the woman answered.

Gawain remained silent as they rode after their caravan.

Mariah looked behind them. The woman was not following. At least not at the now.

As they neared their caravan, Gawain signaled Jae-Sifuentes with his arm. The big man waved back. Plainly, Mariah recognized, these two men could communicate with one another without using spoken word.

Then they took position at the rear of the caravan, behind the older women's bullock cart and the walking man.

Gawain turned to her.

"You saw the woman just as I did," he said. "Tell me what you observed about her."

Mariah frowned. "I do not understand your question, husband."

"Sometimes you encounter a stranger and, in quick time, must determine whether the person is friend or foe, threat or not. What conclusions did you draw when you studied that woman?"

"When I had to run errands back in the city," she answered,

"when I was on the streets, I always assumed all strangers were possible threat and I rarely looked at them. That could result in comment from them or approach."

"You did look at that woman. Tell me about her."

"She was rude and disrespectful. Not a lady."

"And?"

"Uhhh…she wore the clothing of a man."

"Anything else?"

Mariah shrugged her shoulders, at a loss to add any more about the woman. What did husband wish her to say?

"Friend or foe?" he asked.

"I do not know."

"Woman, you need to develop your eye for detail. It could save you from harm."

"What did you see that I did not, husband?"

"Her horse was well-tended, not the mount of a poor person. It did not stir when we approached—well-trained. Like a soldier's warhorse."

"It could have been stolen," she added, hoping that detail would please him.

"That cannot be determined by mere looking," he said. "Her boots were lashed with leather bindings to keep them on her feet. Clearly, they were too big for her. The boots' style was one that an army officer would have."

"She was soldier?"

"Nay. Her speech revealed she is Thurian. There are no females, knowingly I will add, in our King's army. I have met several women over the years who would have been much better soldiers than some men I had under my command." He paused. Then nodded. "At a royal social gathering, I saw King's high counsel, Matthias Duncan. His wife with him. She is slender, modest woman—she is not Thurian, she is a barbarian. Even wearing silk dress, she carries herself as a skilled warrior would. One look and I knew I would hate to face her in battle."

Mariah frowned. "I missed much."

"But you can learn."

"What else did I not see?"

"The woman had a rapier which is a good weight for one of her size and build. While contact with a long sword would break the blade, a skilled fencer would not allow that to happen and a good fencer could do much damage to an opponent."

"I have no skills in fighting."

"I know. Also, she carried a curved-blade dagger. Those are not for stabbing, they are used for up-close cutting and severing. Curved blades are favored by assassins trained in the Eastern Sun fighting arts."

"She was assassin?"

"Nay. But she carried the blade of one."

"You saw much in our brief encounter with the woman."

"Soon you shall have these observations, too. It will aid you in avoiding harm."

"I shall try, husband," she said firmly.

He grunted.

11

ONE HOUR BEFORE SUNSET, THEY FOUND A meadow beside a wooded brook that would accommodate all in the caravan. First, the animals were tended, watered, and fed. Then Gawain, Jae-Sifuentes, and Tybalt quickly raised the tent. Each faction prepared their own evening meal.

Mariah saw that the fisherman family did not have much. As she started toward them with her meal, Gawain stopped her. He put half his portion into her bowl. She divided her meal between the three young lads. Lucille and Kynekka followed her lead. They went to the husband and wife and shared their food with them. The wife blessed them.

Gawain informed her that while she prepared for night bed, he would patrol the perimeter of their camp. He was always the soldier-knight.

She went into their tent and saw the trimmed red rose that had been placed on her pillow. She smiled as she held the blossom under her nose and inhaled its wonderful delicate scent. Her heart filled with elation. Husband had accepted the Queen-commanded bonding. That was true. But had he found their relationship to his liking? Was there more than having available bed companion?

Placing the rose gently back on the pillow, she sat down on the side of the bed. As she removed her boots, the oldest lad of the fisherman family—five, mayhap six, years in age—scampered inside and came straight to her. He grinned, showing that one front tooth had fallen out.

Mariah attempted to be stern. "Never walk into tent or room without first asking permission to enter and receiving that consent."

"I love m'lady," he announced.

"Thank you," she replied, struggling not to smile. "What is your name?"

"Tom."

"Tom, did you understand what I just told you about entering a tent or room? Especially one housing a lady."

"I be yer knight."

"Thank you again." The corners of her mouth edged up into smile.

The lad placed his fists over her lap and opened them. She looked down at two river-smoothed rocks and half of a well-worn wooden soldier. Her heart warmed.

"Didn't take from brothers. I give 'em to m'lady."

Outside, the fisherman wife called for their oldest son.

"Havta go," he said. "I love m'lady."

Tom ran from the tent.

Why, she wondered, did a lad have no trouble speaking those words and a man act as if the very thought of love were a curse?

Mariah undressed and, once she had donned her robe, sat on the bench at the small table. As she finished her teeth cleaning, she heard music begin outside. It sounded like a stringed lute was being played. Then she heard Rain add her singing voice to the melody. She dabbed a drop of the jasmine-scented perfume below each ear and one, wickedly, between her breasts. Hopefully, husband would like the scent.

On the morrow, she reflected, about midday, if the caravan continued at the steady pace they had today, they would reach the Beaudry manor. Where Gawain would leave her with his family. Was abandon a better word? She nibbled at her lower lip. When had his leaving for his soldier duties turned to abandonment in her thoughts? She'd expected Gawain as knight would be like first husband in many aspects. He was, but only in his duty as King's soldier. She sighed. Several unmarried men of proper station that she could have considered in the Queen's decree now came to mind. Gawain should have been at the bottom of the list and immediately crossed off. He had frightened her. She still didn't understand why she had been drawn to him. Had it truly been just two days since they'd been united together in marriage? A mere two days? She'd discovered in that time that she *liked* his gruff manner and contradictions, enjoyed his company. Gawain talked with her. Not to or at her but with.

And...

Yes, the and. That was disconcerting.

Gawain had awakened a passion within her character that she hadn't known existed. He was pagan lover. She understood coupling was only one aspect of a marriage, but it was an important facet. If not, why did the Church Diocese advise on this part of life so often? She'd never questioned before. Now she did. Why was it sinful and wrong that wife and husband lusted for one another and enjoyed pleasuring the other's body? She knew that she could not return to how it had been with Avalon. So tonight, she would initiate as new husband had said—*ordered*—her to. She would give glorious and wondrous body pleasure to him. After tonight, he would leave to fulfill his army duties reluctantly. He would return often to be with her.

She could do this, would do this. Couldn't she? Could, should, would. As she pondered this, she sucked on her thumb for a long moment. Moving it back and forth within her mouth. For practice.

Listening to the music and song, she reached for her hairbrush. Instead she spotted and picked up the opened kaleidoscope. As she tugged the parchment from the cylinder, it tore in half. She fished the second piece out and placed them together at the ripping. There were a few markings written upon it, poorly scrawled as if penned in haste. And they became for her the usual blur.

Outside, she heard Gawain approaching.

She set the kaleidoscope and parchment aside. Tomorrow morning, she would toss both into the fire. Yes, her life with Avalon was done and over. There was no reason to keep mementoes of that time.

Gawain stepped inside. "Good eve, woman."

Mariah smiled. "Good evening, Sir Beaudry."

"I can hear you. That pleases me." He waved her to him. "Come here. You must see this."

She rose and walked to him.

Gawain eased his arm around her waist and pulled the tent flap open wide.

Mariah was astonished. And delighted.

She saw that Lucille sat cross-legged, near the fire ring, in front of Jae-Sifuentes. She was brushing and trimming his beard. The jovial man appeared uncomfortable with the intimate attention but allowed her good friend to groom him. Across the fire from them, Kynekka laid atop her blanket pallet with a contented smile etching her features. Tybalt massaged her feet and ankles. She reached out, taking Tybalt's hand and placed it on the side of her child-extended belly. After a moment, the squire laughed. Mariah knew he had felt the baby moving within her. The coppersmith and his woman perched on a fallen tree. Oakes was the one playing the stringed lute and Rain sang in her glorious, exotic voice. The fisherman husband and wife were dancing in what Mariah believed the couple thought were the steps for the vassedanse. At least it seemed that was what they were attempting. Tom and their other two sons had gathered with the elder women—the oldest female cuddling the family babe—as they all laughed and danced in a circle around the husband and wife. At the perimeter of the camp, the shaved-head man accompanied Oakes' tune on a flageolet flute. Near the man, sitting upon blanket on the ground, was a new couple, both under twenty in years. They held each other and were swaying, back and forth, to the music. When had they joined the caravan? This was the first time she'd seen them.

Tom broke from the others and dashed to them. He faced Mariah.

"We dance?" he asked.

"Sorry, I cannot, sir. I am with husband and we are going to sleep. Mayhap we shall dance at another time."

The lad crossed his arms over his chest and glared, unafraid, up at Gawain. "I love m'lady. She will be mine!"

"Challenge accepted, brave warrior," husband replied.

Tom ran back to the others.

Mariah moved in front of Gawain, sliding her hands onto his shoulders then raised up as high as she could on her toes. She kissed him.

He returned the kiss.

And their mouths caressed. Joyously, intimately.

A flutter rolled inside her stomach. Could she do what she'd planned? Would he be disappointed if she failed? Or worse, what if she succeeded and he disliked her effort. Still, attempt would be undertaken.

She was about to lead him to the bed when he parted his mouth from hers.

"You could have danced with the lad if you had wished," he said.

"Nay," she responded. "I am only wearing my robe. At times, while my body be covered, my intimates could still be revealed. No dancing tonight."

He chuckled.

Warmth settled around her heart. She placed a swift kiss on his mouth.

"You initiated," husband said. "I like that. But before we retire for the night…" He turned her around and placed his arms back around her. "…I want you to tell me what you see."

She smiled as she looked around the camp at their fellow travelers. "They are happy. They are happy because they are safe."

"Safety is always your first concern. Good. To ensure that,

however, I need for you to observe more with your eye. Look about the camp. Tell me what is new."

"Another couple has joined our caravan."

"Actually, they are three. The other one has gone into the woods to attend to body relief. You should have observed him leaving. He is a year, mayhap two, older than the lass. They share similar features. While they may not be sister and brother, they are same bloodline. Continue."

She curled her hands against his muscled forearm. "I believe all the travelers that joined with us are good people."

"Mayhap. A little soon to tell for certain. The shaved-head man warrants closer appraisal. He's from Zar and calls himself Dante. Says he's an experienced stableman with no stable. Heading north to see if he can find work at the manor or one of those around our estate. Earlier, when Tybalt was setting up the fire ring, Dante brought cut-wood and added it to our stack. He asked for nothing for his contribution. But while he walked the camp, he gazed at every female in our caravan. Lingered on you longer than any of the others."

"I did nothing to encourage him!"

"I know. He may be harmless. I have touched every inch of you and I still look."

"You like to look upon me?"

"Aye."

Mariah smiled again. That was nice to hear. 'Twas. *No mouse tonight,* she told herself. No mouse. Initiate. See to conclusion the planned undertaking.

"You have told me what you see, woman. Now tell what you don't."

She glanced up at the underside of his whiskered chin. Don't see? How could she possibly know what was *not* there? This instruction made no sense. She looked across their camp. The missing newcomer had returned. He and the lass did share some features and coloring. As Gawain had said, they had to be of the same bloodline. She counted those in the camp. They were twenty now, and all were within eyesight.

But there was at least one something that husband wished for her to take note of, something not there when it should have been.

She scanned the camp again slowly. Then she believed she saw it. Near their cart was the falcon's perch.

"Your falcon is missing," she reported.

"Excellent. The bird was released after our noonday meal and never returned."

"It became lost?"

"Doubtful. Falcons have two prominent enemies. Man, of course, and eagles. I saw an eagle about mid-afternoon."

"Condolences on your loss, sire."

"'Tis part of the natural order. No matter how skilled and experienced one is, there is always someone more skilled and experienced." He paused. "I want you to study Lucille and Jae-Sifuentes. What do you not see? I'm going to give you a hint this time. Kynekka is laying on her bed pallet. Tybalt's pallet is a respectful distance from hers but close enough that if she were to become distressed during the night, he would be at her aid in an eye's blink."

Mariah looked at her friend and at husband's man. Lucille was checking that her trimming of Jae-Sifuentes's beard was even all around. She thought about husband's obvious clue.

"They have not yet prepared their night pallets."

"But they have. Their pallets have been arranged side-by-side on the other side of the cart for a modicum of privacy."

"Lucille and Jae-Sifuentes intend to—." She stopped. "They've only known one another for less than two days' time."

"They've met before. I accepted invitation to homehold from Sir Ianeillo upon occasion, as I did from Sir Avalon. Jae-Sifuentes always accompanied me."

"You never brought him to our homehold. I would've remembered him."

Gawain chuckled. "He came with me every time."

Mariah shook her head. How much had she missed in her life? Was she so self-absorbed that she only saw what affected her in the immediate?

"You should know, woman, that Jae-Sifuentes assists and watches over you, not because you have become my wife, but because he is fond of you. If he wasn't, you'd never receive a joke or smile from him. He put the rose on your pillow and chastised me most vigorously for not courting you properly."

A disappointed tug pulled at her heart. Tonight, soon, she vowed she would cause good change in their relationship.

"Question, husband." He wanted her to be more observant. This inquiry would show she was becoming so.

"Ask."

"The woman in black we encountered. Is she still following us?"

"She went around us and is camped up ahead near the river bridge. Three horses, two with riders, joined her. I saw their tracks. But they didn't remain with her. She runs cold camp and is alone."

"Is she a concern?"

"She warrants watching." He unbuckled his sword and sheath. Then he eased her inside and closed the tent flap. "Let's retire."

Mariah inhaled and held it for a long moment. 'Twas time to put her plan into motion.

She put out the candles. All. Her intention would best occur in the dark. But she saw, from the fire ring, thin ribbons of light wandering across the interior of the tent. That had not been factored into her plan.

Gawain had taken off his boots and stockings as she moved to him. She assisted in the removing of his tunic, breeches, and undergarment. She touched his flesh—at chest, arm, and thigh—during the disrobing. She skimmed her fingertips over his body scars. Had never done any of that with Avalon.

'Twas time. Mariah slipped off her robe.

Before she could set the robe aside, Gawain pulled her to him, into his embrace, their bodies molding together, and his mouth descended upon hers. All thoughts left her mind as his lips and tongue caressed hers. *Glory, glory be.* The pressure upon her mouth was exquisite with his tongue tasting, sliding, and stroking her.

Then, feeling his cock rising against her flesh, she forced herself to retreat from the dream and released her mouth from his.

"Request favor," she whispered.

Husband's hand feather-stroked her cheek and ear; the other outlined areola of her breast. He said nothing.

"I initiate," she told him.

He grunt-chuckled then traced both hands down her back to her bottom.

"Nay," she said swiftly. No spanking tonight. 'Twas not about him providing her enjoyment. She would do the giving.

Gawain paused, his fingers still against her buttocks. "Speak request."

Mariah would've sworn that the world stopped spinning at that moment. Her heart hammered in her chest and a tornado crisscrossed inside her stomach. Could she this do? She wanted to delight his body as he had hers. Truly.

"Sit, please."

He released her buttocks and sat down onto the side of the bed. Firelight slipped across his face. He appeared to be curious of her actions thus far.

She eased to him and he spread his legs to accept her. Inhaling deeply, telling herself to keep going, she brushed his eyebrows then etched her fingers down his face to his jaw. Steadying herself with hands to his thighs, she went to her knees.

Gawain grunted.

Near her face, at her eye level, was his erect cock. She saw, in the flickering light, that his manhood was at full rise with thick, round head and heavy veins coursing down to his firm bollocks. The fine hair at his intimate was a shade darker than that on his head.

She would've sworn that a low, enticing hum encircled his sex.

Continue, she told herself.

Mariah traced her nails down him. His flesh was like satin, but she felt the hard muscle underneath.

Gawain moaned and placed his hands at the back of her head. He did not direct her to his member, only kneaded her hair and scalp.

She placed her left hand against his thigh to steady her kneeling. Then, with her right, she cradled his cock and lowered it toward her face. *Keep going,* she commanded herself. *Please him.* She brushed her lips against the plump head and felt husband shiver. With lips, skimmed against him again. Another shiver. *Yes!* Now more. With the tip of her tongue, she traced helmet's furrow to opening. He sighed. She paused. He was much bigger, much, than her thumb that she'd practiced on.

Her heart pounded.

I can do this, she repeated. *And I will.*

Slowly, ever so slowly, taking deep breath, she eased her mouth over his manhood's head. Her tongue stroked his flesh. She noted, by her left hand braced on his thigh, that he had become still, his body not moving a twitch. It seemed that he was not even breathing. She nearly cried out in joy. 'Twas a sign. If displeased, he would've stopped her. But he didn't. He *liked* this. She took a little more of him into her mouth. Glory of wonders, she liked the taste of him, and the feel of his warm manhood on her tongue and against the inside of her mouth.

Continuing, she sucked on him as she would fruit to draw out its juice.

"Oh, my god," he whispered hoarsely.

She felt his fingers tighten around the locks of her hair, and he leaned his torso back a tad. Rising, so his movement would not pull his cock from her mouth, she slid both hands onto his stomach. And sucked harder.

Gawain released her hair and dropped back flat onto the bed.

"Mariah."

Yes! She was overjoyed. He had not called her wife or woman. He had said her name.

She slid more of his cock—as much as she could—into her mouth. She nursed him, cherishing his pleasure.

Then, she eased back slowly. Upon reaching his manhood head, keeping her lips and tongue firm around him, she went forward. She continued her steady rhythm. He moan-grunted. Yes, he was truly enjoying this. Her plan was success.

She moved, back and forth, faster.

And faster.

He slipped one hand behind her neck. Again, he was not directing nor restraining her, he caressed her flesh.

"I'm coming," he uttered.

What did that mean? She didn't understand. Paused. A moment later, his body shook one time and his hot seed entered her mouth. She hadn't considered this part of her undertaking. Unsure what to do. Did not seem proper to spit his salty fruit on the ground.

What should she do? Was not ready to release him yet.

She swallowed.

Then she resumed her back-and-forth upon him.

Suddenly.

Gawain sat upright and slid his hands under her arms.

Nay! she would've called out if she could speak. She wanted to keep him in her mouth, wanted to continue to pleasure him. *Do not do this, husband!*

He lifted her, and she sighed, sadly, when her lips and tongue no longer caressed his cock.

In one smooth motion, he laid her in the middle of the bed, on her back, and head on pillow.

He shifted his body above hers. She spread her legs further for him and prepared for coupling.

Gawain kissed, with lips, her chin and followed with another to the tiny apple of her throat. He kissed the vee of her collar bone, the hollow between her breasts, and her sternum bone.

Mariah realized he was going lower when he brushed his lips on her belly and, without conscious thought, she attempted to close her legs, but his body blocked her. *Was he? Couldn't be. Yet it appeared so. Oh, my goodness.* She'd never heard of or considered this act. In the women's gossip about coupling, none had spoken of or even hinted about such as this.

He moved between her legs with his face above her cleaving.

Oh, oh, oh. She lay perfectly still. Her hands clutched the sheet in fists near her sides. *My heavens above!* He *was* going to put his mouth to her intimate. She adored when he love-kissed her mouth; when he kissed her ears, neck, and breasts. Coveted the touch of his lips and tongue, of his whiskered face upon her flesh. Relished the body bliss when he caressed her cleaving with his hand. But this? Wasn't pagan love what she had wanted? Her heart thundered in her chest. His mouth to her cleaving had not been in her wonderings. *Oh, my stars!* What did her intimate smell like? Was there odor? She wanted to escape the bed, craved to run from their tent into the night even if she had to do so unclothed.

He slipped a pillow under her bottom, raising her up, and cupped his hands against her buttock cheeks. His fingers stroked her bottom's flesh.

While her mind called for her to flee, she knew her cleaving had become warm and moist, her folds had swollen and spread wider to reveal her opening to him.

"Lay back and enjoy," he said as if reading her very thoughts. "I shan't harm you. Promise."

She could not reply.

He blew a cool breath across her fine hairs onto her intimate.

She quivered.

Lingering at each, husband kissed her thighs. Mouth-caresses to her left inner flesh and followed with equal to her right thigh. Then brushed his lips along her outer folds going down to her cleaving lowermost.

Touching his tongue to her opening, she nearly leapt from her skin. He had to cease. Had to. She could not survive more.

Yet he continued, teasing and stroking his tongue up and down her folds, across the clitoris pink above her opening. Again, and again.

Surprising herself, not thinking before doing, she moved. She raised her cleaving so his mouth could more fully take her; she grabbed the hair at the back of his head in her fists. This was not to caress him as he had her. This was to keep his mouth from retreating.

Gently, very gently, he took her folds between his teeth and edged along them.

She moaned aloud, tightening her grip on his hair. Too much, too much.

And he paused.

Each tick seemed like eternity to her. Was he done? He had not shifted his position. She knew her most intimate was open to him. Could feel the heat of his face and his breaths upon her. Her body quivered from crown to toe.

Tick...tick...tick...

At last, husband lightly drew his whiskered chin along her revealed intimate. Quiver became tremble. He pressed the tip of his tongue against the flesh above her anus ring and moved up her bridge. *My stars!* He brushed his mouth over her cleaving inner lips. She felt divine throb. *Oh, glorious!* Then he sealed his mouth over her intimate's hood. With flat of tongue, taking his time, he teased and stroked. Down and up, side-to-side, in circle. He sucked at her. *Dear heavens above!* As he continued with his mouth, her leg muscles tightened, her back arched, and she held fast to the hair on his head. *Oh my, oh my!* What was he doing to her?

"*Gawain!*" she called as pinnacle arrowed through her.

He stilled his mouth. *Dear, dear heaven.* She was in a new world, one that was edging her toward swooning faint. 'Twas. Tears of sheer joy crept into her eyes. *Oh, yes.*

The magnificent pinnacle was still lingering when he rose. He shifted his body up hers. Then was above her, her breasts and his chest pressing, but he did not crush her with his weight. She gazed through misted eyes, into his. As always, they were kind and threatening. She released his hair and delicately stroked his face. She wanted to speak to him but was not yet able to. The pinnacle alas was ebbing.

Gawain waited.

"I…," she began. He placed two fingers over her mouth to hush her.

And eased his erect cock within her.

Mariah started to speak around his fingers and, before she could, in one swift motion, he reversed their positions. Now he was on his back, on the bottom, and she was atop.

She gasped as he guided her to upright. His thick manhood filled all of her. She placed her hands flat on his chest to steady herself. Seizing her hips with both hands, he aided her up and down. She swatted his hands away. This might be new to her, as so much had been that husband had shown her, but, for this, she needed no guidance. She knew she had pleasured him with her mouth, and she would do so with her intimate.

He smiled up at her.

She smiled, and began moving her body, up and down, upon him. *Glory, glory be.*

12

A HEAVY RAIN HAD COME OVERNIGHT BUT THE storm had not stayed long.

From the tent, across the muddy and puddled ground, Mariah moved to the fire ring unaided. Her legs had been wondrously weak when she had first put her weight upon them at first rising but she could walk. At least as well as babe learning their steps. Last night had been magnificent beyond imagining. Each had pagan-pleasured the other in manner that she prayed would be repeated. Often. She had thoroughly enjoyed taking husband's cock into mouth and his reactions to her ministering. Then he had put his mouth to her cleaving. *Oh, my heavens. Oh, my!* That had been most pleasurable. And their coupling after, with her on top, had been another delight.

Tybalt was alone at the fire ring.

She handed part of the parchment from the kaleidoscope to him. The other half she'd searched for but could not find.

"What is written on this?" she asked.

He looked at the torn parchment. His brow furrowed.

"Don't know, milady," he replied, giving the parchment piece back to her. "I can't read."

"I cannot either," she said gently. "Are there words on it?"

"Not sure." Then he puffed his chest. "There is the number forty and the number six written on it. Those I know."

"Thank you, Tybalt. You have been most helpful."

Mariah studied the red kaleidoscope and the torn parchment. She would show the parchment to husband. The cylinder from first husband had to be worth a few coins. His message had been that it was valuable. She could sell it. She could use the coins to buy gift for Gawain.

She placed the kaleidoscope and parchment into her cloak pocket then raised the hood over her head against the receding mist. The grand within her faded in the light of day and sadness began to take hold. Last night, she recognized, had not been as momentous for husband as it had for her. When she awoke, not saying a word, she watched Gawain. She had found she liked watching him. He *had* tucked sheet and blanket around her when rising from bed. But she saw that he was not smiling as he dressed. His features were displeased and his body movements abrupt. He did not give her morning kiss, or even glance back, when leaving.

Last night's plan had not achieved her goal.

Lucille and Kynekka crawled out from their shelter under the cart.

"That rain was hard," said Kynekka as Tybalt assisted her in standing upright.

"And came without warning," added the squire.

"We all heard your satisfaction last night, Mariah," Lucille announced, smiling. Then sadness crept onto her features. "The rain arrived at the most inopportune time for me."

Mariah turned from Lucille, not wishing to encourage her friend into sharing more details. If friend did, she would be urged to reciprocate. She needed to try to resolve her conflicting thoughts before sharing.

She looked up the roadway.

Gawain, on his stallion, and Jae-Sifuentes, spurring the she-donkey, rode into camp. They stopped near the fire ring.

Husband remained on his mount, deep in thought, his features grim.

Jae-Sifuentes dismounted and looked at Mariah.

"That animal is most contrary," he growled.

Mariah didn't reply. She watched husband.

Gawain nodded to Jae-Sifuentes. 'Twas another, she realized, of their unvoiced signals to one another.

The big man faced the camp, with hands on hips, and shouted:

"People, people! Gather 'round."

The others hurried to them.

Mariah saw, when all were assembled, that the Zar stableman, Dante, was missing. At another time, she would tell husband that she'd noted this. Hopefully, he would be proud of her.

Gawain studied all the travelers for a long moment.

"Do not break camp," he said at last. "We shall remain here."

"What has happened, knight?" Oakes asked.

"We are so close to destination," said the younger of the cloth women.

Jae-Sifuentes held up his hands for silence.

"The rain last night must've been much stronger up in the mountains," Gawain continued when the travelers had returned to quiet. "The river is overflowing its banks and the bridge was washed away. So, we are forced to stay."

"For how long?" asked the fisherman husband. "Our food supplies are dwindling to nil."

"Jae-Sifuentes and I will ride along the river," the knight replied. "He will go west toward the coast and I shall head east. We will be scouting for a safe-crossing place. At noon sun, we'll turn back and have news when we return to camp."

Oakes waved his arm. "How swift is the river?"

"From what we've seen thus far, anyone crossing would be swept downriver and more than likely drown. I won't stop any fool wishing to attempt to cross."

"What if ye don't find safe crossing place?" the fisherman wife asked.

"Then we shall be forced to remain here until the river drops back to usual level. Even then, crossing would be dangerous. That's why the bridge was built."

Mariah watched as their fellow travelers talked to one another. Mostly they repeated what husband had told them.

"People, people!" Jae-Sifuentes called again. "Listen to Sire."

The travelers focused back on Gawain.

"While Jae-Sifuentes and I scout," her husband continued, "Tybalt will hunt the woods for game. Any wishing to join him, may do so. All he gathers shall be divided equally among us."

"I'll accompany ye," Oakes said to Tybalt.

"I shall also," added the fisherman husband.

"I hunt," Tom called out.

Mariah watched as Jae-Sifuentes remounted the she-donkey. Gawain did not speak another single word. Jae-Sifuentes and he turned their mounts toward the river. They left.

She fought against the tears filling her eyes. Was a swift hello or goodbye too much to ask of husband?

It appeared it was.

Mariah washed the turnips and blueberries the women had gathered. Lucille plucked a wild turkey that Tybalt had taken down with arrow as Kynekka and fisherman wife cleaned three trout and a catfish that fisherman husband had caught in his net at a pond they'd found. Their bounty was a good start for the camp.

She had seen the hunters talking to one another. Tybalt headed toward the river. Oakes moved down the roadway in the opposite direction. Fisherman husband went into the woods back to the pond. Tom trotted to his mother. The young couple and the third man of their group followed the fisherman.

Finishing the washing, Mariah walked toward the tent she shared with Gawain. The other women recognized she needed some solitary time and were giving it to her.

She gazed up at the sky. The only clouds were dark ones on the western horizon. The rain was done here. She stopped and studied the roadway. Tybalt was past the rise in the road and no longer within eyesight. She would miss the squire and Jae-Sifuentes when husband left her at family manor. They, of course, would go with him. The other travelers would not remain at the estate either. They had their new lives to begin.

She bit her lower lip. What if husband was wrong—or had lied to her—and his family did not welcome her? What if they saw her as scheming harlot that had forced him to marry her? 'Twas, in part, true—the Queen's proclamation had taken choice away from him. This new life could be much worse than her previous one, and she would no longer have Lucille as friend and neighbor. She would have passionate remembrances from Gawain. Ones she hadn't had with Avalon, first husband had never given her memorable body pleasures. Only unpleasant and painful joinings. That would make the separation from Gawain much worse than it had ever been from Avalon. She'd heard Lucille refer to coupling with her husband as lovemaking in some conversations. Yes, while the body pleasures had been most wondrous, she believed Gawain and she had made love.

They had, she repeated.

"I do not wish to marry. Ever."

Those were among the first words Gawain had said to her at the camp when she approached him. And he had meant them. She had shown she could arouse him physically, but in all other facets of a husband-and-wife union, she was too stupid to engage his interest.

She wiped a tear from the corner of her eye.

"Milady Beaudry!"

Startled, Mariah twisted toward the calling voice.

Dante hurried down the roadway rise to her.

She stepped back, glancing at camp, as he approached.

"Tybalt sent me to get ye," the Zar stableman reported, halting beside her. "He said to bring you to the river on the run."

"Is Tybalt hurt?" she asked.

"Nay."

An ice chill stabbed her. "Has something happened to husband?"

Mariah didn't wait for answer. She raised the hem of her surcoat with fists.

And ran. As swiftly as she was able.

She rushed over the rise then down. Didn't look back to see if Dante was following. A thick band squeezed her chest. No, no, no! If some harm had taken Gawain, she would not be able to continue onward. She would crumple to the ground and lay there until last breath.

The river came into her view. Tybalt was not with eyesight.

She reached the ruins of the bridge. Looked down at the fast river then to her left and right. The squire was not here.

"Tybalt!" she shouted.

Then, behind timbers the river had thrown onto the bank, she saw him.

The squire was sprawled on his back, unmoving. Blood glistened at his temple.

She took one step toward him and—.

—an arm encircled her chest pinning her arms to her sides and a hand, gripping a curved-blade dagger, went to her throat. She was hauled back against the person behind.

Mariah didn't understand. Then she did as she saw Dante strutting forward.

"This is my partner," he said. "Ye have met before."

A face eased forward over Mariah's shoulder.

Her captor was the woman in black.

"Scream and I'll cut a teat off," the woman said into her ear.

Dante stopped. Mere inches, in front of them. "Where's the map?"

She didn't reply. The stableman's words made no sense at all.

Dante demanded again. "Where's the map, bitch?"

The woman in black tightened her hold. "Talk or I cut. Now!"

"I have…n-no map," Mariah whispered, trembling.

"The kaleidoscope," responded Dante. "Where's it?"

Mariah inhaled. "In my cloak pocket."

Dante pulled the red cylinder from her pocket and broke it in half. He examined both pieces. Frowning, he looked back at Mariah.

"Where's the map?"

"There was no map," she replied, her voice barely above a whisper.

"There was! Avalon told us that's where he hid it!"

The woman in black shoved Mariah to her knees. "My man was the cap'n of that escort troop. Mine an' yers planned the waylay to steal the chest of gold an' jewels. The ambush 'twas disaster for all sides. Our husbands got away with the chest but thought they was bein' followed. They hid it. Then, one or t'other or both decided they didn't want to share. They fought. My man was kilt an' yers badly wounded. Avalon wrote a map to where they'd hidden the chest. Put it in the kaleidoscope. The squire found yer man 'fore we did. Where's the map!"

Now Mariah understood.

"The parchment is also in my pocket," she said.

The woman yanked the parchment out of her cloak and handed it to Dante.

"Where's the other half?" Dante demanded.

"I lost it."

"Shite," he snapped.

The woman in black squatted down next to Mariah then waved her hand high in the air.

Two men came forward from the trees.

Mariah was stunned. One she had never seen before.

The other was Sir Malcolm Avalon.

The knight was being led by the second man. Avalon had

difficulty walking, stumbling every second step, and his arms hung limp and his head rested upon his own shoulder.

As he neared, she saw the ugly scar on the side of his skull.

Dante glared at Mariah then turned to the knight.

"Sir Avalon," he said. "Where did you hide the gold and jewels?"

"Ye have asked that question a thousand times," responded the woman in black. "He's addled an' doesn't know."

The knight, her still-alive husband, seemed to stare at the horizon. His features held no expression.

"Where?" Dante snapped.

"Hungry," Avalon replied.

"This has been a fool's errand," said Dante, sighing.

The woman waved her curved dagger in front of Mariah's eyes. "We kill them and ride out."

"*M'lady!*" a small voice cried.

Mariah saw Tom standing in the middle of the roadway below the rise.

"No, hurt m'lady!" he shouted louder.

"Go to your mother," Mariah yelled.

The lad did not retreat.

"Do not come down here, Tom! Do not!" she shouted louder.

Terror gripped her heart. *Please save the lad from harm,* she prayed.

Then Tom's two younger brothers appeared upon the rise.

No, no, no, Mariah pleaded. Her heart sank. These brigands, she knew, would not spare children.

"Do not come down here!" she called again. "Do not! Not any of you!"

Lucille, clutching a cooking knife, came into eyesight, to the right of the lads.

Fisherman husband moved to her side. Fisherman wife, with babe in arm, scurried to their three sons as Oakes with wood axe joined Lucille and fisherman husband. Rain aided Kynekka beside the wife and lads. Then, the two older cloth women and the young trio, all five holding clubs, appeared. All the camp travelers marched forward. Only Kynekka, the fisherman wife and sons remained where they were.

The woman in black growled in rage and raised her dagger toward Mariah's throat.

Mariah cringed back as she raised her fists to defend.

Dante grabbed the woman's wrist.

"Kill wife," he said flatly, "and Beaudry will hunt us down."

Dante released the woman and ran to the other man.

"To the horses!" he cried.

The two brigands headed into the woods.

The woman in black glared at Mariah for a long moment. Looking at the advancing camp travelers, she rose. She ran after the others.

Mariah wept in relief.

Avalon stood where he was, unmoving.

"Have ta piss," he slurred.

Mariah walked down the road.

She'd left the camp, unobserved, with her small bag. She was unsure where she would go.

Before leaving, she made certain that Tybalt would survive. The squire would have a lump on his head but would heal. Kynekka would see to that. She thanked every member of the camp individually for their bravery and gave Tom a long hug. The lad had been the one that saw her depart, in panic, with Dante, and alerted the others.

Lucille took temporary charge of Avalon. Her good friend told her that first husband had severe and deep wound to skull. That his addled mind would never mend, and he would only grow worse.

As Mariah looked at Avalon, her foremost thought was not about first husband's injury, 'twas that her marriage to Gawain was not binding. Would be dissolved. She had not been widow, free to wed. This had not been known to them but was fact. She knew what her duty was. In their vows, Avalon and she had pledged to tend each other in sickness and in health. That was her obligation to him. Sworn to in church. But she would not. She could not spend her days, mayhap years, nursing *this* stranger who she'd barely known during their time together.

Especially after…

…he was revealed as gambler, thief and murderer, above his harsh acts upon her.

Tears came again.

She had told the others that she needed to rest.

Inside the tent, she had removed her boots and placed them on Gawain's side of the bed. She had put the robe and all she'd purchased with Gawain's coin around the boots.

She was about to leave when she returned to the bed. She stroked Gawain's pillow with her fingertips. Weeping, she had gently kissed the pillow.

'Twas now past noon pinnacle, Mariah noted. She'd been walking the road for over an hour. She should have stayed and talked to Gawain. But there was no point. The church would not allow her to forsake first husband. That was in stone. But she could not spend the remainder of her days tending to Avalon when Gawain had shown her the possibilities of a most wondrous life. Her decision to abandon Avalon was wrong, and she understood that in every sliver of her body. Yes, this would doom her soul to Hell. 'Twould take countless good deeds and selfless acts to lessen the stain of this one sin. She didn't know if it could be done.

She was so lost in her thoughts, in herself, that she didn't hear the horse approaching until the mount was upon her.

Mariah twisted about, dropping her bag, startled to her core.

Gawain gazed down at her from his stallion, his brows pinched. Once again, his eyes appeared kind and threatening at the same moment.

Before she could flee, he leaned down from his saddle, curled his arm around her, and lifted her onto the stallion in front him.

"Where are you going?" he asked softly.

Mariah turned her head, unable to look at him.

"We are not wedded," she said. "I am not widow. You are free."

"I found a safe river crossing and returned to camp early," he replied. "They told me what had happened and that you had left. I admit I hesitated but in that tick of a moment I could hear Jae-Sifuentes, who wasn't even there, say that I was a dumb son of a bitch. And I agreed."

He slipped his fingers under her chin and raised her face.

"Look at me when we talk."

"This morn you did not even nod goodbye to me before you rode off," she said, shaking. "I have not become worthy part of your life in any way."

He sighed deeply. "I was concentrating on the storm, and what I needed to do. Blue hell, I told you I wasn't accustom to the courtesies of a wife-and-husband relationship. My apologies."

"I. Am. Not. Widow."

"Aye."

"You never wanted to marry and, most certainly, not to a mouse like me."

"Aye."

"You are rid of me. You are free again."

He gently cupped her face. "Hear my words. Grab them with your entire body and hold tight. Do you understand me?"

She nodded in his hands. Then she closed her tear-wet eyes.

"You shall look at me when we talk," he commanded.

She did. But she didn't wish to.

"I do not chase after women. When I approach and they say 'no,' then that is the end of it. I do not pursue."

Mariah didn't understand. What was he attempting to tell her?

He smiled.

"I came after you."

The Queen
and the Oracle

The oracle swirled the leaves at the bottom of the cup as she observed them.

"In the mists of the future," she said, "I foresee Kynekka and Tybalt surrounded by children of their own. *Sir* Tybalt will always treat the first child as if the lad was his own blood." She paused. "Lucille and Jae-Sifuentes will not marry but shall remain the closest of dear companions."

"What about Mariah and Beaudry?" Igraine asked, leaning forward.

"Sir Beaudry will petition the church on Mariah's behalf for a divorce from Sir Avalon. Alas, you are well aware of the church's firm standing in matters such as these."

"Yes. However, this petition, if the church received missives from a queen and from the High Vicar of Blackwater in favor of the divorce, it would be granted. Has been done in the past."

"Then a kind woman yer Majesty has never met would say blessing for ye every day."

"Hmmm...an army garrison is near Beaudry manor." The Queen smiled. "I do believe Sir Beaudry could find himself posted there."

"Then ye shall receive two blessings each day. And occasionally one from a knight."

Igraine settled back comfortably into her chair. "I have much to accomplish. But I have time for your last herstory."

The ancient woman's expression slipped from pleased to tight. "This tale reached conclusion only yesterday. Some of the mysteries revealed could leave my Queen...unsettled. Are ye sure ye wish to hear it?"

"Aye. More so now."

"Very well, yer Majesty. We begin at a township north of us, halfway between the capital and the principality of Quantero. 'Tis called Oxham's Mill…"

Celine Duncan, née Thorswald: Barbarian In Silk

13

CELINE HAD NO FOREWARNING OF WHAT would occur in the coming days. If she'd had a hint, she would have forced husband, by physical means if necessary, to leave this township with her before they received the report from the sergeant-at-arms that started it all.

She gazed across the inn's table at husband. Matthias was smiling. She adored it when he smiled at her. His kisses to her mouth and body this morn still lingered. They had finished their joining with her on her hands and knees and husband behind and had pinnacled within moments of the other. Several—she did not attempt to count—smaller crestings followed the first within her and had lasted well over a minute. 'Twas glorious.

Celine wondered what husband was thinking about. His mind fascinated her. Upon occasion, he continued to confuse her but as their weeks together grew, so did her love for him. Some events imposed upon a person seeded sweet fruit.

"We had a fine start to our day, husband," she said.

"We did," he replied. "And today I'm not late for council meeting as I am quite often when we are home."

"Your work is important." Celine lowered her head, pretending timid. "Does husband wish to change our morning greeting when we return to our homehold?"

"Nay," he replied quickly. "I'll just be tardy."

His smile grew.

She knew as much as he had changed her life, in so many wondrous ways, she had become—dare she say *cherished*—wife for him.

Before sitting down, Celine saw that dawn's light barely skimmed the receding rain clouds among the mountains on the eastern skyline, and the serving woman was the only other person in the inn's downstairs at this time. She listened to the sounds of a few lodgers rising from their beds and preparing for their day's tasks in the rooms above them. Back in the kitchen, she heard others join the serving woman. Then, very clearly, from the third floor, the voice of the irksome Lady Glass barked a command at her servants.

Husband and she were waiting for their fast-breaking hot meal to be brought to the table. They knew the stoves and ovens had to finish firing, but enjoyed the wait, for they had each other for company. After four months in the homeland of her husband, Celine still did not care for most Thurian foods. Most meals were overcooked, usually with too many spices and served four and, sometimes, five times in a single a day. Except for bread, ale and wine, the foods served always varied. The largest meal—unless there was an evening celebration gathering with other families—was at midday. Two meals were more than enough for her, and she remembered many a time in her old world only having a handful of grains or a single root or stem vegetable for an entire day. But she, and she admitted this readily, had found a fondness for the royal cook's sweet apple pie. She had never tasted anything more delightful.

"Don't forget," Matthias said, the smile remaining. "The day after our return home, you are to meet with my mother and sisters to plant flowers in the estate garden."

Celine furrowed her brow. "Husband has already reminded me of this."

"Because you will find a way to avoid them."

"Why does your family think I am farmer?"

"They are looking for something you can do together besides horse riding."

"Why do the women in your family only want to do what they call proper lady activities, like needlepoint and drawing pictures?" She smiled. "I very much liked shooting arrows at targets that day with your brothers."

"Father liked it more. You bested my brothers."

"Not all."

"You put your last arrow through Neils's at perfect center."

"We were in same spot. We tied. I should not have been declared winner."

"Father disagrees. Says 'tis good for my oldest brother to be humbled in loss upon occasion. Which, you have witnessed, he rarely is. Father says 'twill keep him from becoming too arrogant. I think Father's a little late on that. I worry about the day Neils becomes the head of family and estate."

"Your brothers remind me of my own. They acted the same way when I competed with them."

His family—Father, Mother, five brothers and four sisters. She continued to confuse the two youngest sisters, the twins, with one another which delighted them. She did not even attempt to keep track of the numerous aunts, uncles, and cousins. It seemed to her the Duncan family had blood ties to half the populace of Thuria. And the people who lived and worked at the manor estate far exceeded the number in her entire Snowbear Mountain clan.

She heard him tapping his right foot, which he did when he was deep-thinking.

"I promise," he said, "I will find an activity, to suggest to Mother, that the ladies and you might all enjoy."

"Please do so."

"I have been meaning to ask you this sooner than now, but this task in Quantero has consumed all my time. Before we left the capital, Mother and eldest sister could not look at me without turning stark red in the face. I understand they had a gathering with you. Is this true?"

She nodded. His mother and his widowed sister had approached her. But the gathering had not gone as she had hoped.

"Aye," she replied, "I was happy. After church meeting on Sunday, when we returned to the manor, your mother told me that I could come to her, or to your eldest sister, if I had any *wifely duty* questions since I could no longer seek advice from my own mother. I thought then she had accepted me as daughter and your sister as sister. I thought they did."

"They do, as do my other sisters and Father as well. They have since the first day we arrived and I introduced you as wife. My only concern with my family had been my brothers. They surprised me, all of them including Neils—happily. What happened with Mother and Alannis?"

"I did have questions. They replied for me to ask. I only voiced two and they ended our gathering without answers."

"That's probably because they expected your talk to be about the wife's part in maintaining a proper household, respectable dress attire, and the hiring of good servants. Mayhap my favorite foods." He tapped his smile with two fingers. "That isn't what you asked about, is it?"

"They said *wifely duties.* The priest's Sunday sermon had been about the responsibility of the woman in upholding your Holy Book's instructions for proper husband-and-wife relations."

Matthias chuckled. "Oh, God."

"Why do the Thurians listen to celibate men about bodily acts between husband and wife? And why are there so many decrees written in your Holy Book about the physical between men and women?"

"That's a long, complicated conversation for another time," he said. "Tell me what you asked Mother and Alannis."

"Priest stated the correct laying between husband and wife was husband atop, and the act should only last until husband's seed was planted within wife and not a tad longer. He said joining was only to produce child and not for body gratiment. Is *gratiment* the correct word?"

"Gratification."

"Aye. Not for body gratification."

"Well, I'm not sure what the sermon was about. I dozed off for most of it. Our priest is a good man, brimming with love for the Lord, our savior, and his fellow men and women, but he is the most boring talker that ever walked, and, from my council meetings, I know boring."

"I listened to every word, husband. I want to learn about your world—."

"Our world now," he interjected.

"Aye," she continued. "I was confused after priest talk. I believed laying together was for both. *My* mother told me when I was a lass, after my first moonflow, that the gods and goddesses of the mountains celebrated the joy bonded mates gave one another, and the more pleasurable the joining the better for the child that could be created from it. I told *your* mother and sister that you always, sometimes more than once in a day's time, pleased my body; I said I liked you atop, me atop as my clan favored, and from behind. Even standing. I asked if we were inviting the wrath of the Thurian Heavens down upon us." She paused. "I was so excited to have females to talk to that I didn't wait for response before asking second question. I asked if they had suggestions that would enhance my sucking of your cock. That was when they ended gathering."

Celine watched Matthias press his lips together tightly. She knew he was trying not to laugh.

"The following day," she added, "strange greeting occurred. Your father came to me. He was in high spirits and told me 'thank you.' Said he hoped your mother and I had more gatherings. Often."

Matthias snorted as he looked up at the ceiling.

"Husband finds this to be amusement. But I offended your mother and sister. Did not intend to."

"You did nothing wrong," he said swiftly, looking again at her. "Despite being unaccustomed to your frankness, they do like you and they want to know you better. Not about all things though. I suggest, strongly, that you do not broach them again about *wifely duties*. They are not *comfortable* discussing the subject. I do have an aunt who would delight in talking to you about this and I shall put the two of you together the next time she visits." He chuckled aloud. "You told Mother and sister I was good lover?"

Celine pretended serious and stern. "I did not say husband was good lover. I do not know if husband is. I have nothing to compare his body ministering to."

He squeezed her hand atop the table. "I love you."

"I love husband. I like husband." She smiled. "I lust for husband."

The outside door opened.

Westen, the sergeant-at-arms, entered the dining room and marched directly to them. Immediately came to rigid at-attention stance beside their table. Celine liked Westen. The sergeant, middle twenties in years, was six-foot tall with gold-red hair—cut to inch from scalp, and was always diligent in duty and proper protocol. At all times, Westen wore an immaculate padded uniform tailored by expert hand to fit trim, muscular body. Matthias, who rarely noticed the dress and fashion of others, had commented that most officers looked like shabby recruits when standing beside Westen. The features that stood out the most for her was the sergeant's beardless baby face and midnight-blue eyes.

"There has been a murder, sire," the sergeant reported.

"Our caravan is only passing through Oxham's Mill," Matthias said. "Unless someone involved in this murder is among the royal circle, it would be a matter for the local sheriff. Does township have a sheriff?"

"Yes. He is former army dragoon. I sent a lad to wake him and I came to find you."

"There, all roles are in their proper place and this matter does not concern us."

"Sire, you will be most intrigued by this murder, and shall wish to give report on the crime to King Richard upon our return. If I didn't believe this so, I wouldn't have disturbed your morning meal with wife."

"Intrigued you say?"

"Aye."

A twinge of warning pricked between Celine's shoulders. Later, she wished she hadn't ignored the premonition.

"Continue then," husband said to Westen.

"The corpse is a prisoner and I believe the killer is one of his guards. Norlow and Irish are holding the man."

"A prisoner of who?"

"All I have learned thus far is that the two guards are from Benbane Prison."

"Two guards. Where is the second man?"

"Sleeping off last night's drunk."

"I am perplexed, sergeant. Part of my mind must be still in bed."

Celine noted his sly glance to her. That look from him overwhelmed all other thoughts in her head. She'd had choices in her life. Bonding with Matthias had not been among the choosings. Father had commanded it. Now she could not fathom a life without walking beside husband. Not behind him, or in the lead, but side-by-side.

"A guard has slayed his prisoner," Matthias continued. "For a reason thus far unknown. You say it was murder. I do not doubt you, sergeant. You have well proven yourself to me. Our soldier-escorts are restraining the guard who is from the capital's hellhole prison called Benbane. Is this the current?"

"Yes, sire."

Matthias frowned. "Sergeant, did you see the killing?"

"Nay. I was on my walking patrol. I noticed an unusual amount of commotion around the gaol and went to investigate. Saw two riders heading toward township from gaol. 'Twas still dark and I did not get good look at them. When I arrived, guard had the corpse lifted onto his shoulder preparing to carry the body to a pack horse nearby. I did see dead prisoner's face under hood covering."

"I am confused again. Why would I be intrigued that the prisoner's head was covered by a hood?"

"Not by the hood, sire. By his face underneath. I shall not say more. Best if you see for yourself first-hand."

Celine set her lust for husband aside in her mind. Concentrated on the immediate. She leaned forward on arms crossed on the table. "A warrior slaying a captive is a crime in Thuria?"

"Depends."

She sighed. She was trying to navigate his world. What was right, what was wrong, what was honored, what was reviled. With her clan, she'd known her place. Yes, she hadn't always stayed within those confines, but she knew what was expected from her. In Thuria, too many people and situations seemed contrary. The richest families in her clan were the ones with the most horses and captives. But they all lived in similar lodges and no one, not even the poorest hunter, was allowed to starve. There was a great divide between the Thurian nobles and soldiers, and a wider one between those classes, as Matthias referred to his fellow countrymen, and farmers, tradesmen, and shopkeepers. But the greatest gulf was between those and the poor street people. She had seen events where a noble would walk away without rebuke and person with no title or lands would be arrested for same offense. Some of her questions would cause Matthias to reply sadly that it 'depends.'

Her husband rose from his chair and extended his hand to her.

"Will you accompany us, my lady?" he asked.

She knew that he already knew her answer. Still, he extended the courtesy of asking.

Celine nodded her consent. He always wanted to hear her observations on the day's events, whether major or small. He respected her keen eye and valued her opinions and had told her to always say what she was thinking and never censor her words to him. Husband was unusual man.

They followed the sergeant-at-arms.

She held husband's arm and allowed him to lead as woman was supposed to do in the Thurian world. She consciously raised the hem of her purple silk dress so she would not become tangled and trip. That had happened often in their first days in Thuria. She'd worn dresses for clan ceremonies, but those garments never extended past ankles. Thurian dress hems went to the ground over feet. She continued to practice being polite and courteous to all she encountered. While Matthias had never commanded her to do so, she knew it pleased him. Still, her first instinct was to battle these *former* enemies.

When sergeant was not looking at them, Celine cleaned with her fingertips a minute trace of her intimate juice from husband's chin beard now glistening in the early dawn sunlight.

It had been four months since they were wedded in the way of his people. She was nineteen years of age then and would remain so for another season. She was learning the expected protocols for proper ladies. Still, to most in the circles they traveled in, she was mainly remembered for the first royal gathering they attended as husband and wife. Matthias had been pulled from her side by two of his brothers wishing to discuss a promising business venture. Alone for less than a full tick, a duke, righteous and sober, confronted her. She did not know all the meanings of the barbarian slurs the man spewed at her but knew they were insults. Matthias heard the last one when the duke said one could dress a sow in jewels and gown, but it was still a damn pig. He jumped beside her; his rage plainly etched on his face. Surprising herself, she had restrained husband by hugging her body to his. He'd lose the clash, she knew, but would fight anyway. As the duke's men rallied behind him, the duke called Matthias a son-of-a-bitch traitor to their culture and heritage. Before first fist was thrown, Queen Igraine, with her knight guard, stepped forward. The pending brawl calmed. Some. Then Celine, in her uneasy Thurian at the time, challenged the duke to a duel. Both Duncan brothers shouted they would be her second. This was unthinkable she learned after—women did not duel, rarely were they witnesses to such events, and a respectable man would never duel with a woman. Despite this the Queen, smiling, informed the duke that he had two choices: He could accept the challenge, or apologize, then leave the Citadelcourt gathering forthwith. There was no duel. The duke left, but words of contrition were not voiced. Not concerned for her own safety in the least, Celine thanked the brothers for coming to Matthias's aid. The older of the two replied they hadn't come to his assistance. As long as fight remained only between the duke and him, it wouldn't have been the first time Matthias got his ass pummeled. They had come to her assistance. The other brother nodded in agreement. She asked why? Older one grinned. "Little brother loves you," he said. The other nodded again. She heard later that the Duncan brothers ruined several of the duke's most profitable businesses.

Aye, husband had been concerned about his brothers and their treatment of her. He should not have worried. While his brothers and he warred about most matters—large and small—their decision about her in the family was simple. Little brother loved her.

Up ahead of them, Celine saw the township gaol. 'Twas a fair distance from their inn, the Swan and Bulldog, which was the last building at the southern edge of the village proper, and 'twas a small stone structure with no windows and three punishment pillories outside. A heavy, sullen man looked fearfully at their approach. The soldier-escorts stood on each side of him. Another man, snoring in deep sleep, lay curled against the stone building with jug cradled in his arms. On the other side of the gaol she saw two horses—one was saddled and the other prepared as pack animal.

"I'll talk to your murderer after we see the body," Matthias informed the sergeant.

"Aye, sire."

Matthias and Celine moved to the gaol doorway. The interior of the stone structure was nearly barren. Dirt floor, worn blankets in corner, water bucket, and another bucket for body relieving.

The corpse was male and lay on his back with dark blood pooled at left side of his tunic at the chest. Chains were at his wrists and ankles. And a hood covered head.

Celine stopped Matthias from entering. She looked at the dirt floor.

"'Tis difficult, husband, to read the signs because the corpse was taken out then brought back."

"Best guess then."

"Two men came inside," she said. "One stood behind the prisoner."

"He more than likely held the man."

"The second man has a cross-cut on his right bootheel. He was the one who did the slaying."

Matthias nodded. "Westen said he saw two riders leaving the gaol."

"I shall look once we are outside for more tracks with cross-cut on heel."

They moved to each side of the body, squatting down.

"Late forties, mayhap fifty in age," her husband noted aloud.

Celine took one corpse hand into hers. "Soft. Not hands of soldier, tradesman, or farmer."

"Clothes are worn but made of good material."

"One blade thrust to body. Between fourth and fifth rib. Straight into the heart."

"Dagger."

"Slender and long blade. Twisted after stabbing."

Matthias tugged the hood off, and leaned, in surprise, back on his heels.

Celine stared. She'd never seen such as this before.

A gray-iron mask covered the man's face

Celine traced her finger around the edge of the mask. "'Twas seared onto his face. Any flesh not burned away would be ripped off if mask was removed."

"Who the hell are you?" Matthias asked the corpse.

14

THE BONDING CEREMONY BETWEEN CELINE and Matthias with her Snowbear Mountain clan had only taken a few minutes. Father had cut the flesh on the palms of Celine's and Matthias's left hands and their blood was dripped into a bowl of white bear, male-and-female, bones that Mother held. While Mother stirred all together, they pressed their cuts against the other. And thus, they were bound in body and soul, and the ceremony was done. The elder clan women immediately surrounded Celine, shielding her from all male eyes, and removed her ceremony dress. Then they took her—without single possession—to the marriage lodge, for all a wife possessed would be given to her by husband. Her father and brothers, and the elder clan men, herded Matthias to the gathering lodge to begin celebration of drinking and man-talk about first night joining.

When Celine and Matthias had been wed in Thuria, their marriage vows were read by his Church's High Vicar and they were surrounded by his loving family, and by King Richard and Queen Igraine. The ceremony had taken an hour. Then there was a long feast, with many toasts and much dancing, before they were escorted to their Thurian wedding-night bed chamber.

During their first days at his home, she asked him what he believed would make a good marriage between them. She expected

him to answer like all men in her clan would, for her to be obedient
and follow his commands. He did not. He replied they must love one
another; they must also be friends and always speak openly; they must
trust and protect each other; that each would have interest in things
and activities that the other did not share and 'twas all right to
continue to pursue those things and activities; and, hopefully, they
would continue to learn what pleasured the other when they coupled.
Then he added, with smile, that if she found a new way to pleasure
his body that he would surely die in bliss. She came to understand
quickly that he meant these words as he had the ones he had spoken
to her on their bonding-night first joining at her clan village. That
night, and she clearly remembered his words, he said: "You may stay
with me only if you wish. At any time, if you decide to leave me, I
shall not stop you."

She had been bewildered. No man in her clan would ever say that
to his wife. She did not believe a man in his world would say that
either. But he had.

She knew Matthias, six and twenty in years, was the youngest son
of the powerful Duncan family. He was fit and trim, near her weight,
and a finger shorter than her; had well-groomed dark hair, mustache,
and chin beard. To her, and from overheard comments from several
Thurian ladies, he was handsome. As one of the youngest Duncan
children, he would not inherit title and lands. He was expected to
succeed on his own merit. He had. Since he was ten years of age, he'd
held trusted position as advisor to the King on the royal high council.
Once again, she could not picture her clan elders listening to a ten-
year-old lad. His King and council did. Matthias could recall what he
saw and read at a moment's notice, had a vast knowledge of the
sciences and world history, had learned several foreign languages
within a day each, could do mathematics without using abacus or pen
and paper, and could envision things that did not exist but could.

Matthias had no warrior abilities. His mind was his skill.

He was the most unusual man Celine had ever known.

Matthias had come to her village in the dark Frontier as King's voice to parlay treaty between her clan and his kingdom. Bjorn the Red Thorswald, their chieftain and her father, had approved the pact then added that part of the sealing of the agreement would, in the way of the clan, be Matthias taking her as wife.

He agreed to the blood-and-bone bonding ceremony. The day after they were bonded, they started their journey to Thuria. The trip had been fraught with more perils than the unforgiving landscape they rode across—vicious barbarians, a rival clan of her Snowbear Mountain people, had hunted and battled them. They nearly did not survive. Yet the dangerous events brought them closer to one another.

When they reached his people at the kingdom capital, Matthias could have easily sent her away. None would have faulted him. They'd been bonded in a pagan ritual. And a short time later—scarring her heart with a heavy sadness that would never leave her—her village, with few survivors, had been slaughtered by rival clans. The treaty between her clan and Thuria was worthless. But Matthias was a man of honor. He had given his word they would be husband-and-wife and he'd keep his oath to her.

She did not understand at the time. In her clan, a female lived with family, and father's instructions were to be always followed, even when wrong. Female would leave father and mother when bonded with male. Then husband would be female's master and he would have voice over all that was done, even when wrong. Mostly that was the way it was in the clan. Mostly. Clan bondings were for the greatest part man and woman. Although bonding of man and man, or woman and woman, was allowed. Proven warriors, usually male, and practitioners in the reading of the bones or the healing arts, mostly women, could choose any for lodge partner. Benefits to the clan surpassed all else. Once bonded, husband and wife were expected to remain true to one another and forsake all others. When it was discovered that one had broken their vows, it led to duel. She had seen fights-to-the-death between wife and husband's lover and between husband and wife's lover. Couples living together were expected to be bonded. Yet there were exceptions. She had seen one husband and wife welcome wife's younger lover into their lodge to live with them and one veteran warrior had three widows tending to all his needs.

So, when Matthias had given her choice, it confused her. She found later it was basically the same male-female hierarchy in Thuria with some differences that were church mandated. However, Matthias did not follow all expected protocols, and, even though he'd once been enemy, she *chose* to remain with him. She hadn't known before their bonding that 'twas possible for a husband and a wife to be *friends* and *lovers*. Their bonding was most unusual in both worlds she recognized, and she cherished him. And he showed he treasured her in his words and deeds.

She discovered, the story coming in tads and bits to her from his sisters and one brother, that five years ago, Matthias had been betrothed to a lady of another noble household. 'Twas said this woman had been the love of his life. But typhus disease came to the kingdom and claimed several hundred lives with no regard between noble and common, between good and bad, between loved and despised. His lady had been among those that died. Since then he had not looked at another woman. His brothers had offered to acquire a paid woman to pleasure his male needs. He had said nay, he had no interest whatsoever. She was surprised, and very pleased, when his closest brother told her that the family had believed Matthias would spend all his days for the rest of his life, sad and alone. Then he returned from his task in the Frontier with her as wife. He was again the happy and spirited little brother he had once been. The family would always see her as a beloved gift given to all of them.

At court celebrations, after the near brawl of their first attending, the Queen insisted Celine be her companion for the events. Her Majesty relished telling her rude, and most often hilarious, stories about the nobles in attendance. 'Twas from the Queen she learned many bawdy and vulgar profanities. A few cusswords, as Matthias called them, were among the first Thurian words she had learned. But the Queen's cusswords were more explicit in visual image and a couple were impossible for a person to do when told to. Celine still used the clan blasphemy, *bax*, most often when she was frustrated or angry.

She knew that if not for her husband she would've been frustrated and angry for most of her time in the world, in both worlds.

She had been, despite her proven warrior skills, an outsider among the Snowbear Mountain clan. She plainly had Father's hazel-colored eyes and Mother's distinctive nose and ears, so her parentage was never questioned. But most among the clan were blonde-haired, blue-eyed, pale-skinned, and large in body. She stood out from the others. She was slender and sleek, light-bronze flesh, small but evident bosom and brown hair at head and eyebrows but no hair anywhere else on body. One repeated whisper was that her mother had offended a forest nymph during her with-child time and Celine was the result. Her brothers and sisters disliked her because she had clearly been Father's favorite among his children.

She was even more of an outsider among the Thurians.

She knew no matter what she mastered in this new world; she would always be seen as barbarian—a wild godless pagan with bloodthirsty demeanor. After her first month at the capital, she could understand most of the Thurian language. By the second month, Matthias said she spoke Thurian better than those who had been born in the kingdom, but that she did not have to add the Queen's new words to every sentence. Still, despite this knowledge, she pretended she did not understand the language. She learned much when people around her believed she did not understand their speech. Now she was attempting to master the Thurian written word. Her clan wrote signs and symbols. This task of understanding written groups of letters was daunting but not insurmountable.

The Thurian ritual she disliked most was the expectation that women would wear dresses. She had worn a few during her clan life but was used to, and more comfortable in, a chainmail vest over her bosom and small breechcloth at cleaving and buttocks, with short-handled club with spiked hammer at top. The least irritating neck-to-foot gowns were silk so most of her dresses were that material, and she liked the colors purple, yellow, and red. Some she had tailored so the hem stopped at ankle. She refused to don undergarments. They were too binding and restrictive. If her husband and she were in jeopardy, she wanted to be able to move without hindrance, even minor. She hadn't used her warrior skills since their arrival at the capital, but she was always prepared.

Matthias was the keeper of royal confidences. King Richard and Queen Igraine trusted him without single misgiving. He informed them he trusted Celine and would not keep secrets from his wife. That led to several meetings but, at last, King and Queen consented. She would know what he knew if he believed she'd be interested. In both the worlds of her clan and Thuria, men had their roles and duties and women had their defined and separate place.

Once again, she marveled at what an unusual man husband was.

Usually she enjoyed their ventures together, there were always new wonders for her to see.

Alas, the current task for Matthias had become a most challenging test for her and her new life.

For the past full week, they had been in the ten-league-wide Principality of Quantero. The independent monarchy had been the kingdom's closest ally since the first Thurian king. The visit was to re-negotiate and clarify trade agreements between Thuria, Quantero, and the kingdoms of Rivenran, Zar, and Cordoba. Matthias was the main voice for their king among the Thurian delegation and had been fully consumed by the debates and final agreements within the long daily talks.

Celine was relieved that the visit to Quantero had concluded. While Matthias attended his meetings, most lasting until after midnight hour, she was expected—compelled, mayhap a better word—to join with a group of Thurian ladies whose noble husbands were also attending the meetings. She declined once feigning illness. The ladies were always utmost courteous when Matthias was present, but Celine knew, since they believed she didn't speak the language, they detested the company of a vulgar barbarian woman. When gathered, the ladies only had three topics of converse. None were of any import to Celine. They talked about the fashions and grooming of other ladies. Some they admired, most they derided. They spoke about the romances of the nobles, single and married. And they gossiped about noble family secrets. As in Thuria, it seemed to her that secrets were expected, and relished.

One afternoon the ladies had gone riding. Celine had been on horses, bareback, since she could walk. In Thuria and the other monarchies, ladies of culture and breeding rode sidesaddle and not astride as a man would. This was exasperating. Toward the end of the ride, one lady's steed turned runaway. The horse raced across a meadow toward a high fence that it could not possibly jump safely, with the woman aboard screaming, terrified, to be saved. Celine switched to astride mounting and caught the horse and woman before they reached the fence and before the male escorts could reach the runaway. Upon returning to the group, the woman muttered a brusque gratitude to her. She was surprised the woman said that much. Had not expected any from her. The ladies, for the next hour, bemoaned again having a barbarian among them. One highborn lady insisted that Celine was cannibal. She'd had enough. Whispering, in Thurian, into the woman's ear, she said when roasted, the ass was the tastiest part of a body. The highborn's face went bloodless, and the woman never spoke another word about Celine within Celine's hearing.

Matthias had laughed, saying "Bravo," when she later told him the story.

As member of high council, Celine learned that Matthias had four soldiers assigned to him as bodyguard-escorts. Captain Geller and Sergeant-at-Arms Westen had been with them since the wedding. Two new soldiers, Norlow and Irish, had joined them shortly before the journey to Quantero.

She had known Geller, ox-chested, face and head shaven, since the treaty negotiations at her village and her bonding to Matthias. The captain was a veteran of many battles with Frontier clans, and he hated all barbarians. At some point during the ride to the kingdom six months ago, he had intended to kill her. Now she had secret. The captain and she, after fighting side-by-side against the vicious Nikota clan, had reached a truce and she was no longer wary of him. When they were preparing to leave Quantero, the principality's empress requested that Captain Geller remain behind to inspect her personal guard and look for weaknesses. There hadn't been any dangers during the journey to Quantero and no reports of any possible perils on the road back. Matthias believed the three soldiers, led by Sergeant-at-Arms Westen, would be sufficient escort. He honored the empress's request and the captain stayed in Quantero.

Westen was good soldier but Celine knew the sergeant's secrets. Matthias had discovered one during the four days they were on the road to Quantero but didn't care as long as Westen performed required duty without incident. An affair had blossomed between the sergeant-at-arms and the Lady Glass. This could have only happened away from the capital. Back home, Celine knew, among the nobles, this would have been deemed scandalous, inappropriate, and most improper. 'Twould ruin the lady's impeccable reputation if it became known, and she would be ostracized from her privileged circles. Celine hadn't shared the sergeant's other secret with Matthias, wondering how long it would take husband to uncover it. Four months had passed, and that secret was still secret.

For Celine, the most infuriating part of the journey to, at, and now from Quantero, without relent, was the Lady Adriana Glass of Blackharbor. She did not know why the Lady Glass had foisted herself into their company, but she had.

After the first full day on the road, Celine informed her husband that any coming ventures that included the Lady Adriana Glass among the entourage, she would decline to participate in. She wanted to be part of her husband's Thurian life, for him to be proud to have her at his side, but this woman's company was asking too much. She'd rather be in outnumbered battle. Matthias accepted her vow.

Then he added, to Celine's chagrin, that the lady's continued support of the crown was much appreciated, and sometimes needed in political matters. Lady Glass was the wealthiest female in the western kingdoms and oft said to be an example of the proper Thurian woman. She was personal confidant of their Queen, and no one ever questioned, even in the minute, her loyalty to the kingdom. She was quoted saying proudly that Thuria was the greatest kingdom in the world and, if their King and Queen ever asked her to sacrifice her life for the realm, she would do so willing.

Matthias said, issuing a rare command, that Celine would not rebuke the woman verbally, or physically.

She had placed her hand over husband's cock and stated that she'd have to be rewarded for her tolerance. She was.

Still, Celine did not want to be in the woman's company. The Lady Adriana Glass, at eight and thirty, was an undisputed beauty with radiant raven-black hair, cool green eyes, and lush figure. This caught the eye of men. The other ladies admired her exquisite fashion and grooming style. Lady Glass was never seen in public unless her appearance was perfect in every detail. She had been married thrice, and thrice a widow. Each husband had been older and had greater fortune than the one before, and none had children for her to share inheritance with. At social gatherings, she was always surrounded by admirers. All the men attempted with compliments and witticisms to have her gift a smile upon them. She never did. Still they tried, despite knowing she would not accept an invitation from any man less than her station. That was not seemly or correct. The only men in Thuria who fit her status requirement were King Richard, the Marquis of the House of Drake, and Matthias's father. The woman openly admired these noble men, but all were wedded, and she would not be mistress even to them. That would be wrong in so many ways. Her stance made her relationship with Westen more exceptional and unique. Yet there it was. The sergeant plainly had charms the Lady's other suitors had lacked.

Their caravan was two coaches. The first, with one of the new soldier-escorts as driver, had the trunks of Matthias and her atop. The interior was plush and roomy. Lady Glass traveled with them. The second coach, with other soldier-escort as driver, was filled with the lady's numerous trunks including a personal bathing tub. There was barely enough room inside the coach for the lady's two indentured handmaidens. Celine had overheard the maidens talking. They hated Lady Glass and, at first opportunity, intended to escape. She did not warn her ladyship of the plan. She wished the handmaidens good fortune.

Matthias had politely informed the Lady Adriana Glass that on the ride to Quantero he had to study previous agreements, documents and ledgers before the trade meetings began, and on the return, he had to analyze the signed agreements in preparation for his review with King. The Lady Glass agreed to allow him the time he needed unless a major disquiet were to arise. Celine knew that husband had all this information already memorized and, at first, didn't understand why he had made this request to the lady. She swiftly learned the reason. And she saw husband silently laughing at her situation. Despite believing Celine did not understand the Thurian language, Adriana Glass talked nearly non-stop to her. She complained about her deceased husbands and their poor attributes, the injustices as a female perpetrated on her in legal court, that people did not show the proper respect she was due, and that the inns along the highway their caravan stayed at overnight were beneath her standard. The last she told in acerbating detail.

Celine could not believe that Matthias was able to ignore the woman's incessant talking. They were close together in the coach. How could he pay no heed to her? And why was husband wearing raised cloak's hood over head during their time in the coach? At their next rest stop, she discovered the answer to both. Husband had placed cotton in his ears. She demanded that he share.

"Nay," he replied with a smile she did not like seeing. "Lady Glass will teach you more about Thurian nobility womanhood than I could ever explain to you." The days in the lady's company would be a good learning event, he added. She vowed aloud she would get revenge on husband. So far, she had not settled on the best method against Matthias. But she would not forget nor forgive despite the love in her heart for the man.

She pondered means of stopping Lady Glass from talking.

When husband was talking too much, which he often did when preparing a speech to give at royal council or in the Great Hall at Citadelcourt before a crowd of the populace, she would go to him and take his cock in hand. As she stroked him, his words became fewer with long pauses between. If she wanted him to be silent, save for calls out to the heavens, she took his manhood with her mouth. She enjoyed both acts and often did them when he was not chatting on. Once, during a minor disagreement, she put hand to him, and he said flatly that she would not get her way by leading him around by the cock. He'd been wrong in that instance, but other times he held his ground. She wondered which of them enjoyed the attempts more.

These acts would not aid her in quieting the Lady Adriana Glass.

During the following morning, after their first overnight at a highway inn, for more than an hour, the Lady Adriana went on and on about the dreadful bed she'd had in her inn room and how she was unable to sleep peacefully. Celine needed a plan to quiet the woman for any amount of time. During a stop to rest the horses, several farmers taking crops to market passed by them. Celine purchased a large, very firm and smooth cucumber from one. Before Matthias rejoined them in the coach, Celine gave the cucumber to Adriana. She pretended limited Thurian but told the widow that it would aid in getting restful night sleep. The lady gazed at the vegetable in her hands and asked how much should she eat at bedtime? Celine shook her head and feigned deep thought before responding. She placed her fist at the woman's crotch then pumped her hand vigorously back and forth. Adriana's eyes widened and her flush was nearly the color of Celine's scarlet dress. The woman acted as if the cucumber had turned scalding-hot, tossing it out the window. Celine had expected the lady to scream or yell but instead she was quiet, wordless, for a quarter hour. Not long enough.

Matthias remarked to Celine that their companion was more solemn and prim than he had believed. And she never smiled.

She replied that husband was not paying proper attention.

Finally, Matthias uncovered her ladyship's secret with Sergeant-at-Arms Westen. Celine teased husband that it had taken him so long to take note. How could Matthias have not noticed that whenever the sergeant was close by, Lady Adriana *giggled* and batted her eyelashes? How could he not have observed that at stops the lady and Westen were often gone from eyesight at the same time. Husband's only comment to Celine was to wonder why the lady, with the great divide between her and the soldier's stations and her well-known view on the subject, would partake in such a relationship. Obviously, Celine replied, our sergeant stirs part of the lady's soul and body that no other does. Matthias grunted and was soon lost once more in his reports.

Once, when they resumed journey after a stop, without saying solitary word beforehand and with Matthias watching, Celine had fixed the misaligned buttons on Adriana's traveling blouse and concluded by tapping the woman's breast so she would know that Celine saw she was not wearing bosom undergarment. The lady remained quiet for half an hour. When she started to talk again, Celine cleaned with her finger a lip-rouge smear at corner of the lady's mouth then had put hand to woman's joining to see if she was wearing that undergarment. She was. The quiet that time lasted for more than an hour. She'd remember that act when the lady's talking was again too much. Adriana never complained to Matthias about his wife's improper behavior. Or, about the time Celine, within the lady's view, stepped to Westen and examined the bewildered sergeant's lips and mouth.

In her four months in Thuria, Celine had learned much from Queen Igraine about the hypocrisies of the noble class. 'Twas deemed common for a husband to have lover—his paramour's station immaterial. After all, a proper wife would not be expected to indulge husband's manly needs of the flesh. Those who did not have lover, and remained faithful, received more gossip. She had overheard that 'twas believed her barbarian ways in marriage bed kept Matthias from straying. However, for noble women, taking a lover was judged wicked and foul, and having one of lower station was sordid and dirty. If found out, expulsion from prominent circles would be the woman's sentence, and, more than likely, with the church's approval if wedded, dissolution of marriage. While the Lady Adriana Glass was widow, there had to be marvelous flare for her ladyship to risk sully on her sterling reputation by consorting with the sergeant.

She also pondered if Lady Adriana knew Westen's other secret.

15

CELINE STUDIED THE SEARED MASK ON THE face of the corpse once more then followed Matthias outside. Immediately, she walked to the two horses and surveyed the ground around them. From the tracks and dung, there had been four horses. The man with the cross-cut bootheel had mounted one that was now gone. She determined that those two had slain the prisoner.

She turned toward the guard as Matthias stepped to the man. The guard was thick-bodied, wearing poorly mended tunic and breeches with one boot separating at its seams. His bare arms were tattooed from wrists to shoulders. The skin inkings didn't fully cover, as they were supposed to, the branding on right forearm that army issued for petty thievery. A full coin purse hung on his belt.

"For your continued good health, my man, I suggest you answer my questions," said Matthias to him. "You work at Benbane Prison?"

"Aye…sirrah, am guard at the Benbane," the man replied.

Matthias pointed at the sleeping man. "Your companion, too?"

"Aye."

"And the corpse was your prisoner?"

"He is…was."

"Why was the prisoner killed?"

"He'll murder me, sirrah, if'n I answer yer questions."

"Who will murder you?"

No response.

Matthias shook his head. "My query 'twould be concluded if you had merely tossed a dagger near the corpse and said the prisoner was attempting to escape."

The guard looked at the ground.

Matthias sighed wearily then issued orders to the soldier-escorts. Norlow went behind the man and pinned his arms. Irish took stance to deliver fist punches.

Celine was surprised. This was not like husband.

Westen appeared to be astounded by the order also.

"Your beating will be distasteful to me," Matthias said, "but it shall commence at my say so if you do not cooperate."

Sweat freckled the man's face as he looked at Irish's raised fists. But he clenched his mouth tight.

Matthias exhaled. "Irish, do not pummel his jaw. I need him to be able to talk. Do what you will to his body. You may break ribs and limbs at elbow and knee. And make sure that for the remainder of his life he's in agony when he pisses."

Irish nodded once. "Sire, may I thumb eye from face and tear ears from head?"

"Wait, wait!" cried the guard. "I will answer sirrah's questions."

Matthias waved the soldier-escorts back. "If I believe you are lying to me, my man, then Irish will punish you. Understood?"

"Aye."

"Let's begin again. First, who was the prisoner?"

"Not given 'is name."

"Where were you bringing him from?"

The guard appeared confused. "From Blackharbor, from the Benbane."

Matthias paused. "Prisoners are taken *to*, not *from*...never mind. Where were you taking him?"

"Pitcairn Isle."

"Pitcairn? That's the most desolate outpost in the kingdom. Only accessible by boat a couple times a year."

The guard glanced nervously at the sergeant and the soldier-escorts.

Her husband looked back at the stone building. "The prisoner had a mask on his face that could not be removed. So why was there a hood over his head, too?"

"Orders from Benbane warden. No one was to see 'is masked face durin' our travelin'. We wanted no questions from the curious."

Celine shook her head. Again, secrets.

"Ah, a hood over prisoner's head would be common but the mask would attract attention," Matthias said. "Why did you kill him?"

"I did not!" the guard nearly shouted. "My oath on it!"

"Two riders were seen coming from gaol and going into township. Did they do the killing?"

The guard slumped, defeated. "Aye."

"Who were they?"

"No names given."

"Why was the prisoner killed?"

"No reason given to me, sirrah."

Matthias removed the pouch from the guard's belt and looked inside. "Twenty-five in gold coin. Newly minted with Blackharbor stamp. Is this why you allowed the killing to take place?"

"Had no choice, sirrah."

"No choice, yet you were paid for your assistance. Who came to you with this handsome payment?"

Celine watched. The guard was plainly debating on whether to continue or not.

"Speak, my man," her husband said impatiently.

"I woke in me bunk night b'fore leavin' Blackharbor," the guard replied, "wit' man standin' over me. He says the prisoner would die on journey an' I could earn gold if'n I helped. While he spoke, he had dagger to me throat. I had no choice in matter."

"What were you supposed to do?"

"Wait in this town 'til the man come along."

"How long have you been here?"

"Two an' a half days, sirrah."

"Didn't that much time raise some suspicions with the local constabulary?"

"*Con-* what?"

"Didn't the township sheriff ask why you were staying so long?"

"He did. Me told him the horses was weak an' needed extry rest an' feed. He called us malingerers but didn't give a shite as long as we didn't want nothing from 'im."

"What was the rest of the plan?"

"Give mate a jug every night. He was 'appy, no bitchin'. After man came, me was to take body to woods an' drop into old mine shaft. Was to tell sheriff that prisoner escaped while I was sleepin'. Mate had duty an' would be blamed. Man wit' dagger an' the second man come tonight."

Matthias paused. She knew he was reviewing all he'd been told.

"Was the man's dagger—blade and hilt—black?" he asked the guard.

"Aye."

Matthias looked at Celine and Westen. "There is a man in Blackharbor that murders for noble coin. He's known for his black dagger."

The guard added, "The man smelled like the devil's smoke, he did. I give oath to that. B'lieve me, sirrah, I had no choice but to help 'im. If'n I hadn't, I would've been killed, too."

Celine studied her husband. She knew that when he was deep in thought he often tapped his right foot on the ground—as he was doing now.

"Sergeant," he said after a long moment. "Lock both men in the pillories. Post guard."

"Shall be done, sire," Westen replied. "The sheriff finally approaches."

Celine and Matthias returned to the inn. Husband needed to tell her ladyship about the change in their traveling plans.

"I do not wish to remain here," the Lady Adriana Glass responded, stamping her small foot. "I demand that we continue on to home. I insist."

"We are staying," said Matthias. "Mayhap for a few days."

Celine ignored the lady's outburst. She thought about what husband had told her when they walked to the inn. There was a man, he said, who called himself Cathedral. He was a trained assassin who sold his skills to noble lineage. Would slay any person for set amount of coin and carried a rondel dagger that's blade—rumored to have been forged from fallen star stone—and hilt were black. His telltale for a killing was one strike to victim's heart. A second was never needed. Cathedral and his henchmen walked the streets of Blackharbor openly with no attempt to shield features. He had never been arrested. No noble would admit to hiring him, no target had survived, and rare witnesses to slaying were soon not among the living. 'Twas said that one murdered witness had been blind. Matthias ordered the sergeant to post sentry on the paid guard. If the killer was Cathedral, he would soon return to slay guard. The man's part was done, and he'd seen the assassin and the second man at their work.

Adriana stamped both feet as heated scarlet colored her cheeks.

"Piffle-tosh, I shall not be inconvenienced for a commoner mishap," she continued. "I shall not!"

"The inconvenience is a murder, milady," replied Matthias. "Our King will demand report on this crime."

"You compel me to request escort from the Baron Longshanks on the final leg of journey home."

"Pardon me? Longshanks?"

"Yes. This inconsequential highway-town must feel blessed to have those from three noble houses within its borders on the same day. Baron Longshanks arrived shortly after we did yesterday eve and is leaving today for the capital. I would rather stay in your company, Mister Duncan, but if lay-about here is intended then I am forced to make other arrangements."

"Milady must do what she believes is best."

"Oh! If this has to do with the two riders, I saw coming from the gaol toward the inn this morn, then go collect them and we can resume our journey."

Celine and Matthias glanced at one another.

"You saw two riders this morning?" husband asked.

"Yes, I awoke early today, and my servants were preparing my bath. Those two women are worthless. I shall replace them as soon as we return home. By the time the miserable creatures finished filling my bathing tub with hot water, the water was already cooling. It had to be redone."

"Please tell us about the riders, milady."

"While my servants were failing at their simple task, I was looking out the window in my dreadful room. I had to open the window to see because the glass was so filthy. On the third floor, one can see a good distance. Because of my miserable servants, it seemed like I stood there forever. The morning air had such chill to it that I had to don wrap over my nightgown to waylay shivers."

"The riders?"

Adriana sighed unhappily.

"Tell us what you witnessed."

"I saw two men riding from the gaol toward township."

"Please, your ladyship, continue."

"One man was covered in cloak. The other had silver hair and beard with no mustache. He had the audacity to look directly at me and *nod* to me. I, of course, turned away. Are there no proper manners in the world any longer?"

"Would you be able to identify the man if he was brought before you?"

"If it shall allow us to continue to home, I will."

"Did you see where they went after they rode past you?"

"Why would I give a piffle-tosh where the ill-mannered ruffians rode to?"

16

ADRIANA POINTED AT THE MAN WITH SILVER hair and beard, no mustache, without hesitation. "That is the rude man I saw this morning riding from the gaol."

"Are you sure, milady?" asked the sheriff. "Ye were a fair distance away when ye saw the rider. This man's features are not that unique."

The lady did not respond but Celine heard the tiny sound that came from her that spoke volumes. How did this commoner sheriff dare to question her statement?

Matthias had ordered a search of the township. Norlow and Irish, aided by sheriff's deputies, discovered this man in the Barbary Tavern at mid-township. Celine had accompanied the others—Matthias, Lady Adriana, Westen, the soldier-escorts, the sheriff, and two of his deputies—to the Barbary. They found the man sitting at a table in the deserted tavern-inn room, smoking a hemp pipe, with another man as companion. Celine noted the cloak draped across the back of the second man's chair. She wondered why they had remained after the killing was done.

The only other person in the room was a lad, about six or seven years in age, Celine reasoned. The boy was cleaning horse shite, clumps of mud, and small animal intestine and bladder—that Celine knew some Thurian men used as cock sheath—from the floor before spreading fresh straw across the planks. The lad smiled every time he found a dropped coin. That, she guessed, was his pay for the chore.

They surrounded the two men.

The second man did not attempt to intervene. He seemed amused.

The lad watched them only for a few moments then continued with his chore.

Celine leaned close to husband and whispered, "The man has cross-cut on right bootheel."

Matthias nodded.

"Your names, gentlemen," he said to the two men.

"My partner is Cathedral," the second man replied. "Today I am called Wiczak."

Cathedral gazed coolly at Adriana.

The sheriff jabbed a finger at Cathedral. "Ye were seen riding to township from gaol. Milady has identified ye." He glanced at Wiczak. "Ye rode with a second man."

"Could not have been me and my partner," Wiczak responded. "We have been at this inn for three days now and there are witnesses that my partner has been at this very table since late yesterday afternoon."

Celine knew this was not a mistake, that the silent silver-haired man was the killer. The guard had said the man who held dagger to his throat reeked of smoke. This tall man with silver hair and beard, no mustache, must've smoked pipe regularly. The smell was from burning of the religious, medicinal Cannabis leaf—that she'd always thought had the same aroma as skunk cabbage. It was imbedded deep in the assassin's clothing.

As Celine pondered Wiczak's lie, he continued, "Is riding into this township a crime?"

"Nay," Matthias answered. "But your partner is known in the capital as a killer for hire. We did not seek out an unknown, innocent personage."

"Is that a question or statement? But aye, his services are sought after by many highborn personages in the kingdom."

"Will any vouch for his character?"

"Your kind, sire, only stand up for your kind, and sometimes not then."

Matthias nodded. "Sheriff Pengler, do your duty."

"What about this other one?" the sheriff asked.

"Her ladyship could not identify the second man."

"There are three of us accompanying our liege," Wiczak said.

"The other arrest can wait for the time being," finished Matthias.

"I think we should," the sheriff said.

"Later if need be."

Pengler motioned for Cathedral to rise. "Stand. You are under arrest."

Cathedral smiled as he placed pipe on tabletop, rose, and was chained at the wrists by the deputies.

As Celine observed Cathedral and his man, a sharp warning stabbed between her shoulder blades despite not seeing sheathed blade on either man. She would have sworn Cathedral was studying Adriana's body with his wolf eyes.

At where the fourth and fifth ribs would be.

Celine wanted to be holding her short spiked mace in hand, and to use it. This was dangerous man.

"May we know the name of the accuser?" Wiczak asked.

"This is the Lady Adriana Glass of Blackharbor," the sheriff said. "She is most esteemed and proper woman."

"Ah, Glass," Wiczak replied directly to her. "We were briefly acquainted with your third husband."

"Obviously, you did not learn any manners from the association," she responded.

Then she turned to Matthias.

"Now we can depart for home?"

"Not yet, milady," Pengler informed her. "The magistrate arrives here tomorrow eve on his travelin' rounds. When court is in session, ye must repeat yer identification in person to learned judge. That is must."

Adriana sighed loudly. "This is too much to endure."

Cathedral smiled again.

Celine nudged Westen as two rough-hewn men appeared on the second-floor landing.

"Wiczak," one rough man called.

"Stand down," replied Wiczak, still sitting at the table.

The sheriff said to Matthias. "We'll hold him in the gaol with the two guards. My deputies will stand watch with yer men."

Matthias nodded in agreement.

At last, Cathedral spoke.

"Anon, my Ladyship Glass," he called as the deputies led him away.

"Interesting," Matthias remarked to Celine. "Cathedral and his henchman didn't ask what the charges were against him. That was the most natural question for them to ask. But neither did."

"You should have had the other man arrested as the sheriff said. He was the second rider."

"One of the three henchmen was. I want to see what they do."

17

CELINE WATCHED MATTHIAS TAP HIS FOOT when he paused as he paced a circle in front of their horseless coach.

She waited patiently, sitting on the coach step-up, knowing that husband was searching his memory for information that was not immediately at his recall. She would not interrupt his process. She bided the time by plucking the white dandelion florets that floated in the breeze from nearby patch from the skirt of her purple dress. Her clan had called the wildflower lion's tooth because of its leaves' jagged appearance and used it as herb to aid in the suffering of constipation and diarrhea.

When they arrived at the coach, the unhappy Lady Adriana, escorted by Westen, had soon joined them.

The sergeant-at-arms adopted attention-stance.

"Sire, with your permission, amidst our regular duties, I will arrange a rotation schedule for Norlow, Irish, and myself to stand sentry posting at the gaol."

"At ease, Sergeant," Matthias replied. "Nay. Give that duty to Norlow and Irish only. Six hours on and six off for rest and food. You will stand all-day and all-night as escort-guard for the Lady Glass."

Adriana appeared incredulous. "You believe my person is in jeopardy?"

The three did not answer.

"No one would dare place hand upon my person, Mister Duncan, let alone attempt to harm me," the lady added. "That is unthinkable."

Matthias bowed courteously from the shoulders. "As we speak, milady, there are those plotting your demise. Do not be naïve about that."

"I am the Lady Glass. I am many things to many people, but never naïve."

"Bax," muttered Celine, chuckling.

The sergeant faced Matthias. "If we are all elsewhere assigned, sire, who shall be escort-guard for wife and you? That is our prime duty."

"You have no need to worry," Celine replied, in Thurian. "I give my oath that no harm shall befall husband."

Adriana stared, in disbelief, at Celine's well-spoken Thurian words. "You can speak our tongue?"

"Aye. But there are times when I wish I did not."

As the pursed-mouth lady and the quiet sergeant walked toward the inn, she heard Adriana complain about her handmaidens and the severe reprimand they would receive for not being at immediate service when she returned from her identification of the disputable man whose name she no longer deemed worthy of remembrance.

Celine found the trunk she wanted. She removed her chainmail breast vesting, joining breechcloth, and short-handled spiked mace. The ankle-high boots she wore under her dress were suitable. She placed her clothing and clan weapon on the seat inside the coach.

Matthias's pacing slowed.

She knew he was close to recalling that which he had searched his mind for.

"There are no current documents about a prisoner in an iron mask," he said to her. "But I recall addendums to old reports and ledgers that noted a special prisoner. No detailed passages because all was merely rumor. There was also mention in a book penned by a monk about the legends of our kingdom."

Celine nodded, knowing he would carry on after shaping his thoughts.

"The eldest speculations couldn't be," he continued. "Both men were long dead before the Benbane had its first stone. But they are intriguing thoughts. One was that a masked prisoner was our first king's most brave and celebrated knight. D'Arth's queen and the knight fell in love and betrayed their vows to the king."

It happens, Celine added silently.

"A second was a priest, a Samaritan and orator whose words are still quoted today. Many common folk named their children—lads *and* lasses—after him and continue to. After his passing, he was anointed saint to stand beside Peter, Augustine, Francis, and Michael. But, supposedly, he had some radical opinions about our Savior and 'twas feared that if his views were to become well-known, it would split the Church."

Celine nodded. Her clan believed in the ancient gods and goddesses of the mountains. But they knew about the Prophet called Jesus, and his life and words were respected.

Matthias paced again. "My own thought is mayhap the corpse is the Duke Frederick Bonham. He was one of the nobles who joined with the Usurper to overthrow our King and sentenced to hang as traitor on the gallows. Before his execution, I heard several debates about him in high council. 'Twas said he had to be publicly executed as example for all on what will befall those who plot against the kingdom. Some disagreed. They held that Bonham was blood descendant of King D'Arth and therefore could not be hanged. Imprisoned but not executed. What if the man said to be Bonham on the gallows was an imposter? Judgment would be believed rendered for the populace, but the bloodline respected."

"Wouldn't King Richard have told you if that had been decided?"

"Not necessarily. The King has said to me that I always side on what is right to do. However, he says, sometimes right is not good politics."

"That is confusing."

"Yes, it is."

"If asked, I would have said that the simplest course would have been to kill the Duke and not engage in all this baxing secrecy and mystery."

"Agreed. And, if you had asked me yesterday about a prisoner in an iron mask, I would have replied that it was tall tale and myth. A good story for our playwrights and ballad tellers to spin."

"Certain things keep repeating in my thoughts," Celine noted to husband. "Cathedral and his henchmen arrived here three days ago."

"It appears they did."

"That was before the prisoner and guards reached township *two-and-a-half* days ago. Why wait until last night to slay the prisoner? Why not kill him the first night they were all here?"

"I have been thinking the same," replied Matthias. "I have surmised there is only one logical reason for the wait. It was so Cathedral could establish his alibi about being in that tavern all night."

"I am not familiar with that word, husband."

"Alibi is saying you were somewhere else, usually with witnesses, at the time of an incident or crime."

"You had him arrested anyway."

"We have two good witnesses against him."

Celine nodded. "I have thought of another reason for the wait. Husband may not think it logical."

"I still wish to hear it."

"They waited until another person came to township."

Matthias exhaled, thinking. "They waited…for the one who hired them to arrive." Then, he muttered, "Bax."

She smiled at his use of her clan curse word.

"What inn is the Baron Longshanks staying at?" he asked.

18

THEIR SEARCH DID NOT TAKE LONG AND, fortuitously, the noble had already descended from his room to the inn's downstairs.

Hiram, the Baron of the House of Longshanks, limp-bowed in greeting.

Matthias bowed in return.

Longshanks took Celine's hand into his weak hand and kissed the air above her flesh. She disliked this Thurian immediately.

And, when he turned back to husband, she wiped her hand on her dress, attempting to remove his touch.

Celine studied the nobleman. Most well-to-do ladies did not possess ball gowns that were more eye-catching than the long-tailed coat, trousers, hat, and ruby-decorated codpiece that Hiram Longshanks was wearing. Then again, Celine thought, the male peacock was more beautiful than the female. But the physical man did not match the clothing. His plump body jiggled even when he stood still. He had a high forehead dotted with powder-covered pimples, string-thin lips, and hook-kneed stance. Continuously he dabbed a satin kerchief to his red-rimmed nostrils. Behind him, a diminutive man with downcast eyes held the tail of Longshanks's coat so it would not touch any furniture in this tavern-inn and, most certainly, not the ground. Celine knew that among her clan a man such as this would have been swiftly beheaded or throat-cut unless he possessed a secret talent which benefited all. Longshanks didn't appear to have any purpose.

"Are you coming from Quantero, sire?" Matthias asked innocently. "As we are?"

"Aye."

"Did you fair well among our allies?"

"'Twas a most disappointing excursion. There is not a decent chef or tailor in the entire province. The empress's gownmaker should not be allowed to design horse blankets let alone dress her Majesty." He huffed. "I was only there because of you, Duncan."

"Me?"

"Aye. Your doing."

Matthias paused. For a moment. "Ah, your cousin, Gabriel, is establishing a merchant's bank on your behalf."

"Thuria's Great Bank of Longshanks. I adore that title." He dabbed his nose again. "Gabriel insisted we go to Quantero while you held your trade talks. Said it was a grand opportunity to strengthen and expand our bank holdings. I had to endure being introduced to potential investors and clients. I am the face of the bank after all. Meeting me was a blessing for those simple folks. I give thanks that I only had to submit to the preambles and not attend the actual discussions. I was so exhausted each day that I had to retire for lie-down nap before midday meal. Can you believe I was too tired to eat without morning rest?"

Celine saw that Matthias was struggling not to laugh.

"Business is necessary," husband said solemnly, "but can be fatiguing and tedious. Is Gabriel accompanying you to the capital?"

"Nay. He remains in Quantero for another week. More bank meetings."

"Please, sire, when he returns, tell him that I would like to gather with him. The King would be very interested in a report on the progress of your banking venture."

"If I remember, I shall." Longshanks looked through the tavern-inn's open doorway at the township street. "I saw that the Lady Glass travels with your entourage. How wonderful for you. I tried to catch her attention yesterday, but she didn't hear my call and seemed to be hurrying to a destination that was not near me. Shame. Her ladyship's knowledge of fashion rivals my own, and her taste is exquisite. You are fortunate to have her company. I truly wish I had known she was in Quantero with you. She would have ended the tedium I suffered."

"You missed the excitement here this morning."

"I heard. The brief asides I was told were adequate for me. I have no interest in the common."

"I'd seen the arrested assassin a few times in the capital. Did you know of him?"

Longshanks shuddered. "Nay! I would never hazard into those parts of the city that someone like him would frequent. 'Tis disgusting enough to glimpse those lazy persons begging for coin near the royal manor. They have no honor."

"Unfortunately, some are former soldiers who were maimed during the war with the Usurper and could no longer keep their stations in the army."

"They would have been better off if they'd been among the honored dead."

"I am remiss, sire. My belated condolences on the passing of your father and brother."

"Their current station is more content than their previous."

"I have overstayed my welcome," Matthias concluded. "As always it was a pleasure to see you again, Baron. I wish you a safe journey home."

Longshanks limp-bowed again. "Adieu, Duncan. And…wife."

As they walked back toward their coaches, Celine turned to husband.

"Is that *man* still a suspect?"

"People have three faces. The first they show in public, the second is for their family and good friends. The last is the face they show themselves. He may well be the narcissistic fop he seems to be.

But the House of Longshanks has a long history of never forgiving injuries done against them. Blood was spilt shortly after the war between the houses of Longshanks and Bonham."

"You believe that man is capable of arranging a revenge killing?"

"I have been surprised many times by what some people do."

"Tell me, husband, do I have three faces?"

Matthias chuckled. "The woman I see beside me is not the woman you present to the ladies you've gathered with, is it?"

Celine started to reply, to rebuke his observation. Instead she remained silent. Bax, at times husband was too perceptive. Not always though. As with her ladyship Glass and the sergeant-at-arms. But sometimes.

"I will meet with Father when we return home," Matthias said. "Longshanks made one comment that stabbed me when he talked about persons begging for coin. There has to be positions at the estate that injured former soldiers can do. Should have done that long ago."

They stopped near the Barbary Tavern where Cathedral had been arrested.

From the shadows, a sheriff's deputy came to them. He bowed.

"What are the henchmen doing?" Matthias asked the man.

"Not much, sire," the deputy answered. "The three is seated around a table, drinking ale and breaking night fast with the eating of pig's knuckle and bread. They just started playing cards using pebbles as betting coins."

"They have not left the table?"

"They has only gone to the shitter." The deputy paused. "Pardon me, m'lady, for my vulgar tongue. To the outside toilet. One did not even go that far. He pissed on the ground from the back steps."

"Has anyone approached them? Mayhap a messenger?"

"Nay, sire."

Matthias frowned. "Keep watch on them, deputy."

The deputy nodded. Then he bowed and headed back to his position among the tavern-inn's shadows.

Celine slipped her hand around husband's arm as they continued back toward the coaches.

"You should have those men arrested," she said. "They all played part if Cathedral is killer."

"I have no doubt Cathedral is the murderer. But several questions remain: who was the masked prisoner, why was he assassinated, and who hired Cathedral to do the killing?" He squeezed Celine's hand. "Cathedral must eliminate the two witnesses against him."

"The Lady Glass and the guard," Celine said.

"Aye." Matthias agreed. "Tell me if my thinking makes sense. If the personage who hired Cathedral wanted to be here when the killing was done, then I would surmise the killing is somehow personal and they wanted the satisfaction in knowing the prisoner was dead."

"They could have wanted proof that it was done."

Matthias nodded. "That, too. Also, that personage must be worried about Cathedral's arrest. Cathedral can identify them to save himself from the gallows."

"Now I understand why you did not have the henchmen arrested and are having them watched. You anticipate that personage will reach out to the henchmen."

"Or the henchmen shall seek them out."

"Why would the henchmen do that?"

"To demand more coin for this unforeseen turn in events."

"Ah. There is no honor among these people."

19

MATTHIAS PACED AGAIN NEAR THE COACHES. He knew one thing for certain, other than Cathedral was the assassin. The other was whomever hired Cathedral had to be a person of well-to-do means because only those could afford the price of the assassin's services.

If he was correct in his deduction that the prisoner was Frederick, Duke of House of Bonham, descended bloodline of D'Arth, and he believed he was, this revelation had many troubling aspects. Bonham had squandered his inherited fortune and had mountains of outstanding debt. The Duke had joined with the Usurper to overthrow King Richard not because he had deemed the Usurper's cause just, but to have his fortune restored when the traitors claimed victory. His choice was mercenary not political zeal and belief. He knew Bonham had not cared a tad who wore the crown of king. The Usurper had accepted the Duke into his highborn fold because of the man's title and family name; the lord traitor had felt the more nobles who joined with him the more his mandate among the populace was strengthened. After Bonham met his fate on the gallows, his two daughters had been auctioned as indentured servants to pay some of the family arrears. This was the ancient law of the land. Matthias personally felt that particular law was reprehensible but that was a lone opinion and challenging it, at that time, would have been futile.

Which was why he was pleased when the daughters were released. 'Twas long believed Bonham had found their first king's sacred sword, Libertykeeper, and hidden it. That turned out to be true. His daughters had located the hiding place and had presented the sword to the grateful King Richard and Queen Igraine. The daughters had then been fully pardoned by royal proclamation.

Two thoughts kept reoccurring to him. Both equally troubling.

First, King and Queen, since he was ten years of age, had marveled and complimented him on his mind; said they trusted him. 'Twas some of his battle strategies the generals followed to defeat the Usurper and his army. If Richard had ordered an imposter to be executed in Bonham's stead and for the Duke to be masked and secreted to Pitcairn Isle, the King had also decided that he should not be told. Yes, he would've argued passionately against the plan.

If first thought was true, just one result would be that he would always henceforth wonder what his King was keeping secret from him. It would change the long-held nature of their relationship.

Second thought was Richard had not planned, or known about, the deceit. Few among the royal high council could have successfully plotted this. That meant there was a person of influence who believed that they knew better than the rest of the council.

That was a chilling notion. But not an unreasonable thought considering the massive egos of those gathered for royal council meetings.

Damn, he thought. Celine had been right. Executing the masked prisoner would have been much simpler than this devious plan.

Matthias stopped pacing, watching his wife.

Celine stood outside their traveling coach naked save for her ankle-high boots. She'd removed her dress and was donning her chainmail vest and breechcloth. He should have been distraught and, mayhap, angry at this improper behavior. As husband and traditional head of their marriage, he should have reprimanded and punished her immediately. He wouldn't. Once again, he marveled at her view of the world. She needed to change clothing, so she did. There was nothing more to it than that. The fact that many in his society would have condemned her for this act in public would have left her confused. Her barbarian way of life was in a thousand conducts much simpler and straightforward than Thurian custom and practices. He was astonished, most days, how much he had come to love and value this woman.

Five and a half years ago, he had been betrothed to Laurel from the House of Sussex. She had been so similar to him in mind and belief. They were, as several told them, the perfect match, and they believed it, too. Many, many of his unusual views about women and their roles in Thurian life had been shaped by Laurel. Then typhus took her from his side.

After what they believed was a proper mourning period, his family attempted to arrange meetings with eligible ladies. They said that Laurel would want him to continue on with his life. The Queen even became involved. She ordered him to be escort for visiting noble families that always included a daughter or niece of marriageable age. Some said he was too driven by his high council duties to see anything outside that task. Others determined he was a soul-sad man and would never marry.

When he negotiated the treaty with the Snowbear Mountain people, he'd known that, to seal agreement with the chieftain, he would be required to marry a woman of the clan. That was their way. He'd decided he would, despite being uninterested in a husband-wife relationship. The bonding would save hundreds of Thurian lives along the border. When he met the chieftain's daughter, feelings of the body and mind that he had never known, not even with Laurel, arose within him. She was different than any woman he had ever encountered. Still, he'd told Celine that she did not have to stay with him if she did not want to, and he had meant it. He pictured Laurel nodding her approval at the declaration. Celine remained with him, but he understood, that, at first, it was because the chieftain, her father, had commanded her to do so. By the end of their dangerous journey to his home, when they had been attacked repeatedly by the ruthless Nikota clan, they had bonded with one another and remained together because both wished it.

Once, after Celine had heard several glorified tales about King D'Arth and his knights, as they lay in their bed after lovemaking, she said that he was her white knight. He did not correct her. He wasn't. 'Twas the reverse that was true. He hadn't realized what a miserable, solitary life he had fallen into after Laurel's passing and would have continued into old age. Celine had rescued him.

He had, even at a young age, considered himself a most logical person. When an issue was presented, he would study all the pertinent facts of the matter then reach the most reasonable and rational conclusion for the best good. Emotions could lead to rash actions and dreadful outcomes. He'd seen that among his own family many times. Logic over emotion first and always. But Celine stirred a myriad of feelings within him. Some good, some plainly not. At times, the primitive in his brain took over and there was no sane reason for his response. And he could not stop his reaction. He knew they would be true to one another as they had vowed in the Thurian marriage ceremony. They were not mere words to each of them. He would never seek another to lay with and she had never given him hint to think she would. Still. He vividly remembered the time at the second royal gathering they attended. The dinner was done, and the dancing had begun. Neils, of all people, told him he should dance with his wife. Eldest brother said she was watching the couples moving to the music and clearly wanted to join them. He'd replied, in a mutter, he didn't dance, couldn't dance. As the first strings of the elegant vassedanse sounded, Neils escorted Celine to the center of the floor. She did not know this dance but, in half minute, had mastered its refined steps. The other couples had actually retreated, and his wife and eldest brother quickly had the floor to themselves. They were vassedanse perfection. The Queen applauded them at conclusion and the others in the ballroom followed her lead. He should've been pleased for his wife. He wasn't. Before leaving the dance floor, Celine had curtsied to Neils and eldest brother had bowed to her and they *smiled* at one another. Rage, black and ugly, overwhelmed him immediately. He knew jealousy was not called for and was a primal response. He'd never felt this way before but could not control the feeling writhing within him. He wanted to take Neils outside and beat brother to a bloody rag. He learned, in the weeks ahead, that this foul emotion would rear within him again and always Celine was blameless in the situation. Studying the reaction, he adopted several solid ways to keep his jealousy at bay. He failed. Every damn time. This woman, his wife, stirred him as no one else, not even his beloved Laurel, did and, he truly believed, as no person ever would again.

During the journey to Quantero, he thought he finally had the ugly emotion under control. Celine and Sergeant-at-Arms Westen had a friendly, at times informal, rapport and jealousy did not flare within him. Watching the interaction between wife and sergeant, he happily determined he was once again master of his emotions. All of them. Then. At the royal palace, he saw Celine looking, a tad too long, at one of the empress's personal guards. The man appeared to have barbarian in his bloodline and shared several physical colorings and attributes with wife. Jealousy rose dark and foul within him once more. Damn. He would learn to govern his emotion. He would.

He was pleased that his family accepted Celine as his wife. As to those in the kingdom, both noble and common, who could not, they could go to Hell's blazes.

He'd been very gratified when Mother told him that Celine was a keeper.

And the past four months had proven Mother was right. Despite his primitive reactions.

20

ADRIANA STARED, AGHAST, MORTIFIED, AT THE tiny room with only a sunken bed and chipped chamber pot inside, and cobwebs at ceiling and corners.

"This is not acceptable," she said, turning to Westen. "When you stated that you'd secured for me a new overnight room in a different inn, I never imagined you would place me in hovel. Half the miserable businesses in this dismal township are inns and this is what you selected. When you said you were taking me to the Rose and Chalice, this is not what I imagined. I know there are vermin in this room!"

"Besides me?" the sergeant replied, not moving a tad from in front of the closed door.

"That is not amusing, sir. I will not stay here a moment longer."

"There are no rooms on either side of this one. No windows, one entry. The stairs groan when weight is put upon them. Here I can protect you and here you shall stay."

"You do not have command over me."

"But I do."

"You do *not*."

"I do, milady, and that shall remain so until your safety is guaranteed."

Adriana huffed. "This is travesty. The Queen will hear of this affront to my dignity. Deserved consequences shall be rendered upon Mister Duncan and you." She stamped her foot. "Go collect my handmaidens. I require their miserable service."

"Can't do that."

"Pray tell why not?"

"First, only Mister and Mistress Duncan know I brought you to this room. The innkeeper believes it is solely for me and did not see me slip you up here, and that is how it shall remain. Second, during this morn's upheaval, your handmaidens ran away."

"What? And you didn't hunt them down?"

"As milady well knows, my duties have been occupied elsewhere. You are not naïve. Do not act so."

The lady's cheeks flushed scarlet. "Do not ever use that word to me again. I demand to be shown proper respect. Do you understand this?"

The sergeant remained silent.

"Did you know she spoke our language?"

"I always suspected Mistress Duncan understood more than she let on. 'Twas shrewd thinking on her part. People can be blunter and more revealing of their nature if they believe one party of the conversation doesn't understand their words."

"Piffle-tosh." Adriana stamped her feet as she stormed about the room. "This journey has been one misery after another. As soon as I believe it could not get any worse, it does. I do not deserve these punishments. I should never have gone to Quantero. Never."

"Why did you go to Quantero? You have never said."

She grimaced. "The banks in Quantero have been longer established than those in Thuria and are more organized and secure. I wanted to meet with some bankers to determine if I would open an account with one. I learned Mister Duncan and wife were traveling to Quantero. They are suitable and respectful company. I dislike traveling alone, enjoy having proper companions to talk with." She furrowed her brow. "I do not have to justify myself to you or to anyone."

Westen sighed. "Apologies. I overstepped my position."

The lady hesitated for a moment. "I never apologize. I always say and do what is correct for my recognized station. I-I apologize to thee, Westen."

"No need to, milady."

"Oh, I must. I have never entertained single thought about engaging in a relationship outside of marriage bonds. Of my own free will, with thee, I have strayed from what is deemed respectable. And, astonishing to myself, I do not wish it different. Yet we cannot continue our rendezvouses once we have returned home. That is not possible. Mister Duncan and wife have already uncovered our liaison."

"They may have deduced us, but there is no eyewitness account of us *misbehaving*."

"I beg to differ. One day, after we parted, I was so befuddled I misaligned the buttoning of my blouse. The woman Duncan re-buttoned me then cleaned a rouge smear at my mouth. That is why the one time she approached thee and studied thy mouth and lips."

"I wondered about that. Listen to me, milady. Sire and Mistress Duncan will not gossip about us. That is not in their character. They are good, honest people. 'Tis to my honor that I serve and protect them."

"At home, mere suspicion of a relationship between us would devastate my standing in the community."

"That is understood, and 'tis why we agreed from the very beginning that we could not and would not pursue relationship at home."

Adriana moved directly in front of Westen. "I must share a truth with thee."

"You do not need to."

"I want to. Truly do."

The sergeant traced her cheek with fingertips.

Adriana smiled. "Thou are beautiful, sir."

Then she took prim stance.

"As I have told thee, I have never participated in any physical relations outside of marriage. Never had inclination to do so. I only allowed my husbands to peck my cheek and hold my hand after we were officially betrothed. Mayhap the occasional kiss to the mouth on special days." She inhaled then exhaled slowly. "In marriage, I did my wife duty but always maintained a clear mind. Yes, I did. I will blush during this confession to thee. During c-c-coitus, I reviewed my planned sojourns for the next day until husband finished. I…I was never aroused nor satisfied when husbands' members were within me. There I said it."

"Very intimate revealing. I am flattered that you shared it with me."

"Then came that second day on our journey to Quantero."

"I believe we began exchanging looks between us since first introduction."

"I do not recall that, sir. 'Twould have been improper. What I remember was that I was returning to coach after secluded body relieving. I was about to wander into a concealed animal trap, and thou pulled me into thy arms to rescue me. I was preparing to thank thee then insist thou release me since thou had not done so immediately. But before I could put voice to word, which is rare for me, I admit, thee kissed me. I fully intended to have thou throttled for thy dastard impropriety."

"You kissed me back."

"I have oft wondered how thee came to be at that most fortunate spot in the woods. Were thou following me?"

Westen chuckled. "Yes. The sound of you pissing on leaves is delightful music to my ears."

"Thy witticisms, sir, are at times crude and not appreciated."

"I was doing the same as you, relieving myself. I knew you were nearby, but I never would have spied on you at a time such as that."

"I know. Don't understand why I said that."

"The first kiss, milady, you kissed me back."

"That I shamefully admit.," she replied.

Adriana did concede she had kissed him back. And that had

surprised her. More astonishing was her mind was filled with two opposing thoughts during the embrace. One demanded she end the breach of etiquette immediately and have the sergeant punished. That was the proper course of action. The other thought, however, was, if it could remain secret, she wanted more kisses from him. Her choice in the two he was well-aware of. Now.

"We agreed," she continued, "we would not engage in more than kissing. If confronted with accusation of improper relationship, we could—with hand to Holy Book—truthfully say we had never had c-coitus nor seen one another naked."

"Yes, that is our agreement."

"When we kiss, and thou strokes my tongue with thy lips, my fingers tingle and my toes curl. 'Tis marvelous. Then thee begins caressing my bosom under my blouse and it is more wondrous. The euphoria thou causes to me is overwhelming."

"I have grown fonder of you, milady, each hour since introduction. You are magnificent, you are miracle. I even have grown very fond of your over-explaining every thought you have."

"Are you implying that I talk too much?"

"You do. I do not mind."

She huffed again.

The sergeant chuckled.

Adriana gazed into Westen's blue eyes. "I have been pondering—."

"That means trouble."

"Stop the poor witticisms, sir, and allow me to finish."

"Apologies. Please continue."

"Thou befuddles me. I have been in correspondence with a well-to-do noble in the kingdom of Zar. We have been hinting in our letters about marriage. 'Twould be a good match. We are equal in station and hold akin views on proper and respectable protocols and politics. We would be excellent companion for one another. But…but thee has raised lingering doubts within me. Marriage to this man would be same as the others had been."

"Milady must do what she must."

Adriana placed her hands at the sergeant's sides and stroked the trim body beneath ribs. "I dislike your padded uniforms. I have never seen other soldiers wearing such as this. Captain Geller never would. They are shield from my touch."

"I had all my uniforms tailored when I was assigned to the soldier-escort post for the high counsel. I knew I would be, at times, in the presence of royalty and nobles. Felt this would befit my station and give good impression. Was I wrong?"

"Nay, thou is beautiful. Oh, piffle-tosh. Thee are diverting me from planned course and this is not the first time thee have done that."

"Apologies. Please stay on planned course."

Adriana stopped her stroking above the sergeant's hipbones. "I have been pondering," she said. "Asking myself if I dared to venture further in *our* rendezvouses before we must cease. As I confided to thee, c-coitus with husbands was duty with no wonder. I believe that…is coupling the correct word?"

"'Tis one word for joining as one. Has milady realized that she is using thee, thou, and thy when addressing me?"

"I have not. Those words are for verses of the Holy Book and in the marriage vows. They are not used in the familiar."

"Those words are also preferred by the poets in their love sonnets."

"I do not use those words. 'Twould be improper. I have never said those words except during marriage vows and…piffle-tosh. *You* are diverting me from planned course once more."

Westen smiled. "Not my intent. Continue on, milady."

Adriana arched her shoulders as she collected her thoughts. Then she began again.

"Thy kisses to my mouth and throat, thy touches to my bosom are wondrous. I believe coupling with thee might be…? That being as one with thee might be…? Thy thought on this?"

The sergeant's smile vanished. "We should not."

"I cannot believe I am the one broaching this and not thee. Thou should be pursuing me, not I pursuing thee. Tell me why not?"

"After we part, as we must, I hope to remain a fond memory for you in the years to come, as you shall for me. If we were to couple, I would eventually not be that fond memory. You would come to believe I took advantage and sullied your good name. You would come to hate me."

Hurt crept into her eyes and onto her features. "I'm not… *desirable?*"

"Do not think that for a moment. When I close my eyes at night, I see visions of us lying beside one another, and I cannot go to sleep."

She smiled. "Then thou do find me desirable?"

"Very much so."

"But thee does not wish c-coitus with me."

"Best that we do not."

She pursed her mouth in pout. "I shall honor your response…if I believe it true."

The sergeant didn't anticipate the lady's next action, did not even suspect it. 'Twas out-of-character for her but then their entire relationship had been so.

Adriana swiftly placed her hand flat against the lacing of Westen's padded breeches.

The sergeant turned rock still.

The lady's mouth dropped agape as she stepped back.

Westen sighed. The Lady Adriana Glass of Blackharbor now knew long-held secret.

"Oh," she whispered, trembling. "You are…there is nothing…c-castrated…"

"Emasculated is the word you seek," Westen replied. "No cock nor bollocks. Accident at birth. I have never missed what I have never known…till this moment."

"Your uniform gives illusion you are intact."

"Another reason for the tailoring. I no longer have to place rolled cloth at my crotch."

Tears welled in Adriana's eyes. "Thou are still more man than most, dearest. My heart aches for thee."

And she threw her arms around the sergeant's neck and shoulders tightly.

She kissed Westen as deeply and passionately as she knew how. And bungled it. Westen took control and soon all was right. Their mouths became perfect fit again.

21

"YOU ARE BARBARIAN," PENGLER SAID ALOUD then he coughed attempting to cover his words.

Celine ignored the sheriff.

Before she and Matthias returned to the gaol, she had stood outside their coach and changed from silk dress into clan. Husband accepted her in warrior attire. This was her heritage, her true self. She had designed the warrior cloaking herself. The chainmail vesting covered her bosom except for swell at the bottom. The breechcloth cloaked her joining, a tick above her cleaving's peak, two fingers below her folding's lowermost, and ran from hip bone to hip bone. A smaller cloth was over her buttocks. She had cut a ribbon of the same material that would have gone over her folding, between her legs, and up the split of her buttocks. But that piece was missing. Didn't matter, she reasoned. She only wore that because husband donned smallclothes under his breeches. Other female warriors in her clan did not dress as she did. Most men were bigger than her however, and some more skilled in battle. She needed every advantage she could muster. She'd been told she was exotic beauty and when she faced enemy, near naked, most men looked at her for at least one disbelieving moment, and that tick of inaction spelled their end.

As she and husband walked to the gaol, she swung the short-handled spiked ball in battle arcs. Yes. For the past four months, her skills had lay dormant but had not been lost to her. This was very good.

She studied the gaol surroundings—saw no one and nothing out of the ordinary—then looked at solder-escort Norlow, the sheriff, and the pug-faced deputy and finally at the two men locked in the pillories.

"Me had no choice, sirrah," the thick-bodied guard pleaded to Matthias as they reached the men.

The second guard had awoken from his drunken stupor. The man had puked, residue of vomit speckled his lower lip and chin and had attempted to free his head and hands from the wood lockdown. His struggle had caused raw scrape to back of neck and his no-belt breeches to fall around his feet. He wore no undergarment, and no one had aided him in regaining some dignity.

Matthias walked to the second man and tugged the breeches back to his waist.

"Blessin', sire," the man muttered. "Can I beg a little water from ye?"

Celine noted that the soldier-escort stood in at-attention stance and keep his eyes riveted on the horizon. The deputy kept side-glancing at the crotch of her breechcloth while Pengler studied her spiked mace. She guessed that the sheriff had encountered barbarian warriors in his past.

Matthias turned to Norlow. "At ease, soldier. Have there been any troubles while you've been here?"

"Several town lads have come by to see what was happening," Norlow answered.

"I run 'em off," added Pengler. "Scamps, they are."

"And one of Longshanks' men approached. Said the baron was curious, the arrests were the talk of the inn during fast-breaking. Did not stay long. Nothing else of note occurred during my current watch."

"We're going to talk with Cathedral." Matthias paused. "Give these men water and, for decency's sake, if that man's breeches fall down again, pull them back up."

"Aye, sir. Shall be done."

Celine and Matthias moved to the gaol. The corpse had been placed in one corner and covered with blanket. Cathedral sat on the dirt floor in the opposite corner. The man did not appear, to her, to be apprehensive about his situation.

They all studied one another for a long moment.

Yes, Celine repeated to herself, *this was dangerous man.*

"Woman, are you some fearsome warrior?" Cathedral said, at last.

She didn't reply. She studied his head for the best kill spot among several options.

"Request, my sire," said Cathedral to Matthias. "May I have my pipe and pouch of herb leaf?"

Matthias nodded. "I will see that you receive them the night before you are taken to the gallows."

"I am innocent man."

Celine squatted down. "We found the tracks of the killers inside the gaol and some outside. One had a crosscut on his right bootheel. You are not the skilled assassin you are said to be."

She pointed at his boot.

For a swift moment, she saw the man's eyes narrow with worry. He curled up his leg until she could no longer see his bootheel. She wondered what he was thinking about. Escape? Vengeance? Last walk to the gallows?

"There are witnesses this time to your crime," added Matthias.

"Her ladyship misspoke. I have people who will say that it could not have been me she saw."

"The King will believe her. And the Benbane guard that you paid shall also testify."

Cathedral shrugged his shoulders, unafraid.

"Her ladyship is in error," he responded. "The son-of-a-bitch guard is damned liar. That will not be disputed."

"Save yourself," Matthias said. "Who is the murdered man, who hired you, and why was he killed?"

"I have no knowledge about the things you speak of." Cathedral paused then added, "If I were the assassin you say I am, and I am not, I would never ask the why of a slaying. The reason would not be of concern nor of interest."

"Only the victim's name would matter after coin was paid."

"Aye. If I was who you say I am, and I am not."

"When the rope is placed around your neck, it will be too late to loosen your tongue."

"I am innocent man being wronged for purpose I cannot comprehend."

"If you change your mind, tell the soldier and he will inform me."

Matthias walked outside.

Celine stared at Cathedral as she tapped the head of her mace against the open palm of her hand. She had seen killers like this man before. Most warriors—clan and kingdom—did in battle what they were trained to do and accepted that slaying foe was sometimes part of their duty, part of their own survival. One man in her clan had been called a berserker. In the heat of battle, he went into a trance-like fury and foamed at the mouth. His companions stayed far away from him during combat until fugue subsided, for berserker could not tell friend from enemy. And then there were men like this one. They lived only to kill others. There was no joy in their life. The only times they felt satisfaction and power, felt their own value, was when they had slain another.

She nearly spat at the assassin then decided he was not worth the effort.

Rising, she followed after husband.

"Anon," called Cathedral.

Celine moved to husband's side.

"Why did you not promise beating if man did not answer your questions like you did with guard?" she asked.

"I knew the threat alone would get the guard to talk. Wouldn't work with Cathedral. He would've invited beating and still not talked. At least in the beginning. All eventually talk. I've never used a beating to gather information, and I rue that a day might come and I will be forced to."

22

AS SOON AS THEY ENTERED THEIR INN ROOM, shortly before noon sun, with the door barely closed behind them, Matthias led her straight onto the bed.

Celine laughed, delighted, as she dropped onto her back. "So, sire, it appears you like me wearing clan."

He took the spiked mace from her hand and placed it on the floor. Immediately he moved over her, cupped her face in his hands, and kissed her hard. She was surprised. He usually began his kisses with a gentle brushing of his lips back-and-forth across hers. 'Twas wonderful. This time he was different, he—without pause— passionately, urgently, plunged his tongue between her open lips and teeth and stroked her. She tugged the breechcloth to the side, then gripped the short hair at back of his head. At her bared cleaving, their bodies pressed together, she felt his cock finish hardening under his breeches.

He was inflamed.

And so was she.

She swept her tongue across his, then sucked.

They feasted upon one another.

Months ago, while the King's man celebrated their blood-and-bone bonding with Father and other clan men in drink, toasts, and vulgar boasts, she waited in the marriage lodge for the stranger to come to her for first joining. Mother, sisters, and the elder women surrounded her. They told the virgin what to expect this night. If new husband was sober, several added. One had warned her about a most curious Thurian practice. They put mouths together in what they called kiss. She had wondered how the pressing of lips, touching of tongues, and sharing of breath could be pleasurable? Thought it most curious. Her new husband *had* kissed her during that first night. After, she had thanked the gods and goddesses. Kiss was such a simple name for this glorious, blissful act. She could not receive enough of his kisses.

She moaned softly into his mouth.

Matthias ended their kiss and traced his tongue and teeth from her ear down her neck to shoulder and back up. Her flesh tingled. As he pleasured her with his mouth, he pushed the chainmail vesting aside, caressing the contour of her breast with his fingers, and circling the large oval of her areola with his thumb. Pinching her nipple, it turned to taut pebble. She knew her folding was blossoming open and growing wet in anticipation. This was incredible. Wave after wave of sensuous heat coursed through her veins. Then, for the first time ever, he kissed and stroked with his fingernails along the underside of her forearm. *Oh, bax!* She believed she would melt into the mattress in glorious bliss. Where had he learned this new marvel?

She knew she was blessed. Among the clan, 'twas the duty of the woman to pleasure the man, and if she crested during joining, 'twas mostly by happenstance not by design. Husband was not clan. He vowed to give her as much bodily joy as she gave him, and she, without qualm, adored pleasing him. She thanked the gods and goddesses of the mountains that husband was the man he was. At earliest opportunity, she would present heartfelt gift to the heavens.

At last, returning his mouth to hers, the kiss growing more passionate and ardent if possible, he shifted his body slightly above hers and started to pull his tunic off. She stopped him. She could not wait for even the scant time it would take for husband to disrobe. Couldn't, wouldn't. Quickly, she unlaced the ties of his breeches.

With erect cock in hand, she guided him to her aroused cleaving and slid him inside her opening. Usually their coupling started slowly and gently then built to deeper and faster. This time they were immediately intense and swift, and in sync with one another. *Faster,* she wanted to shout into his mouth. *Oh, faster!* She clutched him at the back of his head, her mouth sealed against his, and arched her back. Her heart thundered and her flesh grew hotter. Their bodies raced to keep pace with the other. She knew she was plummeting toward the abyss. 'Twas only a matter of moments.

She pulled her mouth from his.

"Yes!" she cried as she fierce-pinnacled and her soul nearly leapt from her body.

He followed and collapsed atop her.

Celine heard someone pounding on the wall from the adjoining room and shouting for them to quiet down.

She slid her hands from his head to his buttocks to keep his cock within her. *Oh, my! Oh, bax!* Cresting after cresting after cresting rippled through her. Her entire body, from crown to toe, trembled and her feet were curled. She knew that if she rose at this moment, her legs would not support her.

Matthias pressed his face to her neck, and they lay joined and unmoving. She felt her cleaving corridor pulsing around his cock. 'Twas wondrous.

Finally, reluctantly, they separated, and a small cresting cried out within her, begging for them to remain joined. But they eased beside one another and embraced.

"Oh, bax," she whispered repeatedly, but no further words came to her. That had been glorious, grand. It was several moments before she noted she was cloaked in honeyed sweat from brow to boot.

"Bax, bax, oh bax."

They lay, holding the other, basking.

"I've been thinking," he said, at last.

Celine rose slightly over him and flicked two fingers across the tip of his nose.

"Why did you…?" he said, in surprise.

"I am struggling to remind myself to breathe," she replied, "and you are laying there thinking?"

"Uh…"

"If I had any strength within me, I'd punish you."

"Hmm…"

She smiled at him and placed her face on his tunic breast and listened to his heartbeat. As she did, she stroked her fingers across his stomach.

"You are growing…what would be the Thurian words? Oh, yes, a little pot belly."

"You're learning to tease, my love," he said.

"Am I, husband?" She placed her hand back over his exposed cock. "You already know this but, upon occasion, I shall remind you. You carry this but it belongs solely to me and I do not share."

"Understood," he said, hugging her tighter to him. "I expect reward for the abuse rendered to my nose."

"Name reward, sire, and see it rendered."

"Not now! More at the moment would finish me. May well be a few days before we can return to this discussion."

She caressed her cheek against his chest. This man had become treasure. In all ways. She would cherish their bonding to end of days.

"What were you thinking?" she asked.

Matthias hesitated, then began. "Remember my guess that the masked prisoner might be the traitor Frederick, Duke of Bonham?"

"Aye. I listen when husband speaks."

"Earlier this year, the houses of Drake and Longshanks were in blood feud. The Marquise Drake—."

"I know Morgana. She is friend."

"She is the daughter of Frederick Bonham. During the feud, the Baron Longshanks, eldest Longshanks son, and one Drake brother were slain. It could be happenstance, but it most is curious that the new Baron Longshanks, Hiram, arrives at township and then the murder is done. That was why I wanted to speak with him."

"We must uncover who the prisoner was."

"That's what I was thinking about. If we don't learn his identity while we are here, I will have the corpse taken to Blackharbor. There I'll have the royal mortician remove the iron mask."

"But the face will be torn off."

"Yes. I shall have the mortician make a death mask."

"Then we'll see his features and learn who he was."

"Yes."

"No one else would have thought of that, husband."

"A few would have, and much sooner than I did."

Celine again traced her fingers across his stomach, thinking. "If the King planned a fake execution and the imprisonment of the Duke Bonham, will he allow death mask to be made?"

"If Richard stops it, that shall tell me much."

"Husband, I saw the corpse. I know 'twas older man. You told me the old story of the prisoner in the iron mask and the many rumors about who the man might have been."

"Talking to you helps me organize my thoughts and, quite often, you have observation or ask question that sheds entirely new light on the subject. I like that."

"Thank you," she replied. "Why is it though, when you share with me your kingdom's history, and its legends and myths, the main personage in the tale is always male? It seems to me that if a female is noted at all, 'tis only in the role of mother, wife, or courted lover. Do Thurian women make no contribution to the kingdom?"

Matthias furrowed his brow. "There are tales about the bravery of women, but they are few, I shamefully admit."

"Name one."

"One," he responded, stroking her hair. "All...right. I'll tell you about—."

"Husband," Celine interrupted.

"Yes?"

"I am about to strike your nose again."

"What! Why?"

"I can tell by your voice alone, without looking at your face and body, that you are about to make a story up. You are terrible liar."

"I'm an excellent liar. Part of my task on high council is to lie and I've never been challenged."

"I always know when you are lying. You have lied to me. Not often. You've only lied to me when you thought the truth would hurt me."

Matthias sighed. "My apologies."

"None needed." She tapped her fingers on his cock then chuckled. "I've lied to you upon occasion, too."

"Oh, dear Lord in heaven," he replied, moaning. "This morning has been humiliating. First, I now believe King Richard does not share all his plans with me. And second, I learn my wife lies to me about my lovemaking."

"Most of the time our joinings are magnificent. Occasionally however you need to be praised when your male prowess is less than the usual."

"Shite."

"Husband."

"Yes?"

"There are no Thurian stories about women who are heroes, are there?"

"None I could recall."

Celine raised her head, listening to the footfalls on the floor above them.

"The Lady Glass and sergeant have returned to her room."

"She needs to be seen going to and coming from her room during the course of the day. That will help ensure the people watching her will not think something is amiss. After darkfall, Westen will secure her in the other room at the Rose and Chalice."

"If she will allow it. I have already heard her new grumbles."

"She has no choice."

"I shall wish Westen good fortune in that matter."

"As do I."

23

I TRULY BELIEVE I AM SAFE WITH THEE BESIDE me," Adriana said rising up, with water splashing over the side of the bathing tub.

Westen stood at the open window with back to her. "I give my oath," the sergeant replied, "that I shall be slain dead before a pinch of harm happens to ye."

She stepped from the tub. Water dripped from her body and added to the puddle at her feet.

"That was most refreshing."

"You bathe more often in a single day than soldiers do in a month's time."

"I like to be clean and the oils in the water keep my skin soft and smooth. As thee have discovered, I pray."

"Yes, milady."

She removed the towel around her head. The black hair cascaded past her shoulders and down her spine. As she dried herself, she gazed at Westen. The sergeant had taken position staring out the open window, with back to her, shortly after the inn's women had brought up the hot water and before she had slipped off one shoe. He had not turned about once. How was it, she wondered, that this man, more than any she'd ever known, stirred these wondrous sensations within her?

"Thou may look upon me," she declared. She was amazed that among the many emotions and delights this man stirred within her, she wanted him to see her unclothed and sought to witness his desire for her in glistening of his eyes and smile upon his lips. Her husbands had lusted for her, which she strived to achieve each day of their marriages and brought her a distinct satisfaction and contentment when accomplished. Never said aloud to another person, she knew she was not a great wit, a savvy in business, nor a robust wanton in bed. She had her beauty, grace, and style. No man had ever been ashamed to be her escort. Now, nearing the end of her fourth decade, she understood she was no longer a young lass—her bosom and buttocks were not as firm as they had once been nor her waist as tiny, and small lines were appearing under her eyes and at the corners of her mouth. She wanted, nay, she *needed* Westen's approval.

"'Twould not be proper for me to look at ye in disrobed state," the sergeant-at-arms said.

"Do you believe if thou saw me in all my glory, thou would not be able to restrain thy passion for me?"

Westen sighed. Did not reply.

Adriana reached her cleaving with towel and silently gasped. This could not be. She saw—not many but definitely a few—new grays rising among her dark intimate hair. They seemed to be sprouting more and more, faster and faster. If she continued to pluck, her cleaving would soon be bald. She'd heard that Mistress Duncan had no body hair, not a whisker. Would her cleaving before long be barbarian? She might have to adopt the Zar style. The fashionable ladies in that kingdom wore undergarments from shoulder to midriff to firm bosom and slim waistline, and stockings from thigh to foot to enhance legs. In-between they donned no garment. This was considered much more sensible for times of bodily relieving than the Thurian custom for complete undergarment covering. In the last few years, the Zar fashion had become to wear a dyed, curled wig adorned with jewels or ribbons over intimate region. Did those ladies reveal their cleaving often? And why was she considering this? Because soon

Westen and she would have to part ways, and thus far the sergeant had not seen her unclothed, had not viewed her glorious womanhood unshielded. She wanted him to.

Drying her thighs and legs, she returned her eye to the sergeant, and lingered upon the tight round buttocks beneath breeches. She wanted to stroke, wanted to explore that magnificent body with her hands. And more.

"Tell me again that I am desirable," she said.

"It astounds me how much continuous flattery you require."

"Thee does not need to say a word. Thy kiss would speak volumes."

"One kiss," Westen said. "After you dress and before we go downstairs for noon meal. It shall be brief. The kiss, not meal."

"When we return to hovel this evening, I shall sleep atop thee. Not a piffle-tosh of me shall touch that ghastly bed. Tomorrow, if I find so much as one flea or lice on my person, Mister Duncan and you shall regret it."

"Yes, milady."

"For night's rest, would thou prefer I wear night-rail or be unclothed?"

"Milady should do as Milady deems best. Please dress so we may go."

Adriana pouted her lips. She had never offered to any man, bachelor or definitely not to married male, what she did to this one. And the sergeant was ignoring her. Until this morning, Westen had been, at every private moment, very generous with kisses and caresses. Despite the relationship being completely inappropriate, she had come to relish it. She knew the change in his demeanor was because she'd learned of the birth injury. Now she had become pursuer and not the pursued. She did not like this reversal in roles a tad. Not one piffle-tosh bit. But these last days should not be wasted. They'd never come again. She willed the tears back. Dammit, when had she turned this emotional? She wouldn't say the words aloud, for they might hurt the sergeant, but she wanted to shout that she was sorry, deeply and truly, that he had been disfigured. In louder voice, she'd say she still wanted his kisses, caresses, and arms around her.

She knew a change had happened in their relationship. And she did not like it a tad.

She was a moment away from accepting this fact and surrendering to it.

Then.

A most joyous thought bloomed in her mind. She giggled into the towel. Yes, this would be wonderful. She knew it would. Westen would no longer be able to ignore her. She finished drying and dropped the cloth to the floor into puddle.

With tiny steps, she crept forward.

She counted to twenty.

Slowly.

"I am now proper, sir," she announced.

"That was quick," Westen said, turning about.

She rushed to the sergeant, placing hands on padded tunic at shoulders. She would not allow retreat to prior stance.

"I do not beg, and yet for thou, I will," she said, rising upon her toes and tilting her face upward. "*Please*. I beseech thee."

Westen hesitated. "First, I must share secret with you."

"*Now? At this moment?*"

"Yes. It plagues me."

"Then speak it. Swiftly I plead, and I pray thee have no more secrets."

"Do you remember when I rescued you from the concealed animal trap?"

"Yes. There was no trap. Thee lied so thee could hold me in thy arms and kiss me."

"You knew?"

"Yes. I told thee I was not naïve."

"But you are, milady, in so many ways. And I give thanks for it."

They kissed.

She felt glorious warmth at her mouth then at her breast when embrace came. Lips pressed; hands caressed. She eased her tongue out from her mouth and Westen captured her between lips. And stroked. *Stars in heaven.* 'Twas wondrous. Utterly it was.

Easing back, but keeping hands to shoulders, she gazed from Westen's face to upper body.

"Thee are so fit and trim." She traced finger along the sergeant's throat. "My husbands' bodies were all slack with age. One seemed to be in competition with me as to which of us would have largest bosom. I well-served each as wife, being more than mere decoration. One, and this was deplorable, but I accepted my role, used me as shield for his unhealthy appetites. None mistreated me, none would have dared, but I earned the inheritances I received."

Westen cupped her cheek and ear. "You are sharing with me again."

"Never had person in my life I could allow myself to do that with. I always kept my own counsel. Then I met thee." She gazed into the sergeant's blue eyes. "As I have said, thee befuddles me, and I have discovered I like that thou does."

Westen grunted.

Adriana moaned.

During the whisper of a moment, the sergeant kissed her deeply then swept her up from raised toe. Westen continued with mouth to hers and carried her to the bed. With one hand, the sergeant placed the bed pillows together at the headboard.

She was puzzled when kiss ceased and Westen set her on the bed against the pillows, sitting upright with knees bent.

This was no coitus position she knew…

…but then there could never be a coupling between them. That was truth.

A sliver of sadness pierced her heart. She believed, if he did have penis and testicles, he would have bodily pleasured as she had never been before.

Westen rose over her, lightly kissing brows, cheeks, chin, and neck.

She sighed, delighted, as beautiful mouth moved to breasts and lingered. *Yes!* She started to stretch her legs out, but the sergeant prevented her from doing so.

Edging down her body, Westen kissed her ribs, stomach, and button then her knees and gently, ever so gently, her inner thighs.

Nay, she nearly cried out. Her first thought, to her horror, was that the sergeant could now see the gray hairs at her intimate.

Then she realized. *Oh, my heavens!* Westen could not be planning to kiss her there! That was unthinkable and—.

That thought and all others vanished.

Blissful joy captured her entire being as lips and tongue possessed her intimate foldings and as finger stroked her anus ring. Panting for breath, she squeezed and captured Westen's head between her thighs.

My stars in heaven!

The sergeant, with tongue, deep-caressed her innermost. Her legs and feet quivered uncontrollably, and her fists gripped the bed covering. She was lost. She was about to weep in sheer pleasure.

Oh, my stars!

As Westen continued with his mouth, the sergeant eased middle finger inside her. He moved fingertip along the upper channel of her opening. She nearly cried aloud as an exquisite and intense spot was caressed. Her leg muscles tightened, her back arched.

Oh my, oh my! What was he doing to her?

Then, not one after the other, at the *same* moment, two pinnacles arrowed through her and joyous wave after wave rippled within her.

Westen stilled mouth and hand allowing the wondrous, incredible sensations to glory within her. *Dear, dear heaven.* She was in a new world, one that was edging her toward swooning faint. *Oh, my.*

Later. Unsure how long the time had been, minutes or hours, mayhap days, her mind began to slowly clear.

Magic, she declared. *True enchantment.* She would've sworn that Westen had caused her to literally soar among the rainbows and stars.

24

CELINE FINISHED DRESSING IN HER YELLOW silk gown and reached for her boots laying in the creek bank's grass beside her chainmail vest, breech cloth, and short-handled spiked mace.

Her bath had been refreshing. Matthias had washed in the room. The maids had offered to bring water for her too. She declined. From the looks on their faces she knew that many, if not all within the Swan and Bulldog, had heard their vigorous, magnificent coupling. The maids were mortified that she didn't intend to wash afterward. Most of her life, Celine had cleaned and bathed in streams, rivers, and lakes. Still preferred those brisk, crisp waters—with the occasional fish nibbling at her toes—to heated water in a cramped tub that the Duncan ladies preferred. So, she had separated from husband and gone to the creek on the west side of township to the secluded wooded spot she had found the day they arrived. Husband had bathed with her that time. And they'd pleasured one another while in the water. This second journey to the creek was not as enjoyable as the first.

Before coming to the bathing spot, she'd watched the Longshanks caravan—with half the day gone—preparing to leave the township, to head southbound on the main roadway to Blackharbor. The baron was mounted on a magnificent destrier albino stallion and was barking commands at his hired men. Most were well into the midst of doing what he was ordering them to do. To her, this added to the weak character of the man that husband considered a minor suspect in the hiring of the assassin. She did not believe the baron was the one behind the murder. *Bax,* she found husband to be a more worthy suspect than that pompous man.

Immediately after observing the caravan, she found the deputy watching Cathedral's henchmen at the Barbary Tavern. They had remained at their table, the deputy reported. The one called Wiczak had left for a three-quarters of an hour. He'd gone upstairs with a bored wench to sard. That was a new word to her. But she understood its meaning. 'Twas coupling—not like husband and she made love— but an act without any import other than a male's physical release and a female's coin payment. She disliked that the henchman had taken that long for a sard. She told the deputy to talk to the woman, to find out if Wiczak had stayed with her the entire time or if he'd left briefly. It appeared to her that the deputy was going to balk at taking orders from a woman—a barbarian woman on top of that. But she had anticipated that possibility. While they talked, she had tapped the spiked head of her mace against her palm and added that husband would want the report. The deputy agreed to query the wench and she had continued on to the creek to bathe.

On the creek's bank, Celine stomped her right foot to secure it within her boot. Then did the left.

Across the creek, she saw movement among the trees. She knew, without seeing it fully, that it was a bear. The snow bear had been her clan's talisman. Many warriors said prayer to the mountain gods to give them the strength and cunning of bear before going into battle. One taken in hunt, without death or wounding of hunters, was considered omen of good fortune coming to the clan. All of an animal taken in hunt was used. In bonding ceremony, the man's and woman's blood were mixed in a bowl with the bones of male and female snow bear to make the union strong. First night bonding beds, as was hers, were topped with white fur that would enhance the coupling.

The bear sauntered into the open and neared the creek.

She sighed. 'Twas brown bear. She knew white bears did not inhabit Thuria as they did in her mountains. But she had hoped for a sign from the elder gods and goddesses.

Then she saw a cub trailing after the bear.

Celine smiled. 'Twas sign for her.

One with hope.

Her moonflow was late. But she had never had the same amount of days between the ending of one and the beginning of the next. Her two older sisters always, and together, received their heavy moonflows every thirty-one days and they lasted exactly four days. Her sisters were more miserable than their usual during that time, moaning about tender teats and cramps to back and gut. Once, feeling devilish, she told them that she could smell their flows from a lodge away and they should remain distant from the camp horses because their stench could frighten the animals and cause stampede. Her sisters had cursed and thrown stones at her—that she easily dodged. She did note later that sisters were walking wide path around horses.

Hope. Her moonflow came between twenty-three and thirty-five days after her last. 'Twas always light, staying only two days, and was minor annoyance. She remembered however the first time Matthias and she coupled during her flow. The look on husband's face when he withdrew from her and saw blood at her intimate and on his erection was one of horror. He believed he had injured her. Yes, her unusual man of the mind had gaps in his knowledge of females. Since then she always announced her moonflow days to him. They would abstain from joining; they would kiss and caress one another, and she would suckle his cock. After flow had passed, he would give her glorious body attention that would have her calling to all heavens in pleasure.

As Celine gathered her clan garments and mace, she knew the bear with cub across the creek were omen from the mountain gods and goddesses. She had never gone this long before. It had been forty days since her last moonflow. She had not said this to husband. She wanted to be sure. But very soon, mayhap before they arrived home, she would tell him—*I am with child*. She had seen him with his nieces and nephews and knew, without single doubt, he would be most wondrous father. She had decided that if son he would be named after both their fathers, if daughter then after their mothers.

She walked back toward the tavern-inn, smiling.

25

CELINE WOKE.

And full aware.

Despite living in the security and safety of the Duncan manor house for four months, she continued to sleep as warrior would—light and alert for strange noises and out-of-place sounds. Deep sleep could mean death from attacking rival clans.

Sitting up, she turned and slid her feet to the floor. Grabbed mace in fist.

She determined that 'twas after midnight, but hours before dawn.

Before going to sleep, she and Matthias had not coupled. They had held one another, with satisfying kisses and caresses. 'Twas enough for this night. She thought about their noontime joining and how magnificent it had been. One they would share again. She liked seeing her husband lose his typical self-control with her. Yes, that was wondrous. She knew husband in his quiet this night was reviewing the prisoner's murder and all that surrounded it. He was attempting to determine who the man in the iron-mask was—although he was fairly certain 'twas the traitorous Duke of Bonham—why the killing, why the killing had been done here in Oxham's Mill, and, most importantly, who was behind it. She decided that if she took his cock in her mouth and pleasured him that he would relax, and it would aid him in his reasoning process. But, before she did, she heard his breathing turn even and soft. She had cuddled against his side with his arm around her and joined him in sleep.

Now she was awake. She immediately recognized the distant sound. 'Twas sword striking sword. All warriors knew the sound well. As they did of arrow in flight, which was usually the last sound they heard save for their own death cry.

She listened, concentrating. Noted that Matthias remained asleep from his even breathing. Downstairs was quiet save the night creaking of walls and flooring planks, and the scampering of tiny claws hunting for food scraps and crumbs. On the same floor as their room, next-door to theirs, the lodger was pissing into chamber pot. Outside, she heard a dog begin to howl. Another hound, then another followed the first.

Then, along with the howling dogs, she heard hooves striking ground. Again, in the distance. There were four—nay, five—galloping horses heading east.

Celine turned to Matthias and placed her fingers over his mouth. His eyes opened.

"Gaol," she said. "Fight, riders."

Matthias, without asking how she knew, rolled from the bed. He tugged into his clothes.

She told him what she had heard.

She was dressed in clan and ready before husband finished.

Matthias headed toward the door. "You shall warn Westen. Tell him to stay with milady. I will get Norlow."

"We should not separate," she replied. "'Tis dangerous."

"The riders you said were eastbound, and our separation shall only be for minutes. We'll go to the gaol together. I'll get a dagger from Norlow."

"Should not separate, husband."

But they parted.

Celine ran straight down the deserted township's main roadway toward the Rose and Chalice where the sergeant-at-arms had hidden the Lady Glass. She slowed only once, as she neared the Barbary Tavern where Cathedral had been captured. There she paused to look inside its downstairs room. The henchmen were gone as was the watching deputy. This confirmed, for her, that the henchmen had attacked the gaol.

Swiftly, she continued her run.

She dashed into the poor inn, surprising the two men and one elder woman inside and ignoring their startled curses. She bolted up the stairs to the rooms.

Westen opened the door after her first knock and before second was needed. He was plainly stunned that she'd been able to come up the creaky stairs without making a single sound. Celine gave him the instructions from Matthias. The sergeant did not like the orders. Said they would be followed regardless. She noted that Lady Adriana had hidden herself on the other side of bed. But she hadn't secreted herself well. Part of her mussed-hair head and a bare shoulder were visible above the bed padding. She saw, then disregarded, that the lady's clothing including night-rail were draped over a stool. Also, there was shining on the dressed sergeant's mouth and chin despite repeated wipes with hand.

Finishing the instructions, Celine rushed back down the stairs, without causing a single step to creak, out of the Rose and Chalice, and ran to the coaches.

As she approached, she saw Matthias and that he was unharmed. No one had been lying in wait for him. Husband spotted her and patted a sheathed dagger at his belt to show her he'd armed himself. She frowned at him. It had been unwise to separate. But it had ended well.

They headed toward the gaol at a swift pace. Norlow accompanied them. He was armed with his broadsword and a short blade. A faint warning pinched Celine between her shoulder blades. 'Twas not about the trouble at the gaol. Something was different about the soldier-escort's demeanor.

As they neared the gaol, Celine saw that the campfire blazed low and there was no sign of any movement around the stone building.

"*Bax*," she muttered.

Soon all was clear to her husband and to soldier-guard.

Irish was dead. He'd caused the sword-bracing-sword sounds that woke her. She told Matthias the tracks in the dirt showed Irish had fought his attackers. However, the soldier had been overwhelmed and slain with blades to chest and back. There was no indication that he'd wounded or defeated a foe opponent. The throats of both pilloried guards had been cut. The thick-bodied man had been slashed to spine, head barely remaining with body. The drunk had his throat knob sliced out. The one deputy-guard had been asleep, wrapped in blanket on ground, and had been stabbed through closed eye.

Cathedral was gone.

As was the body of the iron-masked prisoner.

Celine grabbed a burning limb from the fire and walked eastward, back and forth, studying the ground until she found the tracks. She went a hundred meters further then returned.

"Five horses," she said to husband and Norlow. "All had weight upon them."

Matthias nodded then turned to Norlow. "Go wake the sheriff, tell him what has happened, and to collect his deputies. They are to meet us here at gaol. Then you will return to our caravan. Get three horses ready. Saddle two. Mistress Duncan's mount only needs reins."

"Aye, sire."

"Soldier," Celine added. "Tell sheriff that I did not see the deputy he had watching the three henchmen. His man is more than likely dead."

"Aye, milady, I will." Norlow hurried away on his task.

Matthias paced briefly.

"Wife, you shall apprise Westen—," he began.

"We will not separate again," Celine interrupted. "You cannot deter me from this."

"The villains are gone. You said they rode east."

Celine placed fists on hips and stared evenly at Matthias. "Cathedral could circle back. He still has to deal with the last witness—the Lady Glass. If they have returned, I will not have husband alone. We will not separate."

"Very well." He studied the eastern horizon. "We shall go together to the Lady Glass and the sergeant-at-arms. I dislike waiting till dawn to track these murderers. We may not catch them with two-hour start on us."

"We needn't wait, husband. I can track them by torchlight. However, the torch will be warning to them that we are following."

"No delay then. We speak with Lady Glass and Westen then we, and the others, mount up."

26

ADRIANA WALKED BESIDE WESTEN, KEEPING TO the night shadows, her mind aswirl as they headed back to her original room at the Swan and Bulldog as Mister Duncan had instructed. The sergeant had shortsword drawn.

She was in danger she had been told firmly but she continued to ponder different subject. She'd become gluttonous for the sergeant's company. Now, adding to his companionship, was his glorious pleasuring of her intimate with his mouth. The crestings he created within her were beyond magnificent. She had desired to do the same for him if his injury allowed it. It had not happened. Westen remained dressed during their two-some gatherings, did not even remove his boots. When she touched him between his legs, at his joining, he removed her hand. Her caresses to his padded tunic yielded no pleasurable response. She wondered, with much sadness, what other scars and deformities was he concealing from her. The most he would allow was for her to pleasure him with her kisses, so she did with vigorous enthusiasm.

In a day or so, she would be back at her home and she would no longer take orders from Matthias Duncan and the sergeant. That could be written in two-meter-tall lettering. But—and this was major—there would also no longer be rendezvous with Westen.

In the distance, at the gaol, she saw a band of horsemen riding eastward. One, in the lead, had a torch. She believed that was Mistress Duncan. She knew the woman was barbarian but the many manly skills she possessed was inconceivable. The hunters intended to catch Cathedral and put an end to the hired assassin and his henchmen. Duncan had not said those exact words, but she had inferred it. That was good.

She glanced once more at Westen, and she would've sworn that her heart was swelling more than it already was in her breast. This man, this beautiful man, she thought, was like no other she'd ever known. The longer they were together the more she wanted their relationship to continue. But that could not be, she repeated to herself. At home, 'twould be impossible. Proper societal mores dictated that. Their stations in society were too far part and he was ten years her junior. Never had she wished she were not the respectable, wealthy widow she was. Tonight, however, at least for a short time, she did covet that she was not.

The sergeant-at-arms was silent in their walk. She knew Westen was unhappy. Her man wanted to be with the hunters and going into battle. Did not wish to remain behind. But orders from Matthias Duncan would be followed. He would stay in township as her guard. She would not tell him, but she was pleased he would not be in harm's way in battle.

Adriana sighed. All had not gone as planned. The iron-masked prisoner and now four others, possibly five, were dead. If the missing deputy had been found, dead or alive, she had not been thus informed. This had not been foreseen in the two-fold plan. Only the prisoner was supposed to die here. Later, Cathedral and his henchmen were supposed to be arrested, tried in court, and meet their deserved fate on the gallows. That would restore some order of civility and decency to the kingdom. She would not weep for the four slain. 'Twas said that she rarely smiled but she never cried. She hadn't when her three husbands passed, and she would not now. Tears never changed any event and was a pointless response.

Still, culpability prodded her like sharp forked trident.

What she had learned, what had inflamed her to act, did not assuage those guilty feelings.

No one in proper of mind would believe that she—the esteemed and respected Lady Adriana Glass—was the one that hired Cathedral. Matthias Duncan had been right—the prisoner was Frederick, Duke of Bonham. King Richard and the senior-most member of the high council had planned the ruse. The others on the council, especially Duncan, were not told. Duncan would have argued strenuously against it. He would have said that Bonham's crimes warranted the maximum sentence. She agreed. Nonetheless, what could not be dismissed away, no matter how well worded and Duncan would've been very articulate, was that Frederick Bonham was D'Arth lineage. To sentence one of that bloodline, as one would a commoner, was to dishonor their kingdom's heritage. Each side of the debate had merit. So, King Richard had decided to do both. An imposter, a man already sentenced to death, was put in the Duke's gallows place. That had satisfied the noble and common populace. An iron mask, idea culled from the old legends, was put upon the traitor's face to hide his identity and he was to be taken Pitcairn Isle to spend the remainder of his wretched life.

Adriana supported King Richard and Queen Igraine without misgiving. They had made Thuria the greatest and best kingdom the world had ever seen. She understood they were not perfection to be placed on pedestal; they made errors in judgment. They were, after all, a mortal man and a mortal woman. The King, to her dismay, had his enforcer—the man called Quinn was a black mark on the good soul of the kingdom. And what had the Queen been thinking when she proclaimed a day when widows could order an unwed man to marry them? That went against the natural law of women and men. Still she had meant the words that she would sacrifice her own life for the crown. 'Twas not idle speak. However, she had never considered killing for the kingdom. The Duke's sentence should have been the same as the others who had attempted to overthrow the crown and had intended to slay King Richard in the process. That she believed with her whole heart.

Bonham's punishment was miscarriage of right.

Utter. Failure. Of. Justice.

She learned, after his passing, that her third husband had retained Cathedral's services. How many times, she did not know? But one time had been for the Lord Glass to rid himself of the troubles caused by his malingering, debt-ridden brother. That meant the vile assassin knew who she was and did not feign ignorance when she approached him. She paid him double his usual amount in gold to "execute" the traitor. The extra sum included for him to wait until she arrived in township and signal her when slaying was accomplished. Cathedral said the stipulation was unique, he'd never done it before, but because she was female, he understood she wanted personal and immediate knowledge that deed was done. He never suspected she would then stand witness against him. She knew, at trial, Cathedral would announce she had hired him. That was forgone conclusion. There was no privileged and confidential agreement between them. She'd already practiced in the mirror her shocked then mortified look and her stuttering answers when the accusation was put to her. No one, not King Richard, seasoned judge, nor any noble personages, would believe this possible of her. Her reputation never hinted at any such wickedness. Capital gossip would swirl the names of several patriots who could have arranged the assassination. And many knew about the blood feud between the houses of Drake and Longshanks—the Marquis Drake's wife was Bonham's daughter. The fortunate happenstance of the Baron Hiram Longshanks's arrival in Oxham's Mill would turn most eyes away from her if they lingered on her at all.

Again, she looked eastward. The horsemen were no longer within sight and neither was the glow of the leader's torch. If luck were smiling upon her, and it often favored her, the hunters would catch up with Cathedral and his henchmen and a battle would ensue. And the villains would be slain. Then her concerns about Cathedral coming to assassinate her or voicing accusation at trial would be no more.

She would then return to her favored and suitable life.

Adriana looked at Westen. A life that would contain one deep sorrow.

She eased closer to the sergeant and took his free hand into hers. Without glancing at her, continuing his diligent survey of their surroundings, he squeezed her fingers. Her spirit soared.

Then she sighed. Yes, she would have profound regret upon their return to home.

27

AS DAWN BRIGHTENED THE TERRAIN AROUND them, Celine squatted and dowsed her torch in a mud puddle. No longer needed. She held the reins of her pony and studied the horse tracks and dung. Behind the hunters was a bend in the roadway that passed through a groundswell of jagged boulders.

"They are about a half-hour ahead of us," she announced.

"We are gaining," Sheriff Pengler responded. "Let's keep on the quick and cut their lead to nil"

"Wait," she said.

"Nay!" snapped Pengler, rearing his horse up on its hind legs. "The blackhearts killed two of my deputies. They will not live to see mid-morn. That I swear."

"We shall wait," Matthias commanded. "A few moments only."

He looked at Celine.

"You see something amiss?"

Celine nodded. The villains' course had been steady, not in a rush after leaving township, moving due east along a well-traveled roadway. They had crossed another road two kilometers back that would've taken Cathedral and his henchmen north to, at least, three other trails. But they hadn't taken it. They stayed together and kept to this easterly route. Why? What was she missing?

She did not know this land. Pengler had said if the villains continued easterly on this roadway, that they'd be trapped when they reached a river. Horses could not cross its deep water; the northern and southern shore routes were blocked by high cliffs. They would have nowhere to go. Unless they had a boat. Then they could sail south.

Celine released the pony's reins then walked back into the bend. She studied the boulders on each side of the road. Yes, now she saw it. 'Twas devious plan.

She returned to husband and the others.

"No more waiting," the sheriff called. "We will apprehend them at the river, at road's end."

Celine looked at Matthias, shook her head, as Pengler and his deputies spurred their horses forward. Husband and Norlow waited with her.

She mounted her pony. "No need to go on."

Matthias accepted her words without further explanation.

Norlow grimaced but remained silent.

'Twas three-quarters of an hour later when Pengler and his men returned. They had no captured prisoners. Only five horses, reined together, followed the last deputy.

"They left their horses," Pengler reported. "Had a boat awaiting 'em. Long gone. Damn."

Celine did not respond. She looked at husband. They both knew what was happening.

During the ride back to the township, Celine noted that Norlow kept eyeing her. The soldier-escort seemed uneasy. She had no evidence, only her gut. She believed Norlow had betrayed them, that he'd been paid coin not to interfere in the rescue of Cathedral and the killings of the guards and prisoners.

She wondered why Cathedral had paid Norlow instead of slaying him, too. Then she realized the soldier-escort was needed for one more task. If she was right about this devious turn in events—and she knew she was—then her deduction about the coming night was fact, too.

28

L ATE MID-MORNING.

"They escaped?" Adriana asked disbelieving.

Celine and Matthias had gathered at the coaches with the Lady Adriana and Westen. Only the four of them. Norlow had been ordered to cool walk then rub down the horses. Pengler and deputies had returned to township.

"Sire," the sergeant said. "We encountered the sheriff before joining you. He told us Cathedral and his henchmen fled downriver by boat."

Adriana stamped her foot. "I demand, Mister Duncan, that you order their arrest as soon as we return to the capital."

"No need, milady," replied Matthias. "They are not going to Blackwater."

"You are confusing."

Matthias turned to Celine. "You reasoned the plot. I agree with you. Explain it to them."

She nodded and began:

"The villains dismounted among the rocks at a bend in the roadway. They did this so they would not leave footprints. I realized that four of the horses' tracks were not carrying as much weight coming out of groundswell as they did going in. Three riders dismounted. They carried corpse with them. The last rider led the horses to the river. He hid from sheriff and men, and later I believe joined up with the others."

"Why?" the lady asked.

"They expected us to give chase," Celine continued. "But they didn't plan on us leaving before dawn. That didn't give them as much time as they had planned. We were to find their horses abandoned at the river and deem they had escaped in boat. Which the sheriff did."

Adriana pinched her brow. "I still do not understand."

"Because they are coming back here tonight," Matthias said simply.

Adriana gasped, and backstepped against the sergeant and Westen protectively, without thought of appearance, slid arm around her at waist.

"Cathedral has to come here," added Celine.

"During today," said Matthias, "at some point, they will hide the corpse. And unless one of them is captured and talks, corpse may never be found. It shall be just another tale about prisoner in iron mask."

Celine nodded. "The corpse hidden, the paid guard slain…and, more than likely, Cathedral will have disposed of his boot with cut heel. He does not give the impression that he allows even minor oversights. With those done, that will leave them one witness left that they must dispose of."

She saw Adriana clutch the sergeant's arm. Her entire body trembled. Westen took her tighter into holding. She nearly smiled. The actions of the lady and the sergeant-at-arms, when together, were becoming more out-in-the-open. Unplanned but visible.

"We need a well-thought strategy," Matthias said.

"I have plan," responded Celine.

"I know. And I won't like it, shall I?"

"You won't. But it will work."

"Tell me…tell us."

Celine turned to Adriana. "I shall require two items from you.

Your largest dressing robe so I can easily remove it when time comes. And I require one of your black-hair wigs."

"I don't wear wigs!" responded the lady.

"You shall give me wig. Or I will take the one from your head."

29

MATTHIAS DID NOT LIKE CELINE'S PLAN. NOT a tad.

But he agreed, reluctantly, at last, that it was the best course of action.

So now, well after midnight hour, with no candle lit, he sat alone in the dark of their Swan and Bulldog room glancing up repeatedly at the ceiling and listening for any sound coming from the Lady Adriana's room, or from the stairs. All was quiet. Too much so. Even the other inn lodgers seemed to have settled in for the night. He knew he wouldn't hear Celine moving about above him. She could walk across a bed of dry leaves and twigs without crushing a single leaf or snapping a solitary stick underfoot. She could also hold a waiting position for hours. He traced his finger along the blade of the dagger he'd acquired and knew that Death had joined with them as partaker in the coming events.

Matthias twitched in his chair. After darkfall, Westen had sneaked her ladyship back to the second room at the poor inn. Then the sergeant had left her by herself. Without witnessing the scene, Matthias suspected the Lady Adriana had had another temper tantrum before Westen departed. Both the sergeant and he had been spectator to the fit she'd thrown when giving Celine the wig and dressing robe. That tantrum, he mused, had been about vanity. The lady had been aghast when 'twas revealed that wigs were one of her beauty secrets. Before giving wig to Celine, she made all three of them swear oath to never whisper about it to another person. However, he suspected the outburst had actually been a diversion. Yes, her ladyship was not that shallow of an individual. He'd seen the look of fear of her face, and her tight hold on the sergeant, when she fully understood that Cathedral was coming to murder her. The tantrum was to concentrate her mind on something other than a cold-blood assassin with a black dagger. He wondered if Lady Adriana was having a fitful, restless time alone in her room as much as he was in this room.

If all had gone as planned thus far, he thought, Westen should now be positioned in hiding outside this inn. The sergeant's twin-fold task was to watch both the front entrance of the inn and observe Norlow stationed at their coaches and with their horses. The soldier-escort had not been included in the plan. They agreed that something was off about Norlow's current conduct. There was nothing solid in their suspicions. Still. They would not take a chance on him with the high stakes involved. Pengler and his deputies were also excluded from the strategy. The sheriff gave the impression he had battlefield experience, but he was hot-headed. He had one thought when he had ridden ahead to the river; to avenge his slain deputies. He could not be counted on to wait for the best moment to confront Cathedral and his henchmen.

Matthias flinched as he felt the dagger's edge slice into his fingertip. Sighing, he pressed the cut against the thigh of his breeches. He knew his wife was a skilled warrior. Celine was quick, agile, and bold. He vividly remembered during the journey from her clan village to Thuria the skirmishes with the Nikota clan. He saw one enemy warrior's sword-sweep miss when Celine bent her body backward at the waist and the blade passed over her by a tad. And later, when they'd been trapped by advancing Nikota, she told him to stay behind her as she readied to fight their enemy. He saw no fear on her face. Then he found an escape for them. 'Twas a desperate and dangerous gamble. After she said she would never do such again. If she had to choose between two like that in the future, she'd stand and fight.

Despite his wife's battle skills, he was worried. To his core. Cathedral was an able assassin. The man fought by ambush and deceit. And the coward only attacked face-to-face when his target was restrained and helpless. He had intended to be in the room with Celine. Had. But Celine, caressing his cheek, whispered 'nay.' She said that if husband was with her, she'd fret about *his* safety. That would affect her fight. That could get both slain. Westen had volunteered to wait in the room. But nay Celine had replied. They could not risk the sergeant being spotted and Cathedral retreating. In the light, a half-blind person would not confuse Celine for Lady Adriana. They were much too different. However, in the dark, with Celine wearing the long black wig and large robe, sitting in a chair with her back to the door, it could work momentarily, and that would be long enough.

Slowly, ever so slowly, he struggled to keep his eyes open and his chin from dropping onto his chest. Damn. Sleep was overwhelming him. He snapped his head upright and focused on listening again.

Then the struggle to stay awake began again.

He failed.

Sleep won.

Westen would not fail Mister and Mistress Duncan, would not forsake the Lady Adriana Glass in this harrowing time. Would die first.

The sergeant had taken position at the opening of the alley beside the inn. Had become shadow within shadow with shortsword in hand and battle shield leaning against the inn's wall. The view of the entrance to the Swan and Bulldog was not obstructed. A half-hour ago, laughing and talking, the kitchen workers had departed by the back door. The innkeeper had closed, and locked, the front doors. No one had passed by since. Only a ragged dog had wandered near but not close. That was good. The only thing to do now, as were Mister and Mistress upstairs, was wait for Cathedral and his henchmen to make their play.

Across the roadway, beside the coaches and their horses, Norlow huddled inside his tent. Westen hoped they were mistaken about the soldier. The only repeated grumble overheard from Norlow was that he wasn't paid enough, and payday was time and again late. Irish had agreed. 'Twas a common enough grouse among the regular army troops. Other than that, what stood out of late was Norlow had taken to observing Mistress Duncan more often than ever before. Westen knew the soldier could have been spellbound by her near-naked warrior clan garb. However, and the sergeant had seen this oft, Norlow had the look of a man measuring another before throwing first punch in a brawl. Soon they would all know if the soldier had betrayed them.

Westen glanced down the township roadway. The poor Rose and Chalice was not visible from alley position. Thoughts immediately went to hoping Adriana was not terrified. She did not like being alone under normal circumstances and this situation was not like any she had ever had. Sadness slipped over heart. Their relationship would soon be over. Had to be. Must be. Society's standards demanded it, and the Lady Adriana lived her life by those rules. Their stations in the kingdom were too far apart. Would've ended eventually despite that. If she ever learned the full history of her sergeant-at-arms, it would have been immediately finished, done. Forever. Upon first meeting, Westen was enchanted by the very proper Lady Glass of Blackwater and the attraction grew swift and strong. Never had any woman in the past ever caused this enticement. And, in her eyes and with tiny smiles, she indicated the interest was reciprocated. Had to be wrong in reading of her. Knew that without doubt. That first kiss had been impulse in spite knowing the harsh punishment that could have resulted. Taking her in arms—the lie about a nearby animal trap still fresh in the air—pressed lips to hers. Then, suddenly, she was kissing back. Their next kisses always started the same. Adriana, in a haughty demeanor, would say this was most improper and the sergeant did not know his appropriate place. A moment later, they would be kissing—lips and tongues caressing the other. Their relationship grew in conservative spurts. In their days together, every facet about her became endearing. Even her constant talking and complaining, that most times annoyed Mister Duncan and, especially, Mistress Duncan, were charming. Earlier today, when Adriana became terrified upon learning that Cathedral was coming to murder her, she wanted Westen's protection. That had been more satisfying and, humbling in many ways, than her joyous aloud cries in orgasm. But alas, soon their relationship would only be the fondest of memories.

The sergeant stiffened.

Across the roadway, Norlow rose outside his tent.

Two men approached him out of the darkness.

Westen saw in the pale moonlight that 'twas Wiczak and one of the other henchmen. Wiczak carried a longbow and quiver of arrows as well as sheathed shortsword. The second man had a battle axe. They had plainly come prepared to fight.

Where was Cathedral and the last henchman? the sergeant wondered.

The three men moved to the horses, and quietly saddled five mounts. Norlow tied a crossbow to his saddle.

Westen readied for battle with shortsword in one hand and shield in t'other.

Celine listened. Two men were moving silently, for the most part, across the roof. Only a few creaks moving downward gave them away. The other two men had to be positioned elsewhere, either downstairs or outside. No matter. They were for Westen to deal with. Earlier, the sergeant-at-arms had allowed several witnesses to observe his departure from her ladyship's side. The ruse was intended to make the assassins believe the pampered Adriana was alone tonight in her room.

She heard no one outside the room door or on the stairs. That was, she determined, the most dangerous entry point to the room. Easiest to maneuver, but the one most fraught with lodgers blundering into their path. Dropping down from the roof and using the window required strength and skill, and only one could pass through the window at a time but would work best. The least expected entry for an attack. Those were the only room entries. Of course, the villains could have chosen to come through both at the same time, but the murder of a little gentlelady did not necessitate such a plan. The approaching villains did not know they were in the midst of the last minutes of freedom. Matthias wanted them captured so they could be led to the corpse of the murdered masked prisoner. She would do this for him.

Celine shifted her chair quietly in front of a small table littered with the lady's grooming aids so that her back was to the left-open window. She only had one candle lit to add shadows to the room and to further enhance her disguise. From the window, with her ladyship's silk robe draped down from her shoulders and the black wig positioned atop her head, the villains would not be able to tell 'twas not Lady Adriana sitting at the table. By the time they crossed the room and realized their error, 'twould be too late.

Her short-handled spiked mace lay across her lap. 'Twould be the only weapon she needed. Still she had a slender dagger sheathed in her right boot.

Studying the small standing-mirror, positioned perfectly on the table, she saw a rope drop in front of the window. The rope was knotted every six inches or so to aid in climbing. She heard a man grunt as he eased over the roof's eve.

Celine placed the mirror face-down on the table. Didn't want one of the men glimpsing her reflection. Nothing could be taken for granted in battle.

She heard the first man slip inside the room. Followed shortly by the second. They moved together, silently and swiftly, toward her.

She waited.

Wanted the two closer.

That was *baxing* close enough.

Celine shouted her battle cry as she rose, whipping around, the chair crashing to the floor, the robe and wig flying from her person.

The loud shout and the crash of a chair onto the upstairs floor woke Matthias.

He rushed to the door.

To the stairs.

Straight to Celine.

The henchman froze for a mere disbelieving moment, and during that tick of inaction, Celine's double-fisted swing of mace shattered his right knee.

Without pause, she pivoted toward Cathedral. But the henchman fell between them. Cathedral grabbed his man and pitched him toward her. Then he bolted out the door.

She hammered the mace into the henchman's temple, killing him instantly. And charged after the assassin.

Outside, the three villains all moved at the same time. Toward the inn. As soon as they heard Celine's battle cry.

Westen rushed forward. The henchman with the battle axe was the closest.

The startled man released the reins to his mount and to the one he was bringing with him. Raised his axe. But he was too slow. Westen slashed his shortsword and cut deep into the henchman's side

SILK & SWORDS   291

below the ribs. The man cried out, dropping his axe and collapsing onto his horse's neck.

The sergeant pivoted past the frightened, rider-less horse and toward the next man.

'Twas Norlow.

The grim soldier had his shortsword drawn. Was ready.

Westen advanced.

On instinct, without forethought, the sergeant raised shield. An arrow hit shield, piercing it, and hitting high in left shoulder.

Norlow laughed.

Westen gritted jaw, cursed. Saw Wiczak lower his bow.

On the stairs, below her, Celine heard brief fight.

No!

She swifted down the steps and first saw Cathedral running full-out at the inn-tavern's front doors. The assassin slammed his full body into the locked doors.

The front doors of the inn crashed open and Cathedral bolted outside.

The sergeant started forward again, slower than before, toward the two men.

Wiczak and Norlow spurred their mounts away from Westen and parallel to the inn porch. The wounded henchman rode after them.

"Damn cowards!" Westen called. "Face me!"

Cathedral raced down the inn's porch and leapt into the saddle of the rider-less horse beside Wiczak. The four men galloped toward the southbound main road.

Celine stopped. Only for a tick. All, except one sight, vanished for her.

Matthias sat upright on a stair-step with his back against railing. He had hands to his left side.

Celine jumped, not touching a single step, beside him.

Matthias looked at her, confusion etching his paling features. Even in the dark, she saw the blood pumping from under his hands.

"Ouch," he whispered.

Downstairs, Westen dashed inside with bloody left shoulder and limp arm.

She yelled at him. "Get healer!"

30

CELINE, SITTING ON THEIR BED, HELD unaware husband's hand. His breathing was most difficult. This was her fault. Oh, bax, she'd made grave error. She knew Matthias wanted one, or both, of the villains alive. She had only disabled the henchman at first when she should have slain him outright. Gave Cathedral an escape. All her fault.

The elderly midwife finished wrapping bandage around Matthias's chest. Behind her, were the sergeant-at-arms and her ladyship. Westen had a blood-tinged bandage at left shoulder and arm in sling. Lady Adriana stood, unable to look at Matthias, clutching the sergeant's right hand and plainly struggling to keep her composure.

Celine had learned that Westen had braced the mounted villains. But the four men, with one henchman slumped in saddle, had escaped and ridden south on the road.

The healer midwife studied the bandage on Matthias, and satisfied, looked at Celine.

"If the blade had gone between ribs, Mister Duncan would be dead," she announced. "But it hit lower bone and went up his side. Deep cut. He has lost much blood. All we can do now is keep him comfortable, change bandage on the regular, and wait. 'Tis up to himself, and the angels in Heaven, if he survives."

Celine traced her fingers across the hair at Matthias's temple, then rose from the bed.

"They should not have harmed husband," she said, her words cold and hard.

Adriana, pallid and trembling, stared at her.

"I am going after them," Celine added.

"They have too great a start," Westen replied. "I shall go with you, milady."

"Nay. You are injured and will slow me down, and you are the only person I trust to watch over husband."

Westen frowned.

"I will catch them," she said.

Celine pressed her hand into a bowl holding cloth soaked with Matthias's blood, then drew red stripes across her face.

Adriana gasped.

"And I will kill them all," Celine finished.

Celine leapt from the tiring first horse onto the saddleless second, still gripping the rope of the third pony. She clenched the stallion's mane and heeled the steed, moving faster. No rest, no relent until she'd caught up with the villains.

The sun topped the horizon and she was making good time. A kilometer from the township, she found one, the henchman Westen had wounded, sprawled in the middle of the road. He was dead, whether he'd still been breathing or not when he had fallen from his horse she could not tell. But he had been abandoned by his companions. A quick survey showed the man had bled out from the body wound he'd received from the sergeant. That left Cathedral, Wiczak, and the traitor Norlow. She took a tick longer and studied the men's horse tracks. They were no longer on the gallop. Now they were riding at an even steady pace. That was an ill-fated error on their part.

Kilometer after kilometer, she rode. 'Twas close to midday, with her on the third and last pony, when she saw the Longshanks caravan ahead of her. She was surprised at how slow this procession was traveling. And grateful.

She raced along the side of the caravan. The pony was coated in sweat and she felt its legs weakening, heard its panting.

Celine stopped the pony at the head of the procession, near the Baron Hiram Longshanks riding his albino destrier stallion. The pony collapsed as she stepped from its back.

Longshanks stared at her, aghast. Several men moved around her, weapons at the ready.

"Three men rode past you," Celine said. "How long ago?"

The baron waved his fingers in dismissal at her. "How dare ye address me, woman. Is that blood on ye face?" He shivered. "Go away on the immediate." He paused. "I know ye, don't I?"

"They attempted to murder Matthias Duncan and the Lady Adriana Glass. How long ago did they pass by?"

Longshanks gulped in disbelief.

"Three men rode in the field around us before moving back to the road," one of the men said.

"About a quarter, mayhap, a half hour back," another added.

Celine nodded, moving beside the baron. "The Duncan family and I will be in your honored debt."

"Why?" he replied.

She grabbed Longshanks by the belt and pulled him from his mount to the ground.

The baron uttered a disbelieving, indignant squeal as he landed on his butt. Two men quickly aided him to his feet. A diminutive servant ran forward to brush the dirt from Longshanks's coat and breeches.

A third man moved toward Celine.

Drawing her dagger, without looking at the advancing man, she pointed the blade at him.

He stopped.

She cut the cinch strap and shoved the saddle from the horse. Grabbing its mane, she leapt onto its back.

"I will return horse," she announced.

She heeled the destrier stallion and, a moment later, thundered down the roadway.

Celine heard shouts behind her, but a quick glance back showed no one was following.

Aligning her body with the stallion's, its long mane whipping her shoulder, no further urging was needed. The stallion wanted to run. They rode so swiftly that the landscape became blur to her eyes.

Soon, she told herself. *Damn soon.*

Celine stood, boots planted shoulder-width apart, in the middle of the roadway. The spiked mace was gripped in her right fist at her side and the dagger curled in her left. Her breathing and heartbeat were steady. 'Twas as if ice slow-flowed through her veins. With the clan, in battle, she had no feelings toward the enemy, always centered on the fight at hand. No more, no less. These men she hated with every tad of her being. They would die. Cathedral especially, but also his companions would pay.

When, at last, she had neared the three men on the roadway ahead of her, she'd turned the stallion into the woods and rode around and past them. She had released the destrier near water and grass, then taken her stance upon the road and waited for them to approach.

The men reined their horses to a halt about fifty meters from her. She watched as Wiczak stood upright in the stirrups of his saddle. He spoke to Cathedral. They knew who she was. As the two talked, Norlow drew his crossbow and the soldier-turned-outlaw loaded it with arrow. Cathedral issued orders. All three dismounted.

Wiczak notched an arrow into bow and stepped to her left. Norlow moved to her right. The two eased toward her, moving apart from one another, creating a narrow triangle between them and

Cathedral, but far enough apart that if Celine looked at one then the other would be in blind spot.

The assassin remained in front of the horses.

"I see you are prepared for battle, barbarian," Cathedral called to her. "I know the quick you possess. Saw it first-hand at the inn."

Celine did not respond, there was no reason to speak.

"I am amazed, and impressed, that you were able to catch up with us," Cathedral continued. "We had good lead. If anyone could have caught us, I guess, 'twould have been you. I am surprised that you came alone. Or are there others—the sergeant-at-arms, mayhap—off to the side?"

The assassin was the distraction. She stayed focused and cool.

"Nay, you are alone. So, come now, tell us your intentions. Frighten us with your menacing words."

Wiczak chuckled, amused. Norlow was stone-faced.

"No vows, no threats? I was hoping for something *blood-chilling* in your barbarian tongue." Cathedral sighed; his shoulders sagged. "This is my fault. Should never have agreed to the prisoner's slaying. But the coin offered was too tempting. Greed is among the deadliest sins for good reason. Empires have fallen because of greed. Just look at the recent war among our own kingdom's nobles for proof of this." He paused. "I shall never strike bargain with a lady again."

She didn't understand these last words but felt a twitch between her shoulder blades.

Cathedral shook his head. "I agreed to conditions I never had before. Damn my greed. Then the lady turns witness against me. Now I must leave our kingdom and begin anew in Zar or Cordoba. But I vow to you, barbarian, I shall have my measure of flesh from the lady before I depart."

For briefest moment, she was distracted. She knew who he was talking about. Bax.

Celine again focused fully on the three men. She'd deal with *the lady* later. She could wait, in this spot, without single movement all day if necessary. Wouldn't be required. Wiczak and Norlow would attack momentarily.

"Gentlemen," the assassin said to his companions, "I've decided I want one of her tits. Shall use it as herb pouch."

Norlow fired his crossbow, followed by Wiczak with his bow.

Celine quick-blocked the first arrow with her mace then the second.

She went forward and to her right, screaming her battle cry.

'Twas as if she stepped from her body and was watching herself in berserk fury from above.

And…

Norlow, unable to reload fast enough, dropped the crossbow. Shrieking, eyes wide and nostrils flaring, Celine reached him. The soldier had his sword half-drawn. She shattered his elbow with her mace and saw pain flood his features, heard his grunt. She thrusted her dagger under his breastbone into his heart. Hot blood surged onto her hand.

Pivoting about, leaving the dagger in Norlow, she blocked Wiczak's second fired arrow. And, without pause, raced across the ground separating them as Wiczak released his bow and drew his blade. The henchman no longer appeared amused. He suddenly seemed to understand his own mortality, and his fate was to be delivered in the form of a slender barbarian woman. She swung the mace at him—left, right, again and again. He managed to stave off her blows, barely, as he back-stepped attempting to find attack, not defense, position. Then. She paused, dropping mace to her side. Wiczak hesitated, disbelieving. He appeared to envision that his victor moment had arrived. Swung his blade double-fisted at her. Sidestepping the sword, she swifted her mace upward and crushed his chin and drove his jawbone into his brain.

She turned toward the assassin. Inhaling, exhaling slowly. And merged back into her body.

Cathedral applauded.

Frowning, a tad taken aback, she determined the assassin must have herb worm in his mind. No matter. He was still a most dangerous man. She wiped the blood on her hand across her face.

Cathedral stepped to his horse, to the shortsword in scabbard at saddle. He sheathed his black dagger and drew shortsword. As he shifted the blade from hand to hand, he turned back to her.

"I am not afraid," he announced.

"Good," she growled.

The assassin eased into fight stance.

Celine no longer screamed her battle cry and the berserk fury within her had faded. She was focused, her blood returned to ice.

She marched forward. To him. Stopped. Positioned herself at a forty-five-degree angle with her hips aimed at him, left foot ahead of right and holding the mace handle snug, her fists touching, and her knuckles aligned. This stance allowed attacking from straight down, straight up, from left and right at different angles. She met her eyes with his.

He was prepared and ready, no longer talking at her.

Celine attacked first.

Rotating her entire body in one smooth motion, she feigned level strike from the left but switched and came at Cathedral's right at mid. The assassin, reading her intent, blocked mace with sword that sent a hard rattle down her arms and across her shoulders. Relentless, she continued quick swings at him from left, right, and again left. He blocked each assault, remaining anchored in his position—not moving a tad. His last block caused tremble at her knees.

Finally, Cathedral parried.

And she made error.

He raised his sword one-handed for a downward assail and she, for a mere tick, looked up at sword instead of at his exposed body. With free fist, he punched her in the cheek. Pain exploded immediately in her head and water sprung into her eyes. She staggered back, momentarily blinded. He followed double-fisted and slashed a level chest-high cut. Celine bent her body full-backward at the waist and felt the blade tug at her chainmail vesting. Rolling to the side, she retreated and the assassin's return sweep with sword cut only air.

She positioned once more into assault stance.

Cathedral gripped the shortsword in his left hand and drew his black dagger into his right. She saw him glance at the spot between her fourth and fifth ribs. This time, she knew, he was coming at her for the kill-assault. She'd evaded him, except for fist to cheek, thus far but could she continue to do so? Could she overwhelm him? She was warrior of the Snowbear Mountain clan. She could. Would.

Still, for a moment, a meager tick, she doubted her victory.

Then Cathedral made mistake.

The confident assassin smirked at her and said,

"I enjoyed cutting Duncan."

The berserk consumed her again. Shouting her frenzied battle cry, she charged. She assailed the man with her mace. From side-to-side, at head. Relentless. Attack, attack, attack. Cathedral attempted to retreat. She shattered his left forearm and, before his sword dropped to ground, she crushed the wrist of the hand with dagger. Then she booted him with all her strength between the legs.

'Twas over a few ticks later.

Celine exhaled deeply as the berserk within her slowly faded.

Cathedral lay at her feet. The assassin's face and skull were pulp soaking into the ground and clinging to the spikes of her mace.

She picked up his black dagger. Headed toward the destrier horse. The blade would be saved for the last one.

The woman waiting back in the township.

31

STANDING BESIDE HER GROOMING TABLE, LADY Adriana watched as Westen opened her room's door and Celine stepped inside. Her heart leapt into her throat when she saw the barbarian woman had the black dagger in her fist.

"You've returned, milady," Westen said, relieved. "Have you seen Mister—?"

Celine raised the flat of her free hand, cutting the sergeant off. But she nodded once—yes—to answer unfinished question.

Westen stopped talking, queries etching face.

Adriana knew the assassin was dead and that Duncan's wife had learned the truth. Not the whole of it but enough.

Tears seeped from her eyes. She did not know when she had started weeping.

She pressed her spine to the wall, terrified to her core, her body trembling. There was nowhere to run, nowhere to hide. Her only safety was Westen. Yet the sergeant had no inkling about the danger that had arrived. She understood Westen would not harm Mistress Duncan. The reverse was not true if the sergeant attempted to keep Celine from slaying her. She couldn't allow that to happen. Couldn't.

"Don't hurt him!" Adriana pleaded to Celine. "He did not have any part of this!"

Celine did not respond. Her silence darkened the room as if 'twas a black cloud with thunder and fire behind it.

Westen appeared more confused.

"Our plan was only for the death of Bonham," Adriana continued quickly.

Celine stepped past the sergeant. "*Our* plan? You had partner."

"Was never intended for Matthias to be harmed," she continued. "Or any of the others. I swear."

The sergeant stared at her ladyship, stunned at the revelation.

Celine approached her. "Who were you in league with?"

"Cannot tell. Gave oath."

"Then take baxing oath to grave."

Westen moved toward Celine, easing arm from sling. Fresh blood bloomed on the shoulder bandage.

Celine ignored the sergeant.

"Do not hurt him!" her ladyship cried again.

Celine did not respond.

"Yes, I h-hired…the-the assassin," Adriana stammered to both, "at our Queen's b-behest."

32

MATTHIAS OPENED HIS EYES. HE SMILED AT Celine sitting beside him on the bed.

"Greetings, husband," she said quietly as she caressed his hair and temple with her fingertips.

He noted her bruised cheek. "You're hurt."

"No need for concern. I am fine."

Matthias attempted to sit up, but pain arced across the chest.

Celine pressed her hand to his shoulder to keep him in place.

"You cannot move about yet, husband. Cannot. If you do, you will tear stitching and, if you do—." She tapped two fingers on the tip of his nose. "—I shall punish you."

He looked toward the window. 'Twas night. "How long have I been here?"

"Full day."

Matthias studied the bandage encircling him from breast to below ribs.

"The blade went up your ribs," she said. "'Tis a hand and a half in length."

"Neils will be upset."

"Why will eldest brother be upset?"

"I now have a bigger scar than he does."

Celine lowered her face closer to his. "This is command," she said. "You believe 'tis your bound duty to protect and defend wife. But you are *poor* warrior. In the days ahead, if fight is needed, you shall stay behind me. I will do the battle. This does not make you lesser man. Think on this and you will see the wisdom in my words."

Finishing, she kissed the corner of his mouth.

"Command," she repeated.

It appeared to her that Matthias was about to respond when he decided not to.

"Did Cathedral escape?" he asked instead.

"The assassin has met his deserved fate."

Matthias plainly understood. "And the Lady Glass? Is she safe?"

"As long as I allow her to be."

He furrowed his brow. He plainly did not understand her reply.

Celine caressed his forearm. "Husband was right in several of his deductions in this matter. All, except where corpse is hidden, has been learned. The masked prisoner was the Duke of Bonham. 'Twas King Richard and the council's priest-historian who decided an imposter would be executed in the Duke's place to satisfy populace and Bonham would be taken to Pitcairn Isle to live out his days."

"Because of his D'Arth lineage." Matthias paused, thinking. "The two could not have accomplished this ruse without aid. I would say the prison warden and the King's enforcer assisted them. I shall summon the warden as soon as we are back home. I will question Quinn when he returns from his task at Bella Verde Valley. Tell me the rest."

Celine continued. "This is what I was told."

Months ago, each dawn, for several successive days, the nobles condemned in the Usurpers War were taken to the gallows outside the main gate of Benbane Prison.

Queen Igraine attended every execution. She did not go to quench thirst for revenge. For her own peace of mind, she needed to see justice rendered to the men who intended to overthrow the kingdom and slay her beloved husband.

All the executions proceeded in the same manner. Except one. The traitors were escorted onto the gallows by royal guards and positioned on a stool beneath a high beam with a secured hanging noose. The captain of the guard called out the man's name then announced the charges of which he was convicted. The noble traitor, the captain would continue, was herewith stripped of citizenship, title and all lands and sentenced to death by hanging. During this time, some persons in the assembled crowd of spectators—hundreds watched when the leader of the rebellion, Lord Willem Jaret, was executed—pelted the condemned prisoner with stones and rotting vegetables. The traitor was asked by the captain if they had any last words. Some spoke, some did not. Then the hangman put a black hood over the man's head. The Queen noted that hoods were a new addition to the execution procedure. Hood was followed with the noose. The rope's knot was placed ahead of the traitor's left ear and the noose secured beneath the angle of the lower left jaw. The hangman ensured all was in proper position. If satisfied, he booted the stool away from the condemned. Most kicked and twitched for less than ten minutes before being pronounced deceased. One lasted half-an-hour. The corpse was then carried to the royal mortician and a death mask was cast. Finally, the body was taken to the pyre for cremation.

Queen Igraine knew something was amiss from the beginning of one execution. The condemned noble, hood already covering head and face, was escorted onto the gallows solely by the King's enforcer. While Quinn put the prisoner on stool and draped the hanging noose around neck, the hangman announced the condemned was Frederick, the Duke of the House of Bonham. He had been duly convicted of crimes against the kingdom and was forthwith stripped of citizenship, title and all lands. Then the hangman added that his two daughters were to be auctioned as indentured servants for massive unpaid debts, and he was sentenced to death by hanging. No one in the crowd threw single stone or vegetable at Bonham for fear they might hit the enforcer. Bonham was asked if he had any final words. Igraine, even at the distance she was from the gallows, would have sworn Bonham attempted to talk but it sounded as if he was gagged. The enforcer booted the stool away. When Bonham stopped all movement,

Quinn stabbed him with dagger in the side to ensure he was dead. Then the enforcer cut the rope and carried the corpse directly to the cremation pyre.

Upon returning to the castle, Igraine immediately summoned those among her network of spies and eavesdrops. With the bits and tads of information that came to her, she pieced together the deception the King had perpetrated. She was livid. No man would escape their just punishment for their traitorous act, even with her husband's approval. The Queen devised a plan. Then refined it. When satisfied, she knew she needed a trustworthy confederate. She invited the Lady Adriana Glass of Blackharbor to meet with her. Some would have said the lady was an unusual choice. But Queen Igraine saw beneath the woman's prim, proper demeanor and knew the woman could accomplish the plan.

"I understand our Queen's motivation," Celine said, taking husband's hand in hers, "If I didn't, the Lady Glass would be dead."

"Who knows about this?"

"Only you and I. And Westen."

Matthias looked down at his chest bandage. What was the proper course here? If he gave full report to King Richard and high council, it would cause many reverberations. The council, even those who did not agree with the King's ruse, would demand an edict of censure on the Queen for she had executed plot that went against King's order. 'Twould cause divide between his and her Majesties that might never be mended. The King's political opponents would use it as proof that the so-called honorable Richard had deceived the populace, noble and common, and his word would henceforth always be suspect. He, himself, would now always wonder what King Richard was not sharing with him. If the full truth of the matter was later revealed and 'twas shown that he'd known, 'twould diminish greatly his standing with the King and high council. Some would support the Queen and say that Bonham received his just-and-ordered punishment. But Bonham was not the only person to perish in Igraine's plan. He sighed. If Celine asked him at this moment what he intended to do, he'd reply the miserable 'depends.' This needed much more thought and study.

As if reading his mind, Celine kissed his cheek. "I shall follow, without detour, whatever husband decides to do."

Adriana paced the room, again and again. Captured in maelstrom. Tears stained her face.

Westen watched, not knowing how to comfort the lady.

"My life," she stammered, "as I know it, is done. One word from the Duncans and my standing in society is over. Even those who agree with my aid to the Queen will still say I hired assassin for murder. A proper lady would not do such a deplorable thing. To render justice will be mere token wording. I could be arrested and held for criminal trial." She paused and gasped for breath. "That barbarian woman *hates* me. She was a moment away from slaying me when she decided not to. But she could be back at any time and end me."

Westen started toward Adriana. She waved the sergeant back.

"Mister Duncan will do what he believes is right," the sergeant said. "If Milady Duncan returns, and I do not believe she will, I shall be your shield."

"Thee can destroy me, too."

Westen frowned, hurt. "There is no reason to fear me."

"I believe thy words and trust them right now. But, in the years ahead, unforeseen circumstances could cause thee to come to me for coin or more. These are my black thoughts. I am consumed by them."

"On the morrow, we will journey back to the capital. I give you my solemn oath that I will never bother you again."

"At this moment, I believe thee and thy oath."

The sergeant sighed, devastated. "I shall give you information that will ease your black thoughts about me. With this, you can end my military service and send me to labor prison. And no matter what I said about you, it would be disbelieved."

"I do not understand."

"There is a lie between us that I have allowed to stand uncorrected."

"What lie?"

"When I told you that my cock and testicles were severed from my body in accident at birth. Did not happen."

Adriana stepped back, her eyes widening and her mind a swirl. "T-Thee...thee...?"

"I am female."

Adriana grabbed the bedpost to stay upright. "Nay, this cannot be..." Her knees weakened and she descended to the floor. "...I am cursed."

Westen moved to the door. "I shall never bother you again, milady."

33

DAWN TINGED THE CLOUDLESS SKY ABOVE the eastern mountains as Celine triple-checked the pallet on the floor of their coach. Then she again tucked blankets around husband.

Matthias furrowed his brow. "I can sit up for our journey."

"Nay!" she snapped. "You will allow your body to heal. 'Tis command, husband."

"Yes, my queen."

"Do not make amusement."

"I never do that."

"Never?"

"Well, mayhap once or thrice I might have. Much less than the times you've struck the end of my nose."

"You have deserved the chastising on each occasion."

Matthias smiled. "Deserved? Don't believe so," he replied. "When I was carried out here, did I see Longshanks's white destrier tied to the rear of our carriage?"

"Yes, I borrowed. When I returned, he said to send you to discuss purchase price with him. 'Tis good horse."

"That barter will be expensive." He paused. "Is something amiss, my love? You appear unhappy, and 'tis about more than your worry about my injury. Please share with me."

Celine sighed. "My moonflow started this morning."

Matthias nodded, understanding. "As soon as I am well, we shall make the mountain gods and goddesses applaud our couplings. The heavens will be so pleased with us they will give us most wondrous gift."

She smiled, genuine and heartfelt. "Husband soothes me and gives me much to anticipate."

"Of course. That is the man that I am—glorious and impressive in all ways."

Celine tapped the tip of his nose with her finger.

He chuckled. Then winced. "I believe it may be a day or two before I can laugh."

"Understood. I shall return in a moment and I will *not* amuse you."

Celine stepped from the coach. She raised the hem of her purple dress and walked to the two men hired to drive them to the capital. She reminded them that this would be a smooth ride. Every pothole that rattled their carriage and caused husband to wince would earn the man, along with less coin payment, a wound to body.

As she walked back to the coach, she looked at Westen readying horse nearby. The sergeant appeared downcast and sullen since first meeting this dawn.

Celine suspected the why without asking and, at that very moment, the reason for the malady appeared from the Swan and Bulldog.

Adriana Glass walked toward the carriages followed by those carrying her trunks and bathing tub. She was dressed and groomed perfectly as was her custom. Several townspeople, up to begin their daily tasks, stopped where they were and gazed, amazed, at the elegant ladyship.

The lady raised her chin higher as she strolled past Westen without acknowledgement, or even quick glance to the sergeant. She pointed at the second carriage for the ones following to take her belongings.

Then she moved beside Celine at the open coach door and looked in at Matthias.

"You have my utmost regrets, Mister Duncan," she said, solemnly. "The harm to you was never intended."

"I know," Matthias replied.

Adriana turned slowly, ever so slowly, to Celine. "I thank you, Milady Duncan, for graciously allowing me to ride in your carriage back to the capital."

"Here are the laws for this journey," Celine said. "Break any and I will put you out of the coach to fend for yourself. Husband will not stop me."

The lady inhaled deeply.

Celine saw that Adriana was trembling. The woman's fear of her was justified.

"You will remain silent and only speak when asked question," she told her. "Your answers will be short, on point, and no more. Do not touch husband even by accident. You may not request stop for any reason including body relief. Just piss on yourself and do so in quiet. And, if the sound of your breathing starts to annoy me, I will put you out."

"I understand."

"You understand nothing. I have always thought you a fool. What you deem most important in life are trifles. Today—." Celine glanced at Westen. "—I see you as *baxing* damn fool."

Adriana appeared mortified. She lowered her voice to slip of whisper. "D-Does Mister Duncan, and you, know the sergeant's secret?"

"Husband doesn't."

"It is abomination."

Celine shook her head.

The lady turned toward the open coach door. But she did not get inside. She placed the flat of both hands on the sides of the doorframe and lowered her face.

Celine heard her weeping.

Matthias waved at Celine, saying to do something.

Celine could not believe she felt sadness, and sympathy, for the woman. She patted Adriana's shoulder gently and quoted saying of her mother's. "Life's road has many turns and lows. Disappointments and tragedies are part of the journey. When happiness is found, one should pursue it and clutch to it bosom with all one's strength."

Adriana sobbed harder.

Celine winced. *Shite, bax.* "Milady must do what she believes is best."

Still weeping, Adriana rose and turned about, looking at the sergeant's back.

"Damn society's rules," Celine said. "Pursue happiness."

Suddenly, the lady dashed forward. She cried out as she neared the sergeant.

Westen swung about.

Adriana leapt up, ignoring arm in sling, wrapping her arms around the sergeant and pressing face to neck.

"Please bother me," she sobbed. "Bother me…for the rest of our lives."

Westen kissed her cheek.

Celine climbed into the coach. "I believe her ladyship will cause further delay to start of our journey."

Matthias nodded, struggling not to chuckle. "Appears so."

"She will be horrified when she becomes the main topic of gossip among the noble ladies."

"Aye. The Lady Adriana Glass has a suitor, and he is a soldier who is far beneath her societal standing."

Celine started to correct husband then decided not to. She would continue to see how long it took for him to discover Westen's secret.

"But I have an idea that may aid her," Matthias said. "With the King's and Queen's participation. Before the wedding ceremony, the sergeant will be promoted to the rank of major. After the service, he will resign from the army."

"Major. Why not general or admiral?"

"That might be going a step too far. I think major should lessen some of the gossip about them."

"Stop thinking so much."

Matthias shrugged. "That's what I do."

Celine stroked his temple.

He smiled.

She adored it when he smiled at her. It warmed her from crown to toe.

"I love you, husband. I like you. I lust for you."

The Queen
and the Oracle

T HE ORACLE TAPPED THE TEA LEAVES FROM the cup into her palm and studied them.

"Stories and ballads about a prisoner in an iron mask will be told for generations," she said. "None, however, shall be about the murder of a mysterious masked prisoner in Oxham's Mill. Those who know the truth shall never reveal it."

Queen Igraine nodded, satisfied.

"'Tis not the first event ye have enacted secretly for the King. Nor shall it be the last."

Igraine shrugged her shoulders. "I do what I must for Richard, for the kingdom. His manhood remains strong by not knowing what I have done. He is still a lad in some facets of his personality."

The ancient woman stepped over to a window box of blossoming flowers. The sunlight gleaming through the window reflected on the coils around her neck.

"Before we part," the Queen said, "what becomes of the Lady Glass and the sergeant-at-arms?"

The oracle considered the leaves once more. "With yer Majesty's aid they shall soon be known as the Major and Lady Western. The only gossip about them shall be that a *man* far beneath her ladyship's station seduced and beguiled her. They will be very happy together."

"Will Counsel Duncan and wife have child?"

"Yes. But not soon."

"Is there more?"

The ancient woman brushed the leaves from her palm into the window box. "That is all for today, my Queen. But at our next meeting, I shall find more herstories where yer Majesty had role in the tale."

Igraine rose to her feet. "Then I depart. I have lives I must give my aid to. To better them."

"Aye. So be it."

About Christopher Stires

Christopher Stires lives in Riverside CA. He has written six published novels. *The Thurian Chronicles: Three Tales of High Romance and Adventure* is also available from Deep Desires Press. He has had over 70 short stories and articles appear in print and web publications in the United States, Argentina, Australia, Belgium, Finland, Greece, the Netherlands, and the United Kingdom. See his author's pages on Amazon, Barnes and Noble, Goodreads, and Smashwords.

Books by Christopher Stires

The Thurian Chronicles: Three Tales of High Romance & Adventure
Silk & Swords: A Thurian Chronicles Novel

Don't Miss These Great Titles
From Deep Desires Press

**The Thurian Chronicles: Three Tales of
High Romance & Adventure
Christopher Stires**

*In a Medieval world, three journeys full of
romance and adventure will change six lives
forever.*

Available now in ebook and paperback!

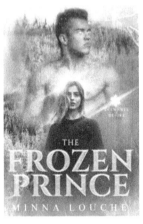

**The Frozen Prince
Minna Louche**

*He is her captor, cursed by ice magic and hiding a
deep secret, yet Genevieve can't help the feeling of
desire growing in her heart as she is drawn into
the mystery of the frozen prince.*

Available now in ebook and paperback!

**The Weeping Forest
James Missaglia**

*When Julieta is captured by her enemies, she is
handed over to a sadistic countess with one
aim—to use pleasure and pain to turn the
demure princess into a pleasure slave for the
sadistic warlord who burned her city.*

Available now in ebook and paperback!